Deadly Deception

Deadly Deception

MARISSA GARNER

WITHDRAWN

**FOREVER
YOURS**

New York   Boston

Copyright © 2018 by Marissa Garner

Excerpt from *Only Obsession* copyright © 2018 by Marissa Garner

Cover copyright © 2018 by Hachette Book Group, Inc.

Forever Yours

Hachette Book Group

1290 Avenue of the Americas

New York, NY 10104

forever-romance.com

twitter.com/foreverromance

First ebook and print on demand edition: January 2018

Forever Yours is an imprint of Grand Central Publishing.

The Forever Yours name and logo are trademarks of Hachette Book Group, Inc.

The publisher is not responsible for websites (or their content) that are not owned by the publisher.

The Hachette Speakers Bureau provides a wide range of authors for speaking events. To find out more, go to www.hachettespeakersbureau.com or call (866) 376-6591.

ISBN 978-1-5387-6073-4 (ebook edition)

ISBN 978-1-5387-6072-7 (print on demand edition)

To my husband, whose enthusiastic support has healed my confidence and whose loving concern has gotten me through many dark days.

Deadly Deception

Chapter 1

Her ten-year-old Buick died on the shoulder of the rural road with a bone-rattling shudder and a belch of smoke.

Molly Freeman smacked the steering wheel. "Couldn't you last one more mile to get me home, you darn bucket of nuts and bolts?"

She massaged her temples. *What a lousy day.* First, the disturbing call with her troubled son had started the day on a sour note. And now her entire afternoon of errands had come to a screeching halt on a deserted road. If only she'd come straight home after the car sputtered to a stop when she'd left the beauty shop in town. But no, she'd swung by the dry cleaners to pick up Jessica's clothes. Once a mother, always a mother, even if her daughter was twenty-nine years old.

Molly drew a deep breath and then exhaled slowly. Crossing her fingers, she turned the key while saying a silent prayer for a miracle. No such luck. No click. No *chugga-chugga*. No nothing. She tried a second and third time but not one encouraging sound came from under the hood.

"Well, damn." She reached into her purse for her cell phone and hoped her husband wasn't napping. Hal was babysitting Callie, their four-year-old granddaughter, and he often slept when she did in the afternoon.

Molly tapped her foot as the house phone rang until the answering machine picked up.

"Hey, Hal, you there? The car died. Can you come get me?" She waited several seconds. "Hal? Answer the phone!" She hung her head and sighed. "Okay. I'm on Wheaton, probably a little over a mile from home. I'm going to start walking in ten minutes. Call me if you get this message."

She dropped the phone back into her purse. Closing her eyes, she pressed her head against the headrest and forced herself to relax.

Relaxation was scarce these days. There always seemed to be more stress and even more work to do. Since Jessica had moved in after her divorce was final six months ago, the commotion of two extra people in the house, one of them a mischievous munchkin, was taking its toll. She loved her daughter and granddaughter, and she would never have turned Jessica down when she asked about living with her and Hal temporarily. *Temporarily* being the operative word.

Molly opened her eyes and checked her watch. Fifteen minutes had passed with no call from Hal, and she certainly didn't want to bother anyone else just to avoid the twenty-minute walk. Besides, the exercise would be good for her.

Leaving Jessica's dry cleaning hanging in the backseat, she locked the car and began her hike. Since there were only two other houses in the area, and one of those was her son's, she didn't have much hope of catching a ride with a neighbor. But her spirits lifted as she scanned the cloudless, late September sky. Nonresidents might make fun of California for being the "cereal land, full of fruits, nuts, and flakes," but the weather was heavenly.

She worked up a bit of a sweat by the time she reached her house. As she'd expected, not a single vehicle had driven by. After trudging through the back door, she dropped her purse on the kitchen table. The blinking light on the answering machine caught her eye. Apparently, Hal had never gotten her message.

She listened for snoring coming from the living room, but the house was silent. So silent, in fact, that the tick of the kitchen clock, which read almost two, seemed oddly loud.

Peeking into the living room, she confirmed her husband wasn't asleep in his recliner. She hurried down the hall to the master bedroom and found an empty bed. Smiling, she quietly opened the door to Callie's bedroom but didn't find Hal or her granddaughter.

Shaking her head and frowning, Molly retraced her steps to the kitchen. Heaven help them all if Hal let Callie skip her nap. Those two hours of midday rest kept the munchkin from morphing into a monster by dinnertime.

With her hands braced on the edge of the counter, Molly leaned over the sink and surveyed the backyard through the kitchen window. She squinted at their huge garden, trying to spot the missing twosome among the long rows of vegetables. Not a soul in sight. She shifted her gaze to the grove of fruit trees. Still no one.

She huffed and headed out the back door. Beneath her irritation, a tiny seed of worry sprouted.

"Hal! Callie! Where are you?"

No answer.

Bracing her hands on her hips, she scanned the property, her gaze lingering on the three-part outbuilding beyond the gravel driveway.

Hal usually parked his old truck in the double garage at one end. The middle section was his workshop, where he and Callie had built a birdhouse last week. The slightly lopsided structure now hung in the same tree with the birdhouse Hal had built with Jessica many years ago when he was getting acquainted with his new stepdaughter. Bless his heart, he'd worked so hard to be a great stepdad to both of Molly's kids after her first husband died in a car accident, and now he was trying just as hard to be an awesome granddad.

The unlit red light bulb over the door of the last section of the outbuilding served as a warning that it was a darkroom. Before Hal had converted his photography business to digital ten years ago, he'd spent hours and hours in there developing film. Fully committed to the changing technology, he'd even taken the time to digitize all his old negatives. So now the space was unused. And always locked.

Unfortunately, no sounds or signs of the missing duo came from any portion of the building.

Molly stomped across the sparse grass of the backyard to the edge of the garden and turned left. She peered into the little forest of eucalyptus trees but saw no figures and heard no voices. She grinned. When Callie was around, her sweet little voice could always be heard because she was a chatterbox.

"Hal! Callie!" Molly's smile faded, and her forehead creased with growing concern. *Where are they?*

She crossed the yard again, but instead of going toward the house, she aimed for the barn. It was a miniature version, but it provided plenty of space for all the supplies and equipment needed to maintain their garden and fruit trees. There was even enough room for Hal to park his small tractor.

As Molly neared the barn, she wrinkled her nose. Over half the load of manure that had been delivered last weekend was still piled in front. Her husband was as far behind on his outdoor chores as she was on her indoor ones because taking care of Callie consumed so much of their time and energy. Wonderful time, well spent, obviously, but still, the chores didn't do themselves.

She opened one of the heavy wooden doors and peered into the darkness. The smells of the packed dirt floor, bags of fertilizer, and gasoline greeted her.

"Callie? Hal?"

After her eyes adjusted to the dark, she scanned the space. No sign of any activity. When her gaze fell on the tractor, she smiled at the thought of Callie's delight when allowed to ride with her grandpa. Just like Jessica had loved it when she was Callie's age. Molly pulled the door shut and latched it securely. The barn held too many dangers for her inquisitive granddaughter.

When she turned around, a brilliant ray of sunlight blinded her like a laser. In that nanosecond of sightlessness, a nauseating sense of déjà vu enveloped her. Memories from two decades ago of another sunny day, a horrible life-changing day, filled her mind.

Gasping and blinking, she dropped to her knees and stared at the outbuilding. She shook her head as if she could dispel the terrible thoughts. Her heart pounded painfully, and she struggled to breathe. *No, no, dear God, not again.*

* * *

Jessica Hargrove parked her Camry in the driveway of her parents' house. The modest, single-story residence had been her childhood home, and the building was showing its age. If only she had the energy or money to help with a rejuvenating face-lift, but she didn't. Like so many things these days, painting and repairs would have to wait for better times.

She pasted on a smile to cover the exhaustion of a draining day. In addition to the stress of her new job in San Diego, she'd spent a tension-packed lunch hour talking to her attorney about options to make Drake pay the alimony and child support he'd agreed to in the divorce settlement. For the thousandth time, she wondered how she could've ever married such a jerk. Sadly, she'd been asking the same question since the day after their wedding. And even worse, she was in denial about the answer.

Drake's refusal to honor his financial commitment had forced Jessie to move back in with her parents, a real blow to her independent nature. Understanding her humiliation, her mom and stepdad were adamant that she save every penny possible so she could afford a place of her own sooner rather than later. But she knew supporting a household of four was putting a real strain on their finances. Although she insisted on paying half the grocery bills, her parents were making sacrifices, such as delaying the purchase of a new car for her mom.

As Jessie strolled toward the back of the house, she sniffed the air, but her nose wasn't treated to the usual mouthwatering aromas from her mother's cooking. Most of the time, she could guess the dinner menu from the fabulous smells. Maybe they were having sandwiches or chicken Caesar salad tonight instead of a hot meal. Her stomach rumbled with hungry anticipation.

Nearing the back door, Jessie smiled at the tricycle sitting on the patio. The pink and purple Big Wheel had been hers, and now her daughter loved it, too. Callie didn't seem to care that the My Little

Pony decals had all but disappeared. A mental video of Jessie racing her brother—Nate madly pedaling his Smurf Big Wheel—made her sigh with fondness for a simpler, happier time, a time long before her problems and Nate's had begun.

A warm breeze blew a strong, unpleasant odor toward the house. Jessie pinched her nose and shot a disgusted glance toward the barn. Her stepdad's tractor sat next to a mountain of manure. Hopefully Callie had *not* been helping him with the chore of spreading it in the garden, for the little tomboy would surely have ended up with some of it in her hair and elsewhere.

Groaning at the prospect of a shampoo battle, Jessie stepped into the house and stopped abruptly. Her gaze swept across the kitchen. The usually bright, noisy room was shadowy and silent. Not only was nothing cooking on the stove, but her mother wasn't even in sight. No loving smile or cheery hello greeted her. She frowned as an odd sensation of foreboding gripped her for a moment before she shook it off as ridiculous. A simple change in routine didn't signal anything ominous.

But something else wasn't right. *Where is Callie?* Her little girl always watched for her mommy from the living room window and dashed to meet her with a huge hug at the kitchen door. Jessie's breath hitched, and she set her feet in motion.

"Callie? Mom?" she called, crossing the kitchen almost at a run.

Hal's snoring brought her up short as she rounded the corner into the living room where he was stretched out in his recliner. She slumped against the door frame with relief. Closing her eyes, she gave herself a mental shake. Whatever had come over her to react in such a ridiculous manner? Things might be off schedule, but nothing was wrong.

She straightened and walked to the recliner. "Dad." She touched his shoulder. "Dad."

He grunted, coughed, and opened his eyes. "Huh?"

She chuckled. "Callie wore you out again?"

He cleared his throat. "Um, yeah, right."

"Did she go with Mom to pick up some fast food for dinner?"

Hal blinked and yawned, struggling to wake up. "Uh, no. Callie's napping."

"Napping?" Jessie checked her watch. "It's almost six. Good grief. We'll never get her back to sleep by eight." She headed toward the hallway, stopped, and looked back over her shoulder. "Where's Mom?"

He rubbed his eyes. "In town, running errands."

"This late?"

Hal shrugged.

"Okay. While I wake the munchkin, you call Mom to see if she's picking up dinner or if she wants me to start something."

She pushed open the door to Callie's bedroom and smiled. Blond curls created a halo on the pillow. Her thumb in her mouth, the little girl was still sleeping soundly. She never slept this late; she must've worn herself out, as well as her grandpa.

Jessie sat on the edge of the bed and brushed the hair away from Callie's face. "Sweetie, wake up. It's time for dinner." She kissed her cheek. "C'mon, honey. Time to get up." With still no sign of her waking, she gently shook the little girl's shoulder. "Wake up, Callie. I want to hear about your day."

Callie mumbled something into the pillow.

"That's my girl. Let me see those beautiful brown eyes."

Without raising her head, Callie opened her eyes and gazed up at her mother. After only a few seconds, her eyelids drifted closed again.

"Oh, no, you don't, sleepy head." Jessie rubbed her daughter's cheek.

She yawned. "I'm tired. I don't wants dinner."

Another exception to normalcy. Callie usually woke up bright and energetic, not drowsy and sluggish. And dinner was her favorite meal.

"What did you do this afternoon to get so tired?"

The little girl gave her mother a blank stare. "I can't 'member."

"*Re*member," Jessie corrected, emphasizing the missing syllable.

Callie pushed out her lower lip in a pout. "I said I *can't* 'member. I really can't."

"No, honey, the word is…Never mind." Jessie sighed. "Did you help Grandpa on the tractor?"

She looked at the ceiling. "I don't thinks so. We didn't gets the tractor out of the barn today."

"Did you ride your bike?"

"I…I don't know."

Jessie struggled not to laugh at the bewilderment on the little girl's face.

"Did a friend come over? Uncle Nate? Or Uncle Chad and his dog?"

Callie shrugged. "I thinks my brain is still asleep."

"No problem, honey. I feel that way a lot." She scooped Callie into her arms and carried her to the living room. Hal still sat where she'd left him, his eyes closed again. "Dad, what did Mom say?"

He started. "Huh? Oh, Molly didn't answer." Frowning, he hesitated. "Went straight to voice mail. I left a message."

"Maybe Mom forgot to charge her phone again. I'll check the fridge and see if I can tell what's for dinner." She set Callie in his lap. "You two wake each other up."

In the refrigerator, she spotted a package of thawed hamburger. "Well, that narrows it down," she muttered. She found spaghetti sauce and pasta in the pantry and a package of garlic bread in the freezer. "I'm making spaghetti," she called to her stepdad and daughter. "Keep trying to get Mom."

By the time dinner was ready, Molly hadn't come home or answered her phone. Jessie glanced at the clock. Almost seven. Her mother never ran errands this late. And why hadn't she called, if not from her cell, then from someone else's or a pay phone? The strange sense of foreboding resurfaced. She swallowed past a sudden tightness in her throat.

"Did you try any of Mom's friends? Has anyone heard from her this afternoon?" she asked, setting the bowl of spaghetti sauce in front of Hal.

"Yep, I did. No one's talked to Molly since this morning." He ladled sauce over a mountain of pasta.

"What about Nate or Uncle Chad?"

"Nope. Not a word this afternoon."

She put a small serving of spaghetti on Callie's plate. Her daughter snatched a long, slippery noodle and sucked it into her mouth.

"Okay, one more before I put the sauce on."

Once Callie had her second noodle, Jessie cut the spaghetti in a crisscross motion and spooned sauce on top. She held up the Parmesan. "Cheese?"

The little head bobbed. "Lots."

"Mom's hair appointment is the only thing on the calendar. Did she mention anything else before she left?" Jessie asked, and served herself.

Hal shrugged. "Nothing specific, but she said the errands would take *all* afternoon."

"She didn't call or leave a message on the answering machine while you were playing with Callie?"

"Nope," he said around a bite of garlic toast. "Maybe she went to a movie."

Jessie frowned. "I didn't know there was a theater in Ramona now. Besides, when has she ever gone to a movie on a weeknight?"

"Before you moved..." He cleared his throat. "She used to go over to the Poway theaters with a few of her girlfriends. Sometimes the prices are cheaper during the week."

A sliver of guilt pricked her. She and Callie had barged into her parents' lives and destroyed their calm, orderly world. They never complained, but she knew it hadn't been easy for them. The added stress and work had resulted in some heated nighttime arguments, which her parents didn't know she'd overheard. Maybe something had happened today that triggered a daytime fight.

She speared a bite of salad and pinned him with a serious expression. "Was everything okay today?"

His fork stopped midair. "What do you mean?"

"You know, did you and Mom have an argument?"

He gulped and blinked. "Well, now that you mention it, we had a...a disagreement."

"About what?"

Hal's gaze darted away and then came back to his granddaughter. "Molly...uh...wanted to sign *someone* up for...uh...dance and tumbling lessons."

Callie's head jerked up. "Dance and tumbling lessons? For me? I'm someone."

"Yes, sweetie, you sure are." Jessie rolled her eyes. "Dad, I've warned you about Big Ears."

"Sorry, honey," he said to Callie, ignoring her mother. "Grandpa and Grandma would love to get you lessons, but we can't afford it right now."

Guilt cut a little deeper. Her daughter's pouty face didn't help. *I should be able to afford the lessons.* If Drake was paying the child support he owed, money for dance, tumbling, finger-painting, swimming, or any other lessons wouldn't be a problem. But without it or the alimony, her finances were tighter than her parents'.

Pushing aside her anger toward her ex, she refocused on the issue at hand. "I understand Mom would be disappointed, but I can't believe she'd miss dinner over it."

Hal did his classic shrug. "Women."

Jessie sighed. "Where else would she go?"

He took a deep breath. "She might be at the coffee shop in town."

They dropped the subject because Callie launched into a pathetic tale about how much she wanted to dance and tumble. Jessie caught herself glancing at the clock every few minutes. She'd never known her mother to act childishly, but staying away, worrying everyone, was definitely childish. As if Jessie didn't have enough problems already, playing referee for her parents might be the last straw.

When Callie finished eating, Jessie pushed her own plate away even though she'd barely touched her food. "Bath time," she announced.

Callie stuck out her lower lip and whined.

"Since you napped so late, I'll read *two* books before lights-out, okay?"

"Okay." She scrambled off the chair and ran toward the bathroom.

"Dad, would you clean up?"

"Sure, no problem."

A bath, three books, a backrub, a glass of water, two trips to the bathroom, and four hugs for Grandpa later, Jessie turned out the light in Callie's room. "Good night, sweetie. I love you."

Callie's eyes were already closing. "Loves you, too."

Hal was half asleep in his recliner when she walked into the living room.

"Did you talk to Mom?"

He raised the back of the chair to upright. "Haven't heard a word."

"This is ridiculous. I can't believe she's acting this way."

"She'll get over it." Scowling, he cocked his head. "You know, maybe she's still upset about the big fight with Nate this morning." He yawned. "But she'll get over that, too. I'm going to bed." He lowered the footrest and pushed himself out of the chair.

"Dad, it's only eight. What did you do with Callie to wear you both out?"

He paused before facing her. "Didn't she tell you?"

"Callie said she couldn't 'member because her brain was still asleep."

He snorted. "I can't believe she doesn't 'member hiking over to the creek to feed the ducks. It was great. Had the place all to ourselves." He shook his head. "Kids. Ya gotta love 'em. Good night."

"Seriously, Dad. How can you possibly sleep with Mom not home? Aren't you worried?"

He shrugged. "Molly's a big girl…and she's done this before."

"She has? Really? This doesn't seem like her."

"Guess things changed while you were gone."

He trudged down the hallway into the master bedroom and shut the door. Jessie glanced at her watch and headed to her own room to change clothes.

She sat down on the bed to slip off her shoes but paused. Closing her eyes, she inhaled and exhaled slowly. As much as she didn't want the blame to rest on her shoulders, she knew her parents' argument was her fault. For so many reasons. She needed to fix the situation before it got any worse.

When she reached the master bedroom door, Jessie raised her hand to knock, but she hesitated. If she told Hal what she was doing, he'd try to talk her out of it and insist she not go. But she had to do something.

Determined to stick with her plan, she returned to the kitchen and wrote a note to tell her stepdad where she was going just in case he got up and found her gone. Leaving it on the table, she grabbed her purse and stepped out the back door.

Her breath caught as the deepening darkness enveloped her. She reached back inside to switch on the patio light. After locking the door and pulling it shut, she hurried toward her car.

Although she'd grown up in this house, the years she'd lived in Chicago with Drake had changed her. Perhaps the fear of big-city crime had followed her home because the lack of streetlights and neighbors here now made her uncomfortable. What had once been precious privacy now felt like vulnerable isolation.

The cloying darkness and quiet pressed in around her. Her eyes searched the shadowy property while her feet raced across the driveway.

She clicked the door lock button as soon as she jumped into the Camry. The instant the car started, she flipped on the headlights. Once on the road, she switched on the brights and sped up. The sooner she got into town and talked some sense into her mother the better.

A mile down the deserted road, she barreled around the corner onto Wheaton. The Camry's lights swept across the asphalt to the opposite shoulder and landed on a familiar car.

* * *

Sean Burke glanced at the flashing lights in the rearview mirror. His eyes widened in surprise and then darted to the speedometer of his Ford F-150 truck. He wasn't speeding, not even close. Scowling, he angled a look over his shoulder at the vehicle behind him.

"What the hell?" he muttered, slowing and pulling onto the shoulder of Highway 67 near Ramona, California.

After lowering the windows and turning off the motor, Sean sat with his hands clearly visible on the steering wheel. Through the glare of the headlights reflected in the mirror, he squinted to see a San Diego County sheriff's deputy get out of the patrol car and approach his truck on the passenger side. The man swung a flashlight in a sweeping motion, but his body was just a silhouette in the vehicle's lights. The crunch of his footsteps on the gravel stopped just before he reached the front passenger window, leaving him partially hidden by the side and roof of the truck's cab.

"Do you know why I pulled you over, son?" a deep, raspy voice asked.

"No, sir. I know I wasn't speeding."

"That's right. Your violation is more serious."

More serious? Sean frowned. He hadn't violated any traffic laws. The Los Angeles Police Department disliked their detectives getting tickets, so he'd become a very careful driver since joining the force. "What did I do wrong, Deputy?"

The man huffed, moved forward, and shined the flashlight directly into Sean's eyes. "You've got a goddamn LA Dodgers bumper sticker, you idiot. This here is San Diego Padres country."

The deputy's voice changed as he spoke, losing its scratchiness and deepness. By the time he finished his reprimand, Sean was laughing.

"Luke Johnson, you son of a bitch. Get your fucking flashlight out of my eyes."

"Watch your mouth, dickhead. Show some respect or I'll haul your ass in." The deputy lowered the flashlight and leaned in the passenger window, resting his forearms on the door. "Heard from your brother that you were coming into town. You need a breath of smog-free air or somethin'?"

More than you could know. LA was a tough place to live for a man who'd grown up in a rural area of San Diego County. In addition to the eye-burning smog that practically made him ill, the SUV-congested freeways, the sardine-can housing, and the gang-related crime made every day a pressure cooker. "Damn right. The smog gets so thick that you have to chew it before you can breathe it."

Luke snorted. "Wanna get some coffee?"

"Sure."

Sean followed his friend to the 7-Eleven, where they both purchased the largest size cup of plain black coffee. As Luke checked in on the radio, Sean settled into the passenger seat of the car. The vehicle's interior brought back memories of his days as an LAPD patrol officer before he was promoted to detective.

"Your brother mentioned you're staying with him," Luke said after a swig of java.

"*With* is relative. Glenn's out of town so much on business, I'll probably never see him."

"Don't want you to get lonely, bro, so I'll call ya on my days off. We can raise some hell like back in the day."

Raising hell wasn't exactly in Sean's plans. He wanted time to think, to decompress. His last case had been such a revelation of the underbelly of LA that he'd burned out. He needed a break. Bad. Technically, he was being disciplined with a brief suspension for not following proper procedures in solving that case, but he was also taking all his available vacation days. Hopefully it would be enough time to decide if he should go back to LA and his job.

Before Sean had to come up with an excuse not to party with his long-time friend, the radio crackled to life. "Check out an abandoned car on the east end of Wheaton. Caller also reported the driver missing," the dispatcher said.

"Vehicle description? Driver's name?" the deputy asked.

"Older model Buick. Missing driver is Molly Freeman."

Sean stiffened.

"Who called it in?" Luke asked.

"Her daughter, Jessica Hargrove."

Sean tensed even more. Painful memories tightened his chest.

"I'm on it. Ten-four." Luke turned to him. "Sorry, bro, gotta go."

"I'll come with you."

Luke nailed him with a you-gotta-be-shittin'-me look. "You're way out of your jurisdiction, Detective Burke."

He played innocent. "Detective who? I'm Sean, your hell-raising high school buddy, just enjoying a civilian ride-along."

Luke shook his head. "Not a good idea. And you know why."

"What's the big deal?" Sean shrugged. "A middle-aged woman has car trouble, decides to walk home in the dark, and her daughter overreacts. C'mon, buddy. How serious can this be?"

Chapter 2

Ten minutes later, Deputy Luke Johnson parked several yards behind the abandoned Buick. The cruiser's headlights shone past the old car to illuminate a Camry parked in front of it. The driver opened the door a crack and peered out warily.

The deputy killed the engine but left the lights on. "Do us both a favor, man, and stay in the damn car."

Sean didn't answer.

Muttering a curse, Luke climbed out and slammed the door. He flipped on the flashlight and spent several minutes inspecting the Buick and the surrounding area. When he finished, he flicked the beam toward the Camry and motioned for the person inside to join him. A woman slowly got out of the car.

Sean swallowed past the boulder in his throat. *Jess.* The sight of her resurrected a long-buried ache in his chest. He knew she'd been married and had a kid, but she didn't look much different. In pants and a blouse, she was still slender, although her curves seemed slightly fuller than eight years ago. He couldn't tell if her rich brown hair was quite as long as he remembered, but it was long enough to be pulled back in a ponytail. His fingers itched to discover if it was still as silky.

And her voice. Would it affect him as it used to? Without a sound, he opened the car door so he could hear better.

When Luke and Jess met at the front of the Buick, she threw herself into his arms and buried her face against his neck. "Oh, Luke, I'm so glad they sent you."

He wrapped one arm around her and stroked her hair with the other hand. "It's gonna be all right, Jessie. Just calm down and tell me what's going on."

Sean glared at the couple. *What the hell?* So this was why Luke didn't want him tagging along. The traitor had hooked up with Jess. *Damn him.*

Luke turned her so she wasn't facing the bright headlights, which meant her back was to Sean. His jaw clenched; he wanted to see her face. And the jerk knew it.

Raising her head, Jessie looked up at Luke. "Mom's missing. She never came home from running errands this afternoon. I decided to go look for her at the coffee shop, but then I found her car." She clutched the front of his uniform. "Where is she?"

"Don't worry. I'm sure everything's fine." He bracketed her shoulders with his hands and put a little distance between them. "You didn't see the Buick on your way home from work?"

She shook her head. "No, I take the other route past the Turners' place."

"Okay. What were your mom's errands?"

Jess let go of his shirt to swipe at her cheeks. "Well, she had a hair appointment."

"Did she keep it?"

"I don't know. We should ask Karla. She'll know. But Mom's appointment is always just after lunch, so it wouldn't make her this late."

"Right, but I'll confirm with my sister just to be sure. Anything else?"

Sean pushed the door farther open and slipped out of the car. As the two continued to talk, he stepped beyond the gravel shoulder into the dirt and quietly approached the passenger side of the Buick.

"My clothes are hanging in the backseat, so Mom must've stopped at the dry cleaners."

"I noticed the clothes, too. We'll call the shop to see if they can tell us what time she was there. Any place else?"

Jess sighed. "Not that I know of, but Dad said she expected to be gone all afternoon."

"Has the Buick been having problems?" Luke shot a quick glance in that direction.

Sean ducked.

"Oh, yeah. It's been giving her fits lately."

"So it likely died on her."

"I get that, Luke, but Mom could've walked home from here by now, been home hours ago. So where is she?" Jess's voice trembled with emotion.

Sean knew where her mother *might* be. And if Molly Freeman was indeed gagged, bound, and dying in the trunk, they needed to rescue the poor woman immediately. Complicating his professional opinion was an irrational longing for Jess to see him, which was probably a mistake but an undeniable desire nevertheless. Regardless of his personal feelings, though, his cop training told him what he had to do. And do it now.

He drew a deep breath, braced himself, and stepped from behind the Buick. "Luke, come here. We need to talk."

* * *

No, it can't be. Jessie froze before whipping around. Her eyes narrowed as she tried to throw daggers at him with her gaze. Quickly moving beyond Luke's reach, she marched across the gravel to stand in front of her former boyfriend. Years of hurt, disappointment, and confusion welled up inside her. Unable to stop herself, she slapped him. Hard. Then she shoved him again and again until Sean grabbed her wrists.

"What the hell are *you* doing here?" she spat, wrenching free of his grasp.

His expression darkened, and he held up both hands in surrender. "Just trying to help."

Her throat grew so tight she wasn't sure she could speak. Her heart pounded like a sledgehammer. "I wouldn't want your help if you were the last person on earth. Go away." She raised her hand and took a threatening step toward the bastard who'd broken her heart.

Luke caught her arm from behind. "Relax, Jessie. Sean's not trying to cause trouble. He just happened to be with me when I got the call."

Sean's gaze hardened with a suspicious gleam. "I bet you wish I wasn't here as much as she does."

Luke frowned. "Yeah. But, as usual, you wouldn't listen. If you had to tag along to gloat, couldn't you at least stay in the car?"

"Gloat? About what?"

"Forget it."

Still stunned, Jessie allowed Luke to lead her to the Camry. "Make Sean leave," she insisted.

"Can't. He rode with me. Now just stay here while I see what he wants." Luke came back after speaking to Sean quietly for less than a minute. "Do you have a key to the Buick so we don't have to jimmy the lock?"

"Oh right. Sure." After yanking her key ring from the Camry's ignition, she separated the Buick key and handed it to him. "They gave me one to both their vehicles when I moved home."

He nodded and trudged to the back of the Buick as he pulled on latex gloves from his pocket. Without a glance at her, Sean joined him.

Tears stung Jessie's eyes. *Only Sean Burke could make me forget for even a moment that my mother is missing. I can't let him affect me like that.*

Despite her resolve, his image swam in her tears. At twenty-nine, Sean—with his ruggedly handsome features—gave the impression of an all-American hero. But she knew better: The guy was a royal jerk.

When she'd stood close to him, she had seen finely etched stress lines, probably the result of dealing with criminals in LA. He now wore his wavy, dark red hair much shorter than when they'd been together. LAPD code, no doubt. And his hazel eyes were world-weary instead of twinkling with love and mischief.

She gulped, blinked her tears into submission, and stared at the two men unlocking the trunk. What they were doing suddenly registered with a jolt. *Oh God no. Please, please don't be in…*

When the lid popped open, she held her breath. Luke and Sean leaned different ways to inspect the trunk without touching anything. After what seemed like forever, Luke stepped away from the car and shook his head no emphatically.

Air swooshed out of her lungs. She splayed her hand on her chest and fell back against the Camry.

Luke hurried over and gave her a reassuring smile. "That's the cleanest trunk I've ever seen."

Jessie managed a faint smile in return while struggling to ignore Sean's piercing stare.

Luke rested his hand on her shoulder. "Do you want to file a missing person report?"

"I do, but…"

"But?"

"I called Dad while I was waiting for you and explained about the car. He said, 'No way in…'" She took a deep breath. "He doesn't want to file an official report."

"Why not?"

"He thinks Mom's just having a temper tantrum."

"About what?"

Jessie shrugged. "Nothing major. Just a disagreement with him about buying something for Callie. Oh, and she had a fight with Nate."

Luke rolled his eyes. "What this time?"

Her gaze wandered to Sean. She yanked it back and cleared her throat before responding. "I wasn't home but probably about the usual: money and meds."

"Is he asking your mom for money again?" Luke asked.

"Most likely. Or she suspects he's not taking his meds."

"Right. I know that's a big issue. Have you checked to see if anyone's heard from her?"

"Of course. Everyone we could think of. No one's talked to her since this morning."

Luke scratched his head and glanced away. "Maybe someone's not telling you the truth to help your mom get away from it all for a little while."

She gulped. God, she hated feeling Sean's gaze on her. It disrupted her concentration, and her mother needed her to concentrate fully right now. Shifting closer to Luke, she braced her hands on her hips. "Seriously, Luke. You know my mom. Would she hide from us? From her problems?"

"I agree. Temper tantrums and running away don't sound like Molly Freeman."

"I know something's wrong, but Dad will have a heart attack if I file a report against his wishes."

He sighed. "At least there's no indication of foul play. And the car isn't damaged, so there wasn't an accident. The shoulder doesn't show any signs of a fight or even a scuffle. In fact, I don't see any evidence that your mother did anything other than voluntarily walk away from the vehicle." He jammed his hands into his pockets. "That should make you feel a little better."

"Not much." Jessie rubbed her hand across her eyes, which were threatening to tear up again.

Luke exhaled. "Look, I can do two things tonight. I'll have the car impounded so we can search it for evidence later if we need to. I could catch some shit, and you might have to cough up the fee if it turns out to be unnecessary. I can also take your and Hal's statements while you find me a recent photo of Molly.

Then you call tomorrow if you convince him to file an official report. Deal?"

She drew a deep breath, and once again, her eyes strayed to Sean. Damn, he was so infuriating. "Fine. But I don't want *him* involved at all."

* * *

The tow truck stopped in front of the 7-Eleven long enough for Sean to hop out before it rumbled down the road, dragging the Buick behind it. He sighed and stuffed his hands into the pockets of his jeans. This helpless feeling sucked.

Especially since it involved Jess.

He ambled into the store and bought another large coffee. He'd lost the first one when Luke drove off to the Freeman house and left him with the Buick to wait for the tow truck. Normally he didn't drink coffee at nine-thirty, but he doubted he'd sleep tonight anyway.

Especially after seeing Jess.

When Sean trudged inside his brother's apartment, it felt emptier than usual. Grumbling to himself, he dropped onto the couch and aimed the remote at the TV. But instead of the images on the screen, all Sean could see was Jess in Luke's arms. *Son of a bitch.* How could his buddy be such a traitor?

Especially with Jess.

Even more surprising was his ex-girlfriend's response to seeing him. Awkward, he would understand. Embarrassed would've made sense, too. But why the hell was Jess so angry? *She* had dumped *him*, after all. Well, technically, her stepdad had been the one to call with the devastating news. And Hal had been more than blunt: *"Jessie doesn't want to waste her life with a pig."* Sean would never forget her reason for breaking up with him. And Jess not bothering to dump him herself still stung. He sighed heavily and drank a swig of coffee.

While he'd dated Jess, he'd known Hal had no respect for law enforcement officers of any kind, but his girlfriend had never shared her stepdad's views. Apparently, with Sean away at college, Hal had managed to brainwash her. But then, why would she be hooked up with good ole boy Deputy Luke? If she'd turned against law enforcement, that didn't make sense.

Closing his eyes, Sean pushed his head back on the cushion. *God, she had looked great tonight.* Even with her ready to bite his head off, he'd wanted to take her in his arms and comfort her. And kiss her. And make…

Shit. Not gonna happen. Deal with it.

He shook his head and straightened. Despite the black cloud of his history with Jess, he remembered Molly Freeman fondly. The lady had always been nice to him, and she had no grudge against law enforcement. But what could he do about her disappearance? Jess didn't want him involved, and her new boyfriend didn't either.

Sean scrubbed a hand across his face. They didn't have to know he was doing a little digging behind the scenes. His training included how to investigate missing person cases, but he'd only worked a few. Fortunately, he knew someone who would know not only how to follow the rules but also how to get around them.

Sean clicked off the TV, tossed the remote aside, and grabbed his cell. The phone rang several times before Jake Stone answered.

"This better be important, Burke."

"Why? You busy?"

"You might call it that," his friend growled.

Sean grinned. Jake's girlfriend, Angela, had joined the men for dinner at Jake's place earlier that evening. In fact, he'd been returning from seeing them when Luke had pulled him over on Highway 67. Angela must still be there, probably in bed since it was now about ten. Too bad. This couldn't wait.

"Sorry, Stone, but I need advice on a missing person investigation."

"Right now?" Jake groaned. "You were here just a few hours ago. Why didn't you ask me then?"

"I didn't know the person was missing then."

"Well, shit. Just a minute."

He heard muffled talking and rustling sheets. He chuckled. Jake would want to kick his ass for interrupting, but Sean knew how to handle the security expert and private investigator, who was a former Navy SEAL and CIA operative. The man's bark was much worse than his bite. Unless you were a bad guy. Sean and Jake shared the common philosophy of not tolerating bad guys. Their philosophy was part of the bond forged while working together on Angela's case, the case that had landed Sean on suspension.

"You owe me," Jake muttered when he came back on the phone. He cleared his throat. "Who's missing?"

"The mother of…uh…an ex-girlfriend. Name's Molly Freeman."

"How ex?"

"Eight years."

"Good. Ancient history. Don't need this to get messy."

Sean cringed. "Right."

"Talk to me."

He released a long breath before explaining the circumstances, conveniently leaving out the part about Jess's angry reaction and slap.

Jake snorted. "Basically, you have no evidence, no motive, and no suspects. Hell, you don't even know for sure she's missing."

"Sums it up pretty tight. I suppose I should start with the males closest to the victim."

"Statistics would say so. Who are the lucky guys?"

"Her husband, Hal. Her son, Nate. And I guess her brother, Chad…uh…Something."

"Hmmm, all relatives. Do you know where the family skeletons are hidden?"

"Nope. Didn't pay attention to that sort of stuff back when I was dating her daughter."

Jake chuckled. "More interested in anatomy lessons?"

Sean grunted. "Give the man a gold star."

"What's *her* name?"

"Jess. Jessica…Hargrove."

"Hargrove?"

"Yeah. Divorced with a kid. A little girl, I think."

"Could her ex-husband have any role in this?"

Sean frowned. "Don't know. I think Jess lived in Chicago while she was married, so the guy may not be local."

"I heard there are these things with wings that can fly all the way from Chicago to San Diego. Ever hear of them?"

"Okay, smart-ass. I'll add Mr. Hargrove to the list when I find out his full name."

"Good. The sheriff's department isn't doing anything?"

"As I said, Hal Freeman doesn't want to file an official report because he thinks his wife is just pouting. Thankfully, the deputy didn't see any signs of foul play."

"Maybe he didn't look close enough."

"I was there, too, and didn't see anything suspicious." Sean grimaced. To be totally honest, he'd been more focused on Jess than on the site as a potential crime scene. He sure as hell wasn't going to admit that to Jake, though. "But I want to take another look."

"Make it quick. Clock's ticking. The first hours are critical in a missing person case."

"I know. I know. I want to come over tomorrow to do my research with those handy-dandy computer research tools you were bragging about today."

"The legal...or illegal ones?"

"Both."

* * *

After watching the darkness swallow Luke's patrol car as he drove away, Jessie closed and locked the front door. She turned around and crossed her arms over her chest. "You didn't have to be so rude."

"You didn't have to call the damn cops. I told you Molly will come home when she calms down," Hal said, pushing out of the recliner.

Her hands dropped to her hips as she marched toward him. "Everything changed when I found Mom's car. How can you not understand that?"

"What I understand is her little hissy fit will be the talk of the town tomorrow. You'll have embarrassed her and, well, all of us.

Hope you're happy." He scowled at her before trudging toward the hallway. "I'm going to bed. Good night. Again."

"Seriously? How can you sleep with Mom missing?"

He didn't even stop when he answered. "Easy. Close my eyes and snore. Try it. Works like a charm." He disappeared into the dark hallway.

Jessie clamped her hand over her mouth. She wanted to scream at him for his lack of concern, but she couldn't risk waking Callie. *Oh, God, how am I going to tell Callie that her grandmother is missing?*

She checked the windows and doors and then checked them again. Feeling the weight of the world on her shoulders, she lumbered into her bedroom and shut the door. After changing into her nightgown, she stood at the window and stared at the moon. Helplessness enveloped her. How could this be happening? Stuff like this didn't happen to regular people.

Tears blurred her view of the moonlit property, the home that had once been her sanctuary. But a lot of the tranquility came from her mother's calm confidence. What would she do if she lost that?

"Mama, don't leave me," she whispered to the night. "I've already lost so many people I loved: Daddy, Grandpa, Grandma, Aunt Sally, and even Drake, in a different way." She paused. "And Sean." She swiped at the tears meandering down her cheeks. "I can't lose you, too, Mama. I just can't."

She closed her eyes and pressed her palms against them to stop the flow of tears. After several deep breaths, she blinked to clear her vision.

She jerked back from the window and stepped to the side. Someone was walking along the road not too far from the house. Size and movement suggested a man, but a bulky, dark hoodie hid the person's upper body and head. He walked with purposeful strides and aimed a flashlight into the deep ditch running alongside the road. As she watched, he stopped and bent down to inspect something on the ground. Although he was heading away from the house, his proximity ignited a spark of concern and sent her heart racing.

Jessie glanced at the alarm clock: almost eleven. Who would be out walking this time of night? What would someone be looking for along the road?

Her breath caught. Didn't criminals often return to the scenes of their crimes? Could this person know something about her mom's disappearance? Was he responsible? Could he be making sure he hadn't left any evidence?

Barely taking her eyes off the man, she ripped off her nightgown and threw on sweats. The man was moving steadily, and by the time she was ready, she could hardly see him anymore.

She snagged her purse and raced through the house. She cursed as she struggled with the locks and then darted out the back door to her car. As soon as she was on the road, she reached into her purse for her cell to call Luke.

Speeding without her headlights, she hoped to catch the suspect by surprise. She spotted the figure ahead of her, his flashlight and attention focused on the ditch. Looking down at her cell, she frantically scrolled through her contact list searching for Luke. The phone wobbled in her hand, and she fumbled it onto the passenger-side floorboard.

"Damn!"

She leaned down, past the console, stretching to grab her cell. Suddenly, the car jerked hard.

She shot upright. Had she hit something?

Thankfully no, but she'd drifted off the asphalt roadway and into a patch of several large rocks on the gravel shoulder. The steering wheel bounced wildly in her hands as she struggled to grip it.

She glanced ahead, and her eyes widened. The hoodie-wearing stranger stood directly in her path.

She screamed and slammed on the brakes.

The man's head whipped around. Their gazes collided.

Just before she hit him.

Chapter 3

A voice called to Sean through the darkness, but he couldn't make out the words over the jackhammering in his head. *Shut the fuck up, already. I can't hear you.* The constant pounding seemed to be pulling him up, up, up, like the crank on the back of a tow truck. If the pain ricocheting around his body was any indication of what awaited him at the top, he wasn't sure he wanted to surface.

The voice came again, louder, clearer. *Damn, I must be getting close.* The rhythmic beating quieted. The cocooning darkness faded. The throbbing pain increased. *Aw, shit.*

"Sean Burke, don't you dare die on me. If I kill you, I want to do it with my bare hands, not my car. Do you hear me?"

"Yeah. Loud…and clear," he mumbled. He managed to open his eyes a slit, but the world was a blur.

Jess squealed. "Oh, thank God, you're not dead."

"I got…the message. You want…to use…your hands." He groaned at the effort required to speak and let his eyes close. His chest ached as if his lungs had been crushed and were working overtime to inflate. Warm liquid ran down the right side of his face. He wanted to touch it, but his hands wouldn't respond to his brain. *Oh shit.* Not good. Not good at all.

"Sean, wake up. Are you all right?"

"What do…you think? You hit me…with a car," he muttered without opening his eyes. "Slapping me is one thing. Running me down…is over the top."

"I'm so, so sorry. I didn't know it was you. I thought you were the person who took my mother. I mean I didn't *try* to hit *him* either. I was calling Luke and dropped my phone. Then I ran off the road."

Her barrage of words bounced off his brain like sleet on concrete. He flinched. *Focus.*

"Oh no, you're in pain. Where does it hurt?"

"Everywhere." When he opened his eyes, her panicked expression gave him some satisfaction.

"Your head is bleeding…bad. I should call an ambulance." She rose from her knees.

"No," he ground out.

She stopped and rubbed her hand across her forehead. "Well…okay. I know. I'll call Luke."

"Fuck no," he snapped, more emphatic this time, and paid the price with a lightning bolt inside his skull.

"But…but…" She dropped back onto her knees next to him. "I've got to stop the bleeding." She leaned across him and moved his hood away from the injury. "Ugh. Your sweatshirt and cut are full of dirt and gravel. I need something clean to press against it. Do you have anything?"

"Not…handy." He grimaced as a wave of nausea swept through him.

Jess glanced around at the darkness. Did she expect something to magically show up? His gaze dropped to her clothes.

"What about your sweatshirt?" he asked.

"My sweatshirt?"

"Yeah. This is your fault, after all. You can at least ruin a piece of clothing on my behalf." He cringed inwardly at the unintended anger in his tone.

"Uh, well, okay." She glanced around nervously.

Well hell, wasn't he worth a simple piece of clothing? All he was asking for was a damn sweatshirt, not some expensive dress or something. What was her problem?

Jess sighed and pulled the sweatshirt over her head. Sean almost choked when her bare breasts bounced into view. And an awesome view it was. *Holy shit.* Despite his blurred vision and nausea, his dick hardened at the sight.

Avoiding his gaze, Jess leaned over him again. Her position put a tantalizing nipple within reach. He bit down on his tongue to keep it in his mouth. If he licked her nipple, he was sure she'd get in her car and run him over. Again. Forward *and* reverse, for good measure.

"Shit!" His attention jerked back when she pressed the soft cloth against his temple. "That fucking hurts."

"Don't be a baby," she scolded, looking down at him. "I'm going to need better light and tweezers to pick the gravel out of the hole in your head. Speaking of holes in your head, what the hell are you doing out here?"

He clenched his teeth for a moment. "Helping."

Jess huffed. "I told you that I don't want your help."

"Well, I don't see Lover Boy out here looking for evidence."

"Who?"

"Deputy Luke," he said in a high-pitched, singsong voice, and then groaned.

She snorted and frowned a moment before pressing her lips together to suppress a smile, which still showed at the corners of her luscious mouth. "Lover Boy's hands are tied. No official report has been filed." Her expression returned to grim. "Did you find anything?"

"Maybe."

"Maybe?"

"Don't get your hopes up. It could be nothing." He drew a deep breath. "Has it stopped bleeding?"

She peeked under the wadded sweatshirt. "Not really."

"I can't lie here all night. Keep pressure on it while I see if anything's broken." *But please get your tit out of my face before I go crazy.* He shut his eyes while he tested parts of his body. His limbs were now responding to his brain, so nothing must be broken, but he'd be black and blue by morning. He reopened his eyes to a firm, puckered nipple tempting his restraint. "Stop, you're killing me," he gasped, catching her wrist. "Help me up."

"I'm sorry it hurts, but you're still bleeding. You need to stay down."

"If you don't let me up, you're gonna be real mad about what happens." He let his eyes point to the Tit of Temptation.

Her breath caught as understanding must have registered. When she jerked her hand away, she scraped gravel across his cut. Then she sat up straight and crossed her arms across her bare chest.

Cursing under his breath, he pushed himself upright with scratched, bloody hands. His left hip screamed with pain. Still, it was better than being tempted by her nipple. Speaking of...

"Put your sweatshirt back on."

"But—"

"Just do it...please."

His tone conveyed how close he was to the edge, and she must've decided not to risk it. She pulled on the messy sweatshirt, leaving a streak of Sean's blood on her cheek. His gut clenched at the sight. He never wanted to see blood on Jess.

Wobbling, he got his legs under him and stood up. She grasped both his arms to steady him. He swiped his filthy hands on his pants. Hoping she didn't shove him back into the ditch, he gently wiped the blood from her cheek with his thumb. He held his breath and her gaze for several heartbeats.

Jess stood statue-still, holding her breath also. Then, apparently realizing she was touching his arms, she let go as if they were scalding her. She gave herself a shake and stepped away. Avoiding his eyes, she glanced over her shoulder in the direction of the house like she might bolt.

"You probably have a concussion, Sean. You should go to the ER."

"I've felt worse." He kept his gaze pinned on her to see if she caught his meaning, but he got no reaction. A good cop watched for such things.

"For the record, I think you should get medical attention. I'll pay—"

"Shit, Jess, I didn't know you'd become an attorney. I'll be fine. And money's not the issue."

She turned back to him with a scowl. "You're just as stubborn as you always were."

"Yeah, some things haven't changed." *Like how your tits make my dick hard.* He grinned.

She crossed her arms over her chest. Maybe she'd read his mind. She huffed and rolled her eyes. "You said you found something."

"No, I said 'maybe' and 'it could be nothing.'"

Jess huffed again. "Okay, what did you 'maybe' find?"

"Shoe prints. This way." He motioned for her to follow him in the direction she'd come but then stopped. "Where's my damn flashlight?"

Jess spotted it in the ditch and ran to get it. Handing it to him, she said, "If it's broken, I'll buy you a new one."

Sean grunted. "A broken flashlight is the least of my worries." He pushed the button, and the light flickered on. "I'll be damned. The Energizer Bunny lives."

Gritting his teeth, he limped along. Harder than walking was trying to ignore Jess behind him. Was she eyeballing his ass? She always used to tease him about what a great ass he had. *Get real, Burke. Her mom's missing.* He gave himself a mental slap.

"What shoes was your mom wearing today?"

"I don't know."

The crunch of the gravel under their feet needled its way under his skin. Of course, all his nerve endings were on edge, and irritability oozed from his pores. Who wouldn't be pissed after being hit by a car? Even though he was limping at a snail's pace, Jess stayed behind him. That annoyed him, too. He needed to curb his anger before he said something that sent Jess running to call Lover Boy. Sean drew a deep breath, blew it out slowly, and then stopped.

Her crunching halted also. "Is something wrong?"

He looked over his shoulder. Jess's face was pale and drawn. *Well, hell. Be nice.*

"It'd be easier to talk if I didn't have to yell so you could hear me."

She lifted her chin and glared at him for a second before taking several exaggerated steps to catch up. "Better?"

"Yeah." He sighed and started walking again. "What kind of shoes does Molly usually wear?"

Jess kept pace with him this time.

"Athletic shoes. In fact, her favorites are a pair just like these." She held up a foot. "Except hers are sevens and mine are eights."

"Let's hope she was wearing them today."

They walked the rest of the way in silence. Sean stuck out his arm to stop Jess before she trampled his evidence. His senses reacted to even that brief contact.

"See there…in the dirt? Where the gravel's gone. Take your right shoe off and lay it upside down to the left of that print," he said, aiming the light at the spot.

After doing as instructed, she remained kneeling. "How did you even see this?"

"Good eyes. Got good pictures with my phone, too. The second print is just ahead. See how it's a short person's stride?"

"If you say so."

He squatted next to her, lost his balance but recovered, and compared the two treads. "Looks good," he said to himself more than to her.

Jess's warm breath fanned across his cheek when she turned to him. Did she pause before speaking because their close proximity was affecting her also?

"You really think these are Mom's?"

Sean shrugged. "Strong possibility. These are fresh or they would've worn away. And how many people walk along this road anyway?"

"Apparently two."

He snorted. "Well, these tiny prints sure as hell aren't mine."

She laughed. The sweet, familiar sound tugged at his heartstrings.

"Did you find more?" she asked.

"Nope, just the two."

"Let's look closer to the house."

"Already been there and back. Molly must've stayed on the road most of the time. Easier walking."

"You already...?" Jess didn't finish her question but whipped around to look toward Wheaton where the Buick had been, her ponytail brushing his neck. He gulped. He used to bury his face in her silky hair while they were...

"The Buick was on the other side of the street. Why was she walking over here?"

"Don't you remember the safety rules? Walk facing oncoming traffic. I bet Molly remembered."

Jess turned to face him, her eyes swimming with tears. "Yeah, she remembers lots of things. She's so smart." Gulping, she blinked rapidly. "So, what does this mean?"

A wave of nausea struck, and Sean swallowed several times. "Let's talk while we walk back to my truck." When he stood up, dizziness threatened. He bent at the waist and rubbed the back of his neck.

"You're dizzy, aren't you?"

He sucked in a deep breath before straightening. "A little."

Her head jerked back. "The great Detective Burke admits to a little weakness. Did hell freeze over when I wasn't looking?"

Frowning, he ignored her jab and took one halting step and then another. "How did you know I made detective?"

She hesitated. "Luke told me."

"Why?" he asked, focusing on the ground for two reasons: one, for balance, and two, because he didn't want her to see the intensity of his interest in her answer.

"I don't know."

So much for gaining any insight. He dropped the subject, and they trudged on in silence. Finally, they reached her Camry. Not trusting himself to know the proper good-bye protocol, he pulled the keys from his pocket and continued on toward his truck parked farther down the road.

"Bye," he said. Short and sweet couldn't be that wrong.

"You aren't really going to drive, are you?" she asked, catching up to him.

"Damn right."

"I'll call Luke," she threatened.

He stopped and waited a moment before turning and pinning her with the steeliest gaze he could muster. "No. You. Won't."

She swallowed hard. "Yes. I. Will. He won't want you to drive either. He's your friend."

"You sure about that?"

She frowned. "Of…of course." She planted her hands on her hips. "I'll drive you home."

Sean studied the rigidity of her posture and the determination in her eyes. The smudge of mascara where her tears had leaked out.

The wisps of hair floating in the night breeze. The fullness of her lips. God, he'd missed her. "I don't think that's a good idea."

"What? Afraid to be alone in the car with me? Afraid I'll slap you again?"

"That's"—his gaze slowly raked her body and then rose to meet hers—"not what I'm afraid of."

Her eyes darkened just enough to be noticeable. "What, then?"

Did the crickets stop chirping or was it just his imagination? The world seemed to wait, breathless, for his response.

Before his slightly scrambled brain cells could form an answer that wouldn't get him slapped, she leaped forward, grabbed his keys, and raced back to the Camry. After locking herself in, she started the car and pulled alongside him. Too injured to react quickly, he hadn't moved since she'd asked the loaded question.

She rolled the passenger window down an inch and said, "Get in."

"No." He crossed his arms, and his ribs objected painfully.

"Okay. I'm going home. Have a nice walk." She switched on the headlights and drove forward a few feet.

Sean smacked the trunk with his hand. "Stop, damn it!" He lumbered to the passenger door. "Unlock it." When he heard the click, he yanked the door open and glared at her.

"Get in," she repeated tightly.

"Fuck." He looked heavenward, searching for divine patience, and then folded himself carefully into the small car. He slammed the door and hoped it rattled forever as a result.

"Thank you," she said primly. "Buckle up."

"Where are my keys?" he asked, doing as told.

She smiled smugly. "Safe."

Her smugness vanished when his gaze dropped to the small tell-tale bulge inside her sweatpants. She pressed the accelerator hard enough to knock him back in the seat, prompting a groan. Afterward, silence settled in. Again.

Jess spoke first. "So, why, then?"

"Huh?"

"Why were you afraid to get in my car?"

"I've seen you drive."

"You are such a jerk."

Sean chuckled. A small victory considering she was driving him home after all. Surreptitiously, he admired her profile until Jess released a long sigh.

"Mom was walking home, right?"

"Yeah. Now we have to figure out why she never made it. Anyone live out that way who could've seen her or picked her up?"

"About the same as when you lived here. There's still only two other houses past where she left the Buick. If you turn right off Wheaton onto Oakdale, instead of left toward us, the Turners live about two miles down the road."

"Any problems with the Turners?"

"No. They've lived there forever and are really nice people. They have a few chickens, so they trade us fresh eggs for fruits and vegetables. And we called them this evening. They hadn't seen or heard from Mom all day."

"Chances are our suspect is a man. Tell me about Mr. Turner."

She shot him a sidelong look that said *Get serious*. "He's in his eighties and uses a walker."

"Okay. Scratch him off the list. Do the Turners have any sons or grandsons? Any other male relatives who could've been visiting and passed your mom?"

"I know there aren't any sons or grandsons but have no idea about other male relatives."

"Get me Mr. and Mrs. Turner's full names, and I'll check them out."

"Sure."

"I remember who lives in the second house, the one a few miles farther down Oakdale past your place. It's another old guy, but single, and we used to pull pranks on him. Even gave him a nickname. What was it?" Sean grimaced in concentration but couldn't access the vague memory. *Damn concussion.*

"Crazy Calhoun."

"Right. How is the old dude?"

"Dead."

"Then scratch him off the list also." He rolled his eyes. "Sure limits the possibilities. Any ideas?"

Jess didn't respond.

Sean angled his head toward her. "What?"

"Nate lives there."

"Huh?"

She let out a frustrated breath. "Strange story. While"—she hesitated—"while you were away at college, Nate sort of befriended Crazy Calhoun. Or maybe it was the other way around. Who knows? Anyway, my brother started spending a lot of time over there. Mom and Dad were not happy and told Nate they didn't think it was wise for him to hang out with the old guy. But since Nate was twenty-two already, they couldn't actually forbid him from doing it."

"Was Nate still having…uh…problems?"

"Was and is. He said Calhoun just let him be. Didn't put any pressure on him. When Calhoun died, his relatives couldn't sell the place, so they asked Nate if he'd like to rent it. He jumped at the chance. I think he pays only nominal rent since he's pretty much acting as caretaker of the property. The arrangement helps him out because he has trouble holding down a job due to his…issues."

"That's why he could've been arguing with your mom about money, right?"

Jess's eyes narrowed as it registered Sean had overheard her conversation with Luke earlier. "Nate would *never* hurt Mom."

"I didn't say that."

"But it's where you were going with your line of questioning." She cleared her throat. "This interrogation is over, Detective Burke."

The remainder of the drive passed in stony silence. He hadn't wanted to upset Jess with his questions about Nate, but if the information helped solve the mystery of Molly Freeman's disappearance, Jess would forgive him. Wouldn't she?

Jess hadn't asked him for directions, so she obviously knew where his brother lived. Sean wasn't aware that they had any common friends or other connections. Which begged the question: Why had she kept tabs on Glenn?

When she parked at the curb in front of the apartment complex, she didn't say a word. She pulled his keys from her sweatpants, tossed them to him, and then stared straight ahead. No thanks for looking for evidence in the middle of the night. No apology for running him down. No wish for him to feel better. Not even a scolding for refusing to get medical attention. *Well, shit.*

"Thanks for the ride. Want to come in and study?" The words

popped out on their own. Sean cringed. He hadn't meant to say them. Hadn't even thought them. They were simply an old habit resurfacing. The phrase was his and Jess's code for *No one's home. Wanna come inside and fool around?* A sharp pang of what he'd had and lost hit him in the chest.

As if that wasn't painful enough, Jess speared him with a damning glare.

"You are one cruel bastard, Sean Burke."

Chapter 4

Jessie's heart ached as Sean stomped away from her car. With a limp, of course, but the stomping intent was obvious.

Damn. Why did he still have such a great ass? And eyes? And hair? And voice?

Sean had broken her heart so badly she'd made some really stupid decisions. Hadn't she learned a lesson? The man couldn't be trusted. Well, really, no man could. Drake had taught her that particular lesson. So why was she noticing Sean's ass, eyes, hair, and voice?

Damn him, too, for making her skin heat and tingle when he'd wiped her cheek. Her reaction to him was wrong on so many levels. *I'm such an idiot.*

Fighting her conflicting emotions, she pulled away from the curb and headed for home. Not only was their dark history reason enough to avoid Sean, but she also had to handle the crisis with her mother. It didn't help that he was the only person who seemed as worried as she was. Her teeth clenched. She could strangle her step-dad for his attitude. And although she understood Luke having to follow the law, he could've worked harder at persuading Hal to file a report. While he was taking the old man's statement, the deputy should've made him feel like a jerk. Instead, he'd treated Hal politely even when he got on his soapbox with his anti-police rant. The situation reminded her of all the times Sean had put up with Hal's crap.

She often marveled that Luke and Sean were so similar they seemed like brothers, not just friends. With Luke's sister, Karla, being Jessie's BFF, things had gotten really awkward after Jessie and Sean broke up. Karla had been totally pissed when Luke didn't tell Sean to go to hell. Although Luke had been sympathetic, sometimes it ticked her off also that he hadn't completely severed his relationship with Sean. But she'd discovered over the years that she was grateful when Luke shared some tidbit of news about her ex-boyfriend. Like when Sean made detective. She shouldn't have cared what was happening in Sean's life, but she did.

Sean's reaction to Luke earlier flashed through her mind. She smiled. *Serves him right.*

When she swung into the driveway, she blinked at the ancient Ford Taurus in her path. What was Nate doing here? Sean's questions replayed in her mind. He'd obviously been exploring the idea of her brother as a possible suspect in her mother's disappearance. But Sean couldn't be right. As she'd said, Nate would never hurt Mom—or anyone else, for that matter. Sure, he had some emotional issues and a quick temper, but he'd never *really* hurt someone. She had to admit, though, he'd been in a few fights over the years that had landed him in serious trouble, but those were always provoked by others.

The night closed in around her as she hurried from the car. The overhead fixture in the kitchen was the only light she could see in the house. Hopefully Nate hadn't woken Hal. The men didn't get along at all. But that hadn't always been the case. When their mother first remarried, Hal had worked hard to fill the void left by their father's death. In fact, Jessie had always been jealous of the close relationship between Hal and Nate when she was little. But something changed. She couldn't remember exactly how old Nate was when his attitude took a nosedive, but soon afterward, her brother became a seriously troubled kid.

She unlocked the kitchen door and stepped inside to find Nate slouched over a beer at the table.

"Where ya been?" he slurred.

Instead of answering his question, she asked one of her own. "What're you doing here?"

His head jerked up, and he gaped at her. "What? I'm such a lowlife now that I can't come check on my own mother?" He shook his head back and forth in a wobbly rhythm. "She's not here, ya know. I even peeked into the bedroom she shares with that asshole husband of hers."

Drawing a calming breath, Jessie took a beer from the fridge and sat down across from Nate. "We called and told you she was missing."

His eyes narrowed. "I'm not stupid, Jessie. I remember. But no one bothered to call me back to let me know if she'd been found."

She took a swig of beer to dampen her annoyance. "Sorry, but it's been a crazy night. As you figured out, she's still gone."

His bleary gaze zeroed in on her. "You look like shit."

She rolled her eyes toward the ceiling. "Thanks. I feel like it, too."

A flicker of a smile passed across his grim face and then it was gone, replaced by an even grimmer expression. "Is that blood?"

She glanced down at her sweatshirt. "Yeah."

"Fuck, Jessie, are you hurt?"

"No, it's not mine. I helped…someone with a nasty cut, and I must've gotten some on me," she said as casually as possible.

Nate studied her a moment and repeated his question. "Where ya been?"

She sighed. "I was going to look for Mom at the coffee shop when I found the Buick abandoned on Wheaton. No sign of Mom. I called 911, and Luke Johnson showed up to investigate. Dad refused to make an official missing person report, but Luke had the car towed in case it's needed later." She stopped when she realized she didn't have to explain about going out a second time and running into—literally—Sean Burke. She cringed inwardly. Why didn't she want to reveal the incident to her brother?

"Were there any clues about what happened?"

"No, nothing."

He swallowed a long drink and belched.

"Nate, you know you're not supposed to drink alcohol with your meds."

"I'm not drinking 'with' my meds. I took them already—with water." He sneered. "You sound just like Mom."

"Is drinking what you fought about this morning?"

A muscle twitched in his cheek. "It's none of your damn business, but no."

"Then what, Nate? Dad said Mom was real upset by the call."

"I know." He hung his head. "I felt bad. I drove over this afternoon to apologize."

"You did? Dad said you hadn't seen or talked to her since this morning."

"I…I didn't. Her car wasn't in the driveway or garage, so I knew she wasn't home. I waited on the patio."

"Why didn't you come inside?"

"I figured Hal was home since the tractor was out of the barn and the place reeked of manure."

Jessie smiled. No wonder Dad was so tired if he'd spread manure and taken Callie to the creek. He worked really hard at being a good grandpa. "What time was it?"

"I don't know. Maybe four-thirty or five. Mom's usually home then. Thought I might hang around until you got home from work."

"And get a home-cooked meal?"

Nate grinned. "Busted. Never hurts to eat decent food once in a while."

"No, it doesn't. You should come over more often."

His smile disappeared. "Can't."

She knew why, so she didn't press the issue. "You never saw Mom walking up the road from Wheaton?"

"Never saw anybody."

"Why weren't you here when I got home?"

His eyes narrowed. "What is this, an interrogation? You think I had something to do with Mom disappearing?"

"Of course not. But you should expect to answer some questions for Luke if Mom doesn't show up tonight."

Nate shoved his chair back so hard it fell over. "Luke thinks I did it? Great, just fucking great." He reached the back door in long, angry strides.

Jessie jumped up. "Wait, Nate. I didn't say that."

"You didn't have to. Suspicion is written all over your face." He opened the door, paused, and then turned back. "I didn't do anything, but I bet I know who did."

* * *

Despite hurting from head to toe, Sean paced his brother's living room before dawn on Saturday. Situations like this exemplified what he loved and hated about being a detective. Putting together the clues in a case reminded him of working a puzzle, and the thrill of solving one couldn't be beat. But he hated all the impediments and restraints. Obey the laws, mind the rules, follow the procedures. He envied the freedom his friend Jake Stone enjoyed in his security and PI practice.

Sean poured another cup of coffee and stepped out onto the patio. He drew a deep breath of fresh, damp morning air and didn't choke on smog. A coyote howled in the distance. A rooster crowed nearby. Damn, it was great to be out of LA.

He sighed and let his mind wander to the subject that had kept him up most of the night. He really should keep his nose out of the Molly Freeman case. Hell, it wasn't even a case since Hal had refused to file a report. Why was her husband being so stubborn? Obviously, Jess was convinced her mom was missing. And not voluntarily, as the old man claimed.

Sean had to agree with Jess. Molly wouldn't hide from her family for any reason, much less because of minor disagreements with her husband and son about money. Something was definitely wrong. And the longer they delayed looking for her, the less chance they had of finding her...alive.

Sean's fingers tightened around the mug. Last night with Jess had ended like shit. *Me and my big mouth.* Part of the time she'd actually seemed grateful for his interest in her mom's situation, especially when he'd shown her the matching shoe prints. Of course, she'd also run him down with her car, which definitely wasn't a sign of appreciation.

He flexed his shoulders carefully. Damn, the car had done a job on his body. *Body...hmmm.* His dick twitched at the memory of Jess's nipple dangling so close to his lips. If he hadn't been lying in a ditch after being run over, he would've pulled her on top of him and...*No, no, no, you idiot.* Maybe eight years ago, but not last night. Why couldn't he get it through his thick skull that Jess wasn't his anymore? He hadn't pined for her like this in LA. At least not in the past couple years. *Proximity.* Yeah, that was the problem. Being in Ramona was just too damn close for his libido.

He rearranged the swelling under his boxers and headed back inside. Enough daydreaming about what couldn't be. Time to get to work. Whether Lover Boy—or even Jess—wanted his help, he had to do what he could to find Molly...before it was too late.

After dragging another buddy out of bed at an ungodly hour on a Saturday morning to drive him to pick up his truck, Sean stepped onto Jake Stone's doorstep at 7:30 a.m. From its hilltop location in Valley Center, the property offered a commanding view of hundreds of massive boulders but no other houses. As Sean surveyed the area, the sense of being in a hidden fortress hit him. The idea certainly fit with the shadowy, secretive image of Jake Stone, former Navy SEAL and CIA operative. It was the "operative" job that intrigued Sean the most. When questioned, the cagey man refused to reveal anything. Sean's research had also turned up nothing. And the CIA wouldn't even acknowledge Jake had worked for them, of course. All of which left Sean with an uneasy feeling that he didn't really know much about the man he'd first met barely a month ago.

He stabbed the doorbell and waited. And waited. He punched it again. None of Jake's vehicles were visible, but Angela's BMW was parked in front of Sean's F-150. He was just about to pound on the door when a voice came through the small speaker in the security console on the wall beside him.

"Go away."

"Good morning, Stone. You, too, Angela." He heard giggling in the background.

"I'm busy, Burke. Go away."

Tilting his head up, Sean grinned at the tiny lens embedded at the top of the doorframe. "But you were 'busy' last night."

Jake snorted. "I'm 'busy' a lot."

"How does Angela feel about you being so 'busy'?"

"Oh, she feels *good* about it, believe me." The sound of skin smacking skin came over the intercom. "See? She can't keep her hands off my ass."

"Good morning, Sean," Angela said. "I'll buzz you in. Help yourself to coffee in the kitchen. We'll be downstairs in a minute."

Jake laughed. "A minute? I better get 'busy' fast."

"Jake," Angela squealed, and the intercom went silent.

A sharp buzz told Sean she'd managed to unlock the door before Jake...whatever. Chuckling, he let himself inside. Those two deserved lots of enjoyable time together after what they'd been through with Angela's case.

Ten minutes later, Jake unlocked the door to his home office on the first floor of the huge house. As Sean walked past, Jake gave him a head-to-toe inspection. "Angela's too polite to ask, but I'm not.

What the hell happened to you? You get in a fight or run over by a Mack truck?"

"A Camry," Sean admitted.

Jake hesitated, but when he realized Sean was serious, he bent over with a belly laugh. "Let me guess: Jessica Hargrove."

"It was an accident."

"You sure?"

He flipped Jake the bird before setting his computer bag down on the desk.

"You said you wanted to use both kinds of my research...tools, right?" Jake asked.

"Well, yeah. You got a problem with that?"

"No, but *you* might if anyone was ever able to trace what we're going to do back to you...or me."

"Good point."

"We should work in my happy place and only on my computers."

"Your what?"

"My happy place." Jake picked up the remote for the large television hanging on the wall. He fiddled with the back, opened a small panel, and then pointed it at the built-in bookcase. The wood creaked softly as the whole piece of furniture slid to the right, revealing a vaultlike door. Jake punched several numbers on the keypad and indicator lights flashed. After he entered more numbers, the door responded with a whir and a loud click before swinging open a few inches.

Sean's eyes widened. "Holy shit. Just like in the movies."

"Not really. Mine's better. I figure if you're gonna pay through the nose to build a safe room, it should be the best possible." He gestured with the remote for Sean to enter.

"You're not going to tase me with that thing, are you?"

Jake gave him a warning look. "Not unless you interrupt me again when I'm 'busy.'"

"I hear ya. Not gonna happen." Laughing, he held his arms over his head as he strolled into the room.

While Jake secured the door behind them, Sean surveyed his surroundings. The "room" was the size of a large studio apartment. At one end, tables were covered with laptop computers, printers, monitors, and other equipment. What Sean guessed was a server sat in a corner. A bank of locked file and storage cabinets lined one wall. A tripod leaned against a padlocked gun rack, which held enough guns for a small army.

Sean turned to the other end of the room. Furnishings included a king-sized bed, an armoire, a love seat, a recliner, and a hanging flat-panel TV. A well-equipped kitchenette occupied one wall. An open door revealed a bathroom with the addition of an unusual bathroom fixture: a rack containing two automatic rifles.

"Expecting trouble, Stone?"

"Always."

"Ever get the impression you attract trouble like a magnet?"

Jake skewered him with a malevolent glare.

After a nervous glance at the arsenal, Sean cleared his throat and dropped into a chair at one of the tables. "Let's get to work."

"Agreed. First, some rules. Don't sign into anything as yourself. I'll give you usernames and passwords. Don't change the settings on the computers. We don't want to leave any trails. I've got my network set up so stuff bounces off servers all over the world. It would be damn near impossible for anyone to trace something back to this room or these computers, but I won't risk it. Don't engage. If there's contact from the other end, tell me, and I'll decide whether to continue or abort. Understand?"

"Got it."

Jake nodded and tapped the laptop in front of Sean so the password prompt appeared.

"The password today for this computer is Granite27, cap the *G*," Jake said with a secretive smile.

Sean wondered if the password was an inside joke. Jake Stone. Granite. Boulders as the primary landscaping. Must mean something.

After entering the password, Sean stared at the mass of icons on the screen. He estimated a couple hundred folders with no obvious organization.

"Open 'Kitchen,'" Jake instructed him.

Sean scanned the folders three times before finding it. "Have you ever considered alphabetizing these suckers?"

"Why make it easy? Now 'Recipes' and then 'Ingredients.'"

Inside the Ingredients folder was a large Word document listing hundreds of food items, from ackee to zucchini. At least these were alphabetized, and they all appeared to be hyperlinks.

"What the hell?" Sean murmured.

"You probably want to start with 'Dates,' 'Sea Salt,' and 'Figs,'" Jake said, his fingers flying over his own keyboard. "Tell me what you're eating, and I'll give you the corresponding log-in."

Sean clicked on Figs and froze. "Holy shit. This is the—"

"Don't freak out on me, Burke. You said you wanted to use *all* my resources. Change your mind?"

"Uh, no. I just don't want to end up behind bars for hacking government networks. Cops don't do well in prison."

Jake grunted. "Don't like the idea of being someone's bitch? Me neither. That's the reason for all the security. Besides, technically, we aren't hacking."

Sean turned an incredulous stare on him. "What the hell do you call it?"

"Borrowing. These log-ins are for legitimate users. They just aren't you and me."

"How did you get them?"

"You don't wanna know. Now quit whining and get to work."

After Jake got Sean onto several sites, twenty minutes passed with no sound except the clicking of keys.

"I'll be damned," Jake muttered.

"What?" Sean asked without interrupting his typing.

"Nathaniel Freeman has quite a rap sheet."

"No shit?"

Jake swiveled his chair around. "You didn't know about this?"

Sean stopped typing and faced him. "Nope. He was just a brooding loner back in the day. What's he been tagged for?"

"Lots of minor stuff. Nothing worse than some county jail time for punishment, though."

Jess's words, *Nate would never hurt Mom*, came back to Sean. He frowned. "Anything violent?"

"Couple of bar fights and one assault charge. It was dropped." His gaze darted back to the screen. "That one's troubling. He attacked his stepfather, but his parents didn't want to press charges. The DA let it go because there were no other witnesses."

"Hmmm. That would've been Molly's call, not Hal's. He was a hard-ass, especially tough on Nate."

"In exchange for no charges, it looks like Nate agreed to a shrink eval," Jake said.

"Too bad we can't see those medical records. Maybe the guy's problems were more serious than people realized when he was younger."

"I can get them if you want."

Sean scowled at him. "Have you no respect for someone's privacy?"

"Now you're talking like a cop, not a private investigator. Make up your mind which you are today. If it helps your conscience, this might be enough. There's a note that Nate was diagnosed as suffering from severe depression and should seek treatment."

"No psychosis, neurosis, disorder, or syndrome?" Sean asked.

"Nope, straight depression. But the notes say it could be related to a childhood trauma."

"A drunk driver killing your dad when you're four would probably qualify."

"Most likely."

"Sounds like I need to have a heart-to-heart with Nate. Jess is gonna be pissed."

"Most likely."

Leaning back in the chair, Sean sighed, scratched the stubble on his chin, and frowned at the computer screen.

"Something wrong?" Jake asked.

"Not sure. Hal Freeman comes up in general searches, but when I look for anything official, there's no Hal. Although I've never heard him called anything else, it must be short for something."

"What're your choices?"

"Apparently, it's been a nickname for Henry, Harry, and Harold. But that use seems more historical and British."

"Don't forget HAL was the evil computer in *2001: A Space Odyssey*," Jake quipped.

Sean shot him an annoyed, sideways glance. "I don't think there's a connection. This Hal was born way before that movie."

"Any other possibilities?"

"So far I've got a Halliburton, Halston, Halroy, and would you believe…Hallelujah? I was just going to cross-reference those names with his Ramona address."

"Logical next step."

Both men returned to their computers. More clicking. More swearing.

"You gotta be kidding me," Sean exclaimed.

"What?" Jake walked up beside his chair.

"The guy's name is Hallelujah Ima Freeman. Freakin' weird."

Jake stared at the screen and didn't respond.

Chuckling, Sean peered up at him. "You don't think that's a weird-ass name?"

Jake didn't crack a smile. "Say it again, syllable by syllable, and don't say 'Emma.' Use a long *I* like *ice*."

"Hal-le-lu-jah Im-a Free-man." Sean paused. "Fuck."

* * *

"Hello," Jessie answered the kitchen phone Saturday morning, saying a silent prayer it was her mother.

"Jessie? We need to talk," her ex-husband said without greeting.

"I have nothing to say to you. Talk to my lawyer."

"Look, I flew all the way out here. Can't you at least spare me a few minutes?" Drake paused. "It's about Callie."

Here? He's here? Oh God, no. The back of Jessie's neck prickled with distrust. "What about her?"

"I'd rather discuss it in person. I drove out to your place yesterday afternoon to see you."

"You were *here* yesterday?" Her stomach clenched. Mom hated Drake for how he'd treated her and Callie. If he'd come to the house, she would've killed him. Or tried to. If Drake had fought back...Jessie gulped. "D-did you talk to Mom?"

"Didn't talk to anyone. No one was home."

"No one? Dad and Callie weren't here?"

"No one answered the door when I rang the bell, okay? I checked around back but didn't see anyone. Before I drove off, I honked the horn a few times in case someone was in the garden or down at the creek. I waited, but no one showed up."

"What time was it?" Jessie asked.

"Huh? What does it matter?"

She didn't respond.

"Fine. Around four, four-thirty, I guess. I don't know exactly."

"Was Mom's Buick parked on Wheaton?"

"Jesus, Jessie. What's with the twenty questions?"

"Answer me."

He hesitated. "Maybe. There was a car parked on the side of the road, but I didn't look at it close enough to recognize it as hers. Damn, Jessie, what's going on?"

She drew a halting breath. "None of your business. Now tell me what you want or you can just catch the next plane back to Chicago."

Drake cursed under his breath. "I got screwed on the custody issue in the divorce settlement. I've hired a new big-shot Chicago lawyer to file the papers to renegotiate. I'm willing to pay all the past-due alimony and child support if you'll agree to let me take Callie home to live with me for the next six months."

"This is Callie's home. Go to hell!"

Chapter 5

Oh, Karla, what am I going to do?" Jessie cried when her BFF answered the phone.

"Calm down. I can barely understand you. What's wrong?" Luke's sister asked.

"Everything." Jessie forced a deep breath and exhaled slowly. How could she be calm when her world was falling apart? "First Mom and now Drake," she finished.

"What about your mom? She was fine yesterday."

Jessie sniffed. "She came for her hair appointment?"

"Yeah. At one, as usual. Why?" Concern crept into Karla's voice.

"I guess you haven't talked to Luke since last night."

"He texted me to call him, but things were getting hot with Troy so I—"

"Mom's missing," Jessie interrupted. She didn't have time to hear the latest about hottie Troy.

"Missing? What do you mean 'missing'?"

"Just what it sounds like. She never came home after running errands. She left the Buick on the side of the road and disappeared. Vanished."

"You're freakin' me out, Jessie. No way would your mother go off without—"

"I don't think she did. I think someone…took her."

"Oh my God. You're serious. Is Luke…? Are the deputies looking for her?"

A sob tore free, and tears filled her eyes. "No. Dad won't file a missing person report."

"He *what*? Why the hell not?" Karla asked.

"Honestly, I can't accept his stupid reasons."

"Then you do it."

"I know. I know. Last night I let him bully me into not doing it. But since Mom still isn't home this morning, I'm going to talk to Luke without Dad."

"Good. The sooner the better. And did you say 'Drake'?"

"He's here." Her throat tightened at the thought.

"You let him in the house?"

"No, of course not. I mean here in San Diego. He wants to change the custody terms and take Callie back to Chicago with him. Over my dead body…"

"And mine. And Luke's. Hell, girlfriend, half of Ramona will beat that bastard to a pulp if he tries anything."

"Thanks, Karla. It may take that. He's hired some new high-powered Chicago lawyer to handle his case."

"Sounds like you need ice cream. I'll be right over."

"It's only ten—" Jessie objected, but Karla was already gone. Bless her best friend. She'd probably been up half the night with Troy, and yet she jumped into action when friendship called. Unfortunately, ice cream wouldn't fix any of Jessie's problems, including the one she hadn't mentioned: Sean Burke.

"Mommy, Mommy," Callie called, barreling through the back door. "Looks what I picked. It's the biggest 'mato in the world. Grandpa said so." She held up a fiery red tomato that was almost as big as a grapefruit. She plopped it on the kitchen table and then peered up into her mother's face, her expression growing serious. "Why's you crying, Mommy?"

Jessie swiped at the remnants of her tears and sniffed. "I-I'm not crying. I just smelled something bad, and it made my eyes water."

"Oh, like Grandpa's 'nure. It stinks. I don't likes it."

Jessie thankfully grabbed on to the change of subject like a lifeline. She had no idea how she was going to tell Callie that her grandmother was missing. When the little girl had asked earlier about her grandmother's absence, she'd accepted a simple explanation that Molly was "out." The easy answer wouldn't suffice for long. "Didn't you help him spread the manure with the tractor yesterday?" Jessie asked.

Callie frowned and shook her index finger for emphasis. "I told him after I gots in trouble for getting 'nure in my hair last time that I don't *never* wants to do it *again*. 'Sides, Grandpa didn't do the 'nure 'terday."

Jessie smiled at her daughter's speech. "Maybe he did it while you took a nap after going to the creek."

Callie cocked her head. "We didn't feeds the ducks. I'd 'member that for sure 'cause I likes them."

She tousled her daughter's blond curls and laughed. "Sweetie, your brain must still be asleep. Go wash up. You smell like tomato plants."

Callie sniffed her hands. "Ugh. At least it's not bad as 'nure."

The phone rang as she skipped off to the bathroom, holding her hands straight out in front of her.

"Hello?" Jessie said hesitantly, hoping it *wasn't* Drake and *was* her mom.

"Jess, it's me."

After the cruel way Sean had ended their encounter last night, her first impulse was to hang up. But she needed to keep him interested in her mother's disappearance. That didn't mean she couldn't set some boundaries. "Good morning, Detective Burke. How're you feeling?"

He hesitated as though he couldn't decide whether she was greeting him as friend or foe. Good, because it was a little of both.

"Uh, good morning. I'm doing okay. Considering you ran me down."

Guilt pinched her. "Did you go to the ER to see if you have a concussion?"

"Real men don't go to the ER." He cleared his throat. "Any word from your mom?"

She swallowed hard. "No."

"Did you get Mr. and Mrs. Turner's full names for me? And their address?"

"Hold on. Let me grab Mom's address book." She opened a kitchen drawer and pulled it out. After reading him the information, she said, "I'm going to talk to Luke about *me* signing a missing person report."

"Good idea." Sean paused and cleared his throat again. "Do you know your stepdad's full name?"

"Huh?"

"Hal. What's his full name?"

"Sean, you're wasting your time suspecting him or Nate."

"Humor me."

"Hal Freeman. That's it."

"No middle name or initial?"

She thought a moment. "Maybe I've seen a *T* or an *I* a couple times."

"Okay. What's 'Hal' short for?"

"Nothing. It's just Hal."

Sean paused again. "How long have Hal and Molly been married?"

"They recently celebrated their twenty-sixth anniversary."

"Interesting. Did you know Nate's been arrested several times?"

Her breath caught in her throat. "No way."

"I didn't think so. Thanks. Talk to ya later."

"Wait just a damn minute," she snapped. "Don't ask me those kinds of questions and then not tell me what you're doing. Spill it."

"Well, hell," he mumbled. "You're not gonna like it. Just let it go."

Instead of sparking more anger, his words spawned a sense of foreboding. She dropped onto a chair at the kitchen table and rested her forehead in her hand. "Tell me. Please."

"Don't say I didn't warn you."

"Fine."

"Your stepdad's name is Hallelujah Ima Freeman."

Jessie blinked. Had she entered the *Twilight Zone*? "You're kidding."

"Nope. And even weirder, I can't find any evidence he existed more than twenty-seven years ago, a year before he married your mother."

She groaned. "What does that mean?"

"Well, since he's in his sixties, it could mean he changed his name at that time. But I can't find any legal record of it."

"Changed it from what?"

"Who you talking to?" Hal asked from behind her.

She whipped her head around, and her heart thumped hard. "Jesus Christ, Dad, you startled me."

"You talking to that goddamn deputy? I told you those people are *not* buttin' into our family's business." He grabbed the phone from her hand. "Stay out of it, Deputy Johnson," he shouted, and ended the call. Glaring at her, he slammed the phone on the table.

"Dad, we have to do something. Mom's been gone almost twenty hours. She doesn't have her car and—"

"Listen to me, Jessie. I didn't want to say this in front of Callie, but Molly was damn pissed I wouldn't let her pay for those lessons. And Nate really got her riled up asking for money to buy a video game console. From the shouting I overheard from his end, he would've strangled her through the phone if he could've." He sighed dramatically. "Your mother had a real tough day."

"But, Dad, why would she—"

He huffed with frustration. "When the Buick broke down, it must've been the last straw. She didn't want to call me for help because she was so pissed about the money thing. Instead, she phoned one of her friends to come pick her up."

"But we called—"

"One of 'em is lying through her teeth to hide your mother. Molly needs a break. Let her have it."

"I can't believe Mom would worry us like—"

"Well, believe this. She'll be so damned embarrassed if her behavior hits the gossip mill that she'll never get over it. Do you want to do that to her on top of all the trouble you've already caused by moving home?"

His words hit like a sucker punch. She floundered for a response.

"I didn't think so," he said with a slight sneer. He started to leave, but then stopped and turned back. "Did you borrow the earrings that were lying on Molly's dresser?"

Still dazed and hurt, she was puzzled by the sudden change of subject. "Earrings?"

"You know, the heavy gold ones I gave her when we got married. They've been sitting there since last weekend and now they're gone."

* * *

"Jess? Jess!" The hairs on the back of Sean's neck rose. Anxiety slithered down his spine. Slowly, he set Jake's phone on the table.

"Well?" Jake asked.

"Huh?"

"Did she know?"

Sean shook his head. "No. Not about Hal or Nate."

"Figures. What're you going to do?"

Standing up, he jammed his hands in his pockets and paced across the safe room. "I don't know yet, but I have a bad feeling about this."

"Me too."

"Who the hell is Hal Freeman? Why did he change his name, other than to celebrate getting out of prison? And what was his crime?"

"Great questions. Got any answers?"

"Not a one." Sean pounded his fist on the wall. "And then there's Nate, who's actually attacked one of his parents before. Maybe after Molly refused to give him money, he took it a little further this time."

"Possible."

"If it's either of them, then Jess could be in danger."

"True. So, I repeat, what're you gonna do, Burke?"

He shoved his fingers through his hair. "I have to protect Jess."

Jake studied him. "You two aren't really ancient history, are you?"

"What?"

"You've still got the hots for Jessica Hargrove."

Sean narrowed his eyes. "Get your mind out of the gutter, Stone. If Hal or Nate have abducted...or killed...Molly, Jess could be next. She poses a threat by insisting on looking for her mother."

"Good point." Jake stroked his chin. "Nate's motive is easy, but what would Hal's motive be? You think Molly found out something about his past and confronted him with it?"

"Exactly. Now we just need to figure out what was in his past that would set him off."

"You're running with Hal as the perp?"

Sean ran his hand over his eyes. "Nope. They're both suspects at this point. But we might be able to eliminate Hal if we can't find anything incriminating in his past."

"Changing his John Hancock to some weird-ass name doesn't count?"

"Changing your name isn't normally a motive for murder."

Jake arched his eyebrows. "Murder?"

"I told you I have a bad feeling about this."

"I haven't known you very long, Burke. Are your feelings usually right?"

"Yeah."

"Mine too."

* * *

"I've already walked to where the Buick was left and back twice this morning looking for any clues to what happened," Jessie said. "And I called Nate, Uncle Chad, and all Mom's friends to see if anyone's heard from her. No one has." The memory of Hal's accusation about one of them lying made her hesitate a beat. "They're going to spread the word and start looking, too. I also called Luke and told him I want to come in and file the missing person report today after Dad leaves for LA. Despite all that, I just feel so helpless." She sniffled as she sucked ice cream from a spoon.

Karla patted her shoulder. "Sounds to me like you're doing everything you can. When I get back to the shop, I'll alert all my peeps, and we'll tell our customers, too. All of Ramona will be looking for her."

Jessie blinked back tears. "What if it's…not enough?"

Her friend swallowed hard. "You'll find her. You gotta have faith."

"I'm trying, but I'm so scared. And this crap with Drake. He couldn't have pulled this at a worse time."

"I understand, but you really should talk to your lawyer."

Jessie rubbed her temples. "My divorce lawyer is in Chicago. She doesn't work Saturdays, and I can't afford another minute of her time."

"Well, you need to be prepared before Drake strikes."

"I agree. I'd like to find out if I can get a restraining order against him so he can't come near Callie or me. But I don't know if I have grounds."

"Ask Luke," Karla suggested.

"Luke is too much in my corner. He couldn't give me an unbiased opinion."

"Anyone else you can ask?"

Jessie went through a mental list, but none of her friends was a lawyer or in law enforcement. *Sean.* The name popped into her head, unwanted and unusable. The irritation produced by his earlier questions on the phone returned. He was wasting his time focusing on Nate and her stepdad. Drake was a more likely suspect, but she hadn't had a chance to tell Sean about her ex-husband being in town before Hal had hung up on him. She needed to get that information to Sean, but how? She'd checked months ago, and Glenn didn't have a listed phone number. Probably didn't even have a landline with as little as he was in town. Did Sean still have the same cell number as eight years ago or had he changed it after moving to LA?

"Earth to Jessie."

"Huh?"

Karla leaned forward. "Is there anyone else you can ask?"

"I…I don't think so." She shook Sean from her thoughts. "Want a Coke?"

"Yeah, thanks."

Jessie opened the fridge. She pushed aside some items to get to the soda cans and paused. The little baggie of breadcrumbs she'd made for the ducks sat where she'd placed it yesterday morning before going to work. Why hadn't Callie and Hal taken it with them to the creek? She smiled for the first time that morning. Callie was probably in such a hurry that her grandpa forgot about the bread. It had happened before. Shaking her head, she grabbed two Cokes and returned to the table.

"Didn't you go to a lawyer with your parents when they were setting up their trust-thingy a few months ago?" Karla said, popping open the can.

"Yeah, we saw Mr. Swanson. Nate, Uncle Chad, and I were there because we're successor trustees. I don't think he's a divorce lawyer."

"Swanson. That's him. He's been practicing law in Ramona since Noah and the flood. He set up a partnership for Troy and his friend to run their pool maintenance business together. Swanson must be more of an all-purpose country lawyer."

"Yeah. Mom told me he'd been such a big help when my birth father died and she had all kinds of legal stuff to deal with."

"See, Swanson knows all that lawyer-y stuff. And since he's your mom and dad's attorney, he probably won't charge you much."

Another memory of Mr. Swanson surfaced. "Hmmm, I'm not so sure. Mom also told me once that he asked her out a couple times before she met Hal. Swanson was never quite as friendly after she remarried."

"Well, that makes sense. The other man beat him out." Karla gestured toward the phone. "Call him. What've you got to lose?"

Jessie sighed. "I want to go to the sheriff's station first to file the report, and I can't take Callie either place."

"You haven't told her?"

"No. I can't even think about telling her without starting to cry."

"Why's you gonna cry 'gain, Mommy?"

She spun around to find Callie standing in the kitchen doorway. She cleared her throat. "Uh…the ice cream's so cold it hurts my head."

"You gots brain freeze," the four-year-old announced.

"You're right. Did you wash the ice cream off your hands?"

Callie nodded and held them out for inspection.

"Hey, I have an idea," Karla said. "Why don't I take the munchkin with me to the shop? I can give her a trim, mani, and pedi to keep her out of trouble while you…um…take care of business. You can pick her up whenever."

Callie bounced up and down. "Say yes, Mommy, pleeeeze. I wanna go with Ms. Karla. Puuleeeze."

Letting Callie out of her sight suddenly felt like a terribly risky idea, but Jessie didn't know how she was going to get her two critical tasks accomplished if she didn't accept Karla's offer.

Her stepdad was leaving in about an hour for a wedding photography job in LA tomorrow, which was scheduled too early for him to make the four-hour drive in the morning. This was the wedding of an old friend's daughter and had been on the calendar for almost a year, so he couldn't possibly cancel. Despite Sean's strange questions about Hal's name and his outrageous suspicions, Jessie would've felt much better leaving Callie home with her grandfather. Hal had a shotgun and knew how to use it. And, more importantly, he wouldn't hesitate to aim it at Drake. Unfortunately, her stepdad just wasn't available. She didn't really have a choice but to let Karla babysit Callie.

"Okay, munchkin, but you mind Ms. Karla and *always* stay where she can see you."

* * *

Sean slouched back into the chair and glared at the laptop screen. "How are we going to figure out who this guy really is? No way he changed his name legally."

"Right. I'm sure it was all done with fake documents. We'll have to come at it from the other side—find him being released from prison shortly before the name change," Jake said.

"Jesus, that could be hundreds, maybe thousands, of inmates since we don't have any idea where he was incarcerated. I mean, federal, state, local jails, anywhere in the country."

"Nothing says it was even domestic."

Sean tunneled all ten fingers into his hair and gripped it. "Fuck. This'll take a while."

"Try forever."

He groaned and then went still.

"I can see your brain working. Should I be afraid?" Jake joked.

"Only if you're Hallelujah Ima Freeman. I'm gonna nail him." Sean stood up and started pacing again. He stopped and turned to Jake. "What if he wasn't released?"

"He escaped?"

"Yeah. There have to be a lot fewer escapes than releases."

Jake nodded. "Better be. Still a lot of geography to cover, though."

"For sure. We'll start with escapes in California."

"Then where?"

Sean stared into space. He'd just heard Hal's voice on the phone when the jerk thought he was telling off Deputy Johnson. The man had a hint of an accent. Nothing strong enough to pinpoint its source, but it was there. It sounded slightly Southern, but not like the deep Southeast. "Hell, I don't know, but let's give Texas a try based on his accent."

"Well, damn, you're not half bad at this. But why couldn't you pick a tiny state like Rhode Island?"

Chapter 6

Jessie's hand trembled as she reached for the doorknob of Mr. Swanson's office. Filing the missing person report on her mother had been an emotional hell. Thank goodness Luke had come to the station to help her through the ordeal even though he wasn't on duty. A person couldn't ask for better friends than Luke and Karla Johnson.

But did Jessie really feel strong enough to draft a battle plan against Drake right now? Drawing a deep breath, she let her hand drop to her side. She closed her eyes and forced resolve through her veins. She had to do this ASAP. If she waited, Drake would have the upper hand. And this was Callie—not dollars, not anything else—at risk. No way could she not act quickly. Squaring her shoulders, she opened the door and marched across the threshold into the empty reception area.

"Is that you, Ms. Hargrove?" Mr. Swanson called from his private office.

"Yes. I—"

"C'mon in. My assistant is smarter than I am; she doesn't work Saturdays."

Jessie walked into an office overflowing with papers, books, and files, quite different from the neat, orderly conference room where the group had met to take care of the trust signing. Behind a desk that looked like a bomb had hit it, Mr. Swanson stood up and reached across the mess to shake her hand. His carefully groomed gray hair, angular features, and piercing blue eyes gave him an aristocratic appearance, and his intense gaze suggested keen intelligence.

"How are you today, Ms. Hargrove?"

She gulped. "I've been better. And please, call me Jessie."

"Of course. Have a seat and tell me what I can do to help with this situation involving your ex-husband."

She explained about the phone call from Drake that morning. Then she gave him some background on their disastrous marriage and even more devastating divorce. He listened intently and nodded his understanding. When she finished, he leaned back in the large leather chair and steepled his fingers under his chin in contemplation.

"What do you think brought on this sudden change of heart regarding the custody arrangements?" he asked.

"I have no idea. Knowing we were moving back to California, Drake was pretty reasonable when we originally negotiated the terms. But he's a manipulative son of…er…person, a real control freak. This could be just another ploy to terrorize me."

"Okay, but couldn't he have made the same demands from Chicago? Why go to the trouble and expense of flying out here?"

The attorney had a point. Why had Drake come to San Diego? A shiver raised the hair on her nape, and she shuddered.

"Are you all right, Jessie?" He stood up.

"I-I'm fine."

Mr. Swanson hesitated a moment before sitting down.

"I don't know Drake's reason for coming, but it can't be good. I'm scared, and I don't want him anywhere near Callie or me. Can we get a restraining order?"

He pulled a legal pad from a drawer and tapped a pen on the yellow paper. "We need to have some grounds on which to request it. Was Drake ever physically abusive with you or your daughter?"

Jessie's gaze dropped to her lap. Even after escaping from him, the memories haunted her. Talking about Drake's behavior would be like reliving the experiences. "Not really. He...he was more of a psychological abuser. He has a terrible temper. When he went into a rage, he was extremely intimidating and frightening."

"Did any of these frightening instances happen in California?"

She thought a moment. "No. Only in Illinois."

"Hmmm. Are there any police reports documenting his violent outbursts?"

Heat flowed up her neck and into her checks as she shook her head. "No. It was never that bad."

"Do you have any witnesses?"

"Not really." She raised her eyes to meet his. "I don't think Drake would actually hurt either of us...intentionally, at least. I'm most afraid he might kidnap Callie. He's used to getting his way, and when he doesn't, he does whatever's necessary to make it happen...or to get revenge."

"Spoiled rich boy?" Mr. Swanson asked.

She cocked her head. "Exactly."

"Such a shame."

"And he's a mama's boy to a woman who defines the word *matri-arch*."

"Terrible combination." He exhaled. "Let me talk to a judge friend of mine who works with domestic violence restraining orders all the time and see what he thinks. You should also gather pictures of Drake, Callie, and yourself, as well as write up physical descriptions of everyone. Do you have a local address for him?"

"No. I don't have any idea where he's staying."

"We'll likely need an address to have him served. Meanwhile, if he does anything—and I mean *anything*—that frightens you, call 911 without hesitation. Better safe than sorry."

"When do you think we can file this?"

"If I determine we can get it approved, we should be ready to go Monday. Will you be all right until then?"

She nodded and stood up. "Thank you so much for seeing me on a Saturday and on such short notice."

"My pleasure." He smiled. "Every time I see you, Jessie, you look more and more like your mother," he said with a hint of longing for what might have been in his voice. "I haven't run into her in a while. How is Molly?"

Jessie gulped, and tears filled her eyes. How was she going to cope with all this: Mom, Drake, Hal... Sean?

The attorney's expression morphed from curious to concerned. "Is something wrong?"

"M-Mom's missing," she stammered.

Mr. Swanson froze, and his gaze hardened. "Tell...me...what...happened," he said, emphasizing each word.

Her legs wobbled so she grabbed the back of the chair and lowered herself onto it. She opened her purse to rummage for a tissue.

When she looked up, his eyes were still riveted on her. "Mom never came home from running errands yesterday. I found her Buick abandoned on Wheaton, but she's vanished…without a trace, as the saying goes."

His face paled to ashen as she spoke. He didn't blink, just stared right through her. "How did she know?" he mumbled so softly Jessie wasn't sure she heard him correctly. After several seconds, he cleared his throat. "What's being done?"

"I filed a missing person report with the sheriff's department right before I came here. We've notified Nate, Uncle Chad, and all Mom's friends and asked everyone to be on the lookout for her and to spread the word. This afternoon, I plan to distribute flyers."

"What can I do to help?"

She shrugged. "Check places you think she might be. Spread the word. Anything you do is appreciated."

He nodded, still looking dazed.

She gathered her composure and stood again. "Thank you for your help with…both matters, Mr. Swanson."

"My pleasure," he replied absently.

He didn't make a move to stand, shake her hand, or show her to the door. He seemed totally distracted. Should she stay and be sure he was okay? No, she couldn't; she didn't have time. She wanted to make flyers on the computer and distribute them before picking up Callie at the beauty shop. She turned to say good-bye as she stepped through the doorway into the reception area.

Mr. Swanson still sat at his desk, his head cradled in his hands, and muttered to himself, "Why, sweetheart, why?"

* * *

This sucks. Sean's level of frustration maxed out. He and Jake weren't having any luck finding an escape report on the man now known as Hal Freeman. And Sean's focus was shot to hell with worry over Jess. *"Stay out of it, Deputy Johnson."* Freeman's words ricocheted around in his brain. They were joined by all the man's hate-filled comments from years past about law enforcement. His attitude fit the profile of a convict perfectly.

Gnawing at the back of Sean's mind was the crucial question of what crime the man had committed. Petty theft? No big deal. Aggravated assault? Big deal. Rape? Big fucking deal. Murder? Biggest fucking deal. The possibilities and the corresponding danger to Jess were driving him crazy.

"I gotta go," he announced.

Jake swiveled in his chair and eyed him solemnly. "To check on Jessica?"

"Yeah. I can't shake this bad feeling."

"Understood. Stay in touch. I'll keep looking."

"Thanks, Stone."

Jake pressed something on the high-tech remote. The safe room door buzzed, clicked, and opened. He nodded. "I turned off the electrical current. Hurry up so I can rearm it."

Sean thought his friend was kidding, but he couldn't be sure. He hustled out, grabbed his computer bag, and passed through the "normal" office as the bookcase slid back into place.

"Angela?" he called when he reached the foyer.

A laugh came through the speaker beside the front door. "She left hours ago, Burke. Get out before I decide you were planning to flirt with my girlfriend."

The front door lock clicked. Sean saluted the security camera in the corner and escaped the fortress.

His truck shot down the steep, winding driveway and past the boulder sentries. Careening onto the two-lane road at the bottom of the hill, he raced away from the isolated citadel toward the freeway, urgency increasing with each passing mile.

Pulling his cell from his pocket, he pondered calling Jess. Would she talk to him or tell him to go to hell? He didn't want to take the chance so he headed to Ramona without making the call.

Bad traffic increased his trip to almost an hour. When he finally pulled into the Freeman driveway, the property looked deserted except for Jess's Camry. Stepping out of the truck, he listened for signs of life but heard nothing. No kid chattering. No equipment running. No music or voices. His gut clenched.

He leaped up the two steps to the front door and poked the doorbell several times. No response. He banged his fist on the wooden door. Still no response. "Jess! Answer the door." Nothing.

Sean dashed around the house to the back door. Without knocking, he grabbed the knob and twisted. Locked. "Fuck." He yanked his wallet from his back pocket, fished out a credit card, and slipped it between the door and frame. Frantically, he slid the card up and down against the old lock until it gave way. He shoved the door open. "Jess!"

He flew through the kitchen, which he knew at a glance hadn't changed since his last visit years ago, and landed in the living room. A quick sweep confirmed it was also empty. His heart pounding, he hit the hallway at a run.

Halfway down, he slammed into someone emerging from the bathroom. They both went down, sprawling onto the floor.

Jess screamed and pummeled Sean with her fists. "Stop, Drake, don't hurt me," she cried with her eyes closed, arms and legs flailing.

Drake? Is that her ex? With Jess struggling frantically beneath him, Sean captured her wrists with one hand and pinned them above her head on the carpet. "Jess, stop. It's me. Sean."

"Sean?" Opening her eyes, she gasped for air and stopped squirming. "What...what're you doing here?"

"Looking for you. But the real question is why did you think I was Drake?"

Her eyes still blinking with surprise, she stammered, "H-he's here."

Here? Sean's head whipped around, his eyes searching the hallway in both directions. Then jealousy bit him. Hard. His gaze dropped to the woman beneath him. "You're here...alone...with your ex. How does Lover Boy Luke feel about that?"

In that jealousy-laden moment, he noticed Jess wore only a towel. A towel that their struggles had pulled down to barely cover her nipples. He knew because those delicious points were protruding noticeably beneath the terry cloth. The swell of her breasts rose and fell with each labored breath. His dick decided to do some rising and swelling of its own.

Jess's eyes widened and darkened as his erection pressed into the V of her thighs. She swallowed hard. "Sean? What...what are...?" she asked breathlessly.

His gaze locked on hers. Without his permission, his hips pumped. Once. Twice. He waited for the rage he was sure would follow.

But it didn't.

Instead, Jess's lips opened in a gasp of pleasure. Eyes still held by his, she rubbed herself against his hardness.

He almost lost it.

His breathing accelerated but not as much as his heart rate. Separating her legs with his knee, he settled between them. *I must be dreaming.* Still watching her dark chocolate eyes for any sign of rejection, he lowered his head. When his lips touched hers, he couldn't keep his eyes open. They closed as the feeling of their lips touching swept him away. God, he'd missed her. More than he'd ever admitted to himself or anyone else.

Her lips opened and invited him inside. He leaped at the opportunity to rediscover her warm, wet, sensual mouth. He groaned. Jess tasted the same, felt the same.

His hips moved again, and he couldn't stop them, didn't want to stop them. Jess's hips joined the rhythm. Faster. Harder. They moved together, seeking…

"What the hell? Is this how you behave around our daughter?"

Sean launched himself off Jess and into a battle-ready stance.

She screamed and clutched the towel tighter around her body while scrambling to her feet. "Get out of my house, Drake," she yelled. "And don't ever come here again."

"Your house? That's a joke." He glanced back toward the living room with a disgusted sneer. "Of course, why anyone would want to live in this place is beyond me."

"Get out," Sean said, his tone threatening.

Lazily, Drake's gaze swung back. "And who are you? Jessie's latest sugar daddy?"

Sean's hands clenched into fists, and he took a step toward the other man. "The lady told you to get out, asshole."

Drake's right hand disappeared into his sport coat pocket. "Lady? A moment ago she looked like a bitch in heat."

Sean took another step.

Jess grabbed his arm. "He's not worth it. I'll call...Deputy Johnson."

Sean's jaw tightened when jealousy bit him in the ass again. Didn't she think he could handle the situation?

"No need. I just came by to see my daughter. Callie?" Drake called.

"She's not here. She wouldn't want to see you anyway. Now leave," Jess said.

"Well, then, maybe you'll at least tell me if Molly's been found."

When had her ex, who was supposed to be in Chicago, joined the search? Sean shot a sideways glance at Jess. Her expression told him she was just as surprised that Drake knew about Molly's disappearance.

"M-my mother is none of your b-business."

"I think a judge would disagree. Vanishing grandmothers don't lend stability to a child's life. Your mother is my business because she affects my daughter's well-being."

Jess gasped. The jerk was doing a damn good job of intentionally scaring her.

Sean wrapped his arm around her shoulders and pulled her against his side. "Did you have something to do with Molly's disappearance?"

"No, country boy. I heard about it at the coffee shop. Don't you just love *little* towns?"

"Actually, I do. Small towns are great; big cities suck. Now get your ass back to yours"—Sean's gaze dropped to the man's pocket and then rose slowly to glare into icy blue eyes—"before you do something you'll regret."

Drake stared back, his expression cold and calculating. His eyes shifted from Sean to Jess and narrowed as if he was evaluating his options. The bulge in his sport coat pocket moved.

Sean tensed. His grip on Jess tightened, preparing to push her behind him.

With a frustrated sigh, Drake pulled his hand from his pocket and shook his index finger at them. "You haven't seen the last of me. I'm not going home without my daughter."

* * *

Drake stormed down the hallway and through the living room. The back door slammed a few moments later.

Jess slumped against Sean. "Oh God, what am I going to do?"

"You can start by explaining why you didn't tell me Drake was here," Sean said, his tone accusatory and stern.

She jerked away from him. Their behavior on the floor flashed through her mind. *I'm such an idiot.* She should never have let it happen. But he felt so good, and it had been so long.

Raising her chin, she crossed her arms over her middle. "I didn't know he was in town until this morning. I was going to tell you on the phone, but then…then Dad interrupted."

Sean grunted. "Where is…Hal?"

"In LA until tomorrow evening for a wedding gig."

"And your daughter?"

"At…a friend's." *Why didn't I say Karla's?* Drake was the one she needed to hide Callie from, not Sean. But now was not the time to second-guess herself. "Are you through interrogating me, Detective Burke?"

He scowled. "Not even close. What the hell is your ex doing packing heat when he comes to see his daughter?"

"What?"

"Carrying a gun."

She willed away the light-headedness threatening to swamp her. "I *know* what it means. I just didn't see a weapon."

"In his pocket. He had his hand on it."

Jessie lost the battle with dizziness. She put her hand on the wall to steady herself. "Oh God."

"You okay?"

He reached for her but she held her hand out to stop him. "I want to get dressed and then sit down to digest all this."

Her Jell-O legs carried her into the bedroom. Her hand shook as she shut the door. Collapsing onto the bed, she closed her eyes against the tears. She couldn't let Drake do this to her. And she couldn't let Sean do what he'd done to her either. Catching her in a compromising position gave Drake fuel for his hateful fire. She couldn't—wouldn't—let it happen again.

A gun. Oh my God, he'd brought a gun to the house. What if she'd been alone or with Callie? She didn't really have to play *what-if.* She knew exactly what Drake would've done. Callie would be on her way to the San Diego airport, taken at gunpoint by her father.

When she gave in to the sobs, she buried her face in a pillow. Could she protect Callie and look for her mother at the same time? Did she have the strength?

A knock on the bedroom door jerked her upright. "Jess, you okay?"

She gulped. "Sure. I'll be out in a minute." It actually took her ten.

When she walked into the kitchen, Sean sat at the table with two glasses of amber liquid.

"I don't—"

"You need it," he said, pushing one across the table to her. "The bottle was on the counter so I figured it wasn't anyone's extra-special stash."

She sipped the whiskey and coughed. "You wouldn't be trying to get me drunk to seduce me, would you?" She cringed inwardly. What a stupid thing to say.

He studied her for several beats and then raised the glass to his lips. "I don't need booze," he said before downing his drink in one gulp.

Her cheeks burned. "About that. I'm sorry."

"I'm not."

"It didn't mean anything. It was just a natural reaction from not having sex for a very long time."

He gave her a sexy smile. "I can fix that."

She set the glass on the table with a loud clink. "Stop it. Our behavior was inappropriate. I won't let it happen again."

He poured himself another drink. "Whatever you say. Shame, though. Felt pretty damn good to me."

Other parts of her body began to burn along with her cheeks. Another sip did nothing to extinguish the spreading flames.

Sean leaned back in the chair, all casual and sensual and hot.

She swallowed hard. *Down, girl, down.*

"Why did Drake have a gun in his pocket? Didn't sound like it was because he was glad to see you."

"He wants to renegotiate the custody terms and take Callie back with him for six months. Over my dead body…"

"He might be okay with that."

Her breath caught. "He has a temper, but…" Her voice trailed off because she wasn't so certain of anything anymore.

"How'd he get along with Molly?"

"She never liked him, and after I filed for divorce, she hated him. The feeling was mutual."

Sean nodded. "You and Callie can't stay here tonight."

She sighed. "Yeah, I know."

"You should spend the night with me."

Chapter 7

"Not going to happen, Sean."

Mentally, he prepared for battle. "Why? Even your boyfriend would agree."

Jess rolled her eyes. "Luke isn't—"

"You're right. He isn't going to like it. But hell, he's a good guy even if I'm damn pissed at him. He'll understand why Glenn's apartment is the safest place for you to stay."

"And why is that?"

"Okay, I'll tell you." He stood up and paced through the kitchen. "You dated Drake while you attended San Diego State. I'm sure you brought him to Ramona to hang out with your friends. Therefore, he knows Luke, Karla, and several other people. Chances are he also met Nate and your uncle Chad. But *me*"—he tapped his chest—"he never met. Remember Drake asked who I was. Neither of us ever told him."

"He heard me call you Sean."

"Nope. You never said my name."

She cocked her head. "Really?"

"Yeah. I notice stuff like that. Makes me a good detective."

"You probably are, but this is different."

"You mean it's personal."

"Right. *Too* personal. But I have the perfect solution. Callie and I will stay at the hotel on Main Street." She gave him a self-satisfied smile.

Sean shook his head. "All Drake has to do is provide his out-of-state driver's license and tell the clerk his wife and daughter, Jessica and Callie, checked in earlier, and he needs a room key. His ID with the same last name makes it believable."

"I'll tell the front desk not to give anyone else a key."

"And you'd trust Callie's safety to a teenybopper wearing her iPod earbuds and smacking gum to remember your instructions? And for sure, the info would get lost or forgotten by the graveyard shift when you'd be the most vulnerable."

Jess pressed her fingers against her eyelids. "Staying at your place is so not a good idea. And you know why, Sean."

"No, tell me." Stuffing his hands in his pockets, he leaned against the cabinets. If he got any closer, he was afraid he'd touch her, shake some sense into her, kiss her, lay her on the table and…

"I know it's been years, but I'm still hurt and angry about what happened."

His jaw clenched. "You? What about me, Jess? Maybe we should talk about it."

"What could you possibly be hurt and angry about?"

The jiggle of the doorknob startled both of them. Sean spun around and grabbed a butcher knife from the wooden holder on the counter behind him. He was armed and ready by the time the door opened.

A disheveled Nate Freeman stepped through the doorway. He snapped to attention when he saw Sean with the knife. "Fuck! What the hell's going on?"

"Sorry. Thought you were Drake." He chuckled and stuck the knife back in the holder.

Jess's brother shook off the shock and assumed a more macho stance. "In case you haven't heard, her other ex-asshole lives in Chicago."

"Drake's in town," Jess said.

"What the hell for?"

Jess explained her ex-husband's demands and described his visit, leaving out the specifics of where he found her and Sean. And what they were doing.

"That bastard," Nate muttered. He glared at Sean. "And why is this bastard here—alone—with you?"

"I've offered to help look for your mom," he said before Jess could answer. "You don't know anything about her disappearance, do you?"

"Sean," Jess snapped.

Nate bristled. "No. But if Drake's here, I'd take a serious look at him."

"Already on it," Sean said.

The air crackled with tension and testosterone.

Jess looked ready to strangle both of them. "What do you want, Nate?"

His gaze swiveled back to his sister. "Mom always puts Dad's gigs on the calendar, so I knew he was leaving today. I came to see if there was any news?"

"You're lucky you caught me. I've been gone most of the afternoon, and I'm leaving again shortly."

A hint of a smile twitched Nate's lips, and then it was gone.

Sean's eyes narrowed. "Maybe he hoped you'd be here alone."

This time they both glared at him.

"What's that supposed to mean? I thought *no one* was home until I saw the car and truck in the driveway." Gulping, he stopped talking abruptly.

"If that's what you thought, how did you expect to learn any news?" Sean asked.

Jess jumped up. "Stop it, both of you. I have enough *real* problems without the two of you going at each other's throats." She turned to her brother. "You need to help. I printed flyers to tape up all over town. You're going to distribute some." She stomped out of the kitchen.

The two men sized each other up.

"Don't you dare hurt her again," Nate warned.

"Never have, never will." Why did everyone, including Jess, keep making him out to be the bad guy?

"Bullshit." Nate scrutinized his face. "You get in a fight or something?"

His hand went automatically to the bandage on his temple. "Or something."

Nate snorted. "Guess the other dude won."

"Jess won."

Her brother's eyes widened. "Damn, she's good. I knew she was pissed, but I didn't know she was capable of…of that." He waved his hand at Sean's injuries.

"Help me out here. Tell me why she's so pissed, and I'll forget why you were really coming to the house when you thought no one was home."

Nate's lips curled into a sneer. "You think you're so smart now that you're a big-city cop. But you don't know shit about this family. Deception should've been our last name."

"I know you need money."

"Go fu—"

"I told you boys to stop it," Jess said, marching into the room and straight to Nate. "You hit Main Street above Tenth, and I'll do the rest. Cover the residential neighborhoods at that end of town as well. I want to see these plastered everywhere." She shoved a large stack of flyers into his hands. When he didn't move, she leaned in close. "Go. Mom needs us to find her."

* * *

After Nate's rusty Taurus rumbled off, Jessie turned to Sean. "Why do you have to be so hard on him? He already suffers a lot with his problems." Her shoulders slumped. Fatigue was settling in, but she had to keep going.

"One of his problems is lack of money." Sean rubbed the back of his neck. "Listen, Jess, I know you don't want to hear this, but your brother was coming to look for cash or something he could pawn."

"Did you borrow the earrings that were lying on Molly's dresser?" Her dad's question hummed in her head. No, it couldn't be true. Nate hadn't resorted to stealing from their parents. *"Did you know Nate's been arrested several times?"* Sean's question joined the first one. Confusion swirled like a dust devil in her mind. Her mother was missing or having a temper tantrum. Her stepdad had changed his name to a friggin' weird name she'd never heard before. And her brother had an arrest record and might be stealing from their parents. She grimaced. Surely she'd wake up from this nightmare soon.

"I'm sorry, Jess. I know it's a lot to take in."

She glared at him. "Yes, it is, and you're not helping."

"Telling you the truth isn't helping?"

"You're confusing me. It's like I don't know these people anymore. Who are they? While I was gone, everyone changed."

"I haven't changed, Jess."

"You changed sooner, before I left. Your change was the reason I left."

He looked at her so oddly that she almost laughed, except there wasn't anything humorous about the situation.

"You have to leave. I need to post these flyers."

He sighed. "Fine. We'll talk later. Let's go." He started toward the back door.

"You're not going with me." She couldn't handle having him with her. Her emotions were already so overloaded she might explode if he stayed close.

"Like hell I'm not. You can't go anywhere alone until Drake is back in Chicago."

Well, damn, he has a point. She gazed up into the face of the man who used to make her feel safe and loved. Until he deceived her. Until he broke her heart. Now she couldn't trust him. But that didn't mean she couldn't use him to protect Callie and her from her ex-husband. Unfortunately, the idea added another question to her confusion: Who was going to protect her from Sean?

She sighed. Ex-boyfriend versus ex-husband. It held a certain poetic justice. They'd both deceived and hurt her, so she shouldn't care if they hurt each other this time. But she did. And she didn't dare wonder why.

* * *

Sean watched Jess's changing expressions as she carried on an internal debate. Would she reach the right decision, the one he needed her to make?

"Okay, fine. Make yourself useful, then. Go find the duct tape in Dad's workshop," she finally said.

He narrowed his eyes. "Give me your keys."

She pulled back. "What?"

He held out his hand. "Keys…please."

She pulled them from her purse and dropped them in his palm. "Why?"

"You wouldn't send me on a fool's errand so you could drive away without me, would you? Besides, Hal always kept the workshop locked."

Jess glanced away guiltily. "He was out there this morning, so it's probably not locked…today."

After giving her a gotcha look, he hurried to the workshop. The door was indeed locked, just as he'd expected.

Once inside, he scanned the room and scratched his head. Not seeing any organization to the mess, he began opening drawer after drawer in the main workbench. It yielded nothing.

"If I were Hallelujah Ima Freeman, where would I keep my duct tape?" he muttered, surveying the rest of the room.

Sean attacked a six-drawer cabinet in the corner, starting at the top. He yanked the bottom drawer open so hard it came all the way out and landed with a thud on the floor. Cursing under his breath, he replaced the items that had flown out. As he moved things around to make room, he spotted something in a plastic baggie at the rear of the drawer. He lifted it out for a better look.

The black object was an external hard drive.

Glancing back at the drawer's other contents, he frowned. Odd place to keep a portable hard drive, among old tools, boxes of nails, unidentifiable pieces of stuff, and a roll of duct tape.

He snagged the tape and laid it on the workbench. Returning his attention to the baggie, he examined it from all angles. The clear plastic was dirty, but spots were smudged. Fingerprints? Recent enough that new dirt hadn't covered them. Inside, the device appeared spotless and intact.

Normally, people kept their backup hard drives in a safe place, but this one wasn't here for safety. It was hidden. Well hidden. Which begged the question: Why?

Sean peered over his shoulder, out the open workshop door. Jess stood by the corner of the house, waiting for her keys. His gaze shifted to the item in his hand. *I need a warrant.*

He frowned. *Maybe not.* Detective Burke hadn't found the hard drive. Detective Burke wasn't investigating the case. As an LAPD detective, he didn't even have jurisdiction. Sean was simply acting as a past friend of the family, helping with the search.

If he discovered and examined something that had no obvious connection to Molly Freeman's disappearance, he wasn't tampering with evidence. Hell, no one knew yet if a crime had even been committed. If he *borrowed* the item for Jake and him to inspect but then returned it undamaged, he wasn't even guilty of theft. Besides, Hal was gone until tomorrow evening. He'd have it back in place by then. No one would ever know.

He glanced at Jess to be sure she couldn't see him pocket the hard drive. Surveying the workshop, he confirmed everything was where it had been. No need to raise a red flag that someone had rummaged through the place.

Stepping outside, he pulled the door shut and pretended to lock it, knowing he needed access tomorrow without a key.

"Took you long enough," Jess complained when he handed her the keys. "Find something you like in there?"

Sean did a double take. "What?"

"You know, guy stuff. Tools, junk, scraps, and pieces of anything left over from past projects. I can't stand to go into the workshop myself, but Dad loves it."

"He spends a lot of time in there?"

"Fair amount. He spends more time in the house on his computer these days since he converted his photography business to all digital."

"Interesting. People's pictures from special events are priceless. I bet he goes to great lengths to back up everything so nothing gets lost."

"Oh yeah. When I helped move his photography stuff out of the bedroom Callie's using, he pointed out his two large-capacity external hard drives. He also uses them to back up their personal laptop."

He followed her to the Camry. "Where did he move them? To the workshop?" he asked.

She stopped abruptly and shot him a disbelieving look. "Are you kidding? The workshop is filthy. All his photography stuff is in his and Mom's bedroom. I feel bad they're so crowded, but it didn't work for Callie and me to share a bedroom."

Sean's curiosity skyrocketed. If Hal kept his business and their personal computer data on hard drives in the house, what was he keeping on the one hidden in the workshop?

* * *

"Before we start distributing the flyers, I want to stop by Mom's closest friends' houses…unexpected," Jessie said as she turned out of the driveway.

"I thought you already talked to them."

"We have, multiple times."

"Then why take the time to visit? To give them flyers?"

She released a long sigh. "That's my cover. Actually, I'm following up on something Dad said."

Sean arched his eyebrows in question.

"He thinks one of her friends is hiding Mom so she can have a break. He gave me a real guilt trip for trying to ruin it for her."

"That's bullshit."

"I agree. But if I can disprove it, maybe he'll finally get past the denial phase."

"Denial phase?"

She shrugged. "I don't know what else to call it. His lack of concern is so totally unbelievable."

Sean's lips thinned to a tight line. She could tell he was holding back what he wanted to say about her stepdad's behavior being suspicious. He probably wanted to lecture her on Hal's weird name and what it might mean. When he turned to look out the side window, a muscle in his cheek twitched.

Jessie swallowed hard. She remembered that muscle well. It always twitched when Sean was forced to listen to her stepdad's anti-law enforcement rants. She had appreciated Sean's restraint then and even more now.

After the last friend's home visit without any sign of her mom,

Jessie's cell rang as they trudged to the Camry, disappointment weighing heavy on her shoulders. Yanking the phone from her purse, her breath caught at the caller's name. "You drive. Take us to the south end of Main Street." She tossed the keys to Sean and then answered her cell. "Hey, Luke. Any update on Mom?"

As she climbed into the passenger seat, her heart pounded in hope of good news.

"Nothing…yet. I just wanted to let you know everything's in process. All the alerts, notifications—everything we can do. A couple of off-duty deputies even came in to get up to speed before heading out to do some searching on their own."

Her eyes filled. "That's nice of them."

"Yeah. They knew your mom back in the day and wanted to help. How did your visit go with the attorney earlier?"

"Swanson was real weird when he learned Mom was missing."

"I wonder what that was about. Are you going to get a restraining order against Drake?"

"Swanson is going to talk to a judge about it. The bad news is Drake paid me a visit."

Beside her, a soft, deep growl came from Sean.

"Shit. You okay?" Luke asked.

"Yeah, but only because Sean was there."

"Sean? Double shit."

"No, it was a good thing. Drake had a gun."

"Fuck. He pulled it on you?"

"No, Sean could tell it was in his pocket."

"Jesus, Jessie, your ex is an asshole. I still don't understand why you hooked up with the guy."

She knew, but she didn't like to admit it even to herself.

"Be sure Hal has his pistol handy," Luke continued.

"Dad's in LA until tomorrow evening." She chanced a glance at Sean and found him staring at her. She gulped. "Sean thinks Callie and I should stay with him tonight."

Her statement was met with silence. A long, thoughtful one.

"What do *you* think?" Luke finally asked.

She pulled her gaze away from Sean. "I understand his reasoning. Drake doesn't know who he is or where he lives. But..."

"But? Sean's right, damn it."

"It's...it's just..." An eight-year-old ache cut off her words.

"Just don't...get hurt," Luke warned.

"I...I—"

Another growl from the driver's seat interrupted her. "Shit. Tell Lover Boy he can stay in Glenn's bedroom with you and Callie. I'll take the futon in the office."

Chapter 8

Jess tapped End and stared, mouth gaping, at Sean. Did she realize she'd disconnected without saying good-bye to her boyfriend? "What did you say?" she whispered.

While she'd been talking to Luke, Sean had parked the car in a strip-mall lot on Main Street. Gripping the steering wheel tighter, he kept his eyes focused straight ahead. "I said…you and Luke can have the bedroom. I'll sleep on the futon in Glenn's office. If you want…more privacy, your daughter can stay in there with me."

Tentatively, she rested her hand on his arm. "Why would you do that?"

He drew a deep breath. "Because your safety is more important than my jealousy."

"I see."

Her fingertips traced the inside of his forearm, something she knew he liked. Sean tried to ignore the desire firing along the nerve endings to his groin.

"What if I said I didn't want…Luke…in the bedroom with me?"

He whipped his head around to face her. "I wouldn't"—he gulped—"believe you."

She withdrew her hand, shook her head, and gazed out the side window. "Of course you wouldn't. You've always been so damn sure you're right about everything."

He snorted. "It's called trusting your instincts. I have good ones."

Eyes blazing, she turned on him. Gold flecks flashed in the darkest brown. "Well, your good instincts fucked up this time. Luke and I aren't together. Never have been. Never will be."

"But I saw you in his arms, crying on his shoulder. The way you…um…connect. Your relationship is totally different than it used to be. It's…you know."

"No, I don't know. Luke's like a big brother to me."

Sean scoffed. "You and Nate never acted like that."

"I wish we did. After my divorce, I needed that kind of support. Nate wasn't there for me; Luke was. There's nothing romantic—or sexual—between us. We're just good friends. He's my best friend's older brother, and he treats me like another kid sister."

"Isn't girl-falls-in-love-with-BFF's-older-brother a favorite plot for chick flicks?"

"Thank God this isn't a movie. It'd be a horror show." She pressed her head against the headrest. "Forget it. Think what you want. It doesn't matter." She reached for the car door handle.

Sean caught her other arm and pulled her around to look at him. Had he misinterpreted her behavior with Luke? Were his emotions clouding his good instincts? Was he still hurting so badly that he was eager to blame someone else because he'd never made sense of what had happened between them? He frowned. "You wouldn't be punking me, right? I'll kick Luke's ass if you are."

"Grow up, Sean. Of course I'm not punking you. Let's go. I need to get these flyers distributed and pick up Callie."

He released her, and she climbed out of the car. *Well, damn. This is a strange turn of events.* And, under the circumstances, did it mean anything? Or, as she'd said, it didn't matter.

* * *

Two hours later, the Camry barreled into the parking lot at Karla's salon just before the shop closed. Fatigue and frustration weighed heavily as Jessie scooted out of the car.

"Stay here, Sean," she ordered.

"Why?"

"Do you want Karla to scratch your eyes out?"

Sean huffed. "Big surprise. She's mad at me, too." He waved his hand dismissively. "Go."

As Jessie scurried to the shop, she mused about Sean's reaction to her not being involved with Luke. Although he hadn't voiced it, he'd been clearly relieved that they hadn't hooked up. *Men. Impossible.* Despite all the years since he'd dumped her, he still didn't want her to be with another guy. Was it an ego thing? A selfish thing? Whatever it was called, it sucked. And she resented it. She grinned. At least she'd made him suffer with jealousy for a while.

"Mommy, Mommy," Callie shouted when her mom came through the door. "Lookie what Ms. Karla did."

Jessie squatted in front of her daughter and surveyed her face and hair. Her little girl had on enough makeup to make a hooker proud. "Wow, aren't you *something*." She smiled and then turned to shoot a scowl at her friend. "Ms. Karla, you outdid yourself."

"Hey, the customer is always right, and she picked out every bit of it."

Jessie stood up. "Callie wasn't a customer; she was your charge for the afternoon."

Karla's eyebrows rose. "You're mad at me? Seriously? I was just keeping her entertained."

She exhaled and shook her head. "Sorry, I'm exhausted. I'm sure Callie had awesome fun. Thanks, girlfriend. I owe you big-time." She gave her BFF a hug.

"Any news on your mom?" Karla whispered in her ear while holding her tight.

"Nothing. But Luke says everything's in process. My brain's so fried, I can't think of anything else we can do. And I'm so scared, I feel like breaking into tears all the time. But that won't solve anything."

"Then go home and get some rest. Let the system work."

"I just hope it does. I'm still stunned that this is even happening."

"I'm sure it's perfectly normal to find this unbelievable. No one ever thinks it could happen to them. You gonna be okay tonight or do you want me to come stay with you?"

"Thanks. We'll be fine." Jessie shot a worried glance toward the parking lot and hoped they would be.

As she and Callie approached the car a few minutes later, the munchkin stopped in her tracks. "Mommy, there's a strange man in our car." She wrapped her arm around Jessie's leg, almost tripping her.

"It's okay, sweetie. He's…he's an old friend." Her daughter refused to release her leg, so Jessie hobbled the rest of the way like a peg-legged pirate.

Sean got out of the car and crouched to eye level with Callie. He gave Jessie a meaningful glance before extending his right hand.

"Hi, Callie. I'm Sean. I knew your mommy before you were born. We were…the best-est friends. I'm really happy to meet you."

Callie looked from his face to his hand to her mommy. Jessie nodded. Her gaze came back to his, and she slowly let go of her mom. Hesitantly, she took his hand and shook it once before snatching back her tiny fingers.

"Do you like Happy Meals?" Sean asked.

Her whole face brightened. "Yeah. Lots." When he straightened to his full height, her head angled back as he grew higher and higher.

"May I buy you ladies dinner?" he asked, grinning. "I think your daughter approves of my choice of cuisine."

"Thanks. I'd eat almost anything tonight to avoid having to cook."

She let him drive, and twenty minutes later, he turned left onto Oakdale toward the Freeman house. Her stomach growled from the mouthwatering aroma of french fries and hamburgers coming from the bags in her lap.

"Isn't that Nate's car pulling out of your folks' driveway?" Sean asked.

She straightened in the seat. "Yeah. Maybe he came by to tell me some news."

"Your car's not there, and he could've called."

Her brief bubble of hope popped.

"I know you don't want to hear this, but he was probably—" Sean continued.

"Not now and not ever in front of Big Ears." Jessie jerked her head toward the backseat.

He rolled his eyes. "I'm not used to having an ankle-biter around."

"I do not bites ankles," came an indignant little voice from behind him.

He snorted. "Sorry, kiddo."

Jessie grinned. "Your life is never the same and never your own once you have a child."

"I'll take your word for it."

* * *

All during dinner, Hal's external hard drive burned a hole in Sean's pocket. Curiosity and suspicion gnawed at his attention so he didn't hear Callie when she first spoke to him.

"Mr. Sean, looks at me when I talks to you," she scolded.

"Callie, you know better than to talk to someone like that," her mother scolded in return.

"But…but you says it all the time."

"She gotcha," Sean muttered out of the corner of his mouth to Jess. "I'm sorry, Callie. I have a lot on my mind. What did you say?"

"Do you likes 'nure?" she asked in a serious tone.

"Good Lord," Jess mumbled, and rolled her eyes.

His gaze flicked to her. "Translation, please."

She hid a smile behind her hand. "Manure."

He pulled back. "Manure? As in bullsh—"

In a flash, Jess's hand covered his mouth.

Callie's eyes widened. "Were you gonna says a bad word? Mommy does that to Grandpa all the time."

Sean barely heard her. His eyes locked with Jess's while her palm rested against his mouth. He slipped his tongue between his lips and stroked her soft flesh. Once. Twice.

Her breath caught, and she swallowed hard. But her hand remained.

He stroked again and again. His dick twitched.

Her chest rose and fell with shaky breaths.

They both started when the phone rang.

Jess snatched her hand back and held it to her chest as she jumped up to answer the call on the kitchen phone.

"Hi, Dad." She turned toward the wall. "Yeah, we're fine. Just finished dinner." She listened for several seconds. "No word from you-know-who. And I stopped by to see each of her close friends today. They're as worried as I am, so I'm sure she's not staying with any of them." She waited, huffed, and then planted her free hand on her hip. "I don't care what you think. No way is she hiding in a hotel. Open your eyes, Dad. Someone took—" Her volume increased until suddenly she gasped and glanced over her shoulder at Callie.

"Hey, kiddo, what were you going to tell me about manure?" Sean asked to divert the little girl's attention from her mother's rising voice.

She turned bright, sparkling eyes on him. "Oh yeah. We gots 'nure," she said proudly. "Wanna see it?"

"Absolutely."

Callie hopped down from the chair and took his hand. While she led him to the back door, he waved over his shoulder at Jess.

Outside, Sean surveyed the property. Not much had changed over the years. The place could use some maintenance, but overall, it was still in good shape. The quiet hit him more than anything else. Even quieter than Glenn's neighborhood in town. So unlike LA. *Nice.*

He shortened his strides to keep pace with Callie. She skipped instead of walked and carried on a steady stream of conversation, only about half of which he understood. And she seemed to have completely overcome her initial shyness.

When they reached the barn, she pointed at the huge mound of manure. "See. 'Nure."

Sean grimaced at the odor and breathed through his mouth. "Awesome."

"No, it's yuck. It stinks." She let go of his hand and moved closer. Cocking her head, she studied the pile. "Mommy was right. Grandpa did do the 'nure yesterday." She turned to Sean with a mystified expression. "How comes I don't 'member?"

At a loss, he shrugged.

A moment later, she skipped to the garden. "Wanna pick a 'mato?" she called to him.

"Sure." *Definitely better than looking at a mountain of shit.*

Callie guided him to a plant with tomatoes larger than her hands. "Aren't they 'mongous?" she exclaimed.

"Uh, yeah." He picked one and sniffed. The sun-warmed tomato smelled delicious. He inhaled deeply.

"The 'mato smells good, but the green part stinks," Callie announced with profound certainty.

Sean smiled. How long had it been since he'd eaten a homegrown tomato? A homegrown anything, for that matter. Probably not since his parents moved from Ramona to Phoenix when he went away to college. Savoring the memories, he collected two more tomatoes to enjoy later.

"We gots 'chini, too. Lots." She made a disgusted face. "It's squash. Yuck."

He helped himself to a couple zucchini. "May I have some corn?"

"Yeah. It's yummy. It gets all over my face when I eats it. Up to my ears, Grandpa says."

Sean snapped off three pieces of corn and glanced toward the house. "Your grandpa sounds like a fun guy."

"Yeah. He likes to play tickle and wrestle. Mommy thinks he wishes I was a boy."

"Why?"

"So I could plays boy stuff."

He adjusted his armload of vegetables. "Does he tell you stories about when he was a little boy?"

Her mouth twisted to the right as she thought. "Nope, 'cause he never was a little boy. He's always been old."

Sean chuckled. "I bet Hal has some funny stories about where he used to live. Has he told you any?"

She pondered again. "No, 'cause he and Grandma always lives here." She turned in a full circle, surveying the property. Her cute face quirked with puzzlement. "Where *is* Grandma?"

Damn. Not in my job description. "Uh…let's go see if Jess…er, your mommy, is off the phone."

She scowled and stiffened with defiance. For a moment, he thought he might have a "resisting arrest" situation on his hands. He exhaled with relief when she decided to come along peacefully. In fact, she took off running.

By the time he reached the empty kitchen, she was racing through the house, hollering for her mother. As he reached the end of the hallway, the bathroom door opened. Memories of that afternoon gave his dick a yank.

"Callie, I'm right here," Jess called. She scooped up her daughter, who barreled out of a bedroom.

"Mommy, Mommy, where is Grandma? When she coming home?"

Jess turned red-rimmed eyes and a blotchy face to Sean. "What happened?"

Shit. Obviously, the phone conversation with Hal hadn't gone well. *The bastard.* Even if he didn't give a damn about his missing wife, he should at least care about Jess and Callie. Sean fought the urge to wrap his arms around both of them.

"Sean, what happened?" she repeated.

"We were talking about Hal, and…and Molly just came up."

"You were interrogating my daughter? A four-year-old. How dare you?" She tightened her hold on Callie.

"We were just *talking*. Lighten up."

"Easy for you to say. You don't have to answer her question."

Callie's eyes had grown larger and larger with their rising voices. *Well, shit, we're scaring her.* He stepped closer and ran a hand down her hair. She laid her head on Jess's shoulder.

"It's okay, kiddo. Grandma had to go away for a while, but she'll be back as soon as she can," Sean said, hoping he sounded soothing and, even more, hoping it was the truth.

Callie's lip quivered. "Where did she goes?"

Shit. Think, Burke, think. "She…uh…she didn't tell us, so it's like a…a game to guess where she is. Your mommy and I and a lot of other people are looking for her."

Another lip quiver. "Likes hide-n-seek?"

He gave her a reassuring smile. "Yeah, like that. You're smart."

Callie blinked and sniffed. "I'm a good hider, too. Wanna finds me?"

"Sure. I'll count to fifty, okay?"

"Yeah." She wiggled out of Jess's arms. "No peeking," she called, running down the hallway to the living room.

Jess wiped at her eyes before meeting his. "Thanks. Crisis averted. You were great. I-I'm sorry about—"

"No problem. Hmmm. I have forty more seconds. What should we do?" He glanced down the hallway. "I have an idea."

He tangled his fingers in her hair, and before she could object, he gently pulled her to him. His eyes drifted closed as their lips met.

He still had ten seconds left when Callie screamed.

Chapter 9

Before the reality of the scream even registered in Jessie's brain, Sean had pushed her aside and raced down the hallway. "Stay behind me."

When he stopped abruptly at the entrance to the living room, she bounced off his back and landed on her butt. Dazed, she blinked up at him when he turned around and extended his hand.

"Callie?" she gasped, her heart pounding.

"Uncle Chad has her in a tickle hold. My God, she sounded like she was being skinned alive." He pulled Jessie up and snaked his arm around her waist to support her.

When she saw her uncle playing with her daughter, she sighed with relief, and her heart slowed to a normal rate. She chuckled and then laughed. "It's a girl thing. We scream. It's in our genes."

"Does that mean I can use my Y chromosomes as an excuse when necessary?" he asked, giving her a squeeze.

"Don't count on it." She drew a deep breath and pulled away. "Uncle Chad, what're you doing here?"

Unsmiling, he released Callie, who crumpled into a giggling, gasping heap at his feet.

"I came to find out where the hell my sister is. No one's keepin' me in the goddamn loop." His eyes narrowed when he recognized the person with her. Her uncle marched across the living room to where they stood. "And what the hell is *he* doin' here?" A scowl creased his forehead as his gaze bounced between the two of them.

Jessie put a finger to his lips. "Uncle Chad, language." She jerked her head toward Callie. "You guys grab a beer in the kitchen, and I'll put on a movie for her."

Uncle Chad stomped away, but Sean stayed behind. "If he tries to gouge my eyes out, am I allowed to defend myself?"

"He wouldn't attack your eyes." She grinned wickedly. "Be careful, though. Before he became a cement contractor, he used to castrate bulls."

* * *

Chad Brown was already nursing a beer at the kitchen table when Sean entered. The older man hadn't gotten him one from the fridge. Figuring the omission was intentional but refusing to be intimidated by it, Sean helped himself to a cold brew. He chose the out-of-reach seat on the opposite side of the table, sat down, and balanced the chair on its rear legs. The two men sized each other up for several moments. Chad's eyes held undeniable dislike.

"No one answered my questions. Let's start with why the hell you're here," Chad growled.

"I'm helping Jess look for Molly."

He snorted with cynical disbelief. "And where the hell is my sister?"

"If we knew, we wouldn't be looking," Sean said with a straight face.

"Smart-ass. You always were too smart for your own good. Except when you decided to break Jessie's heart. That was stupid…and cruel."

"Now wait just a damn minute. I didn't—"

"Shut up. I'm not interested in your excuses. I fucked up thinkin' you were a good guy. Turns out you aren't any better than the dickhead she ended up marryin' to get over you."

Sean frowned. "That's why she married Drake Hargrove?"

"*Duh*, as you kids say. You damn well broke our hearts as well as Jessie's. Only one happy about the whole mess was Hal."

Sean's frown deepened. "Why was Hal happy?"

Chad scoffed. "No way did he want a pig for a son-in-law."

Puzzle pieces that had been floating around in Sean's head for eight years started falling into place. *No fucking way. That bastard wouldn't…*

Before he could explore the shocking possibility, Jess joined them. She poured a glass of wine before sitting down.

"How you holdin' up, baby girl?" Chad asked.

She closed her eyes. "I'm scared. I'm confused. I'm exhausted. And that's the good news."

"It's gonna be okay. We'll find her." Chad patted her hand. "I've been out lookin' all day. And callin' everyone I can think of. Where does other stuff stand?"

Jess described in detail what had been done to find Molly. Sean wasn't surprised when she chose not to disclose his suspicions of

Hal and Nate. Granted, Molly had been missing only about twenty-eight hours, but he had hoped Jess would start to open her eyes to the closest-male probabilities.

The mood in the kitchen grew more somber by the second. When Jess described Drake's phone call and revealed he'd come to the house armed, Chad shot out of his seat and bellowed with rage. Callie even came running from the living room.

"What's wrong with Uncle Chad? Is he hurt?" she asked, clinging to Jess.

"No, munchkin, he's okay."

"Good. I don't likes people to gets hurt." Her mouth opened in a long yawn.

Jess gave her a hug. "You're tired. Go put your jammies on to watch the movie."

The little girl trudged out of the kitchen.

"What're you gonna do about the son of a bitch?" Chad asked, still standing.

"I saw Mr. Swanson—remember the attorney—today about getting a restraining order. We're going to talk again on Monday."

"Restrainin' order or no restrainin' order, if that bastard comes near you again, I'm gettin' out my old tools and cuttin' off his gonads. Too bad they're probably so small we won't be able to make us even an appetizer of Rocky Mountain oysters."

Sean's balls shriveled like they'd been dunked in ice water. Jess arched her eyebrows with an I-told-you-so grin. He swallowed hard.

"Your little one needs to get to bed. I better go." He sighed. "You keep in touch better, baby girl. Let me know if there's anything else I can do."

Jess stood up and hugged him. Chad's eyes glistened while he held her tight. The closeness Sean remembered between uncle and niece was still there.

After the hug, Chad cleared his throat and turned to Sean. He did the classic two-finger, I'm-watching-you gesture. Then he sighed again, his shoulders slumped, and he lumbered out the back door.

Before it closed behind him, he yelled to his dog, "Goddamn it, Buster, quit diggin' in that manure. You're gonna earn your sorry self a bath."

When the barking faded away, Sean asked, "You haven't changed your mind about staying at my place, have you?"

She hesitated. "Callie's so tired. She won't sleep as well if she's not in her own bed." Jess shrugged. "And Nate's just down the road. Maybe I should stay—"

The back door swung open.

Chad loomed in the doorway, his face grim. "Sean…out here." He jerked his thumb over his shoulder.

Something in the man's expression told Sean this had nothing to do with his gonads. He nodded. "Stay here," he ordered Jess.

"What in the world?" she asked, and took a step.

He grabbed her shoulders and glared directly into her eyes. "Stay…with…your daughter."

Her eyes widened, but she nodded.

Wordlessly, he followed Chad outside onto the patio.

"Don't be obvious, but look at Jessie's car," her uncle said.

Sean kept his face directed at Chad, but his eyes focused on the car beyond in the driveway. The problem was immediately obvious: She had two, possibly four, totally flat tires. They'd been slashed, not deflated. *Drake*.

"Fuck," he muttered.

"Yeah, fuck."

While keeping his head stationary, his gaze swept across the property. Lots of places to hide. But the asshole had to get here somehow. Where was his rental car? Sean's eyes scanned the road in both directions until he spotted a vehicle sitting on the shoulder about four hundred yards toward the Wheaton intersection.

"He's parked down the road toward town," Sean said.

"I couldn't see him—eyesight's not that great anymore—but I figured the asshole might still be around. I'm takin' Jessie and Callie home with me." Chad pushed past Sean, heading for the house.

Sean grabbed his arm before he got there. "That won't work."

"Why the fuck not? They sure as hell aren't safe here." He yanked his arm free.

"I already knew that from Drake's visit this afternoon. I convinced Jess to stay at Glenn's apartment, but now she's wavering."

"Your brother's place? With you? No way."

"Listen to me. Drake knows everyone but me. He doesn't know my name, and I don't live here. I'm staying at Glenn's apartment, which he damn well wouldn't be able to figure out. The girls will be safer there than with you."

Chad's eyes narrowed. "Safer in some ways. Maybe not in others."

"I won't hurt her. I want to protect her…and Callie."

Chad jammed his hands in his jean pockets and glared at the ground. "I get your goddamn point, but I still don't like it."

"Deal with it. I've thought it through. It's the only scenario that makes sense. You, Nate, Luke, Karla, her other friends—no good. Besides, I'm a cop. I'm trained to handle assholes like Drake."

Chad exhaled with resignation. "Okay. You're right. But how are you gonna get them out of here without him seein'?"

Sean thought a minute. "We'll go back inside and turn off the patio light. After Callie falls asleep, we'll check if Drake's still there. I'm sure Jess can find some binoculars…and…and a lamp timer. See where my truck's parked?"

Chad glanced out of the corner of his eye. "Yeah."

"It's not that visible, and in the dark, I can get them into it without Drake seeing. You'll watch from inside with the binoculars to see if he follows me."

"Gotcha."

"You wait another half hour and turn on the patio light as you're leaving. We'll set the timer to keep a lamp on in the bedroom for another hour. We'll all be safely home by the time the asshole discovers no one's here," Sean explained.

"What if the bastard trashes, or worse, sets fire to the place?"

"Even Drake's not that stupid."

* * *

"You should go to bed, Jess," Sean said, sitting down next to her on the couch in Glenn's living room. "You're exhausted."

"Yeah, but going to bed would be a waste of time. I'm so tense, there's no way I can sleep."

He ran his hand down her arm. "Relax. Drake can't find you and Callie here."

But it wasn't just Drake making her nervous, as Sean's gentle touch reminded her. "I want to believe that, but I can't."

"Look, I have two loaded guns in the apartment—"

His words, meant to reassure, added another layer of tension instead. "What if Callie—"

"They're hidden up high. She can't get to them. I don't expect to have to use them. I just want you to know I'm prepared for anything." He tucked a stray strand of hair from her ponytail behind her ear. His fingers lingered before trailing down her neck. "Relax, babe."

Yeah, right. Wishing she didn't like his touch, she scooted away on the couch. "I can't stop worrying about what Drake might be doing to my parents' house. If he—"

"While you were putting Callie to bed, I called Luke. He's on duty, so he's going to check things out. If Drake's still hanging around, he'll tell him to get lost. And he said he'd set up a patrol to keep an eye on the place all night."

Why did Sean have to be such a nice guy—most of the time? He made it hard to remember she hated him.

"As usual, you have it all figured out," she said, hoping being bitchy would douse any inappropriate ideas—by him or her.

He leaned back against the cushions and crossed an ankle over his other knee. God, why couldn't she feel as calm as he looked?

"You're wrong. I don't have it 'all figured out.' But I had a breakthrough today." His jaw tightened, and his hazel eyes grew icy. "And when I do figure it out, believe me, you'll be the first to know."

"What're you talking about?"

Sean didn't respond. He seemed lost in thought.

Just as well. She was too tired to put on a kick-ass front, too exhausted to even talk. She scooted down on the cushion so she was more reclining than sitting. With her eyes closed, she flexed her shoulders and rolled her head from side to side, but the muscles remained stiff. Her chest felt tight; her head ached. No way was sleep in her future.

She heard and felt Sean move but kept her eyes shut. Maybe he'd head for the futon, which he'd made up earlier. His absence would at least remove one source of her tension.

Her eyes popped open when she felt his hands on her waist. Unbelievably, her whole body tensed even more than it had been.

"What are you doing?" she asked, trying to push herself upright.

"Relax, babe. I'm gonna get rid of your tension. You look about to snap."

"I'm…fine," she said.

"Liar."

She huffed. "Even if I am, you…you shouldn't be…uh…lessening my tension."

"What's the problem?" He undid the button on her shorts.

Yes, what was the problem? As Sean probably remembered from years ago, sex had always been a wonderful stress reliever for her. And honestly, she might be tempted—if he wasn't Sean Burke. Anyone but *him*. Because no way in hell would she, could she, or should she have sex with *him*.

"The problem is you," she answered. The flash of pain in his eyes stabbed her with guilt. Mentally, she shook it off. He deserved it after the pain he'd caused her. "Besides, my daughter is in the bedroom."

"You closed the door. I'll hear her if she comes out. Anything else?"

When she didn't respond, he stared directly into her eyes and unzipped her shorts. Her breath caught.

"If you want me to stop, Jess, tell me and I will. Instantly." He slipped his fingers beneath the elastic band of her panties, slid them back and forth, back and forth, moving the sides of the shorts more out of the way each time.

Her gaze dropped to watch his fingers. Her breathing quickened.

Cupping her with the palm of his hand, he moved his fingers to where the panties circled her thigh. He traced up to her hip, down to her groin. Up. Down. Up. Down. Up...down.

She should say stop. Really she should. But his touch felt so damn good that her mouth wouldn't cooperate.

His fingers mesmerized her. She got lost in the sensations.

When his finger ducked under the crotch of her panties, she gasped. Deftly, gently, he separated her folds and stroked her center. He groaned right before she did.

He raised his eyes to hers. "Hot. Wet. Ready...for me."

Two fingers probed until she spread her legs and opened for him. Without hesitation, they thrust inside. In. Out. In. Out. His wet thumb found her sweet spot, pressed, circled.

Her head lolled to the side. Her eyes closed. Her lips parted to release her panting breaths.

Faster. Deeper. In. Out. Press. Circle.

Inside, she coiled tighter and tighter around his fingers. Release, oblivion, beckoned.

Her orgasm exploded with such massive spasms that her thighs clamped together around his hand.

"Sean," she cried.

Waves of pleasure washed over her for the longest time. She floated, weightless, relaxed.

She didn't even open her eyes when Sean lifted her from the couch, carried her to the bedroom, and laid her on the bed. He fluffed the sheet over her before kissing her forehead.

And then left.

Chapter 10

At 6:00 Sunday morning, Sean sat at his brother's kitchen table, watching a four-year-old scarf down a bowl of Cheerios. This was a first for him. Not the time or location, but sitting alone with a little girl. One who talked incessantly, often leaving off the first syllable of words, making comprehension difficult.

He yawned and scratched the stubble on his cheek. Would he and Jess have had a child by now if things had gone according to his plan? Their daughter wouldn't have blond hair, though. That gene had definitely come from Drake Hargrove. Callie *Burke* would have had darker locks like his deep red or Jess's rich brown.

Resentment bit him in the ass. The same emotion had kept him awake most of the night. Of course, last night's sleep deprivation was also the result of several other issues: Molly's disappearance, Drake's threat, Hal's hard drive, Jess's proximity, and the futon's size, to name a few. But resentment at the developing solution to the eight-year-old puzzle of why they broke up was definitely high on the list.

How was he going to confirm his suspicions before discussing them with Jess? He suspected only one person—the guilty party—knew the truth. And the bastard would never confess. Would Jess believe Sean without objective evidence or would she conclude he was lying in a case of Hal-said versus Sean-said? Every attempt he'd made with Jess, Luke, Nate, and Chad in the last two days to declare his innocence had been met with disbelief or disgust. Was there any way to convince them without the testimony of the one responsible for their breakup?

The sound of water running in the master bathroom pulled him from his thoughts. He shook his head and refocused on the babble pouring from the miniature person beside him. What was Callie saying? What the hell were "efants"? Did she mean…?

Several minutes later, footsteps in the hallway warned him of Jess's approach. Despite bracing himself, seeing her sleepy and tousled in the doorway almost drew a moan from him, a sound of longing for what might have been.

"How long have you two been up?" Jess asked around a yawn.

"Mommy, Mommy." Callie scrambled from her chair and wrapped herself around her mother's legs.

"Morning, munchkin."

"Guess what? Mr. Sean is gonna takes me to see the efants."

Jess arched her eyebrows in question.

"Elephants," he translated proudly. "But, Callie, remember I said I couldn't take you today. It'll probably be next weekend."

"I 'member. Can Mommy come?"

His eyes connected with Jess's. "Sure. I think she likes to come."

A bright blush blossomed on her cheeks, and her eyes darted away.

Sean pushed back from the table. "Callie, let your mommy

sit down while I get her some coffee. She looks like she could use it."

Callie stayed in the doorway as Jess shuffled to the table and plopped into a chair. "Do you have 'toons?"

"Yeah. I have an iPod, and Glenn has a stereo. What kind of music do you like?"

She looked at him like he was speaking Greek.

"What?" he asked Jess.

"Car*toons*."

"Oh. Do I? Have them, I mean."

Jess rolled her eyes. "Does Glenn have the Disney channel?"

He shrugged.

"Nickelodeon?"

"Nickel what?"

"Netflix?"

Relief. "Yeah."

"Good. Find the children's movies category, and she'll pick one."

Ten minutes later, he returned to the kitchen. Mission accomplished. After refreshing her cup and pouring himself another, he joined Jess at the table.

"What's the deal with dropping the first syllable?"

"Her mouth can't keep up with her brain, so it takes shortcuts."

"Hmmm. Interesting."

Silence settled around them. Too long to be comfortable.

Sean pretended to listen to the TV noise emanating from the living room. Jess seemed fascinated by her coffee mug. Was she going to say anything about last night? How good it felt? How he still knew how to pleasure her? Was she angry, grateful, embarrassed or some combination of all three? Seconds stretched on…

"I—" they said at the same time.

"Ladies first."

"Okay." She gulped. "I…I need to tell you something about last night."

Her expression was cautious, not angry. *Good sign.* Instead of prodding, he waited for her to continue.

"Last night…" She faltered, stopped.

His hopes rising, he held his breath.

Looking past him at the cupboards, she tried again. "Last night, while we were packing up to leave the house, I went into my parents' room to *borrow* forty dollars from their 'quick cash' envelope."

His hopes collapsed.

"They always keep two hundred dollars on hand for…you know, quick access or emergencies." She sighed. "Anyway, the envelope was empty." Her eyes came back to him. "Do you think Nate…?"

She quit speaking as if the thought was too difficult to voice.

He took pity on her. "Maybe. Maybe not."

"Did I tell you about the earrings?"

He went still. "No."

"Yesterday morning, Dad asked if I'd seen the gold earrings that had been on Mom's dresser. Apparently, they've disappeared, too."

"Could she be wearing them?"

"She'd never wear anything that expensive to run errands." Jess buried her face in her hands. "Nate was there, in the kitchen, when I got home Friday night after…you know, hitting you. Hal and Callie were asleep. He admitted coming over that afternoon to apologize to Mom for the fight they'd had on the phone that morning. He'd waited on the patio because he thought Hal was home. He claimed he never came inside. But what if…?" Her voice trailed off.

Sean's pity dissolved. Finding Molly took precedence over maintaining Jess's opinion of her brother. "What if Nate actually did come in and steal the earrings and cash?"

Her hands dropped to the table. Disappointment lined her face. "I don't want to believe it."

His mind produced another scenario. "You also have to consider that he could've been here when Molly walked home. Maybe she caught him leaving with the stuff and confronted him." Sean paused. His words were going to hurt, but Jess had to face the facts. "They could've gotten into a fight, something snapped, and things went terribly wrong."

Jess blanched whiter than Glenn's walls. "Oh my God. You think Nate killed Mom."

* * *

The roaring in Jessie's ears drowned out all other sounds. She scrunched her eyes shut. Just the idea that her brother might have killed their mother made her head spin and her stomach roil.

"Don't panic, Jess. I'm only theorizing. We don't know anything for sure," Sean said.

Panic? I can't panic. I have to be strong. To take care of Callie. To find Mom.

Jessie fought her way through the haze of shock. When she turned her head and blinked her eyes open, Sean was kneeling beside her.

"I'm sorry. I shouldn't have pushed you," he whispered.

Her head shake was more of a wobble, so she added, "No, I have to deal with all of it." She drew a deep breath. "It's on my shoulders."

He stroked her cheek. "You're not alone in this. I'm here for you."

"You don't understand. It's not about me. Once you're a parent, your first thought is always how something is going to affect your child. I know I'll be able to...to handle whatever happens, but I'm terrified about how this might affect Callie...for the rest of her life."

"She's oblivious—"

"No, she's not. She may not know exactly what's happening, but she can *feel* something's wrong. I believe she isn't insisting on a full explanation about her grandmother because the last time she felt something was wrong, her world collapsed."

"The divorce?"

"Yes. It's been really hard on her."

"I'm sorry."

"I don't expect you to understand. You're still single, only looking out for number one. I've been a wife, now an ex-wife, a mother. We live in separate worlds."

Concern creased his forehead. "You haven't changed that much, Jess."

"Yes, I have, Sean." Her eyes filled. "I'm not the Jess you knew. And our time together is *ancient* history."

He stared into her eyes for the longest time. She struggled not to look away. The emotions changing his expression were indecipherable. He seemed to battle with himself. Finally, he shook his head and stood up. He'd obviously decided against saying what was on his mind.

"I need to go see a friend of mine," he said instead.

She hated the disappointment his statement prompted, the briefest twinge of panic that he was leaving her. Again. And why did he say "friend" instead of naming the person? A tendril of jealousy wound through her.

She lifted her chin. "Fine. It's daytime now. Callie and I will be okay at the house."

"I don't think so. After I arrange for a tow truck for your car, I'm calling Luke to come stay with you."

"I don't need a babysitter."

"Not to protect you from Drake. He can't find you here. It's to protect you from yourself. I don't want you going anywhere on your own."

She sighed. "Other than buying new tires, I don't know what else to do. I'm all out of ideas."

"Use the phone. Keep calling people. Motivate them. Call the station or have Luke call for an update. Just don't tell *anyone* where you are."

"Fine. Go see your 'friend.'" She cringed at her catty tone.

He peered at her oddly and then smiled. "In a minute. First, I gotta show you something. C'mere," Sean said, moving to the refrigerator. He stepped to the side away from the cabinets and placed his hand halfway across the top. "Can you reach up here?"

She had to stand so close she could feel his body heat. When she stretched up on her tiptoes, her backside brushed against his front. Her body's awareness of him was unsettling, but she vowed to ignore it.

Her fingertips touched something cold and hard. She jerked her hand back.

"It's not gonna bite you, Jess. I might, but it won't," he said from close enough behind her that she felt his breath in her hair. "Can you grab it?"

Her fingers wrapped around the grip. "Yeah."

"Good." His warm, large hands grasped her waist to move her aside. "Follow me." He led her into the master bedroom and opened the closet. "Up here," he said, pointing to the highest shelf.

She stood on tiptoes again but couldn't get her fingers high enough. "I can't."

"No problem." He moved the gun to the lower shelf. "Still way out of Callie's reach."

Jessie surveyed the closet for things her daughter could climb up on and found none. "Should be fine."

He guided her out of the closet and closed the door. "Luke will bring his own but show him where these are." He studied her. "You still know how to shoot, right?"

She stiffened. "Of course. It's like riding a bike, only deadlier. You may get rusty, but you don't forget how. Anyway, because of the high crime rate, Drake had me take a class in Chicago."

Sean smirked. "Good. Maybe it'll help you shoot him if necessary."

* * *

"I've been looking at prison escape records for so many hours I'm about to go blind," Jake Stone said after he'd locked them in the safe room. "What've you got?"

Sean withdrew the baggie from his pants pocket. "An external hard drive. Belongs to Hallelujah Freeman."

"A backup?"

"I'm not sure. He keeps two of them in the house. This may be stuff Hal doesn't ever actually allow on his computer, so technically not a backup," Sean explained.

Jake peered at the dirty plastic bag. "I take it this one wasn't in the house."

"Nope. In the bottom drawer of a chest in Hal's workshop."

"Hidden?"

"Definitely." Sean paused. "I also want to check it for fingerprints. Maybe we can nail the sucker's identity that way. But I'm hesitant to involve Luke and the sheriff's department since they haven't officially identified Hal as a person of interest or suspect. You don't have a fingerprint kit, do you?"

"Of course I do. I've got all kinds of CSI equipment. Let's see if we can pull a print off this baby."

With skill earned through experience, Jake managed to get two partial prints. Afterward, they stopped to celebrate with a beer.

"If Hal was incarcerated, his prints will be in the FBI's system. I could run the prints myself if I was in LA, but since I'm not, I need to come up with an alternative," Sean said.

"You're looking at it."

"Are you telling me you can access the FBI fingerprint identification system?" Sean asked incredulously.

"Hell no, but I've got friends everywhere. Let me handle it."

"Okay." Sean glanced at his watch. "We better get busy. I have to get this back in the workshop drawer before Hal gets home tonight."

"Right."

Jake connected the external hard drive to one of his computers and hit the appropriate commands. A box appeared asking for a password.

"Fuck," Sean muttered. He jammed his fingers through his hair.

"Let's try the obvious. Open the Freeman file on that laptop. We have all kinds of the common possibilities: address, phone number, social, birthday, anniversary."

Two hours later, both men were ready to tear their hair out. Sean checked his watch again. "I gotta get that damn thing back. Can we copy it onto one of your hard drives?"

"I'm not fond of downloading unknown data. Besides, often these external devices can't be copied if you don't know the password."

"Just try, damn it."

"Down, Burke," Jake said in a warning tone.

"Let me outta here. I need to call Jess." Sean stomped to the vault-like door and waited for Jake to open it.

"Use my phones."

"No. I want to call her on my cell."

Jake glared at him. "Don't trust me now?"

Sean returned the steely gaze. He didn't know what he felt at the moment. Distrust? Yeah, of the whole world. Frustration? Yeah, at everything going on. Concern? Yeah, for Jess and Callie's safety.

"Just let me the fuck out."

Jake waited another few seconds before tapping the commands on the remote. "Why don't you go cool off by the pool?"

Sean trudged through the empty house, worry gnawing at his gut. Their progress was too slow. Molly had been gone almost forty-eight hours, and they hadn't found a single trace or any evidence. All he had were theories.

"What's happening?" he asked without greeting when Jess answered her cell.

"A lot, but nothing's yielding any results."

"A lot? Meaning what?"

She sighed. "Luke and I talked to the sheriff's department. We met the deputies at my parents' property so they could look around. From there, they went to interrogate Nate and Uncle Chad. Both of them also voluntarily consented to searches of their places. The deputies called Luke afterward and said they didn't get anything helpful from any of it. I've talked to everyone about Mom so much they're sick of hearing from me. Karla called to check on us before she headed up to LA with her boyfriend for a show they've had tickets to for months. She offered not to go, but I said no way. She'll be gone until Monday afternoon."

"Anything from Drake?"

"No calls, thank goodness. Luke has someone checking on the house regularly. It seems okay. We got new tires put on the Camry. Luke says I should file an insurance claim, but I can't deal with it right now."

"I'll help you with it this week."

"Oh, Dad called, and he's coming home earlier than expected. The photographer he was helping with the wedding said he didn't need to stay for the reception."

"Shit," Sean muttered.

"Excuse me?"

"Nothing. Does Hal know I'm in town?"

She hesitated. "I don't think I've mentioned it, but he could've heard it from someone else. By the way, Dad's attitude was really different when he called. I think our argument on the phone last night finally hit home. He said he was going to get in touch with a couple of Mom's friends who moved down to San Diego in the past couple years. And he wants to put up flyers in Julian because Mom always likes to go there."

"Okay," he responded absently. "When will Hal be home?"

"I'm not sure. He was already on the road, but he said not to wait on him for dinner. After Luke's on duty tonight, he and another deputy are going to interrogate Dad again. I'm not sure what time, but his shift starts soon, so I think—"

"No. Wait for me before you go back to the house. I'll be there as soon as I can."

"Are you sure you want to leave your...*friend*?"

"It'll be hard, but I'm willing to make the sacrifice. For you." He pressed his lips together to stop a laugh.

After they said good-bye, Sean hurried back inside and through the house to Jake's office. As he approached the open safe-room door, he heard Jake's voice. Curiosity and caution made him stop and listen.

"Salami, it's Granite."

Salami? Granite? Sean arched his eyebrows. Jake was a former CIA operative. Were those spook names?

"I need a favor. I have to open a password-protected external hard drive. I was able to copy it, but I still can't open it."

He copied it. Great, maybe I can get it back in time.

"Yeah, yeah, I tried the perp's birthday. Screw you."

Sean grinned.

"No, I don't know what's on it. And, yes, it could be full of fuck-ware."

Fuckware? As in malware? Sean almost laughed. Too bad he couldn't hear the other side of the conversation.

"I'll send it ASAP. Thanks. You guys-that-don't-exist have the coolest toys. And I'm in a bit of a hurry." He gave a snort of laughter. "But I've told you that's not physically possible."

Sean strained to hear, but the talking had stopped. Jake must've disconnected.

"If you've heard enough, Burke, you can come in now," Jake called to him.

Embarrassed at being caught eavesdropping, Sean walked into the room. "Sorry."

"Nothing wrong with you being curious, but also remember, I'm always careful." Jake gestured toward a large monitor.

One square showed a picture of the outer office where Sean had just been hiding. Others displayed every step of the way to the pool. Jake had known exactly where Sean was and what he was doing the whole time.

"Go." The former spook held out the baggie. "I'll call if I get anything on the fingerprints or get the file open."

Racing from Valley Center to Ramona in his truck, Sean mulled over Jake's phone call with Salami. He obviously still had connections with active operatives. *Granite?* He'd heard that before. Oh yeah, the password for Stone's computer yesterday: Granite27. *What does the twenty-seven stand for?*

Sean pondered a moment and decided he didn't want to know.

Chapter 11

Sean flew into his brother's apartment. Empty. *Damn.* When he hadn't spotted Jess's Camry in the parking lot, he feared she'd left already. Had she run an errand or gone home? He suspected the latter but hoped for the former.

He yanked the roll of duct tape from under the futon. Knowing he'd need an excuse to get back into the workshop, he'd hidden it there before leaving for Jake's so Jess couldn't put it in her purse or something. However, an excuse might be the least of his worries if he didn't beat Hal there.

As Sean approached the Freeman driveway, he breathed a sigh of relief at the absence of Hal's truck but also cursed the presence of Jess's lone vehicle. Did the woman not understand the danger Drake posed? Or the risk represented by whoever was responsible for Molly's disappearance? Until someone figured out the motive behind her mother's abduction—and Sean was pretty damn sure that or worse was what they were dealing with—Jess and Callie could also be on the perp's radar.

After parking his truck, he resisted the urge to race to the workshop. He didn't want to raise any suspicions if Jess saw him. Wrinkling his nose at the smell of manure, he strolled toward the three-section outbuilding with the baggie in his pocket and the tape in his hand. When he reached the door, he did a slow 360-degree turn, surveying the property, and glanced down the road in both directions. No sign of anyone or any traffic.

The workshop doorknob twisted in his hand, and he smiled with satisfaction. He checked over his shoulder one last time before stepping inside. As he squeezed around the main workbench to reach the cabinet in the corner, his pants pocket caught on a protruding hammer, sending it to the floor with a loud clang. *Shit.* He scanned the floor for the wayward tool. Unable to spot it, he knelt and peered beneath the adjacent furniture. Spying it under a small table where it had skidded, he stretched across the dirty concrete to recover the tool. After replacing the hammer on the workbench, he more carefully circumvented the mess to reach his target.

Pulling the baggie from his pocket, Sean bent over and opened the bottom drawer of the cabinet. The contents were in such a jumble that he couldn't remember exactly where the tape had been, but he knew the hard drive had been buried in the far back.

"Hands up, you bastard! Nobody steals from me!" Hal's booming voice filled the cramped space.

Fuck. Hesitating only a second to drop the baggie, Sean straightened and turned toward the door. He froze when he met a rifle pointed at his chest.

The older man's eyes widened, and his jaw dropped. It was hard to tell who was more shocked.

When the rifle shook in Hal's hands, Sean tensed. His mind

scrambled for a plan. "Hey, Mr. Freeman. It's just me," he said, hoping to defuse the situation.

"You? What the fuck are *you* doing here?" Hal's face reddened. "The pig's a thief now?"

"No, sir." Sean held up the duct tape. "Just returning this."

Hal frowned, confusion mixing with his anger.

"Jess and I used it to post the flyers about your missing wife. I was just putting it away." He bent quickly, snagging the baggie and shoving it to the back of the drawer with one hand while placing the tape in the front with the other hand.

"Get your hands up here where I can see them," Hal yelled.

Sean stood up and smacked the drawer shut with his shoe. He held out his empty hands. "Jess sent me out here to get it yesterday. Sorry if that wasn't okay. I'll buy you a new roll."

"Smart-ass, bastard. You think for one minute that I believe Jessie would do anything with you? She hates your guts."

Rage erupted inside him. This wasn't the best timing—with a rifle aimed at his chest—but enough was enough. Time to get the truth out of the lying motherfucker.

Sean's eyes narrowed. "Whose fault would that be?"

"Yours," Hal sneered.

Despite the gun, Sean dropped his arms to his sides. His hands clenched into fists. "Bullshit. Since I came back to Ramona, I've discovered that everyone thinks I broke up with Jess. But that's not what happened, is it...Hal?" Damn, he wanted to shock the asshole by calling him Hallelujah Ima Freeman. But with the man's finger on the trigger, Sean thought better of it.

"Don't know what you're talkin' about." Hal sighted down the rifle barrel.

Eight years of pain and frustration kept fear and caution at bay. Sean's heart pounded with the need to finally do battle with the source of that pain and frustration.

"Liar," he snapped. "*You* called *me*. Told me Jess never wanted to see me again." Sean's voice rose with each word until he was shouting. "I'll never forget what you said. Your exact words were 'Jessie doesn't want to waste her life with a pig.' Ring any bells, Hal?"

"Dad?"

Hal whirled around. The rifle slammed into the door frame, jarring Hal's hand and firing.

Jess screamed.

Sean vaulted over the workbench, tackling Hal on his way down. The men fell through the doorway onto the ground. The rifle skittered across the gravel.

The scuffle was short and one-sided. In the end, Sean straddled Hal and cocked his fist.

"Sean, don't," Jessie yelled. "Please."

Heart hammering, he froze but didn't lower his fist. "You all right, Jess?" he asked without taking his eyes off her stepdad.

"Yeah," she said, her voice shaky.

"Get the rifle," he ordered. "Be careful."

"Let me up, you prick," Hal growled.

"If your stepdaughter wasn't here, I'd beat the shit out of you. I wouldn't even care that you're an old fart. You're *sick* for what you did to me…to her…to *us*."

Jess's footsteps crunched on the gravel. "Got it."

"Take out the ammo." He listened as she did. "Hand it to me."

When Sean turned his head and extended his hand, Hal took a swipe at him. Sean jerked back, the blow brushing past his jaw.

He raised his fist again. *God, this is gonna feel good.*

"Sean, please," Jess cried. "Callie's watching."

This time he pinned the man's arms to the ground before glancing toward the house.

The little girl stood like a statue, her eyes wide and her mouth gaping. Then Callie screamed, covered her ears, and raced into the house.

* * *

No, no, no. The word pounded in Jessie's head as her feet pounded the ground. *No, no, no.* She barged in the back door, through the kitchen, and down the hallway. At Callie's bedroom doorway, she stopped. Sobs came from under the bed.

She braced herself and lay down on the floor. "Callie, munchkin, Mommy's here. Everything's okay."

"N-no, i-it isn't," Callie sputtered.

"Yes, it is. Don't be scared. Mommy's here." She touched her daughter's arms, which were wrapped over her head. "C'mon out, baby. Let Mommy hold you."

Callie shook her head and whined.

"Wouldn't you like Mommy to hold you? I'm too big to crawl under the bed. Come out so we can cuddle." Jessie sighed. What she wouldn't give to have someone cuddle her right about now.

"What that big noise?" Callie mumbled into the floor.

Oh God, she heard the gunshot. Jessie searched for an answer that wasn't a lie but also wasn't the whole truth. "Uh, it was something in Grandpa's workshop. You know what it's like in there."

She turned her head to look at her mother. "Something b-broke?"

"That's a very good guess. Grandpa will have to check later to see if something is damaged. Why don't you come out so we can talk easier?"

She hesitated but then crawled out from under the bed. Jessie pulled the little girl onto her lap and embraced her. Callie snuggled in close.

"Why was Mr. Sean fighting with Grandpa?"

Jessie drew a deep breath. "I'm...not...exactly sure. But they were naughty to fight."

"Yeah. Bad boys. Use your words, not your hands. That's what Grandma always says."

"She sure does. I'm glad you remember." Tears threatened, and emotion clogged her throat.

"Are they gonna get a time-out?"

"Do you think they should?"

Callie nodded vigorously. "It was a biiig fight."

"Okay. I'll give them a biiig time-out."

"Good."

Callie fell silent for several minutes.

Jessie's initial panic subsided. Those feelings were immediately replaced by recriminations. She'd failed to protect her daughter. Granted, Callie hadn't been physically hurt, but she was traumatized. And Jessie knew from her marriage that emotional hurt could be worse than physical pain.

She closed her eyes and tightened her grip. It had all happened so fast.

She'd glanced out the kitchen window as her dad raced from the side garage door to the workshop with the rifle in his hands. Startled, she had run to the kitchen door and spotted Sean's truck in the driveway. Horrible scenarios had flashed through her mind. She'd hollered to Callie that she would be right back and for her to keep watching the movie. Then she'd bolted from the house, arriving at the workshop doorway as Sean shouted at Hal.

And, of course, the four-year-old did exactly the opposite of her mother's orders: Callie followed her out the door.

"Was that a gun?" Callie whispered.

Jessie started. "Huh?"

"Was that a gun in your hands?"

Crap. This is your fault, Dad. Why did you have to overreact? "Do you know what a gun is, honey?"

"I sees them on TV."

"Right." Jessie's stomach clenched. "Yes, it was. You should never touch one. It can hurt you or someone else if you don't know how to handle it. Promise me?"

"Okay, Mommy." She yawned.

"Why don't you rest while I go put Grandpa and Sean on time-out?"

Callie's eyes were already closing as Jessie lifted her onto the bed. She slipped off her daughter's shoes and kissed her cheek. By the time Jessie reached the bedroom door, Callie's thumb was in her mouth, her eyes closed. At four, she only sucked her thumb when she needed soothing from serious stress. Not a good sign about her current state of mind.

Jessie held her own thumb up in front of her face. If only it were that easy for a twenty-nine-year-old. But oral soothing could take many forms besides thumb-sucking: smoking cigarettes, drinking alcohol, eating chocolate, sucking... Her mind jumped to Sean on top of her in the hallway and between her thighs on the couch. Yes, sex could be a very effective soother.

She gave herself a mental shake. Her life was overflowing with problems. She didn't have time for frivolous sexual relationships. Her mother was missing. Her daughter was suffering. Her ex was threatening. She had to keep her head in the game and not let herself get distracted by sexual needs.

Taking a deep, fortifying breath, she closed the bedroom door quietly and marched down the hall to face two of her problems.

* * *

From the love seat, Sean stared across the coffee table at the man pretending to relax in the recliner. How had Hal managed to sneak up on him? And armed, no less. Thank God no one had been hurt when he accidentally pulled the trigger. Sean didn't even want to imagine the possibilities. After Jess dropped the rifle and raced after Callie, Sean had locked the gun and the ammo in his truck. Hal probably had other weapons hidden somewhere, but at least that one was out of reach.

Now the burning question was: Had he seen the baggie with the hard drive? Or had he already been in the workshop and discovered it was missing? Was that why he'd been so upset? Sean would just have to bide his time until he could figure it out.

Both men's heads whipped around when Jess stomped into the living room. She glared at them with obvious disgust. Without a word, she disappeared into the kitchen. Did she want them to follow her?

By the time Sean stood up, she reappeared with three beer cans.

After handing one to each, she sat down on the couch, which was conveniently situated between the recliner and love seat. All she needed was a black-and-white-striped shirt and a whistle to play referee.

"Do you realize what you've done?" she asked, the question apparently meant for both men.

"Jess, I'm really sorry Callie witnessed any of it," Sean said. He set the unopened beer on the coffee table. Drinking wasn't high on his list of priorities just now.

"Yeah, me, too," Hal muttered.

She turned to her stepfather. "What the hell were you planning to do with the damn rifle?"

He shrugged. "You know I'd gone back to get my suitcase out of the truck in the garage. I heard a noise in the workshop. When I looked out, I saw a strange truck in the driveway. I thought some guy was helpin' himself to my tools, so I grabbed the rifle and went after him."

"Did you consider calling the police?"

Hal narrowed his eyes. "Not for a second."

"Of course not. You'd rather risk shooting your granddaughter than involve the law."

"It was an accident," he snapped.

"Accident or not, Callie would've been just as dead. Or it could've been me."

They glared at each other for several seconds before Jess pivoted to Sean. He braced himself.

"What the hell were you doing in the workshop?" she demanded. "Why didn't you come to the house?"

He met her angry gaze. "I was putting the duct tape back," he said simply. He arched his eyebrows. Did she appreciate that he didn't mention she'd left the tape in Glenn's apartment where she'd spent the night?

She swallowed hard. Oh yeah, she appreciated it.

"Right." Jess cleared her throat. "Thanks again for helping me."

"You're welcome."

Hal shifted the recliner to upright and leaned forward. Anger reddened his face again. "What the hell is *he* doing here?"

"Sean learned that Mom was missing. He offered to help. He was kind enough to hang flyers in town with me."

"I can't believe you're even talking to the bastard," Hal sneered.

Jess stared at her stepdad for a full minute. Her gaze hardened, and her jaw clenched with determination. Then her eyes filled with tears, and she gulped repeatedly.

Sean frowned. *Something's wrong.*

"Why, Dad? Because *you* decided I didn't want to waste my life with a pig?"

Chapter 12

All the red rage drained from her stepdad's face. Color kept disappearing until his skin was ashen. Normally, concern would've taken over, but Jessie knew this was no heart attack. Mostly because the man must not have a heart, considering what he'd apparently done to her and Sean.

"Well?" she prompted, glaring at him through her tears. She didn't dare glance at Sean because she'd fall apart.

"Wh-what?" Hal stammered.

"Don't play dumb, Dad. I overheard you and Sean in the workshop."

Hal's expression morphed from stunned to cautious. "I don't know what you're babbling about."

"That's hard to believe. You're lying, just like you lied to me about Sean's phone call."

"Jess…," Sean said softly.

Without looking at him, she held up her hand for him to stop. "This doesn't involve you."

"*Excuse me*? It most definitely does," he countered.

"I can't deal with *both* of you right now, okay?" Her voice cracked. "We'll talk later. Just…wait for me, please."

"Always."

She shut her eyes to regain her composure. Battling the sensation of falling, she wondered if this was how Alice felt dropping down the rabbit hole. After several calming breaths, she returned to questioning her stepdad. "Why did you lie to me?"

He bristled. "I don't know what you think you heard, but I won't put up with this bullshit."

He scooted forward to get up, but Sean was beside the recliner before Hal's feet touched the floor.

"You're not going anywhere," he said through clenched teeth. "You owe us both an explanation."

Hal's gaze darted between the two while he seemed to weigh his options.

Jessie held her breath. She didn't want another fistfight, but damn if she didn't feel like pummeling the man herself.

Probably realizing there was no escape, Hal pushed back into the chair. "Fine. What is it you think you heard?"

Sean looked ready to explode, but she didn't ask him to sit down. His towering presence might do a good job of loosening her stepdad's tongue.

She swallowed hard. "You called Sean; he didn't call to talk to me. You told him that I never wanted to see him again because I didn't want to waste my life with a pig."

The unbelievable words hung there.

No one spoke. No one moved.

Finally, Hal scrubbed a hand across his face. "Okay, I admit it."

Her breath hitched at his confession, her trust in him shattering. Tears spilled down her cheeks. She didn't bother trying to wipe away the torrent. The emotional agony became physical, and she whimpered at the searing pain in her chest.

Sean turned to check on her, but she ignored him. She didn't want to think about what he was feeling.

"Why?" she whispered.

Hal pounded the arm of the recliner. "Because he's not good enough for you."

She saw Sean's hands ball into fists.

"The asshole wouldn't give up his plan to be a cop. Moving to LA was more important than being here with you." Hal's bushy eyebrows pulled together in a scowl. "No way was I going to let you marry a *pig*." He spat the last word.

Jessie's throat was so tight she wasn't sure she could talk. She kept trying to swallow, but the lump wouldn't go away. Her voice didn't even sound like hers when she finally spoke.

"It wasn't your decision to make. I was okay with Sean being a cop. Of course, I was afraid of the risks, but I knew I could handle it." She swiped at her tears as agony gave way to anger. "You. Had. No. Right."

"A father has a responsibility to protect—"

"But you distorted that responsibility to fit your own agenda. You hate cops. I've never understood why, but you're the hater, not me."

She dabbed at her tears again. How could this be the man who had been her father for twenty-six years? The man who had swooped in, dazzled her mother, and adopted two children without any reservations. How could he have intentionally broken her heart?

Jessie began to shake. Scrunching her eyes shut, she searched for her happy place. But the events of the past two days must've destroyed it, for there was no solace anywhere in her mind.

When Sean knelt in front of her, she opened her eyes.

"You should go to bed," he said. "We can talk tomorrow."

Her eyes cut to her stepdad, but she couldn't stand the sight of him. "I…I can't stay here tonight."

Sean's eyes searched hers. "My place?"

She nodded. "I'll get Callie."

Jessie raced into her bedroom to grab the duffel bag that was still packed from spending last night away from home. In the other bedroom, she scooped her daughter into her arms and hurried back to the living room. She found Hal brandishing the fireplace poker at Sean.

"Jessie is *not* spending the night with you." He jabbed the makeshift weapon at the younger man. "She's upset. She's vulnerable. I know your type. You'll take advantage of her."

Sean didn't seem concerned, but he was circling, staying just out of reach.

"Stop it, Dad. Put that down."

When Hal glanced in her direction, Sean snatched the poker from his hands in a flash. Cursing, Hal lumbered to the front door and turned to face them with his arms outstretched, blocking their exit.

"I'm leaving, Dad. I can't stand to stay in this house tonight. I suggest you spend the time figuring out how you're going to convince me to forgive you. Because right now, I sure as hell don't see how I can."

"You're not going anywhere. You're gonna sit down and listen to me." Hal's chest heaved with labored breaths.

"We're leaving, old man," Sean growled. "Get out of the way. I don't want to hurt you, but I will if I have to."

The doorbell rang.

Everyone froze.

It rang again.

"Mr. Freeman, it's Deputy Luke Johnson. I need to ask you some questions regarding your wife's disappearance," a voice called from outside.

Hal spun around and yanked the door open. "Arrest this man, Deputy. Sean Burke threatened and…and assaulted me. *Arrest him.* Do your job, goddamn it."

Sean gripped Jessie's arm and pulled her and Callie with him to the door. He elbowed past Hal and pushed through the doorway. Surprised, Luke and a second deputy stepped off the front stoop to make room.

"Question him *real* good, Deputy Johnson. If you decide to arrest me, you know where to find me," Sean said as they passed.

* * *

Sean checked the rearview mirror for the hundredth time and let loose a long sigh of relief. Jess wasn't having problems driving. He didn't really think she was in any condition to drive, but she'd insisted on taking her car.

Thankfully, Callie had remained asleep through all the commotion and the transfer into her car seat. He rolled his eyes. The contraption had more straps and buckles than an F-16 pilot's seat.

After parking his truck, Sean jogged over to Jess's car so he could carry Callie. Halfway to Glenn's apartment, the little girl opened her eyes and instantly began to wail. Once inside, Jess took her daughter straight to the master bedroom. Did this mean Callie wouldn't go back to sleep? *God, I hope not because Jess and I really need to talk.*

Crooning the lyrics to some kid's song, Jess's voice drifted into the living room. He marveled that she was able to tamp down her emotions and deal with Callie so calmly. *Must be a parent thing.*

He found a beer in the fridge and settled on the couch with his feet propped on the coffee table. After a long swig, he leaned his head back and closed his eyes.

What a clusterfuck the evening had been. The only good—admittedly, a major good—to come out of it had been the revelation of the truth about their breakup. He frowned. How did he feel now that he knew the truth?

Without opening his eyes, he took another drag of beer. Hard to sort out the influx of emotions, especially for a guy. He groaned mentally and started the inventory.

Relieved? Hell, yes. Jess hadn't broken his heart; her stepdad had. *Cheated? Damn right.* The eight years they could've been together were gone forever. *Resentful? Shit, yeah.* How dare that son of a bitch screw up their lives? *Hopeful? Maybe.* He still loved Jess, but what did she feel for him? Although he'd felt protective of Angela Reardon while investigating her case—which was long before she was Stone's girlfriend—Sean hadn't loved Angela or anyone else since Jess. But she'd fallen in love with Drake Hargrove, married him, and had their child. Of course, now she knew the guy was a prick, so at least she wasn't pining for him. But what scars had her failed marriage left? Had she sworn off love? Or was she looking for a second chance?

He remembered the feel of her beneath him on the hallway floor.

The way she'd responded like she wanted him. And he'd made her come last night on the couch with just his fingers. Yeah, their chemistry was still hot.

But those situations could've been nothing more than lust. They didn't tell him a damn thing about what she felt for him. His heart squeezed. Even learning their breakup had been bogus didn't mean her love would return. Unlike his love, which had never gone away.

"May I join you?" Jess asked.

He opened his eyes. Leaning against the hallway door frame, she looked ready to collapse. No surprise. First her mom, then Drake, and now Hal. Who wouldn't be on the verge of a total breakdown?

"Sure. Make yourself comfortable," he said, hopping up. "Wine or beer?"

She straightened. "Wine would be great."

When he came back, she'd curled up in a corner of the couch, her bare feet on the cushions, her arms wrapped around her bent legs, holding them to her chest. Yep, she was hurting bad. Even her body language was setting up barriers.

Sean handed her the glass of wine and sat down at the opposite end of the couch. He didn't want to invade her space if she was feeling that vulnerable. And he also decided to wait her out on talking about…anything. As a result, they sat in silence for at least a half hour.

"Dad told me that you said you'd outgrown me," Jess finally began, so softly Sean had to strain to hear. "Going to college in a big city had opened your eyes to all sorts of opportunities Ramona and I couldn't offer. He stressed your point that a small-town girl like me would be a burden in a big city like LA," she continued without looking at him.

When she stopped to take a drink, he responded, "I didn't say any of that shit, Jess."

She shrugged. "I know that now, but at the time, it played right into my insecurities. I don't know how many times I confided in Mom or cried on her shoulder because I was afraid of those very things. Dad might've heard me or she could've told him."

"Hal took advantage of your fears."

"Yeah. It was a smart strategy because it made me believe you were breaking up with me. If he'd said you'd found someone new, I probably wouldn't have believed him. If he'd said you got cold feet about our relationship, I would've known he was lying."

"Why didn't you call me? To yell at me if nothing else."

"Because 'your' reasons played on my existing fears, it shot my confidence to hell. I...I just couldn't bear to talk to you, to hear those awful words from your own lips." She turned her face toward him. "Why did *you* believe what Hal told you?"

Sean massaged the back of his neck. "I struggled with it for months, long after I moved to LA and got into the LAPD. What made it marginally believable was his tying it to his own hatred of cops. I figured he'd finally had enough time to brainwash you into feeling the same way."

"And you didn't call me because...?"

He grimaced. "Are you sure you want to know? It won't make you feel any better about what he did...to us."

Jess squared her shoulders. "I want to know everything."

"Okay." He sighed and hoped she was really ready for another dirty little secret. "Hal threatened that if I tried to contact you, he'd accuse me of..." He gulped.

"Of what?"

"Of…raping you."

She gasped. "Was he out of his mind?"

"Didn't sound like it to me back then. Of course, I was only twenty-one. He was very convincing. He said that if he couldn't get me actually charged with rape without your cooperation, he could still make enough of a stink to keep me from ever getting hired by any law enforcement agency." He shrugged with defeat. "I believed him. And when you never called, I decided you agreed to go along with his threat. Then, well, I gave up hoping…for a miracle." He ran his hand across his mouth and chin. "Look at the bright side. Now we know the truth."

"But it's too late for the truth to set me free." Jess's lips quivered. She put her hand over her mouth to try to still them. One tear and then another and another created a stream to her chin. Her chest jerked with silent sobs. "You don't understand the extent of the consequences of what Dad did."

Oh God, he wanted to scoot across the couch and take her in his arms, kiss her until her pain went away. But her body language still said *Don't touch me.* He cleared his throat. "Yeah, I do."

She set her glass down with a distinct thunk. "No, you don't. No one can. I never admitted this to anyone."

What is she talking about? He waited.

She drew a tremulous breath. "I…I never loved Drake."

Sean swallowed the cheer rising in his throat. *C'mere, Jess, come to me,* he pleaded with his eyes.

But she didn't move.

"He'd been hitting on me for months. He was hot and rich and drove a convertible BMW. Other girls on campus thought it was cool that he was from Chicago and fawned all over him, but I wasn't interested. I became a challenge, and he just wouldn't give up. Later, I figured out he wasn't used to being told no…by anyone."

Sean's jaw tightened. *And he still isn't.*

"After the breakup, I agreed to go out with him. He swept me off my feet easily because I was so vulnerable on the rebound. Before I knew it, we were married, and I was living in Chicago. I hated it. But I tried. I honestly did. I just didn't fit in with his wealthy friends and relatives. Drake's family shunned me. I became the burden I believed you said I'd be in LA. It was like the prediction came true, just with another man in another city. Drake resented that I wasn't what he'd hoped for. He became verbally abusive. When I got pregnant, he was even angrier, although his parents' attitude changed immensely. They doted on Callie, but they couldn't run interference for either of us. The last straw was when Drake started being verbally abusive to Callie."

Her dark chocolate eyes swam with tears and pain when she looked at him.

"God, Jess, I'm sorry. I'd do anything to erase those bad times."

"But you can't, and neither can I. And worse, they changed me. Some stupid stuff, like fear of the dark and being isolated. But also in ways I can't really explain."

His eyes narrowed. *What is she trying to tell me? I'm not going to sit back and let her push me away. Not after what she just admitted about not loving Drake.*

"Babe," he breathed, "maybe I can't erase your past with Drake, but I can make your future better."

She shook her head, hopelessness flowing off her in waves. "I have too much baggage. And it's only getting worse."

Enough. He couldn't stand to see her in agony a second longer.

Sean scooted across the couch. Before she could react, he lifted her onto his lap and enveloped her in his arms. His lips found hers, and he let his kiss do the talking.

At first, she resisted. But slowly, very slowly, she went from board-rigid to relaxed to melting. She wiggled around until she straddled his lap. Her hands went behind his head, her fingers playing in the hair at his nape.

As their tongues tangoed, desire shot to his groin. He couldn't stop his dick from swelling into a lightning rod, but he didn't have to act on it. He refused to prove Hal right by taking advantage of Jess when she was so vulnerable. But it was going to be damn difficult because he wanted to make love to her so badly.

Her breasts pushed against his chest like she couldn't get close enough. Through their clothes, the heat in her crotch burned his dick. If she didn't quit riding the rigid line, he was going to embarrass himself.

"Sean," she gasped, "help me escape for a while."

He came up for air, too. "Like last night?"

Her head lolled back, and he left a trail of kisses down her neck to the hollow at the base. "No. More."

"Babe, it wouldn't be right."

She pressed herself harder against his dick. He groaned as his hard-on went into overdrive.

"It was always right with you, Sean."

"Jess," he pleaded, "have mercy."

"No." Her hands dug between their bodies and found his zipper.

He covered her fumbling fingers with his hand. "Are you sure this is what you want? Are you *sure* it's a good idea?"

"Damn sure."

"Well, hell, who am I to disagree?" he murmured.

He swatted the two sofa pillows, sending them to the floor. Grasping Jess's waist, he lifted her off him and laid her on the cushions. She unzipped her own shorts while he undid his.

The moment his stiff dick sprang free, the doorbell rang.

Chapter 13

What's that noise? Jessie's mind tried to focus through the sexual haze, but her hands continued to tug at her shorts to get them down her hips. The sound interrupted her frenzy again. She shook off the confusion. *Screw it. I want Sean.*

"Babe, stop. Door. Gotta get it." Sean bit out the words like it was hard to speak.

She blinked as he climbed off the couch. The ache between her thighs made her whimper. She closed her eyes. *Door? Pizza delivery? Cable guy?* A hand touched her shoulder.

"Jess, it's Luke. He needs to talk to us."

The fog cleared instantly. Her eyes popped open. "Mom? Did they find her?"

Sean's expression provided the answer before his lips. "I don't think so. Luke just has some questions." His eyes shifted to her exposed panties. "I'll stall him for a minute."

"Oh my God." She jerked upright and then stood. She zipped her shorts and smoothed her blouse. Nodding to Sean at the door, she inhaled a calming breath as she plopped back onto the couch.

When Luke stepped inside, his eyes shot from Sean to the pillows on the floor and then to her. *Crap.* Heat ignited in her cheeks. Gulping, she self-consciously ran a hand over her tousled hair and waited for the other deputy to enter.

"Relax, Jessie. I dropped my partner at the station. I figured I could handle the two of you by myself." With a Cheshire cat grin, he ambled to a chair. "I guess you set Sean straight about our relationship. Pretty damn funny where his mind went, if you ask me."

Sean ran his fingers through his disheveled hair and rolled his eyes before closing the door and dropping into another chair. Suddenly, she felt uneasy on the couch alone, flanked by the two men. She imagined a stark, solitary lightbulb hanging over her head and a disembodied voice saying, *Where were you on the night of…?*

Luke withdrew a notebook and pencil from his pocket. "I can see you were busy so I'll keep this short and sweet," he said, the corners of his lips twitching with a smile.

"Any news on Mom?"

All humor drained from the deputy's face. "No, sorry. Trust me. We're doing everything we can. We've had a few calls, but when we followed up, they didn't amount to anything. Don't give up, though. It's only been two days."

Sean grunted to express the sentiment that two days was two days too long. "What do you need from us?"

Luke's gaze fell to his notepad. "I never got an official statement from *you.*"

"Me?" Sean's mouth gaped with disbelief.

"Luke, seriously," Jessie said. "You can't possibly think—"

His eyes rose and, with them, a frown. "Look, it's a formality. Mostly. There is"—his knowing gaze lingered on the pillows—"*was* bad blood between Sean and your family. I mean, just an hour ago, your father was yelling for me to arrest him." He turned an all-business expression on his friend. "Detective Burke, where were you last Friday from approximately one in the afternoon until about eight that night?"

A muscle in Sean's jaw worked. "I was visiting a friend in Valley Center. Got there about noon. I was on my way home when you pulled me over on Highway 67."

"Your friend got a name and number?" Luke asked.

"Yeah. Jake Stone. He's a security expert and a PI." Sean shot Jessie an amused glance, and she recalled her earlier bout of jealousy about him visiting a friend. He pulled his phone from his pocket and read off the contact number. "We done?" he asked, slapping the cell on the coffee table.

"Not quite." Luke sighed. "Tonight, Hal repeated the same statement he gave Friday night about his whereabouts during those hours. But I need to verify it. That means talking to…" He cleared his throat.

"No way," Jessie snapped. Her chest tightened. "My daughter has been traumatized enough already, and she doesn't even know the truth about her grandmother yet."

Luke stroked his chin. "I understand where you're coming from as a mother, but without some collaboration, Hal doesn't have an alibi for much of that time on Friday. Especially if we put any stock in the shoeprints Sean found that seem to indicate Molly was walking home." He arched his eyebrows. "Did Callie say anything to you about what she did Friday afternoon with her grandpa?"

A tingle of foreboding raised the hair on Jessie's nape and arms. Remembering Sean's suspicions, she angled him a glance and then just as quickly dropped her gaze. *Hallelujah Ima Freeman. Who are you, Dad? Please don't be involved in Mom's disappearance. No way could I handle that.* Her heart rate picked up speed, and she shuddered.

Sean moved to sit next to her on the couch and wrapped his arm around her shoulders. "Easy, Jess. Luke's just doing his job. He doesn't want to hurt Callie or you."

She nodded shakily. "I know." She leaned into him, appreciating his warmth, support, and strength. "When I asked Callie Friday night what she'd done with her grandpa that day, she couldn't remember."

The deputy exhaled frustration. "Jessie, you gotta trust me."

"I do, Luke. I'm telling the truth." She offered a faint smile as she remembered the conversation with her daughter. "Callie was still napping when I got home about six. I woke her and asked about her day. She was really groggy and couldn't remember what they'd done. She even said something about her brain still being asleep."

"Is that normal?" Luke asked.

She stared down at her hands. "No. She never sleeps that late, and she always wakes up bright and full of energy."

He scribbled a note. "Did Hal say anything to you about the afternoon?"

Her bottom lip began to quiver with the memory. "Dad said they went to the creek to feed the ducks. But…" She hesitated.

He cocked his head. "But?"

"Work with him, babe," Sean coaxed, and gave her a reassuring squeeze.

She swallowed hard. "But…I found the baggie of breadcrumbs for the ducks in the fridge Saturday morning. Hal…he could've simply forgotten them or made another bag himself."

Luke studied her for several beats before adding something to his notes. "Anything else?" he asked, not looking up.

"I don't recall if Dad mentioned it when you took our statements that night, but he must've spread some of the manure Friday afternoon because the place reeked when I got home. And I noticed the tractor was out of the barn."

"Yeah, I remember the smell when we went to the house after you found the Buick. Would anyone else have been there during that time frame?"

"I told you about Drake, right?"

"Yeah, but we haven't been able to get our hands on him. After you gave me the phone numbers for his parents earlier today, I called. They didn't even know their son was in California. We have a deputy working on tracking down his rental car or hotel. Don't worry. We'll find him."

Sean snorted. "Talk about bad blood between Jess's family and someone. Drake's your guy."

Luke stiffened. "I said we'll find him."

"I also told you my brother stopped by but said he didn't see anyone," Jessie added.

"Yeah, Nate told me the same thing. Like your stepdad, though, he's way short of a solid alibi."

Luke's gaze locked on Sean's with a silent message. Jessie cringed at what it might be.

* * *

By the time Sean locked the door behind Luke, he knew the mood had changed. He felt it in his gut, heard it in the silence, and saw it in Jess's body language. For the best, probably. Although his dick wasn't convinced, his heart and brain remained steadfast against the possibility he might be taking advantage of Jess's vulnerability.

Still standing by the door, he studied her. She'd pulled her legs up in front of her like a barrier again. Her closed expression told him her thoughts were far away—with her mother, no doubt. The dark circles under her eyes were more pronounced now than they'd been just an hour ago.

"You should go to bed," he said, returning to the couch. "You look exhausted."

"You're right, but I know I can't sleep." She rolled her head from side to side to loosen her neck muscles. "I feel like I should be doing something—anything—to find Mom."

"There's nothing more you can do tonight."

"I just hate this helpless feeling. And I'm getting so scared that…you know."

"We'll find her," Sean said with certainty. He just wasn't sure they'd find her alive. Those critical first hours had come and gone without a solid lead. And no ransom demand, although that had never been a serious consideration given the family's lack of wealth. Unfortunately, most abductions that went on this long didn't end well. The total lack of clues at the scene hadn't helped. This case seemed the classic example of "disappeared without a trace."

"Do you really think so?" Her eyes pleaded with his, probing, searching for the truth.

After their discovery of Hal's relationship-ending deception, Sean didn't think she wanted another lie, but that meant giving it to her straight. *Well, shit.* "Yeah, I think we'll find Molly…just probably not…" Fuck, he couldn't say the word.

Her face crumpled, and her eyes filled. "Not *alive*, right? That's what I've started to think. And I feel like such a traitor for losing hope."

"Having a loved one abducted is an agonizing ordeal. People cope with it in all sorts of ways. There's no right or wrong. And no one's a traitor for being realistic. It softens the blow when reality finally strikes."

"Oh, Sean, I can't imagine losing Mom…forever." Burying her face in her hands, she shook with heartbreaking sobs.

In three long strides, he was beside her. "C'mon, Jess. You need sleep to deal with this."

He pulled her up from the couch, wrapped his arm around her waist, and guided her into the master bedroom. With her seated on the side of the bed, he knelt to remove her shoes and socks. His eyes panned over the rest of her clothes. Nope, he couldn't handle undressing her.

Standing, he swiveled her legs onto the bed and laid her head on his pillow. After fluffing the sheet over her and Callie, he kissed Jess's forehead and left the bedroom.

Stopping in the hallway outside the closed door, Sean wrestled with himself. His Y chromosomes urged him to return to the bedroom and crawl into bed beside Jess's warm, supple body. He didn't have to make love to her; he just wanted to hold her, comfort her, and protect her. His brain, on the other hand, believed she needed to sort this out for herself. And pushing her while her emotions were overloaded could only produce bad results.

He trudged back to the living room and slouched onto the

couch. The need to do something to get his mind off Jess or to help find Molly burned in his gut, but he couldn't leave the apartment. He could, however, give Stone a kick in the butt. Sean slipped his cell from his pocket and dialed.

"Yes?" Jake Stone answered.

"Any news on the prints or the hard drive?"

Jake hesitated.

"What?" Sean came to his feet. "You got something?"

"Not exactly."

"Stop with the word games, Stone. I'm not in the mood."

"Down, boy, down. It's what I don't have that's interesting."

"Meaning?"

"My FBI contact called me. Said he had a 'situation' with the prints I'd sent him. I tried to press him for more info, but he clammed up tight."

Sean began to pace. "What's the problem?"

"Well, if the prints do, in fact, belong to an escapee, the feds might want to get their hands on him. And that puts my guy in a bind because he was running the prints on the down-low for me."

"Damn, this guy escaped twenty-seven years ago. Why the hell would they care that much unless…Fuck." His gut tied itself in a knot.

"Yeah. Fuck."

"When will you know something?" Sean stopped pacing, shoved his fingers through his hair.

"Not sure."

"Look, we're well past forty-eight hours since Molly disappeared."

"Relax, Burke. I know that, but there isn't a damn thing I can do.

I explained to my guy that the prints could be evidence in an abduction case, so he understands the urgency. He'll get back to me ASAP."

"Sorry, man. It's killing me to see Jess suffer."

"Are you preparing her for the worst?"

"A little." He sighed. "She...understands."

Stone swore. "If it's Hallelujah, let's nail his ass for her."

"Yeah, finding out it was her stepdad will make it *so* much better."

"Sorry, wasn't thinking. Anyway, when I know, you'll know."

The phone went dead.

Sean paced the living room for another hour. But the activity did little to uncoil him. The news about the prints still had him on edge. Knowing Jess was sleeping in his bed again didn't help either. And what the hell was on that hard drive? Stone hadn't mentioned any progress on getting past the password prompt.

Finally giving up, he got ready for bed and crashed on the futon. Still, he couldn't unwind. He tossed and turned.

Memories surfaced that hadn't appeared in years. He allowed them to crowd out the present. Of course, Jess was the star in every one. Meeting at a high school football game freshman year. Homecoming dances. Making out at the movies. Stolen kisses in odd places. Making love the first time. Prom. Discovering their insatiable desire for each other. Saying good-bye when he left for college. Coming home to see Jess. Skinny-dipping in the creek. Loving all summer long.

Slowly, gradually, the stress eased, replaced by the hard-on from hell. Damn, he just couldn't catch a break.

"Sean?"

He bolted upright.

Wearing only her bra and panties, Jess stood in the doorway. He gulped.

"I want you," she whispered.

"I want you, too, babe…so bad it's killing me."

After closing the door, she tiptoed to the futon and fell into his arms. He toppled backward with her on top.

"Were you expecting me?" she asked.

Don't blow it, Burke. "Uh, no. Why?"

She giggled. "You're already hard."

"What can I say? You have that effect on me even from the other room."

"It was always like that…back in the day."

"Yeah. I remember having to carry my backpack in front of my fly so often that the guys caught on and teased the shit outta me. They made it even tougher. Especially Luke."

"Did you…ever think about those days? After we broke up, I mean."

"For a long time, Jess. But it was ripping me apart, so I finally quit. How about you?"

She rolled off and snuggled against him. "Because I was married, I tried not to. But you often showed up in my dreams. I lived in fear that Drake would hear me mumble your name in my sleep."

"Would've served the asshole right."

"But it would've been me who suffered."

He shifted so he could wrap his arms around her. "I wish I could undo those years."

"Wishing doesn't make it so. Those years came and went, changing both of us in innumerable ways. Forever."

He wiggled his eyebrows and pumped his swollen dick against her thigh. "Some things haven't changed."

"Thank God."

When her expressive eyes connected with his, he read want and need in them. *Yeah, thank God.* Gently, he pressed his lips to hers. She moaned as she shut her eyes. Teasing her lips apart, he deepened the kiss, his tongue probing, stroking. He groaned with the realization she tasted the same. Something else that hadn't changed.

She leaned forward so he could unfasten her bra. After disposing of it, Sean turned Jess onto her back and positioned himself between her legs. He inhaled the sight of her like a starving man gorging on gourmet food. His hands cupped both breasts, molded, kneaded. Slipping his lips over a puckered nipple, he sucked and licked until Jess squirmed. His breath came faster, and his heart beat a happy, rapid rhythm.

Then his mouth made a leisurely journey down her body—kissing, sucking, licking—to her navel and beyond. He slid his fingers under the elastic of her panties, back and forth, back and forth, farther each time until he reached her pubic hair.

She gasped.

He froze. "Jess, babe, you're good with this, right?"

She blinked her eyes open. "Damn right I am. But if you don't get inside me quick, I'm gonna come without you."

"Not a problem. But let's get these out of the way."

While she lifted her hips, he grasped the panties and removed them. But instead of settling over her, he scooted down the bed until his face was between her thighs. His tongue darted out for a taste.

"Sean, I…I…"

"Come for me, Jess. Like you always did."

He pressed his mouth to her, his tongue furrowing between her folds, dipping into her hot wetness. His thumb found her most sensitive spot. Tongue and thumb stroked in perfect harmony. Moments later, she cried out with her climax.

Only after she'd floated back to earth and recovered did he move over her. His rigid dick caressed her before the head probed the entrance.

"Look at me, babe," he whispered.

Once their gazes met, he plunged inside. He clenched his teeth and stilled or he would've come right then. Slow, deep breaths pulled him away from the edge. After he regained control, his hips began a measured rhythm. But urgency built toward frenzy when Jess wrapped her legs around him. Unable to hold back any longer, he thrust hard and deep. She grabbed his shoulders and held on. Faster. Deeper. Faster. Deeper.

At the first wave of her orgasm, he exploded with a climax that seemed to go on forever. His entire body shuddered from the welcome release. Then he collapsed and rolled to the side, pulling her with him.

They lay entangled for a long time.

"I have to go," Jess said.

"Pee?" he mumbled, half asleep.

She snorted softly. "No, back to sleep with Callie."

"Stay." He tightened his embrace.

Jess grimaced. "I tried to tell you I've changed. I'm a mother now. I can't just do what I'd like; I always put Callie first. And she'd be frightened if she woke up alone in an unfamiliar bedroom."

"Aw, c'mon. We'll leave both doors open. You'll hear when she wakes up. You don't have to go."

"You don't understand. It's not an obligation. I *want* to be there for her." She pushed the sheet off and stood up. "Things are different, Sean. It can never be the way it was."

As he watched her leave, he wondered if her words were a warning.

Chapter 14

Monday morning, a small finger poked Jessie's shoulder. Repeatedly. "Mommy, Mommy, is he still on time-out?"

"Huh? Who?" Jessie mumbled into the pillow.

"Mr. Sean. You know, for fighting with Grandpa. He keeps looking at us."

Yawning, Jessie rolled over and stretched. The nightgown she'd put on after returning from Sean's bed slid sensuously over her body. Her nerve endings were still super sensitive, but her limbs felt like limp linguine. The tension and tight muscles were gone. Amazing what great sex could do for a woman.

"He's here again." Callie squealed and hid under the sheet. "I don't likes him."

Jessie raised her head.

Holding two cups of steaming coffee, Sean stood in the doorway. "Okay if I come in, ladies?" he asked, his tone uncertain.

"No," Callie snapped from beneath the covers.

"Callie, behave. This is Sean's bedroom. We should be thankful he let us sleep here."

He arched one eyebrow as he strolled across the room. Warmth crept up her neck all the way to her cheeks. If he'd had his way, she would still be on the futon in the other bedroom. And definitely not wearing a nightgown.

"I wanna go home," the little girl whined. "To my own bedroom."

"We will," Jessie said. *I just don't know when.*

Sean handed her a cup and then reached into his pocket. "You got a call about five minutes ago."

After a sip of coffee, she took her cell phone and tapped the screen. "Oh, sh—" She bit off the end of the forbidden word. "Work. I forgot to send them an email about not coming in today. They're looking for me because I'm an hour late. I can't believe I slept so long."

"I can. You were exhausted."

"Yeah. Well, now I've got another problem." She set her cup on the nightstand and scrambled out of bed. The phone to her ear, she hurried out of the bedroom. "Good morning, Rita. Is Mark in?"

"You okay, Jessica? We tried to call you," the receptionist said.

"No, I'm not okay. I have…a personal emergency. I'll explain to Mark, and he can spread the word."

"Fine. Take care, honey."

Fifteen seconds later, her boss came on the phone. "Not like you to be late, Jessica. We got worried. Is everything okay?"

"Actually, no." She gave him a brief description of the situation.

"That's awful. You must be devastated."

"Yes, I am. I really don't think I can work until…we find her."

Mark hesitated. "How long will that be?"

"I…I don't know. I'm so sorry. Is this going to be a problem?" *Translation: Will I still have a job?*

"I can get a temp in here within the hour. However, I don't have time to bring someone up to speed on your responsibilities since you're working on so many projects. Could you come in briefly to handle that?"

"Sure. I'll be there as soon as I can. Thanks." Jessie immediately disconnected and then called Karla.

"H'lo," a sleepy voice answered.

"Karla, sorry to wake you. I thought you'd be at the shop already. I need someone to watch Callie for a little while."

"Um, girlfriend, I'm still in LA with Troy."

"Oh, crap. I forgot. It's been crazy here."

"Any word on your mom?"

"No, nothing."

"Do you need me to come home?"

"No, thanks anyway. You couldn't get here fast enough. You enjoy the day with your hottie and call me when you get back."

"Okay. Hang in there, Jessie."

Her chin drooped after she disconnected. She needed to get herself oriented. Unfortunately, this was definitely Monday. Not only did she need to take care of the work situation, but she also wanted to stop by Mr. Swanson's office to discuss the restraining order against Drake. Four slashed tires sent a strong message of violence. The update might make a difference.

She sighed. No way could she drag her energetic four-year-old daughter along to either her job or the lawyer's office.

"I can watch Callie, babe," Sean said from behind her. "How hard can it be?"

She turned and chuckled. "You'd be surprised."

"I might miss having a translator, but I don't think I can do much harm."

Callie sprinted down the hallway, flung herself against Jessie, and clung to her mother's legs. "No, no, I don't wants to stay with Mr. Sean. He might fights me."

Raising his hands in a gesture of surrender, he took a step back and looked to Jessie for support. His phone saved him from an awkward moment. "What's up, Stone?"

Jessie frowned as a dark shadow crossed Sean's face. His hazel eyes hardened, and a muscle ticked in his cheek.

"Right. On my way." He disconnected. "Callie wins. I have to go see my friend."

Without waiting for a response, he hurried into the master bedroom and shut the door.

Jessie stared after him for several moments. *Stone?* That was the name of the friend he'd given Luke last night, the PI who was Sean's alibi for when her mom disappeared on Friday. Was Stone the friend Sean had also gone to see yesterday? What was he doing with this private investigator that would prompt such an ominous reaction? It couldn't have anything to do with her problems, could it?

Callie tugged on her nightgown. "Can Uncle Nate watch me?"

"Oh, good idea, munchkin. Let's call him."

"Any news?" Nate answered.

"Not about Mom." She crossed her fingers. "Are you…feeling okay?"

He paused. "You mean, have I taken my meds?" Frustration vibrated in his voice. "Yeah, with tequila…for breakfast."

"Don't be a smart-ass. I need to know if you're feeling up to babysitting Callie."

"I'm not a baby," Callie announced loud enough for her uncle to hear.

Jessie rolled her eyes.

"Why?" Nate's tone turned suspicious.

"Because I have to go into work to get things organized so I can take time off until...until things calm down. Then I need to stop by the attorney's office to talk about Drake. Obviously, Callie can't come with me. Besides, it could take a few hours. Can you help me?"

"Sure. I'll be over in a few minutes."

"Uh, no, no, wait." She couldn't let him know she and Callie weren't at home. Or about spending the night with Sean. "I need to get us both ready. And I think she wants to play at your place. With your Legos."

He chuckled. "No problem. We had fun with them last time."

"Great."

"And I'll clean up. You know, put all the booze and pills away."

"Nate, please. We're all just worried about you."

"Not everyone."

"Who—"

"Forget it. See ya when ya get here."

Before Jessie got herself and Callie bathed and dressed, Sean had left for Valley Center. He'd worn such a grim expression it frightened her, but she didn't have time to ask him what was wrong.

Driving past her parents' house on the way to Nate's, she didn't see any signs of her stepdad, but he could be inside and the truck in the garage. She glanced down at her clothes. Way too casual and wrinkled for the office, but she didn't want to risk running into Hal if she stopped to change. Her boss would understand the extenuating circumstances, wouldn't he? Otherwise, her appearance was the least of her concerns at the moment.

Nate seemed genuinely pleased to have Callie visit, and she was bouncing gleefully by the time Jessie pulled out of his driveway. She didn't even get a good-bye wave from her daughter. She sighed with relief that she'd been able to make acceptable babysitting arrangements on such short notice.

On the thirty-minute drive to San Diego, Jessie tried to get her mind around how to efficiently transfer her job to the temp. But focusing was hard. Her organizational thoughts were disrupted by worry for her mom, anxiety about Drake, anger at her stepdad, and hot flashes from memories of last night with Sean. She shook her head with frustration. It was a miracle she could even remember her name and the date.

As promised, Mark had the temp waiting for her in the conference room when she arrived. Her boss's genuine concern eased Jessie's fear for her job. Hopefully his reaction meant job hunting wouldn't be added to her growing list of battles.

She was almost halfway through the pile of files with the temp when her cell rang.

"Sorry, gotta check this. It might be about my daughter." Her mind added *or Mom or Drake*. But when she snagged the phone from her purse, no familiar name was on the screen. The local number looked vaguely familiar, but she couldn't place it. Without answering, she laid the cell next to her purse.

She opened another file and started an explanation. Her cell dinged with a text. Scowling, she leaned over to see the screen. *Urgent. Call me. S. Swanson.* The message had come from the same number as the call. Apprehension gripped her. Good news or bad?

"Guess I need to check on this after all," she said, turning to the temp. "Shouldn't take but a few minutes. You can read these papers in the meantime."

Standing at the end of the empty hallway, she called the attorney.

Mr. Swanson skipped the normal pleasantries and answered with, "Any news on Mol…your mother?"

His voice sounded strained, and his brusque intensity ratcheted up her concern.

"Unfortunately, no. The sheriff's department is doing all they can. And, frankly, I've run out of ideas of things to do myself."

"As have I." He sighed. "I need to see you, Ms. Hargrove, as soon as possible."

"I was planning to come by your office after I finish here at work. Did you talk to the judge about the restraining order?"

"Yes, but that's not why I'm calling."

She frowned. "It's not? What…?"

"This is a rather delicate matter, Ms. Hargrove."

Delicate matter? What's he talking about? Does he know where Mom is? No way.

"So you won't be able to get here until after five?" he continued.

"Normally. But I'm just showing someone how to cover for me until…until Mom comes back. I should be done in less than an hour."

He exhaled loudly. "Good, good. Can you be in my office by one?"

She glanced at her watch. "I think I can make that."

"See you then."

He was gone before she could ask about the "delicate matter."

Back in the conference room, she went through the rest of the files as fast as possible with the temp. As she worked, her mind kept returning to the odd comment by Mr. Swanson. What could be delicate about a restraining order? Was there something else going on with Drake that she was unaware of?

Finally, she finished the work, thanked her boss, and hit the road to Ramona. Thoughts flew through her head as quickly as the passing scenery. Sean hadn't called. Should she call him? No, she wasn't sure she wanted to know what had caused his grim mood. Was Callie doing okay with Nate? Her daughter was definitely showing signs of stress from the recent events. Should she call? No, Nate would've texted if anything was wrong. Better to finish up her business and then pick up Callie. But where would they go? Jessie was still so angry with her stepdad that she wasn't sure she could stand being in the same house with him. Worry grew with each passing minute. *Oh God, my life is a mess.*

Releasing a perplexed sigh, she parked down the street from Mr. Swanson's law office. *Please, please have some good news for me.*

"Good afternoon, Ms. Hargrove," the receptionist greeted her. "We've been expecting you."

"Hi. Sorry I'm late."

"Not a problem. The others are already in the conference room." She blinked. *Others? Who?*

"May I get you something to drink? Coffee, tea, bottled water?"

"Water would be great. Uh…who—"

"Fine. Go on in and have a seat." She gestured toward a closed door. "Mr. Swanson will meet with you all shortly."

You all?

* * *

Sean's truck careened up Jake's steep, winding driveway. Stone's call had upset him more than he'd realized. The PI generally had ice in his veins, so for him to sound urgent on the phone meant something—something bad.

And Sean hated leaving Jess to deal with her problems alone. Before he'd bolted out the door, she'd mentioned going to the attorney's office after taking care of stuff at work. He'd warned her to stay alert for Drake in case the asshole tried to follow her. But being with her would be much better than warning her.

He slammed on the brakes and jumped from the truck. At the front door, Stone buzzed him in without even a greeting, much less their usual banter. Sean hurried through the house and found the safe room door open for him.

Inside, Stone sat at a laptop connected to three large monitors. He didn't turn when Sean entered. "Close the door."

"What the hell's going on?"

Jake spun the chair around. "We have a problem."

"Tell me something I don't already know."

"My FBI contact finally got back to me on the prints. I wondered why the hell it was taking so long." Jake glanced over his shoulder at one of the monitors. "The system found five potential matches for the partial fingerprints."

"That's good news, right?"

"Yes and no."

"Stone, I'm not in the mood. What's going on?"

Jake slammed his fist on the desk. "The son of a bitch won't send them to me unless I tell him where I got the prints and who I think they belong to."

"That's not the usual MO," Sean said, his mind processing the possibilities.

"Fuck no, it's not. It's blackmail."

"You think they figured out this guy's an escaped con?"

"Damn right," Stone snapped.

Sean shrugged. "They can have him once we're done with him."

Stone shook his head. "Ain't happenin', partner. The FBI wants him ASAP. That tells me the real person behind the Hallelujah Ima Freeman alias is a very bad man."

Chapter 15

Jessie's jaw dropped when she saw the two men sitting at the conference room table. Confusion, then fear, stampeded through her and lodged in her throat. "Nate, where's Callie? Is she all right?" she choked out.

"Yeah, yeah, she's fine. Gave me grief when we had to put the Legos away," he said, smiling. "Feisty, just like her mother."

Jessie's eyes darted back and forth between her brother and uncle. What was going on? Didn't they share her anxiety about Drake? "B-but where is Callie?"

Nate frowned and shrugged. "With Hal. He didn't have any gigs today."

Exhaling with relief, she shook her head to clear it. Having Hal babysit when she was so angry with him wasn't her first choice, obviously, but she could live with it. And she knew Hal wouldn't hesitate to use his rifle against Drake to protect Callie. So her fear faded, but confusion remained. "Why are you two here?"

Her brother cocked his head. "Not sure. I got a weird-ass call from Mr. Swanson. He said he absolutely had to see me in his office at one. The weird-ass part was that I wasn't supposed to tell anyone I was coming here."

Uncle Chad nodded. "Exactly what Swanson told me, too, baby girl."

"I don't understand." Despite the almost out-of-body feeling engulfing her, Jessie managed to make it to a chair and sit. "Then what did you tell Dad?"

"Well, when it became clear he didn't have a clue where you were or that Callie was with me, I had to think fast." He gave her a look saying he expected an explanation, sooner rather than later. "So I told him you had to work today. I just didn't say how long. He'll assume until five."

"Ooo-kay. But how'd you explain having to leave without mentioning Swanson's call?"

"I said I'd forgotten about an all-afternoon group counseling session in San Diego, which meant I couldn't babysit Callie the rest of the day. You know me—always forgetting things. That's why he bought it."

She turned her attention to Uncle Chad.

He shrugged. "It's just me, ya know. I didn't have to make excuses to no one since I didn't have any cement jobs scheduled today."

"Okay, but I still don't understand why we're all here." Jessie flexed her shoulders and blew out a long breath to lessen the tension. "Callie really is okay, then?"

"Yeah, sis, of course. Now you tell me why Hal didn't know where you and Callie were this morning. Did something happen?"

Closing her eyes, she let her head fall back against the chair cushion. She was enveloped by a longing, physical as well as emotional, for Sean to be at her side to deal with whatever was coming. She forced herself to push the feeling aside. "I found out Dad lied about Sean calling to break up with me."

"What?" both men exclaimed, and leaned forward.

She sighed and opened her eyes. "Dad had called Sean and told him I didn't want to waste my life with a pig. And you know the story Dad gave me about Sean. It was all a big lie. He made up every word of it and deceived all of us."

Uncle Chad's eyes narrowed. "That SOB broke my baby girl's heart on purpose. I should break his neck."

"He says he didn't believe Sean was good enough for me. I don't buy it. I think it was all about him hating cops. The whole deception was based on his own agenda."

"The prick," Nate muttered.

"Sean was at the house last night when Dad confessed what he'd done. I was so angry, so hurt, I just couldn't stay there. So Callie and I spent the night...at his brother's apartment." Her statement was met with silence. She looked from one to the other. "What?"

"Holy shit. You and Sean Burke are back together," Nate said, a silly grin on his face.

"So *not* happening. Too much time has passed. We've changed a lot in eight years. And I have a daughter who doesn't like him. He has a career in LA, a city I detest. It's impossible, so don't even go there, big brother."

"Listen, baby girl, you got too much shit goin' on in your life right now to make such an important decision. Don't slam the door shut just yet," Uncle Chad advised. "Give it some time."

"Sure," Jessie said, forcing a smile. She couldn't forget the look on

Callie's face when she thought Mr. Sean might be babysitting her. Sheer terror came to mind.

The conference room door swung open. All three heads turned.

Mr. Swanson handed Jessie a bottle of water and proceeded to the head of the table with a folder in his other hand. His expression was as grim as Sean's had been that morning.

"Good afternoon. Thank you for coming on such short notice. Sorry to keep you waiting, but I had a minor fire to put out." His gaze moved slowly around the table. "This is a delicate matter, and most uncomfortable for me. Please forgive any lack of objectivity on my part, but I feel personally, not just legally, involved in this situation."

Jessie snuck a quick glance at her brother and uncle. They appeared as bewildered as she was.

Mr. Swanson opened the file and held up three envelopes. "I think a little background would be helpful before I give these to you." Carefully, deliberately, he laid them one at a time on the table in front of him. "You may not remember that I helped Molly with the legal paperwork after David passed away. We became...very good friends. When she started to recover from the shock and grief, we even dated a few times, but it was quickly obvious she wasn't as attracted to me as I was to her. Once Hal Freeman burst onto the scene, I wasn't surprised that our relationship came to a screeching halt. When Molly told me she and Hal were getting married, she explained that she couldn't see a future for us because I would always remind her of David's death. Despite that unfortunate connection, we did manage to remain friends all these years."

Jessie stole a glance at Nate. His lips were pressed in a thin line. Did he remember Mr. Swanson dating their mother? Had he been disappointed when Hal Freeman won the competition for her heart?

The attorney cleared his throat. "After Hal and Molly had been married about a year, she came to my office unexpectedly. She was…completely distraught. She told me something had happened, and she was thinking of divorcing Hal—"

"Divorcing him?" Uncle Chad interrupted. "I don't remember that."

Mr. Swanson shrugged. "I don't know if Molly ever told another soul, Mr. Brown, so don't be hurt."

"Did the bastard cheat on her?" Chad asked.

Jessie cringed, not sure she really wanted to know.

"Molly never told me what happened."

"Nate, did you know anything about this?" their uncle asked.

All color had drained from her brother's face. He stared straight ahead as if lost in his own thoughts.

"Nate?" Chad touched his arm.

He jerked and glanced around, clearly embarrassed. "What?"

"You were only six, but do you remember any of this?"

His gaze dropped to his hands. "Nope. I was…too young."

"I thought Molly had come for me to write up a trial separation agreement, but she hadn't. Instead she gave me these envelopes. As you can see, she sealed them with red wax. They've remained in my safe for the past twenty-five years."

"What the hell are they?" Nate's voice sounded strained, his tone anxious.

"I don't know."

"Her will?" Chad asked.

"Maybe, but I don't think so. I'd written new wills for her and

Hal after they married. They were already in my files when she gave me these." He tapped each envelope in turn. "If these are a codicil to that earlier will, it's been superseded by their recent living trust anyway."

Foreboding sat on Jessie's chest like an elephant. "Why are you giving them to us now? If they're related to her will, superseded or not, aren't you jumping to a terrible conclusion? *We* haven't given up hope."

Mr. Swanson rubbed his forehead. "This is the delicate part because it requires me to make a judgment about the current situation."

"What judgment?" Chad said, frowning and obviously mystified.

"Molly's instructions were to give you these only in the case of"—he gulped—"her death or disappearance *under suspicious circumstances.*"

Jessie gasped. Nate and Chad swore under their breath.

"As you'll see, she even wrote that on the envelopes." The lawyer stood up, his expression stern. He handed each of them an envelope. "Remember, Molly wrote these when you were twenty-five years younger. Your age at that time could've affected her perspective." He sighed heavily. "I hope I'm doing the right thing. I'll give you some privacy. Stay as long as you like. If you have any questions, let me know. Although I'm not sure I have any answers." He left the conference room, closing the door quietly behind him.

Silence draped the remaining occupants like a shroud.

Jessie dropped the envelope on the table. The words in her mother's handwriting stared back at her: *To be given to my daughter, Jessica, in the event of my death or disappearance under suspicious circumstances. If she is under thirteen, please have my brother, Chad*

Brown, or my attorney, Steve Swanson, read it first and explain it—gently—to her.

Her throat constricted until it was unbearably tight. Her insides trembled. *Oh God, oh God, oh God.* What could've been so terrible for her mother to write something like this? Surely a husband's infidelity didn't produce concern for one's life. Or did it? Novels and movies portrayed love-triangle murders, but in real life, how often did it happen? Especially so many years later.

Mr. Swanson's strange comment on Saturday—*How did she know*—suddenly resurfaced and became crystal clear. Upon first hearing of Molly Freeman's disappearance, he had remembered the envelopes with the odd instructions entrusted to him two decades earlier.

The sound of ripping paper raised her gaze. Nate was the first to open his envelope. His eyes moved across the paper, widening, glaring. Transfixed, she watched his ashen complexion regain color, progressing past normal to redden with…what? Embarrassment? Rage?

"Mom didn't know. The fucker lied to me," he mumbled almost incoherently. His gaze flicked to Jessie and then darted away as though humiliated by his words…or something else.

She watched Uncle Chad almost reverently break the wax seal, remove the sheets of stationery, and begin to read. He stilled. His eyes shifted to Jessie for a second before returning to his sister's words.

Finally, after drawing a fortifying breath, she opened her envelope.

My dearest Jessie,

I don't know how to begin because I don't know how old you'll be when, if ever, this envelope is opened. I see my four-year-old baby girl today and can only imagine the beautiful woman you'll become.

The opening of this envelope means something has happened to me. Hopefully, I'm just feeling paranoid after what I discovered about your stepdad, but I've never suffered such a shock in my life. Some days, I worry that I don't really know the man.

My life-changing discovery occurred a month ago. Hal was babysitting you while I ran errands. I started feeling ill and came home early. After searching the house and property, I found both of you down in the bomb shelter.

Jessie frowned. "Bomb shelter? What bomb shelter?" she murmured. She shook her head in disbelief and continued reading.

What I saw was so horrible that I can hardly put it into words. But you must know. You were asleep on a red silk sheet. You were naked and had been posed in a suggestive manner. Hal was taking pictures of you.

"Oh God! Oh Mom. No, no, no," Jessie exclaimed, and dropped the pages on the table. Bile rose in her throat.

When she looked up, Nate and Uncle Chad stared at her, their eyes filled with sympathy and their expressions angry. Their letters must have told the same story.

Tears filled her eyes. Outrage swelled inside. She splayed her hand over her mouth to restrain an eruption of disbelief, disgust, and despair. Her mind struggled to accept that her stepdad had taken horrible pictures of her. And why had her mother allowed the despicable man to remain part of their lives? Shock and disgust gave way to the need to comprehend. With trembling fingers, she lifted the letter.

I screamed and grabbed you. Never before had I experienced such rage. My heart is pounding as I remember the panic I felt as I ran into the house with you limp in my arms.

Hal pleaded with me to let him explain before I called the police. I'd never seen him so upset, and he actually frightened me until he started crying. He told me that his photography business was failing. His male pride and confidence had been crushed. Fearing his new family would hate him if they ended up on welfare, he made the gut-wrenching decision to raise money by selling child pornography. How the horrid idea even came to him, I can't fathom. He swore this was the only time he'd taken pictures of you. He promised to destroy the film and never do it again if I could find it in my heart to forgive him.

I don't know if I can.

I am still very angry, but I am also torn. On one hand, I can't stand the sight of the man, much less treat him as my husband. On the other, the thought of you and Nate losing a father for the second time rips my heart apart. And I have to admit, before this unspeakable act, Hal had worked very hard to earn his role as your daddy.

I'm so upset that I can hardly think straight. I'm going to wait another month before I decide whether to divorce him. I pray I make the right decision, my darling daughter, because I would never forgive myself if any harm came to you in the future. As I told Hal, if he ever does this again, I'll turn him in to the police or kill him.

The words *if he ever does this again* pulled Jessie's gaze back like a magnet.

Then she rocketed out of the chair. "Callie! Oh God, not Callie."

* * *

Sean massaged his temples, hoping to ease the headache threatening to make his head explode. His eyes burned from staring at computer screens for several hours. Stiffness in his neck and back made it impossible to get comfortable even in the large leather executive chair.

"Take a break, Burke," Stone said, as if reading Sean's mind.

"Can't take one until we catch one."

Jake grunted. "I'm glad you haven't been holding your breath for one or you'd be dead by now."

Sean groaned as he stood. He stretched and flexed until his muscles relaxed enough to move easier. His mind went to Jessie, longing to call her. Was she safe? Had she finished working with the temp at her office? Had she gotten a restraining order on Drake? Where was she now?

The weight of the phone in his pocket tempted him, but he resisted. He shouldn't call. Not until he had some concrete news.

One of Stone's burner phones rang. Both men stared at it for a moment before the ex-spook grabbed it.

"Talk to me, Salami. Wait a minute. You mind if I put you on speaker? The other guy"—Jake hesitated, sliding a sideways glance at Sean—"who's working this with me is here. Bur..." He paused again. "Name's... Badge, and he's highly invested in this."

Several tense seconds passed.

"Cool," Jake said. He pushed a button and set the phone on the desk. "Shoot."

Another few seconds ticked off before a gravelly voice spoke. "The password is RAU259078. You're not gonna like what's stored on that drive." The phone went dead.

Sean blinked. "Not much of a talker."

"Nope. But that was short even for Salami. I thought he'd

have more to tell us, but he's probably pissed I let you hear his voice."

He shrugged. "Like I'm gonna track him down or something. Gimme a break."

"Hey, don't second-guess him. In our business, you never know."

"Gotcha." He studied the password Jake had jotted on a piece of paper. "You know what that looks like?"

"Yeah. Initials and a prisoner ID number. We should be able to match up the initials against the list of escapees I accumulated. Maybe we won't need the FBI's help after all."

"Yeah, but first let's see what the hell is on Hallelujah's drive."

Jake removed a flash drive marked AVOCADO from the hidden safe.

"What's with all the food names for files and stuff?" Sean asked.

"*Avocado* doesn't sound like something important, does it?"

"Well…uh…not really."

"See. It works."

The password prompt appeared after he plugged the device into the laptop. He typed in the letters and numbers Salami had provided. Folders, labeled by gender and a number, filled the screen.

Both men glared at the screen.

"Fuck," Sean muttered.

"Fuck," Stone agreed.

Sean's gut twisted into a knot. Jerkily, he pointed to the icon identified as "Girls 4."

"You sure?" his friend asked.

He nodded once.

Stone clicked on the icon. Several folders with girls' names appeared.

Sean's heartbeat pounded in his ears. He gulped, pointed again.

Jake opened the Callie folder. They stared at pictures of Jess's daughter. She was naked in all of them.

"Shit." Sean scrunched his eyes shut. "Go back."

After the click of the mouse, he opened his eyes. He scanned the screen of names. The knot in his gut tightened. He indicated another file.

Stone sent him a questioning look.

"Open it, damn it," he snapped.

His breath caught at the sight of another naked little girl. Her brown hair fanned across the red silk sheet where she lay. In others, the child was sleeping on a white bearskin rug. "Son of a bitch," he yelled. He twisted around and pounded his fist on the wall but then stopped. Spinning back, he said, "Open Boys…uh…six."

A few clicks later, Sean and Jake stared at pictures of naked six-year-old Nate Freeman. Some of the horrible pictures included his sister. Little Jessie always appeared to be asleep, but Nate was definitely awake.

"Goddamn bastard. He was in on it," Sean seethed. He slammed his fist into the wall again.

Jake stood up and grabbed Sean by the shoulders. "Listen, Burke, the kid was only six. Give him the benefit of the doubt. Who knows what coercion Hal could've been using on him," he said calmly, reasonably.

But Sean didn't want to listen to the voice of reason.

"Not that it makes a fucking bit of difference, but I damn well intend to find out." He stomped to the door and waited until Stone opened it with the remote. "I gotta warn Jess about Hal and Nate. Call me when you figure out who the hell RAU is and what he was locked up for. Although I think we already know."

Chapter 16

I'm driving," Nate announced, catching up to his sister outside the office building.

Jessie started when he grabbed the keys from her hand, but she never slowed her racing footsteps. "But your car—"

"I don't give a shit about my car. I'll pick it up later. You're too upset to drive."

She couldn't argue with that. She was trembling all over, and her nerves felt ready to spark an explosion. Just when she thought her life couldn't get any worse, it did. And this time it might be directly hurting her daughter.

As Nate peeled out of the parking space with Uncle Chad close behind, Jessie covered her eyes with her hand and drew slow, deep breaths. How could this be happening? How could her mother have kept such a horrid, dark secret all these years? *Oh, Mom, how could you?* She was guilty of a more serious deception than Hal. *Wait a minute. Mom wasn't taking pictures of me. Dad was.* Her mother was just trying to hold a fragile new family together.

Even if it meant giving a man who'd done a terrible thing a second chance.

Jessie lowered her hand from her face. "Mom's letter to you explained what she'd caught Dad doing with me, right?"

A muscle in Nate's jaw twitched. His Adam's apple bobbed with three quick gulps.

"Yeah," he said, keeping his eyes on the road.

"Obviously, she decided not to divorce Hal, so she must've believed he just made one horrendous mistake to raise money. After that one time, nothing's happened again in all these years. Maybe I'm overreacting. Maybe I should trust Mom's judgment."

"*Maybe* Mom didn't know everything," he spat.

She cocked her head. "What do you mean?"

After a moment, he shook his head. "Forget it."

Jessie studied her brother. Was he hiding something, too? Was everyone in her family capable of deception?

"Speaking of not knowing everything, do you know Dad's full name?" she asked.

He turned to her with a puzzled expression. "You mean more than Hal Freeman?"

"Yes."

He arched his eyebrows. "Can't say I do. Don't remember ever hearing a middle name."

"His full name is Hallelujah Ima Freeman."

Nate snorted. "You're kidding."

"Totally serious."

"How do you know?"

"When Mom first disappeared, Sean did some investigating on Dad—"

"I thought I was his only suspect."

Jessie scowled. "No. He was following the closest-male theory, looking at everyone in that category. Anyway, I don't know exactly how he found out, but he says it's definitely Dad's name."

"Fucking stupid name, if you ask me. Makes me think of slaves or"—he turned to her, his eyes widening—"convicts."

"Exactly. And adding to the weirdness, apparently Sean can't find any evidence of Hallelujah's existence earlier than a year before he married Mom."

"Which means what?"

"I don't know for sure, but it raised some serious red flags in Sean's cop mind." She rubbed her forehead, another headache hammering into existence. And yet more longing for Sean's stabilizing presence. "What do you think Mom's letters were telling us—other than the obvious?"

"Seriously? You don't get it?"

"Of course, I have an idea, but I want to hear yours."

"Okay." He huffed. "Mom thought if something 'suspicious' happened to her, it could be related to her catching Hal taking those pictures. Of course, she feared it might happen *two decades ago*. But obviously, he didn't hurt her. At least I never saw any signs of abuse over the years. Did you?"

"No. And she must never have caught him taking horrible pictures again. So why am I jumping to the conclusion that Callie's in danger?"

Their gazes connected and an unspeakable possibility passed between them.

A sob escaped before she felt it coming. "Oh God, Nate. He couldn't. He just couldn't."

His eyes grew hard. "The man's capable of far more than you realize. You suspect it, but you don't want to believe it. You can't even say it, can you?"

"You're right. I don't want to believe it." Her voice rose, sounding panicky to her own ears. "Who would want to believe a man she loved had taken horrible pictures of her and her daughter and…and made her mother…disappear? That man, her father, hurting three generations."

"*Stepfather*," Nate said, the word a hateful slur. "You're thinking exactly what I'm thinking. Mom caught him taking nasty pictures of Callie, and he killed her this time. Damn good reason to think Callie's in danger."

"My brain just doesn't want to accept that a man I've known and loved practically my whole life could be a pervert and a…a killer. How can you—"

"Because I know a different Hal than you do."

Her eyes narrowed. There it was again: the feeling her brother was also hiding something. "What aren't you telling me, Nate?"

His jaw worked as though chewing on his next words. What could he be holding back that was so awful he couldn't bring himself to tell her?

A horn blared just as he spoke. "I knew."

Her mind clutched at the two words, but they skittered away because the horn sounded again, louder, closer. And this time, Uncle Chad's truck flew past them on the two-lane road. He swung back into their lane and raced down the highway.

"Catch him, Nate. Who knows what he might do if he gets to Dad first."

Nate floored the accelerator, and her Camry shot forward. Jessie's head bounced off the headrest before she braced herself with her hand against the dashboard. Her heart pounded in her ears as familiar scenery rushed past.

Uncle Chad kept a rifle in his pickup, and Hal also stored one in his truck, plus a handgun in the house. No way did she want Callie caught between the two men.

When the Camry careened into the driveway, Hal's truck was parked in front of the garage. Her uncle, gun in hand, was disappearing through the back door of the house.

Jessie and Nate bolted from the car. By the time they reached the living room, Chad burst from the hallway, the rifle clutched at his side.

"They're not here. He must have Callie in the bomb shelter," Chad said.

Jessie struggled to breathe. Her world had gone crazy. "We don't have a fucking bomb shelter," she shouted at him.

He didn't even slow down, just pushed past her and Nate, back to the kitchen.

"Yeah, we do. It was probably built in the sixties like a lot of others," Nate said, taking off after Chad.

She willed her rubbery legs to move. Stumbling out the back door, she yelled, "Wait. Where're you going?"

Nate headed back to intercept her. He grabbed her shoulders and gave her a sharp shake. "Stay here!"

"Like hell—"

"Listen to me. You don't want to—"

"I won't be able to live with myself if I don't help Callie. Let go of me," she gasped between sobs.

He stilled and studied her with haunted eyes. "You're right. Doing nothing is worse." He released her shoulders but clasped her arm to steady her as he led her across the yard.

Her gaze darted around the property, searching for signs of a bomb shelter she never knew existed. "Where…?"

"In the darkroom."

Her eyes widened as she watched Chad slamming his body into the door beneath the unused red light. Finally, the door gave way, and he dashed inside. Her brother dragged her through the doorway a few seconds later.

Stale air and a whirring noise filled the darkroom. Dust tickled her nose.

Blinking in the dim light, she gaped at the three-foot-square steel door protruding from the concrete floor and at the hole beside it.

The top of Chad's head was barely visible as he descended into the ground. "You fucking son of a bitch," he roared. "I'm gonna kill you!"

A muffled yell responded.

Nate released her and scrambled down the steps. "Fucking bastard."

Her whole body shook as if she'd stepped into a freezer instead of an old, dusty darkroom. Only the adrenaline pumping through her veins and her white-knuckled grip on the railing saved her from tumbling down the steep metal stairs.

As soon as her head cleared the concrete floor, she scanned the surreal scene, searching for Callie. So intent on finding her, Jessie almost tripped over Chad's rifle on the bottom step.

The three men were a blur of motion, locked in a struggle. They yelled and threw punches. Arms and legs swung wildly. Bodies bounced off walls and furnishings. Flesh connected with flesh. Hard.

But no sign of Callie.

"Where is she?" Jessie screamed above the din.

The men froze.

Nate and Chad exchanged a silent message and then together shoved Hal several feet to the right, pinning him against the wall. Behind where they'd been fighting stood a camera on a tripod. Beyond that was a table.

* * *

Sean pounded the steering wheel for the hundredth time. He glared at the ribbons of brake lights ahead of him on southbound I-15. Not a single vehicle was moving.

He'd been stuck in this exact spot for forty-five minutes. Multiple sirens had blared and stopped at least thirty minutes ago. People were turning off their engines and milling around between the vehicles.

This stretch of freeway had few exits and entrances. Surface roads were almost nonexistent, meaning there were no alternate routes. If the accident had blocked all lanes, it could be hours before the highway patrol got traffic moving again. Swearing under his breath, he called Jess's cell again. And again, it went directly to voice mail. With everything that had besieged her in the last three days, maybe she'd forgotten to charge her phone. He swore before leaving another message.

"Hal's dangerous. Stay away from him. I'll explain later. I'm stuck on I-15. Call me. I…I…" He shook his head. Now was not the right time. "See you ASAP." He slammed the phone onto the passenger seat. Again.

* * *

Jessie's keening cry filled the concrete room as she rushed to her daughter. Sweeping Callie into her arms, she said a silent prayer for the little girl to stay asleep.

Then she turned on her stepdad. Her body shaking, she glared at the man who'd deceived and hurt them all.

"Where's Mom?"

He glowered at her, his lips curled in a disgusting sneer. "I don't know."

"Liar," she shouted. "What did you do to her?"

He responded with an evil chuckle. "I'm guessin' *someone* got tired of the bitch meddling in their business, but you got nothin' on *me*." He smirked with confidence.

Jessie stepped closer. "You're gonna rot in hell, Hallelujah Ima Freeman."

His eyes widened.

"Yeah, we *know*." She paused. "This is for you, Mom." She rammed her knee into his groin.

Hal bellowed with pain. His legs buckled, and he sank to the floor.

Chad grabbed his rifle and pinned it against Hal's head. "What did you do to my sister, asshole?"

Hal snickered. "I took good care of her."

"Did you kill her?" Nate yelled in his face.

"Damn right. The bitch should've stayed out of my business."

"Your business of child pornography," Jessie growled.

Hal's face paled.

"Mom outsmarted you," Nate spat.

Their stepdad snorted. "Well, I outsmarted all of you. You'll never find your precious Molly."

Jessie sobbed. "You'll pay for this. For all of it." Her world was spinning out of control. She swayed.

Nate caught her arm. Blood dripped from his busted lip. "You take care of Callie. Chad and I will call the cops when we get Hal tied up in the house." His eyes dropped to his little niece. When they reconnected with Jessie's, they were filled with anguish.

Her brain seemed unable to process his words. Dazed, she just nodded before heading to the stairs with Callie in her arms. *Protect my baby, protect my baby,* repeated like a mantra in her head. Primal maternal instinct replaced rational thought.

Overwhelming urgency clawed Jessie's mind as she climbed the stairs. She wanted to run, to flee from the depths of the hell surrounding her. Her left hand clamped over Callie resting on her shoulder, while her right hand gripped the railing like a life preserver. Miraculously, she reached the top of the stairs despite her rubbery legs. Without pausing to catch her breath, she ran out of the darkroom, across the driveway, and into the house, only stopping when she arrived safely in Callie's bedroom.

Jessie collapsed onto the bed, sobbing and hugging Callie to her.

"You're safe, baby. You're safe," she whispered over and over.

Cradling Callie in her arms, she swept the sheet over them and snuggled down into the pillows. Her daughter showed no signs of waking despite all the movement and noise.

Jessie brushed the hair out of her daughter's face and stared down at her baby. Tears dripped from her chin onto Callie's rosy cheeks. Carefully, she pressed her fingers to the pulse in the little girl's neck. Strong and regular. Jessie breathed a sigh of relief.

Mom's sleeping pills. That would account for Callie's current deep sleep and her lethargic state after her nap last Friday. Hal had drugged her to avoid the possibility of her waking up while he took his god-awful pictures. Her mother's letter had mentioned Jessie was asleep. Had Hal used sleeping pills on her also?

She closed her eyes and let the events of three days ago march through her mind. Everything took on a new significance.

Just like today, Hal had thought he would be alone with Callie for several hours. There'd been no hike to the creek to feed the ducks. He'd drugged his granddaughter and taken her down into the bomb shelter where they couldn't be accidentally discovered. But Mom had come home early and found them. Had her mother felt the déjà vu? Jessie could only imagine the horror and anguish she'd experienced, realizing that her decision twenty-five years ago had been terribly wrong and had precipitated this current atrocity.

"Oh, Mom," she breathed.

Reality hit her like a sucker punch. Her mother wouldn't be coming back.

A new wave of sadness swamped her. How could she, her mother, and her daughter have loved a man capable of such evil? How would she ever be able to explain all of this to Callie in a way that wouldn't leave lifelong emotional scars? Hal's heinous actions threatened to destroy three generations of her family. *Not if I can help it.*

"I won't let you win," she said through clenched teeth.

The roar of engines roused Jessie from her thoughts. How long had she been lying with Callie? Why hadn't she heard Uncle Chad and Nate bring her stepdad into the house?

Throwing off the sheet, she jumped out of bed. She tore down the hallway, through the living room, and into the kitchen. Racing past the window, she noticed Hal's truck was gone.

"Noooo," she screamed.

Tires squealed.

She barreled out the back door and stopped in the driveway. With her shoulders slumping, her arms hung limp at her sides.

Hal was already a hundred yards down the road with Uncle Chad's truck in close pursuit.

She fell to her knees, buried her face in her hands, and sobbed.

Chapter 17

Please, God, don't let him get away," Jessie prayed, picking herself up off the ground.

She peered down the road in the direction the two trucks had disappeared. Defeat and helplessness weighed heavily. Her world hadn't just gone crazy; it was crumbling into a million pieces.

Wiping tears away with the back of her hand, she trudged into the house. Her head pounded, and her chest ached. Her body was now encased in the concrete of hopelessness instead of buzzing with the adrenaline of panic. This nightmare continued to worsen, not improve. Was it ever going to end?

When she picked up the kitchen phone to call the cops, she paused. Nate had said that he and Uncle Chad would call after they got Hal tied up in the house. Why hadn't he wanted her to call immediately? *Why? Why? Why?* Rubbing her forehead, she scrunched her eyes shut and forced herself to push aside the day's traumatic events and to concentrate.

Moments later, Nate's reason hit her. Hard. *Oh my God.* Still gripping the phone, she dropped onto a kitchen chair.

Thank God for Nate's foresight. He knew that once they called the sheriff's station, the deputies would arrive at the house with a million questions. She, Nate, and Uncle Chad needed to decide beforehand what they were willing to disclose. Obviously, they'd report Hal's confession to killing Molly, but what about where they'd found him, what he'd been doing, or how they'd known to look in the bomb shelter? She groaned at the thought of revealing the horrible truth.

She glanced toward the back door. Now things had changed because her stepdad had gotten away. But surely Nate and Chad could catch Hal in his old truck. And if they needed help, didn't it make more sense for them to call the cops?

As Jessie hung up the phone, she made her decision. She'd wait an hour. Only one hour. If she didn't hear from her brother and uncle by then, she would call the cops. *Heaven help me.*

Then she hurried into the bedroom to check on Callie. Her little angel still slept soundly. In an ironic way, her drugged sleep was a blessing because she didn't rouse when Jessie carefully dressed her in a nightgown. What would Callie have thought if she'd woken up naked?

Convinced her daughter would be all right alone for a few minutes, Jessie rushed out to the Camry. She hoped against hope that her purse was inside, but honestly, she couldn't recall leaving the attorney's office with it. Her life was beginning to blur.

She sighed with relief when she spotted her bag on the passenger side floorboard. She retrieved it and pulled her keys from the ignition where Nate had left them. After locking the car, she stared down the road again, listening, hoping for the sound of a vehicle. But only the early symphony of crickets reached her ears.

Back inside, she dug out her cell. The battery was totally drained. After setting the phone up on the kitchen counter to charge, she noticed she had several messages and missed calls, but she was too exhausted to care. They could wait; Callie couldn't. Jessie needed to be with her daughter. Not that Callie needed her; it was the other way around.

Battling exhaustion and despair, she climbed into bed beside her little girl to hold her close until Nate, Uncle Chad, and Hal returned. Or until a fateful hour had passed.

* * *

Finally, traffic was moving. Sean had been stuck on I-15 and then on the long detour for three hours. Now he was flying toward Ramona on Highway 67.

Why wasn't Jess answering her phone? Was it dead? Had she turned it off? Had something happened?

The last question raised the hair on his nape.

Knowing about Hallelujah's perverted photos made him damn scared for Jess and Callie. And while he'd sat paralyzed on the freeway, he'd had plenty of time to speculate on possible scenarios connecting Hal's child pornography activities with Molly's disappearance. None of them good. The shit just kept getting deeper and deeper.

His cell rang, and he grabbed it from the passenger seat. "What ya got, Stone? Who's RAU?"

"Ronald Arthur Usborne."

"Your FBI contact caved?"

"Nope. Figured it out myself. I worked my way through the list of escapee reports we made. Found a few with the right initials. One RAU was from Texas. Remember, you thought Hal's accent might be Texan. So that fits. And the asshole was incarcerated for the production and interstate sales of child pornography. Bingo."

"No murder charges or convictions?"

"No. But self-preservation kicks in when you're cornered."

"Damn right."

"How do you want to play this, Burke?"

"I need to talk to Jess first. But I don't want to give Hal…er…Ronald up to the feds before we know for sure whether he's responsible for Molly's…disappearance."

"Agreed. I'll keep ignoring my FBI guy's calls."

Sean sighed and slid the phone into his pocket. *Poor Jess. She's going to end up losing both parents.*

* * *

The pounding and buzzing in her dream was damn annoying. Jessie yawned and rolled over. Then her eyes popped open, and all the horrible details of the day came flooding back. She groaned. At least Callie was here, safe, next to her.

The noise started again, proving it wasn't just a dream.

What the…? Was it Nate and Uncle Chad with Hal?

Why didn't one of them open the door with his key? Did they have Hal? Maybe they couldn't risk using their keys if they were restraining him.

Jessie jumped out of bed. *Oh God, I didn't mean to fall asleep.* But she obviously had because she could see through the bedroom window that night was already falling. How long had she slept? Had poor Nate and Uncle Chad been chasing Hal all this time?

The pounding and buzzing resumed as she pulled the bedroom door closed behind her. Envisioning her brother and uncle struggling with her stepdad, she ran down the hallway to the living room and reached for the doorknob.

"Open the door, bitch! I want my daughter."

Jessie gasped. *Drake.* She yanked her hand back as though burned and backed away from the door.

"I know you're in there. Open up or I'll break down the damn door," Drake yelled.

A louder thump suggested he'd switched from hammering with his fists to ramming with his body.

Do something, her paralyzed brain screamed. *Lock myself and Callie in the bedroom? Call the sheriff? Call Luke? Do I have time? No, help can't get here fast enough.*

Another wham against the door sent her flying to the master bedroom closet. When her hand closed around the handgun on the shelf, her gut clenched. *Please, God, don't let me have to use this.*

"Callie, honey, it's your daddy. I want to see you, but Mommy won't let me. Tell her to open the door," Drake was shouting when she ran back into the living room.

"Go away, Drake. Callie's sleeping. She doesn't want to see you anyway," Jessie called, pressing her back against the door.

"You better be nice to me, bitch, or I'll take her away permanently." He emphasized his threat with another assault on the door. "I'm coming in whether you like it or not." The door shuddered again.

"Stop, Drake. I…I have a gun."

"So do I," he sneered.

Something cracked when he hit the wooden door again. The impact jolted Jessie.

She took several steps away from the door and aimed the gun. The pistol shook in her hands. "I'm warning you. Go away."

"Or what? You're going to shoot me?" Drake's laugh was an ugly bark.

"If she doesn't, I will," came another male voice, calm but steely. "Move away from the door, Hargrove. Keep your hands where I can see them."

Jessie's fear evaporated at the sound of Sean's voice. Her knees went weak with relief. She lowered the gun and sank onto the couch.

"Don't kid yourself, Jessica. This fight isn't over. You know I don't give up until I get what I want. My daughter is *not* going to live in a house where people go missing."

Jessie whimpered. If that was true, what would Drake do if he discovered Callie had been living with a man who took pornographic pictures of her? She didn't have to speculate. She knew. With the court's blessing, her ex would take her daughter away…forever. And that would be more unbearable than losing her mother.

An epiphany struck like a bolt of lightning. Drake Hargrove must never know about the pictures. Correction: *No one* could ever know what her stepdad had done to her and Callie.

But she'd fight to her last breath to be sure he was convicted of killing her mother. There could be consequences to hiding Hal's other crime, but Jessie's brain was too fried to figure them out. She just couldn't sacrifice Callie to ensure Hal's punishment.

The men's angry voices grew fainter, and soon she heard a car engine. Tires squealed, and a distinct "Fuck you!" reached her ears.

Moments later, Sean knocked softly on the door. "Jess, he's gone. Let me in."

Relief surged through her. She hurried to the door and opened it.

After one last look at Drake's receding vehicle, Sean stepped inside and locked the door behind him. He reached for Jessie, but his gaze dropped to her hand.

She looked down at the gun she'd forgotten she was still holding.

Gently, Sean took it from her, set the safety, and shoved it in his waistband next to his Glock. He led her to the couch and pulled her down onto his lap. Cocooning her in his arms, he rocked her for several minutes.

She pressed her head against his muscular chest. He felt so strong, so solid. Like a rock. Too bad he couldn't be her rock.

"You okay?" he asked.

"Not really. I don't know whether I'll really be okay ever again."

He tightened his embrace. "Sure you will." He glanced toward the hallway and then the kitchen. "Where's Callie?"

"Sleeping."

"Is...Hal here?"

She tensed. "No."

"Where is he?"

"I...uh...don't know." She hoped she sounded nonchalant even though her insides were roiling.

Sean opened his mouth as if to ask another question, but a vehicle roared into the driveway, cutting him off.

* * *

Sean shook his head. Drake Hargrove wasn't only a stupid prick, he was also a persistent one. As a cop, Sean had dealt with his type many times. But this was personal.

He yanked Jess's gun from his waistband and shoved it toward her. "Lock yourself in with Callie. Don't come out until I give the all clear."

She scrambled off his lap and hurried toward the hallway. Stopping halfway there, she spun around. "He's dangerous. Be careful, Sean."

He gave her a reassuring smile. "I know. I will."

Once he heard the bedroom door shut, his focus moved outside. No engine noise. Running footsteps. Toward the back door.

Sean darted to the archway leading to the kitchen and flipped the wall switch to turn off the lamp in the living room, cloaking the space in darkness. The back door lock clicked, and the door swished open.

He frowned. Drake didn't have a key. Was this Hal coming home? The horrible pictures he and Jake had uncovered flashed through his mind. His eyes narrowed, and he relished the feel of the gun in his hand.

Heavy footsteps stomped across the linoleum floor and exited the kitchen just a few feet from Sean.

"Police! Hands in the air," he ordered, flicking on the light switch with his free hand.

"Fuck," Chad exclaimed, reaching for the ceiling.

"Fuck," Sean echoed, and blew out a frustrated breath. "Relax, Chad. It's me."

Wearing an angry-bull expression, the older man turned on him. "What the hell? You tryin' to gimme a goddamn heart attack?"

"Sorry, man. Thought you were Hal." Sean zeroed in on the other man's bruised left cheek, the cut over his eyebrow, and his busted lip.

Chad's gaze dropped to Sean's gun, now pointed at the floor. "Why would ya be aimin' that thing at Hal?" His eyes rose to meet Sean's. Something in his expression said it wasn't a casual question.

"Uncle Chad?" Jess stood in the hallway entrance, her eyes wide and her face ghostly pale. So much for waiting for Sean's all clear. "Wh-where's Da…H-Hal?" she stammered.

Chad's lips pressed into a thin line.

Her eyes grew even rounder and filled with tears. "D-don't tell me you lost him. Dear God in heaven, don't say he got away."

Sean frowned. *Lost him? Got away? What's she talking about?*

Chad pulled Jess into his arms. "It'll be okay, baby girl. Hush now. Everything's gonna be fine."

He brushed her hair aside and said more into her ear that Sean couldn't hear. She raised her head and peered at him questioningly. Then her expression hardened, sadness faded, and determination took its place. She glanced at Sean before whispering to Chad for several seconds.

Chad pulled back. "But—"

Jess shook her head. "I mean it."

"What's going on?" Sean asked, bristling at being excluded.

They turned in tandem, wariness and uncertainty on their faces. Jess regarding him with suspicion rankled…and hurt. How could she not trust him after all he'd done to help?

Before either answered, another vehicle drove into the driveway and stopped. Everyone froze and listened. No one spoke. Sean brought his gun up again and waited.

"Careful, Sean," Chad warned. "It's probably Nate." He angled his head toward Jess. "I dropped him off to get his car."

A piece of the puzzle: Chad and Nate had been together before they lost Hal or let him get away.

A few minutes later, Nate unlocked and opened the front door. His gaze darted around the room to each person before landing on Sean's Glock. While he remained in the doorway as though unsure what to say or do, his hands shook so badly that his keys jingled. His T-shirt was torn at the neck, his left eye was swollen and bruised, and blood had dried beneath his nose and on his lips.

Mentally, Sean aligned another puzzle piece: Chad and Nate had been in a fight, probably with Hal, not each other.

"C'mon in, Nate. I was just gettin' ready to explain to Jessie how Hal got away from us. But I'm thinkin' we could all use a drink right about now," Chad said. "Sean, would you do the honors? The whiskey's…in the pantry." Jess started to say something, but he silenced her with a stern look.

Sean surveyed the scene. Obviously, Chad wanted to talk to Jess and Nate—alone.

He snorted. He could play along…for a while.

In the kitchen, he first looked for the whiskey bottle where it'd been on the counter the other day, but it was gone. Then he searched the pantry and found no whiskey, no alcohol at all. *Wild-goose chase. Big surprise.*

As he approached the doorway, he attempted to eavesdrop, but only a low hum of whispering, with no discernible words, came from the other room. He poked his head around the corner. The three huddled in front of the fireplace with Nate in the middle, whispering and gesturing emphatically. When Sean cleared his throat, three pairs of eyes cut in his direction.

"The booze isn't in the pantry, Chad. Where is it, Jess?" His annoyed scowl delivered a distinct message.

"Oh…uh…I think Mom…um…moved it to the cupboard over the stove. You know, so Callie can't reach it," she said.

"Right."

Several minutes later, he returned to the living room with four tumblers of Jack Daniel's on the rocks. After distributing the drinks, he settled in the recliner opposite the couch where the others now sat. He sniffed. "What's that smell?"

"Um…we thought a fire would be nice, but we changed our minds," Nate said, avoiding Sean's eyes.

Seriously? Sean's gaze traveled deliberately to each person. Then he pinned them with a don't-fuck-with-me-again glare. "We need to talk."

Chapter 18

Jessie cringed inwardly under Sean's penetrating glare, but she was determined not to let him intimidate her. She had to follow her chosen course of action. Despite their glorious lovemaking last night, Sean Burke was her past, not her future. And that future required Jessie to protect herself and her daughter—at all costs.

"Yes, we do need to talk," she said. She raised the whiskey to her lips, annoyed that the ice tinkled against the glass because her hand shook so badly.

"What the hell happened?" Sean demanded impatiently.

"Well…uh…," Uncle Chad began.

Jessie patted his knee. "It's okay. I'll tell him this part." She drew a bracing breath. "The three of us decided to question Da…Hal…about Mom's…disappearance."

Sean surveyed the living room. "Here?"

She gulped. "Yes."

He grunted. "Doesn't look like a fight—"

"The fight happened outside," Nate interrupted.

Sean studied him. "Hal didn't much like being questioned?"

Jessie shot her brother a silencing glance before continuing. "No, he got really belligerent when we suggested he had something to do with…you know."

"I'll bet he did." Jessie trembled under Sean's disbelieving stare. "You've adamantly refused to even entertain my suspicions of your dad. What changed your mind?"

She glared back. "*You* did. Okay? That and the absence of any other suspects. Look. You were right. H-Hal c-confessed," she stammered.

Her brother's and uncle's heads snapped around, but they didn't speak.

Sean frowned. "He confessed?"

"Yes."

"To what, *specifically*?"

"To…k-killing her."

"And you idiots didn't call the cops immediately because…?"

Sean's unfinished question dangled like bait. Jessie held her breath, hoping the other "fish" were also too smart to take it. Thank God no one responded. When she finished fabricating the story in her mind, she answered.

"Of course we were going to call the police. That's why I came back inside. But then I saw both trucks leaving. I didn't know what was happening, where they were going. They could've been headed to the sheriff's station for all I knew. Besides, I figured if the guys needed help with Hal, they'd call 911 themselves."

After a moment's consideration, Sean gave a grudging nod of agreement. "You could've called Luke."

"He may be a good friend, but he's not a one-man police force."

Sean huffed with frustration. "Well, are you gonna call *someone* now?"

She gulped. "Yes. Definitely. I want the bastard caught."

"Then you better decide first what you're going to tell them about"—he paused—"about the…pictures."

Dread gripped Jessie's chest. She shuddered. "What p-pictures?" Her voice trembled because she knew that he knew. She couldn't fathom how, but he'd discovered the awful secret.

Sean studied her for several beats before zeroing in on Nate. "Hal's pictures of…naked kids."

Humming buzzed in her ears. Black edged the periphery of her vision. Her stomach churned. When his gaze shifted back to her, she shut her eyes against his simmering anger. "How…how do you know?"

"I'll share if you will. Why don't you start over at the beginning? And this time, tell me the truth."

If she kept her eyes closed long enough, would it all go away? Darkness beckoned, coaxing her to give up the fight. Maybe reality was overrated. Would anyone blame her for escaping from the shambles of her life? *Yes, I would. I'd blame me.* She drew a long breath until her chest swelled and then let it out slowly. *I can do this. I have to do it…for Callie.*

"Baby girl, I think Sean's right," Uncle Chad said, giving her hand a squeeze.

Calmly, she opened her eyes. "First, you have to swear that nothing—and I mean absolutely nothing—about those pictures ever leaves this room."

Sean frowned. "You don't want Hal punished for what he's done?"

"Of course I do. He's an immoral bastard, so we'll just have to be sure he gets the maximum sentence for killing Mom."

"Jess, there are no guarantees. We don't even have the perp or the victim."

"Then we'll just have to find both."

Nate made a strangled noise before clearing his throat. "I agree with Jessie. The death penalty for Mom's murder would be good enough."

"I'm not a lawyer so I'm not sure—" Sean began.

"Deal or no deal?" Jessie demanded.

He sighed. "Deal. Now tell me what really happened."

Steeling herself, Jessie recounted the day's events, starting with the meeting in the attorney's office and the shocking letters from her mother.

Sean looked like he'd been sucker punched. "What bomb shelter?"

"Beneath the darkroom. I never knew it was there either. The entrance has been hidden for decades under the worktable and rug."

"Damn."

"Hal wasn't in the house when we got here. The bastard was in the bomb shelter"—she closed her eyes against the images—"taking pictures…That's where we confronted him about Mom. He flew into a rage and fought with Nate and Uncle Chad. Then he bragged about killing her."

"Fuck."

"I…I just had to leave, so I grabbed Callie and got the hell out of there. After getting her into bed, I was waiting for the guys to bring Hal inside so we could call the sheriff. Then I saw the two trucks leave…like I already told you. I didn't know what was happening so

I lay down with Callie to wait an hour before contacting the police myself. But then I accidentally fell asleep." Wringing her hands in her lap, she finished with, "And that's when Drake showed up. You know what happened after that."

"Drake? What the hell was he doing here?" Nate asked.

"He's threatening to take Callie away from me," Jessie said. "I'll explain later."

Silence settled over the living room. Apparently, she wasn't the only one stunned by hearing the tale spoken aloud. Beside her, both Uncle Chad and Nate stared at the floor, lost in their own thoughts.

"Next," Sean finally prompted. "How did Hal get away?" he clarified.

"I'll take this one," Chad offered. He glanced nervously at Nate, who kept his gaze focused on the carpet. "It happened real fast, ya know. After Jessie left with Callie, Hal simmered down and didn't put up much of a struggle climbin' out of the bomb shelter. We were all hurtin' from the fight, especially us old guys. Anyway, comin' across the driveway, the prick jerks around and kicks Nate in the nuts. Bad, real bad. Poor kid went down like a bag of cement. I let go of Hal for just a moment to help Nate, and the bastard took off runnin'."

Jessie cringed. Hope slipped away as her uncle talked. Tears threatened, but she was too drained to actually cry.

"Hal locked the door to his truck just as I got there. I yanked on it anyway until he started moving. 'Bout ran over my feet haulin' ass outta here. Nate and me jumped in my truck and took off after him like—"

"Where'd he go?" Sean interrupted.

"We followed him all the way to San Ysidro, not too far from the border crossing. Real surprised neither of us got stopped for speedin'. Just lucky, I guess. When we got off the freeway, it got real dicey." He rubbed a hand across his face. "Lost him when he ran a red light right in front of a semi. Looked and looked but never did spot his truck again. So we came home. So sorry, baby girl." He shook his head, disappointment weighing on him.

"You got anything to add?" Sean directed the question to Nate.

He shrugged and kept his eyes down. "Nope. Happened just like they said." Nate glanced briefly at Chad. "I suspect Hal's heading into Mexico."

"Yeah. Bet the SOB plans to sneak across the border," Chad said. "You know, they say it's full of holes. If tens of thousands can come this way, what's to stop one old fart from goin' the other, huh? That way there'd be no record of him crossin' into Mexico either."

He reached around Jessie and patted Nate on the shoulder. Her brother gave their uncle a grateful smile.

Sean didn't look convinced. He speared each of them in turn with his intimidating glare.

Jessie huffed. They'd kept their end of the deal. Too bad if he didn't believe them. She could barely believe it herself. And if he didn't like what had happened, too fucking bad. It couldn't be undone.

She raised her chin. "We need to call Luke so they can get…whoever…to start looking for Hal and his truck. But remember, no one breathes a word about the letters from Mom, the bomb shelter, or the pictures. And while we wait for Luke to arrive, it'll be your turn to tell us what you know."

* * *

Sean listened to Jessie make the call to Luke. The deputy was on duty, so he'd be coming in his official capacity. But now she, Chad, and Nate sat on the couch, glaring at him, waiting for him to keep his part of the deal. He wasn't sure how they were going to take it.

"Remember when you sent me out to Hal's workshop to get the duct tape?" he began.

Jess nodded.

"In the drawer with the tape I found a baggie containing an external hard drive."

"That can't be. Hal has them in the master bedroom."

"This isn't one of those. My friend, the one who's a private investigator, and I were able to open the files." He left out the part about a CIA spook named Salami helping them with the password. "Hal was hiding the hard drive because it contains hundreds, maybe thousands, of child pornography pictures."

Jess gasped. "Oh God. All those innocent children."

Chad and Nate swore.

"How did Mom ever fall in love with such an awful man? How could I have loved him, too?" Jess asked. "D-did you see…?" She wasn't able to finish the question.

"Yeah. He had the files organized by gender, age, and first name."

"Damn him. He was lying when he told Mom he'd only done it that once."

"Yeah. From the dates on the files, it looked like it'd been an ongoing…activity. He'd obviously taken the time to digitize photos he'd originally taken with thirty-five millimeter film."

Her eyes widened. "That bastard. He hadn't stopped even after Mom caught him?"

Sean shook his head. "No, except maybe with you. There were

plenty in the past twenty years. But you gotta understand, we didn't look long. It was too disgusting. Callie's were the most recent I noticed."

"Shit. You mean he'd taken pictures of her before today and Friday?" Nate asked.

"Afraid so."

"Oh my God. Hal was hurting kids all this time. I know Mom would've reported him if she'd even suspected. But how could she not find out? Maybe…maybe he never took the pictures here again…until now," Jess said.

Another stunned silence enveloped them. Everyone looked pretty shaken up. And rightfully so.

Should he tell them that he and Jake had figured out Hal's true identity? How would they react to learning that the man who'd been their brother-in-law and stepdad was also a convicted felon? Previously convicted of the same crime he'd committed against their family. He understood Jess's adamant opposition to letting the child pornography become public knowledge. Uncomfortable, unanswerable questions would invariably be raised. But damn it, they needed to know how evil this man was.

"One more thing," he said, drawing their attention back to him. "Hal's previous name was Ronald Usborne. He was in prison for child pornography until he escaped about a year before he married Molly. He went to ground, changed his name, and successfully hid from the feds ever since. But they'd damn well love to get their hands on him. If they figure out the missing Hal Freeman is their guy, the shit will hit the fan."

The three people on the couch looked shell-shocked.

Jess buried her face in her hands and sobbed. After a few minutes, she raised her head. "I can't stand the idea of that pervert hurting more kids. If we have to, we can tell the feds who Hal really is, and he'll go back to jail for his previous conviction and for escaping, right?"

"Yeah," Sean said.

"So they don't need to know about me and Callie to keep him from preying on more innocent children."

Although he understood her reasons for wanting to hide the child pornography, he wasn't sure how they were going to pull it off. Especially without breaking the law. Especially without him breaking the law. One wrong step, and he could kiss his career good-bye.

There were so many factors: the lawyer, the letters, the bomb shelter, the hard drive, the FBI. So many possible connections that would reveal the truth. *Shit.*

"Did you tell the attorney what Molly's letters said?" he asked.

Chad looked up. "No. We didn't even see him after we opened them. Why?"

"So Swanson can't raise the pornography issue."

"He said Mom never told him what had happened with Hal or what was in the envelopes, and we sure as hell didn't," Nate said.

"But if the cops interrogate Mr. Swanson, he'll mention the letters. Where are they?"

Nate squared his shoulders. "We burned them. It was my idea. We'll claim…uh…Mom said Hal had an affair, but she forgave him. We were so angry that we decided to burn the letters. You know, kill the messenger."

Damn. Sean hadn't seen that coming. He'd have to figure out the ramifications later. "You two, go make sure the darkroom is put back together," he ordered, pointing outside. "That means putting the rug and worktable back in place to cover the bomb shelter entrance. When you're done, lock the door. Of course, if it's searched, they'll be able to tell stuff's been moved because of the dust being disturbed. But nothing we can do about that now."

Chad and Nate darted toward the kitchen.

"What about…?" Nate gulped.

Chad gave him a stern look.

"What about Hal's…camera and stuff?" he finished.

"No time. Leave it. Hopefully we'll have a chance to deal with it later," Sean said.

"Grab Callie's clothes. She might realize they're missing and start asking about them. In front of the wrong people," Jess said.

Nodding their understanding, the men raced out through the kitchen.

The despair on Jess's face made Sean want to take her in his arms and make all the hurt go away. But he couldn't. All he could do was try to protect her from more pain. "Spray some air freshener," he called over his shoulder as he ran toward the kitchen.

"Where're you going?"

"To get the hard drive."

When he reached the workshop, he could hear Chad and Nate arguing in the darkroom next door.

"No," Chad said. "We stick to the plan."

"But…but…what if…?" Nate said.

"Hurry. Luke will be here any minute," Sean hollered before darting into the workshop, thanking his lucky stars that no one had locked the door since his confrontation with Hal yesterday. After retrieving the hard drive, he yanked the workshop door shut and glanced down the road. Sure enough, headlights were speeding in their direction. "Shit."

He raced across the space to the darkroom door. Nate and Chad were just setting a large worktable on top of an old area rug. "Luke's coming," he said, flipping off the overhead light and closing the door.

The musty room turned pitch dark. Since there were no windows, Sean couldn't watch Luke's approach. Crouching beside the door, he heard the patrol car pull into the driveway and stop. A car door slammed, and gravel crunched under shoes heading toward the house.

Behind him, either Chad or Nate knocked something onto the concrete floor with a crash that probably seemed louder than it actually was.

But the footsteps outside stopped. Sean held his breath. The heartbeat in his ears counted the seconds.

"Hey! Someone out here? Show yourself," Luke called.

The footsteps started again, heading away from the house and toward them.

Chapter 19

After checking on Callie, spraying air freshener, and lighting a fragranced candle, Jessie stood at the living window watching for Deputy Luke Johnson. Her stomach cramped with knots, and exhaustion threatened to swallow her whole. Honestly, she didn't know where she'd find the energy to continue to spin their tale. But she had to. For so many reasons.

Thank goodness Sean had agreed to go along with her plan not to disclose the child pornography. Was he endangering his career for her? Hopefully not, but if so, it couldn't be helped. He'd be gone soon, back to congested LA, but she, Callie, Nate, and Chad would continue to reside in Ramona. No way could they live in this small town with a black cloud like that hanging over them. God, she hated Hal for what he had done and for what he was doing to her family.

Approaching headlights caught her eye. *No, not yet.* She ran into the kitchen. From that window, she spied Sean darting into the darkroom. Oh God, were Uncle Chad and Nate having problems putting things back where they belonged? Was there some trick to closing the bomb shelter door that none of them knew? When the light flicked off and the door closed, she knew there was trouble. Panic kicked in.

A car door slammed in the driveway. After racing back to the front room, she watched Luke turn toward the outbuilding and holler something she couldn't make out. Then he marched in that direction. Her panic rising, she yanked open the door and stepped outside.

"Hey, Luke, where ya going?"

He hesitated a moment before angling his head toward her. "I heard something. Thought I'd take a look."

She stepped off the front stoop and strolled to the driveway. She clenched her trembling hands behind her so his cop Spidey sense wouldn't notice them. "Oh damn. I'll bet it's rats again. We were going to put out traps on Saturday, but with Mom missing and all, it never got done." She shook her head. "And the workshop and darkroom are locked up. Thanks anyway. C'mon in. Would you like a drink?" She took two tentative steps toward the house.

Narrowing his eyes slightly, Luke peered at the outbuilding again. Jessie held her breath. Finally, although obviously still curious, he joined her.

On the front stoop, she stopped, put her arm around him, and turned him toward the opposite end of the house. Sniffling, she leaned into him and rested her head against his shoulder, hoping he couldn't feel her wildly beating heart. "Oh, Luke, I can't believe this is happening. I'm so glad we get to deal with you and not some stranger."

He hugged her and propped his chin on her head. "I know all

this is unbelievable, but you'll make it through. You have lots of support."

She shifted to peek over his shoulder, through the open doorway. No sign of anyone. She sniffled again and made her voice whiney. "How could Hal do this? I mean, he's been my dad for twenty-six years. We loved him."

Luke shook his head. "I'm shocked, too. But don't worry. We'll figure this out."

"But how are you going to find—"

"You gonna question us out there or in here where it's more comfortable?" Sean asked from just inside the front doorway.

Jessie barely contained a huge sigh of relief. She gave Luke another squeeze and a peck on the cheek. "He's just calming me down, Detective Burke."

Sean reached out and pulled her from Luke's arms. He looked none too happy about her delaying tactic—the delay, yes, but not the tactic.

"Chad and Nate are working on drinks to help all of us calm down."

She clung to Sean as he guided her to the couch. He settled her in the middle before sitting down beside her. Wrapping his arm around her shoulders, he nestled her against him like a mother bird protecting her young under her wing. Strong. Warm. Comforting. It couldn't hurt to accept his support while he was still here, right?

Luke closed the door and claimed the recliner. Chad and Nate entered the living room, carrying the four refilled tumblers of whiskey and a can of Coke for Luke since he was on duty. Nate sat on the couch next to Jessie, and Chad chose the love seat.

No one spoke. Could Luke sense the tension, the apprehension she could see in their grim expressions and their jerky movements? More deception in the making.

After a long swig of Coke, Luke pulled his notebook and pencil from his shirt pocket. "We already put out a BOLO for Hal and his truck. I also called the highway patrol and the southern division of the San Diego Police Department since they provide law enforcement in San Ysidro."

He took another drink, and everyone followed suit. The whiskey burned all the way to Jessie's knotted stomach, reminding her that she hadn't eaten since breakfast.

"The detective from the Ramona substation isn't available until morning. And by then, this case may be turned over to one of our homicide investigators from San Diego. I've been ordered to question you separately. I'll start with Jessie. Chad, you go wait in the master bedroom. Nate, you take one of the other bedrooms." He pinned them with a no-nonsense look. "With the doors closed."

Grumbling, the two men trudged down the hallway. Luke watched them until the bedroom doors closed. Sean took one of her hands in his and gave it a reassuring squeeze.

"Okay, Jessie, let's start at the beginning," Luke said.

Numbness crept through her like ice covering a pond. First the extremities, then progressing up her limbs to her torso, and finally overtaking her heart, freezing her emotions. Maybe frozen feelings were a self-preservation ploy. Maybe she was in shock. Maybe Sean's presence gave her strength. Whatever the explanation for her composure, she managed to recite the story they'd all agreed to. The version without the evil in the bomb shelter.

When Luke finished questioning her, she sighed with relief. What she wouldn't give to be able to simply collapse on the couch.

Unbelievably, thankfully, she'd survived another ordeal with Sean's help.

His arm protectively around her waist, Sean led her to the master bedroom and then sent Chad to the living room. "Just rest," he said, pulling the sheet over her. He swallowed hard. "I wish I could stay, but it's really best if I listen to the other interrogations." He kissed her forehead.

"I understand." She grabbed his hand. "D-don't let…"

"I won't."

* * *

Sean wore his cop hat—figuratively, of course—because if he didn't, he would give in to the impulse to curl up on the bed with Jess and hold her forever. The pain in her eyes tore him inside out. He had to do everything in his power to make it go away. With that goal in mind, he forced himself to leave her and return to the living room.

Grim-faced, Chad was just sitting down with a fresh whiskey. Hopefully, the liquor wouldn't loosen his tongue but would strengthen his courage instead.

"Do I need an attorney?" he asked, taking a seat on the couch. He leaned forward, resting his forearms on his legs, holding the glass with both hands. The ice tinkled from the trembling. Chad looked ready to crack.

"I don't know, Mr. Brown. Do you?" Luke asked, straight-faced.

"Back off, Johnson," Sean hissed. "Don't play mind games. The man's just learned his brother-in-law killed his sister."

"Shut up, Burke. I'm here as a deputy, not his friend. If you interfere, I'll make you leave."

"I'd like to see ya try."

"Boys, boys." Chad shook his head. "Y'all are actin' like teenage bucks. I knew ya back then, remember?" He leaned back against the couch cushions, a slight grin lifting the corners of his mouth.

Sean hid his own smile as he sat down. Good, he'd managed to relax the old guy a bit. Now, if Chad could just hold it together and tell the story exactly as Jess had done. When Luke started the questioning, Sean held his breath.

Chad did pretty well until Luke asked, "Who was driving?"

"I was drivin' my truck, and Nate—" His eyes widened, and he coughed.

Sean leaned toward him. "You okay?"

Chad cleared his throat. "Yeah. I...I get choked up when I think of Hal...gettin' away."

Sean could feel Luke's eyes burning into him. Did his friend think he was trying to coach the witness?

The old man drank a long swig of whiskey. He tried to camouflage wiping the sweat from his upper lip by rubbing the back of his hand across his mouth. He cleared his throat again. "As I was sayin', I drove down and Nate drove home."

Luke studied him a second before scribbling something. The interrogation finished without further incident.

Now came the wild card. Nate's high-strung personality and behavior would make his reaction to the questioning unpredictable. After ushering Chad to the guest bedroom, Sean tried to calm Nate as he escorted him to the living room.

"Just stay focused, man. Keep your answers as simple and honest as possible. Take a second to think before you speak," Sean whispered.

Jess's brother nodded like a bobblehead doll. *Shit. Not good. He's a nervous wreck.*

After the two men sat down on the couch, Luke eyed Nate closely. "You feel okay?"

"What you really mean is have I taken my meds."

Sean cringed. *Down, boy, down.*

"No. What I 'really mean' is are you up to answering my questions?" Luke explained.

Nate huffed. "Yeah. Sure. It's just been a helluva day."

"Sounds like it. When you're ready, start at the beginning," Luke instructed with a hint of concern.

Sean was feeling more than a hint.

Nate had only made it through the meeting at the attorney's office when Luke interrupted. He frowned. "Where was Callie when you got here?"

The color drained from Nate's face, and he shot a panicky glance toward Sean.

Hoping the rattled man would understand, Sean closed his eyes and nodded very slowly.

Nate blinked and drew a deep breath. "She…was sleeping."

Luke made a note. "Go on."

The story progressed smoothly until Luke asked about Hal's getaway. "Who drove?"

Just like Chad, Nate fumbled.

Sean frowned. What was so difficult about that question?

"Who drove?" Luke repeated.

Nate seemed to gather his wits and squared his shoulders. "Uncle Chad drove to San Ysidro. I drove back because he was exhausted."

Luke spent a good deal of time picking his brain about where they'd searched for Hal in San Ysidro, but the answers clearly indicated Nate was unfamiliar with the area. He couldn't remember street names or in which direction they were going. The lack of information would make tracking down Hal's truck more difficult. That realization made Luke a frustrated interrogator. He scowled and held the pencil in a death grip. After making several more notes, Luke slapped down his notepad. "You can get the others," he said to Sean, jerking his head toward the hallway.

Sean opened the bedroom door and poked his head in. Chad slouched on the bed, gazing out the window into the night. "Luke's done. You can come out."

Chad nodded.

Soundlessly, Sean pushed the master bedroom door open. Lying on the bed, Jess stared at the ceiling, her arms crossed over her middle. She didn't react when he stepped into the room.

He sat next to her and took one of her ice-cold hands in his. "It's gonna be okay, babe. You all did fine."

She blinked at him. "Nothing's *fine*." She pulled her hand away and rolled out the other side of the bed.

When they reached the living room, things had gone downhill. What in the world had happened in those few minutes?

"What the hell were you thinking?" Luke said in a volume just below yelling. "You confronted someone you suspected of murder without...without..." His shook his head in disbelief.

"It was three against one," Nate said defensively.

"Yeah, and the *one* got away. You're lucky he ran instead of shooting you. I know he keeps a rifle in that truck of his." Luke smacked the arm of the recliner. "You should've called me before you left the attorney's office."

"All we could think about was Hal…and Mom," Jess added from the hallway entrance.

Luke's head whipped around. "No. You didn't *think* at all."

"Look. We'd just read Mom's letters about Hal having an affair and how she was…was afraid of him," she tried to explain.

"Wasn't that enough of a warning?" He rolled his eyes. "And I'm gonna need those letters."

The three witnesses automatically turned to Sean. *Shit.* He'd hoped the deputy wouldn't ask for them tonight. *Well, hell.* He swallowed hard. "They burned them."

Luke sprang out of the recliner and stomped across the living room. Leaning forward, he got in Sean's personal space. "They what?"

"Burned them."

A flush worked its way up the deputy's neck to his face. "You're fucking kidding me, *Detective* Burke. You let them destroy evidence."

"FYI, they didn't ask me first." Sean lifted his chin and glared back. "Evidence? Of what? Those were twenty-five-year-old letters. Molly disappeared only three days ago. What relevance did they have?"

"You're not an attorney, Burke."

"Well, at least I have a degree in criminal justice." Resentment tightened Luke's expression, making Sean immediately regret his statement.

"The letters proved she'd been afraid of him before," Luke said.

"That was *twenty-five fucking years ago* with not a shred of proof—no domestic violence reports, no restraining orders, no anecdotal incidents—that she's ever been afraid of him again. And that one *ancient* instance was…uh…apparently after discovering he was having an affair, as they just explained. More than two decades ago. No one's suggesting he's having one now."

"He could've been. Who knows what made him snap? When Molly was at the beauty shop Friday afternoon, maybe she learned he'd been screwing around and came home to confront him," Luke said.

Actually, four people knew what had made Hal snap, and the old letters weren't relevant in his child pornography crime either. Dear God, Sean hoped it was never necessary, but if Hal was tried on new charges, the pictures on the hard drive and the testimony of today's three witnesses would be enough evidence. Suddenly, he felt much better about the burned letters.

"Luke, isn't Hal's confession about murdering Mom more important?" Jess interjected, pulling Sean from his thoughts. "Especially since three of us heard it."

"Possibly." Luke swore under his breath. "Unless you're all suspects in *his* disappearance."

* * *

"What the hell are you talking about?" Sean growled.

"Down, Detective Burke. Don't say it hasn't crossed your mind," Luke said, bristling.

Jessie looked from one to the other. Had she missed a turn in the conversation? "I-I'm confused. We just told you how Hal got away. He didn't *disappear*."

"Tell her, smart-ass." Sean pressed his lips together and crossed his arms over his chest.

Luke pinched the bridge of his nose. "Look, Jessie, I'm not saying I believe it…"

"Why do I hear a big 'but' coming?" she asked indignantly.

He sighed. "But others may see it differently."

"What 'others'?"

"The sheriff's department detectives working the case. Unfortunately, I'm not a detective." He shot what appeared to be an envious scowl at Sean.

"And what, specifically, are the detectives going to see differently?"

"Whether any or all of you had means, motive, and opportunity."

"You asshole," Nate yelled, and stepped toward Luke.

Sean's hand shot out to stop him. "Cool it, man. That won't help."

Jessie's mind scrambled to make sense of it. She couldn't fathom how the means, motive, and opportunity formula applied to Uncle Chad, Nate, and her. Trancelike, she stumbled to the couch and dropped onto it. "Are…are you…saying we might've done something to Hal because we were so mad he killed Mom?"

"That would be the motive. Means could be all the guns around this place. And opportunity presented itself when you three had him here with no witnesses." Luke switched his attention to Nate and Chad. "Or the two of you could've offed him when you caught up to him in San Ysidro."

"How dare you say we're the bad guys?" Nate exclaimed as he lunged for the deputy.

Sean grabbed him from behind and restrained him in a bear hug. "Getting arrested for assaulting a deputy is only going to make things worse."

Chad came up beside them. Standing toe to toe with Nate, he

got in his face and hissed, "Shut the fuck up, son, before you say...something stupid."

Uncle and nephew glared at each other for several seconds.

Then Nate groaned and hung his head. "Right. Gotcha."

Chad gave his head a jerk to signal Sean to release him.

"You sure?" Sean asked.

Chad studied Nate for a few more moments and then nodded. "Yeah. Let him go."

Sean did, but remained Nate's shadow.

Tension crackled through the room like static. Everyone's eyes shifted from person to person, on guard for the next explosion of emotion.

Jessie massaged her temples. When she lowered her hands, Sean was watching her. He was on her side, right? On their side? What if his sense of duty pulled him in the opposite direction? What if he turned against them? Against her? Better to know now than to have an unpleasant surprise.

She swung her gaze from Sean to Luke and back. "Anything else we should know about what these 'others' might think?"

The two law enforcement officers exchanged a knowing glance. Shoving his hands in his pockets, Sean moved to the couch and sat down next to her.

"Promise not to shoot the messenger?" he said.

Not appreciating the humor, she stared at him stonily.

He drew a deep breath. "Thinking like a detective, I'd have at least one more theory."

"Can't wait to hear this," Nate sneered.

"Just spit it out, Sean," Jessie said.

"Inheritance."

Chapter 20

Inheritance?" Jess echoed.

Sean nodded. He could see her trust in him fading like a brilliant sunset going to the blackest night.

"Get real," she huffed. "Money has been so tight my folks can't afford to replace the Buick. And have you noticed the overdue maintenance on the property? Hal's photography business has never been that successful. I wouldn't be surprised if they're up to their armpits in debt."

"What about life insurance?" Luke asked.

"I have no idea. They didn't talk about stuff like that."

"Well, expect to be asked about 'stuff like that.' The detectives will want access to all their financial accounts," Luke said. "Obviously, we'll also watch their credit cards for any usage that might indicate Hal's whereabouts."

"Why bother?" she said snidely. "A dead man can't charge things."

"Jess, be reasonable," Sean said.

"Reasonable? Two friends just accused me, my brother, and my uncle of murdering my parents, and *I'm the one* being unreasonable?"

"She's right. This is bullshit," Nate said, joining the fray.

Chad frowned and puffed out his chest in support of his niece and nephew, but he remained silent. Maybe the old guy understood what he and Luke were trying to do.

"Everyone calm down." Luke patted the air with both hands. "We're not accusing anyone of anything."

"Sure sounded like it to me." Nate again.

"Listen. We don't believe you folks killed anyone. Right, Luke?" Sean shot a sideways glance at his friend, thankful when he received an emphatic nod in response. "But we won't be running the investigation. Those people don't know your family like we do, and they'll be looking at every possible angle."

"Tell them we didn't do it," Jess urged.

"Doesn't work that way. They have to perform an objective investigation, keeping all options open."

"Depending on the detectives, they might ask my opinion, but it won't be taken as gospel," Luke added.

"So be careful what you say and do because all of you will be under suspicion in the disappearance of both Molly and Hal," Sean concluded.

"Mommy, what does that means?"

Five heads whipped around.

Wide-eyed, Callie stood just outside the hallway.

After a moment of stunned paralysis, Jess rushed to her daughter. She flashed everyone a go-to-hell glare as she swept Callie up into her arms and carried her to the kitchen.

"That's my cue to leave," Luke said to the remaining group. With a quick pat, he confirmed the notebook and pencil were in his pocket and headed for the door but stopped. "None of you should be alone. Just in case Hal comes back."

"He's not coming back," Nate said adamantly.

"How do you know?"

"He wouldn't dare." Nate gulped. "He…he'd be a fool to show his face after what he confessed."

"Hal wouldn't be planning to 'show his face.' He might sneak in to get his computer or checkbook or prescription meds. Or he could come looking for revenge or to silence you," Luke said.

Chad placed a hand firmly on Nate's shoulder. "I'd appreciate if you'd stay with me tonight. And tomorrow, I got a job to pour a concrete patio in Lakeside. I could use an extra hand. The pay's good. Interested?"

Nate hesitated as if trying to determine if his uncle had an ulterior motive. "Yeah. Sure. I can do both."

"Keep your cell phones handy," Luke advised. "I'm sure the detectives will be contacting you sooner rather than later. Stay in touch, Sean." He glanced toward the kitchen, sighed heavily, and then left.

"You gonna take them to Glenn's place again?" Chad asked.

"Yeah. Safest place I know."

"Agreed. Take care of my baby girl." Chad exhaled like the weight of the world was on his shoulders. "C'mon, son. It's been a helluva day. I gotta hit the sack." He headed toward the door.

Nate stared at the floor for a few moments before meeting Sean's gaze. "Don't let anything happen to my sister and niece."

"I won't."

* * *

After Jessie heard the front door open and close a second time, Sean strolled into the kitchen. She looked up from the kitchen table where she sat while Callie ate a bowl of Cheerios. She didn't know what to say. Just when she'd thought things couldn't get any worse, they had. Again. Would this nightmare never end? If her daughter hadn't been sitting at her elbow, she would've fallen apart.

But that couldn't happen. Not now. Not ever. She had to be strong for Callie.

Digging deep for strength, Jessie said, "I assume we're staying at Glenn's place."

"Yeah. Now you have two reasons not to be here." Sean nodded at Callie. "She all right?"

"Groggy. Confused that it's nighttime."

"What about…the other?"

She cocked her head in question.

He nodded toward the living room.

Ah, he meant Callie's earlier question. "Distracted by cereal. It'll resurface, I'm sure."

"Let me know the appropriate answer." He wiggled his index finger for her to come closer.

"Chew slowly, munchkin," she reminded the little girl before getting up and joining Sean by the counter. "What?"

"We should pack up as much as we can and take it with us."

"Like what?"

"Hal's computer. The guns. Lockbox. Checkbooks, financial records. Anything you wouldn't want to…disappear," he whispered.

"You think Hal's coming back?"

He shrugged. "No, but why risk it?"

"I guess you're right. Will you sit with Callie while I grab everything?"

"No, Mommy, he might fights me." She scrambled out of the chair and grabbed her mother's arm.

Callie's opinion of Sean had completely reversed after seeing him struggle with Hal. In the long run, maybe disliking Sean was better than getting attached to him. It would save her daughter from disappointment when he returned to LA. Despite that, she would never want Callie to be afraid of him.

Jessie crouched down to eye level. "Mr. Sean's…our friend. He won't hurt you."

"Mr. Sean hurts Grandpa, so he might hurts me."

Her heart squeezed. Sometimes the right answers were so hard to think of, especially when the answer was so complicated. She couldn't tell Callie that her grandpa was the one who had hurt her, had hurt a lot of children. Her daughter knew him as the loving character he played in his charade to hide the evil lurking beneath the surface. She prayed Callie would *never* know the truth about her grandfather, but certainly not when she was only four.

Jessie gulped back tears. "Mr. Sean had to fight because Grandpa was doing something that could've hurt him or me or you. Mr. Sean was right. Grandpa was wrong." She glanced over her shoulder and met Sean's grateful gaze.

"You means Grandpa's gun." Callie pondered a moment. "Okay. Mr. Sean can sits in that chair." She pointed to the one on the opposite side of the table.

"Good girl." She helped Callie back into her seat and patted her head. "I'll be quick," she said to Sean.

She scurried from room to room, gathering the items Sean had mentioned plus anything else that looked important. After accumulating everything on her bed, she dumped the contents of one of her moving boxes from Chicago, which she'd never needed to unpack. She piled the stuff inside the box and hauled it to the kitchen.

Sean stood at the sink, rinsing Callie's bowl. He turned. "Ready?"

She nodded. "Callie, let's put your shoes on and grab a jacket."

"But, Mommy, I'm ins my gown."

"I know, munchkin. We're going to Mr. Sean's for another sleepover."

She hated her traitorous body's reaction to the simple statement.

* * *

Sean didn't breathe easy until he ushered Jess and Callie into the apartment and locked the door. After setting the box on the floor, he flicked on the living room light.

Callie was already asleep on Jess's shoulder. "I'm going to put her to bed and get ready myself," she said, heading toward the bedroom.

He didn't ask where Callie would be sleeping. Although he wanted Jess in his bed, in his arms, he knew it was a selfish wish. She needed to be with her daughter. Sean didn't pretend to know anything about being a parent, but he damn well understood being protective. And most likely, protectiveness was a big part of parenting.

His cop imagination had been filled with several scenarios involving Hal or Drake, so he released a long sigh of relief that nothing had gone wrong after leaving the Freeman house. He wandered into the kitchen and snagged a beer from the fridge. He might even need two to relax his taut nerves. Dropping into a kitchen chair, he downed an icy gulp.

With his eyes closed, he let his head fall back. *God, what a day.* If he felt like a Mack truck had run over him, Jess must be feeling like she'd been laid out on Interstate 5, problem after problem slamming into her. She was so strong not to have crumbled under the constant barrage. Pride swelled in his chest.

But it wasn't over yet. Sean grimaced. He couldn't even say with certainty that the worst was over.

His cop hat settled into place. If he were working the case and did *not* know the players, he'd be looking long and hard at a possible double homicide. Committed by Jess, Nate, and Chad, or some combination thereof. With money as the motive. Obviously. It was almost always about the money. Even when there appeared not to be much.

Of course, the evidence to make that theory blow up in the detectives' faces was Hal's child pornography. Surely Jess wouldn't withhold that information if it meant someone being wrongfully convicted of murder. *Right?* Protecting Callie from the taint of her grandpa's heinous activities was important, but if Jess was wrongfully convicted of murdering Hal and/or Molly, her daughter would end up in Drake's hands. Sean just couldn't see her accepting that outcome.

"It's almost midnight. Aren't you coming to bed?"

Your bed? The damn thought popped into his head as he opened his eyes.

Wearing a short gown, Jess leaned against the doorjamb. Her rich brown hair hung loose on her shoulders. Dark shadows underscored her chocolate eyes. If he didn't know the source, the image could've been sultry. As it were, he marveled at her ability to even stand up-right.

"Yeah, as soon as I finish my beer."

"Oh."

How could one syllable, two simple letters, pack such a punch?

Sean didn't break eye contact while he deliberately set the almost full can on the table without taking another drink. Then he stood up slowly and stalked toward her.

Stopping close, gazes still connected, he cocked his head. "Where are you sleeping?"

* * *

Jessie gulped. "With…you." She stepped away from the door frame and into his arms. "I feel like I'm going to shatter into a million little pieces."

"If you do, I'll glue every one of those pieces back together. I'm here for you, Jess."

He held her tightly against him and rested his chin on her head. The warmth of his embrace seeped into her very core. Strength and courage seemed to transfer by osmosis from his body into hers. "You know, I believe you."

"Damn straight. Now, what was that about sleeping with you?"

Without waiting for a reply, he lifted her into his arms and car-ried her to the home office. After shutting the door, he leaned against it and watched her remove the gown. His hazel eyes dark-ened with desire, igniting her own lust. Was their chemistry as insa-tiable as it had been eight years ago?

Not likely. Highly improbable. Nearly impossible.

Eight years was a long, long time, after all. Back then, they'd been young and carefree. Sex was still new, exciting. Sean had been her first lover, so of course their lovemaking held a special place in her heart.

Their early awkwardness had progressed to more skillful techniques. She remembered always being satisfied but also even more eager for the next time. Last night, Sean showed he'd acquired a few more skills over the past eight years, and the sex had been mind-blowing. The most amazing part, though, was how she'd been left with the same combined feelings of total satisfaction *and* the insatiable need for more.

Seriously? How could a twenty-nine-year-old single mother with the weight of the world on her shoulders even care about sex under these circumstances, much less ache with desire? But there it was. As she watched Sean get naked, her whole body throbbed with need. For him and only him.

He'd barely tossed away his boxers when she rushed to him. Clasping her hands behind his neck, she jumped up to wrap her legs around his waist. He smiled with surprise that quickly turned to understanding. Supporting her bottom with one hand, he used his other to guide his engorged dick into her hot wetness. She groaned and arched her back as he filled her.

"Ride me, Jess," he whispered.

And she did. With wild abandon. His hands cupping her butt cheeks and his hips pumping in time with her rise and fall, she rode him into oblivion. She had to bury her mouth in his neck to keep her scream from ricocheting through the apartment and waking Callie.

Without pulling out, Sean lowered them both to the futon. His dick swelled even more inside her, and she gasped.

"Not…yet. Too…sensitive," she said.

"No rush." He passed the time by assaulting her lips with a demanding kiss, stealing her breath and rekindling her desire.

His mouth moved lower to her nipples. He licked and circled and sucked, sending shock waves through her. Then he trailed hot kisses across her breasts and back up her neck.

By the time he reached her mouth, she barely had time to say, "Ready," before he claimed it again.

He eased almost all the way out and then plunged in deep. Slowly out, fast thrust. Again and again and again. She coiled tighter and tighter.

He chuckled near her ear. "Come already. You're about to cut off my circulation."

With one more thrust, he pushed her over the edge.

"Your turn," she breathed as she floated all the way down.

"As you wish."

He clasped both her hands in his large one and held them on the futon above her head. Supporting himself on his other arm, he peered down at her while his hips pumped double-time. His eyes darkened. His neck muscles strained. He felt so huge inside her that she marveled she didn't burst.

He changed his angle slightly, catching her by surprise, because amazingly, she was right there with him, hanging by a thread. Again.

"Now," he gasped, and muffled her cry with his mouth.

* * *

His eyes closed, Sean reveled in the natural feel of Jess draped across him. They'd recuperated from the first round of mind-blowing sex only to rally for a second, albeit less strenuous, round. He didn't think he could ever get enough of her.

Just lying here with her, no words necessary, his world was complete. A peacefulness he hadn't experienced in eight years calmed his soul.

"When do you leave?" Jess asked, her head lying on his chest.

He blinked, the heavenly bubble burst by reality. He swallowed hard. "Probably Sunday. I have to work Monday."

"I see."

He waited for more. But silence stretched on.

That was it? Two words? What about "Don't go" or "I'll miss you"? Even, "It's been great seeing you again."

Maybe he should say something. Like the "great" or "miss" sentiments he had hoped to hear from her. What if he asked Jess to come live with him? Shit, that wouldn't work. And the invitation would probably make her mad because he knew how much she hated LA. What if he told her that he liked her and wanted to keep seeing her? No, that sounded too much like a proposition for a friends-with-benefits thing. His throat tightened. What if he confessed he…loved her? Because he did, damn it. Despite his brain knowing it was a horrible idea, his heart had torn down the walls he'd built around his old feelings for her. And now those old feelings were his new feelings. How would Jess take the news? Only one way to find out…

"Jess," he whispered, "I love you."

Slow and steady breathing was her only answer.

Chapter 21

Jessie fought to keep her breathing soft and regular. Not an easy task with her heart in her throat.

Had she heard Sean correctly? Had he really said he loved her? How could that be true?

So many years had passed. So much had changed. So many problems complicated her world and weighed her down.

That's why she wasn't soaring with joy, right? That's why she didn't open her eyes, fling her arms around his neck, and tell him she loved him, too.

How could this be happening at the worst possible time? In addition to all the current crises, Sean would be leaving in six days. He'd go back to LA, to his career, to his friends, to his life…without her. He'd be so busy that he'd probably even forget to call. In no time, the little town of Ramona and unsophisticated, small-town-girl Jessie Hargrove would fade from his thoughts.

Their second chance was going to end in failure. And it would be her fault. But she had no choice. She was first and foremost Callie's mom. A primal instinct stronger than romantic love ruled her life now: a mother's protectiveness of her young. She choked back a sob.

Sean let out a soft groan. She held her breath.

Once she was sure he was asleep, she slipped out of his arms, rolled off the futon, and found her gown. Standing at the door, she let the tears fall as she watched him. The man she had loved and lost, loved now, and would soon lose again. Fate was so damn cruel.

She turned away and closed the door, literally and figuratively.

* * *

"They've got a search warrant already?" Sean said, gripping his phone tighter.

He sat with Jess and Callie at Glenn's kitchen table on Tuesday morning as the little girl inhaled a bowl of cereal. They both looked up at his harsh tone. Jess arched her eyebrows.

"They gave the case to some hotshot new homicide investigator from LAPD who just joined the sheriff's department. Folks say he's trying to make a name for himself. The jerk acts like he's smarter than us just because he came from a big…" Luke's explanation trailed off.

Sean let Luke squirm in his own words for several strained moments. "Yeah, I know the type. But how could he have had time to go over the file?"

"Shit, how do I know? Don't shoot the messenger. I could get in big trouble for this heads-up."

"Sorry, buddy. Anything else?"

"Yeah, it's all three properties: the Freeman's, Nate's, and Chad's."

"Well, sh—" Catching himself just in time, he slanted a glance at

Callie, her mother's "Big Ears" warning rising to the surface. "Hang on, Luke." He left the kitchen table, moved to the living room, and lowered his voice. "Nate and Chad aren't even home. After checking to make sure the old homestead was still in one piece, they headed down to Lakeside for some concrete work."

"Might want to warn them so they can hoof it on home."

"Will do. Any sign of Hal's truck?"

"Not yet. Oh, and the new guy's getting a court order for access to Hal's credit card and cell phone records to see if they can locate him through a charge or call. And he wants their bank accounts frozen."

"I figured that. Sounds like he wants it both ways."

"How's that?"

"Hal's alive and on the run for killing Molly, *and* the three suspects knocked him and Molly off for the inheritance."

Luke snorted. "Covering all the bases and his ass."

"Yeah, but he's at a disadvantage because he doesn't know the family like we do. You gonna be part of the search team?"

"Not a chance. The guy's already figured out I've got a conflict of interest and doesn't want me near his case. Besides, I'm not on duty. After I catch a few Zs, I'm heading down to San Ysidro to put in some time searching for Hal and his truck. As a private citizen, of course."

"Of course. Good luck."

"Thanks. Gonna need it. Same to you and Jess."

Sean blew out a long breath as he stuffed the cell phone in his pocket. Foreboding prickled the skin at his nape. This could be a bad, bad day.

Jess hurried into the room, interrupting his depressing thoughts. "What's happening?"

"I'll tell you in a minute. I need to call Nate and Chad ASAP."

After Jess gave him their numbers from her cell phone, Sean went to the bedroom and shut the door. He called Chad to warn him and Nate about the searches of their properties. As expected, they were really unhappy with the turn of events.

"What the hell do they expect to find at my place?" Chad demanded, the rumblings of what Sean guessed was the cement truck making it hard to hear him.

"They're looking for any clue as to what happened to Molly or Hal."

Chad snorted. "Like I know? They should be searchin' down in San Ysidro or across the border in Tijuana, if you ask me."

"Yeah, well, I'm not sure the detective's buying the family's story. I expect he'll want to separately question each of you himself."

His statement was met with silence.

"How soon can you be back to your place?" Sean asked.

"My guy Jimmy rode down in the truck with me. I'll leave him to finish up. I can catch a ride with Nate and be in Ramona in, say, forty minutes."

"Make it thirty. Call me when you get home. Have Nate call me, too."

The bedroom door swung open, and Jess stood in the doorway. "I put a movie on for Callie. What's happening?" She dropped onto the bed.

"The sheriff's department got warrants to search all three properties."

"What does it mean?"

Sean sat down next to her and took her icy hand in his warm one. He pasted on his most reassuring smile. "Nothing more than standard procedure."

She looked him directly in the eye. "For suspects, right?"

He exhaled. "Yeah. They need time to conclude you guys are innocent."

"Whatever happened to innocent until proven guilty? In the meantime, Hal's getting away in Mexico."

"We don't know that. Coyotes charge big bucks to sneak people across the border. They deal in cash, not checks or credit cards. Hal can't get that kind of cash from an ATM. Most coyotes aren't totally stupid either. A gringo wanting to sneak *into Mexico* is gonna raise some eyebrows. They might not take him across if they think it's too risky for them."

"Can the sheriff freeze Mom and Hal's accounts so he can't get the money?"

"They're on it."

"What if…?" She gulped, and her voice dropped to a whisper. "What if they search the darkroom and find the bomb shelter?"

He tried to think of a way to soften the blow. *The dark Freeman family secret is out of the bag* didn't sound very supportive, but it was the truth. "Assuming Hal took pictures of Callie before you guys interrupted him, the photos are gonna be on his camera. I don't know how you can deny the pornography issue then. The silver lining is that it would provide motive for Hal murdering Molly."

"I want it proved some other way."

"I know. But you can't make the darkroom disappear. They're going to search it. Today."

* * *

Karla had just left with Callie to babysit her at the beauty parlor when a patrol car pulled into the Freeman driveway. Probably a good thing, since a long wait would've driven Jessie up the wall. Of course, being separated from her daughter brought its own worries.

Sean stood behind her as she opened the front door.

"Ms. Hargrove, I'm Deputy Lungreen, and this is Deputy Anderson. We have a search warrant for this property," the older one said, handing her a paper.

She passed it over her shoulder to Sean. "Only two of you?"

"Yes, ma'am. We're just gonna keep an eye on things here while the team searches the other two properties with Detective Cramer."

Sean's phone rang, and he walked away from the door to answer it.

Jessie squared her shoulders. "So, how does this work?"

"Deputy Anderson will wait inside, and I'll stay out here."

"Okay." She moved aside so the younger deputy could enter. He stepped around her but didn't go any farther. Then she offered them both something to drink, but they declined. After shutting the door, she gestured into the living room. "Have a seat."

"I'll stand, thanks."

The deputy set his feet in a wide stance and clasped his hands behind him, looking like a soldier. Appropriate, since Jessie felt embattled.

Sean motioned her to the kitchen doorway.

"That was Chad. Detective Cramer and his search team just arrived. I'm going over there to observe."

"You're leaving me here? Alone? With them?"

His gaze darted to the deputy and back. "If you're comfortable with them staying here without you, I don't think they'd object to you going with me."

"What if…?" she whispered.

"They're not going to do anything until the boss arrives. Trust me."

"If we leave, will both deputies wait outside?"

"That would be my guess."

"Will they think we're…uh…running?"

"Nah. The property will eventually be searched even if we never come back."

"I see." She released a shaky breath. "Let's go, then. It'll drive me crazy just waiting here."

After they explained to Deputy Lungreen where they were going, the deputies settled in the patrol car. Jessie locked the house and also checked the outbuilding doors. She'd known they were locked, but she couldn't help herself.

When they arrived at Uncle Chad's, the search was in full swing. She counted five deputies in addition to the detective, who introduced himself immediately before leaving to supervise the inspection of a shed.

The five-acre property included several small structures in addition to the modest two-bedroom, ranch-style house. Eucalyptus trees dotted the land, but there wasn't a grove of fruit trees or a garden. Not since Aunt Sally had died, at least. Jessie's aunt and uncle had lived here for as long as she could remember. Since they'd had no children, they'd borrowed her and Nate occasionally for the joy of spoiling them rotten. The warm memories seemed a lifetime ago, and she had to fight back tears.

"Never thought I'd see the day," Chad muttered, shaking his head. He jammed his hands into the pockets of his work overalls. "Sure as hell don't like bein' made to feel like a criminal."

Jessie gave him a hug and stayed at his side. "It'll be all right."

"They should be putting their effort into looking for Hal," Sean said.

Jessie nodded.

Suddenly, ferocious barking came from inside the house. A wide smile lit Uncle Chad's face.

"Wait for it…," he murmured.

A deputy rounded the corner of the house at a trot. "Mr. Brown, we need you to restrain your dog."

"What's the problem? Buster loves everybody."

"Not us. He's growling and barking something fierce."

"You boys do somethin' to piss him off?"

"No, sir." The deputy grinned. "Bet he was a damn good hunting dog in his younger days."

Uncle Chad puffed up with pride. "That he was. Still got a damn good nose, though I don't have much use for it these days. Gave up huntin' when my hands got unsteady." He turned to Jessie. "I'll be right back, baby girl."

Sean and Jessie watched as he led Buster to his truck and helped him into the cab. He rolled both windows down and gave the dog a good rub before closing the door.

After Chad rejoined them, it seemed like forever before the deputies finished scouring the property. They packed up to move on to Nate's place without bagging a single item of evidence. Jessie breathed a sigh of relief even though she'd never imagined there could be any sign of wrongdoing since her uncle was completely innocent.

Chad hopped in his truck with Buster, and Sean and Jessie followed in his Ford F-150. Five minutes later, the caravan of vehicles passed the Freeman house and continued down Oakdale a couple miles. When they pulled up to Nate's house, he stomped out the front door, belligerence reddening his face and resentment seeping from every pore. Jessie prayed he'd taken his meds and not been drinking. Otherwise, the situation could go downhill quickly.

Nate's rental was smaller, and the property contained no out-buildings, so Jessie had hoped the search would take less time. However, the lack of space must've been offset by higher suspicion, for the search took even longer than at Uncle Chad's. Obviously, the deputies were aware of her brother's arrest record, even though she'd been benignly oblivious to his law-breaking behavior. They asked question after question about the numerous bottles of pills, but thankfully, the medications were all legally prescribed by doctors and filled by legitimate pharmacies.

As time dragged on, Jessie's insides coiled tighter and tighter. The future was a double-edged sword: She dreaded with all her heart the search of her parents' property but also dreamed of the process being over.

Finally, after a few hours, the deputies had confiscated only Nate's computer, a work glove with a spot of dried blood, and some financial files.

As the caravan headed down the road to the Freeman property, Jessie fought the nausea churning in her stomach. She'd be damned if she'd give the obnoxious sheriff's detective the satisfaction of knowing he'd upset her to the point of throwing up.

"It's going to be all right," Sean said, although the grim look on his face belied his calm reassurance.

"I'm just so afraid they're going to find the bomb shelter and the…the horrid stuff down there."

"Granted, it's 'horrid stuff.' But it's incriminating of Hal, not the three of you." His tight expression told her there was something he wasn't saying. She thought she knew what it was.

"Unless his pornography represents another motive for the three of us—in addition to the inheritance."

He sighed. "There is that."

"This is just surreal to me. Hal's the criminal, but we're the ones being investigated."

"Most of this is standard MO. Don't take it personally."

She snorted. "Don't take it personally? Are you crazy? Of course it's personal."

"Okay, look at it this way. The process will *personally eliminate* you three as suspects."

"Only if it works right."

"O, ye of little faith."

"Today, yes."

As they neared the Freeman driveway, Sean slowed the truck and leaned forward, squinting through the windshield. A muscle in his cheek twitched.

"What's wrong?" she asked.

He pointed down the road. "See that car on the shoulder?"

"Yeah. I don't recognize it from here."

"I do. It's Drake's rental. Remember, I saw it the other night when I escorted him away from your front door."

Her eyes narrowed. "What's he doing?"

"I don't know. Let's go see."

As soon as the patrol cars in front of them turned into the driveway, Sean pressed hard on the gas and sped past. If it was Drake in the car, he probably recognized Sean's truck and decided he didn't want another confrontation because the sedan executed a fast U-turn and raced away. Sean pulled onto the shoulder instead of chasing the disappearing car.

"Why was he here?" Jessie asked.

"He might've been planning to pay you another visit but then spotted the patrol car sitting in your driveway."

"He knows Mom's missing so he'd probably think they were here about that. But it'd be great if he thought I'd filed a complaint against him. Or do you think he's heard about Hal?"

"If he hasn't yet, it won't take long in this small town."

Her throat tightened. "A family murder will just be more ammunition to help him take Callie away from me."

"We can't stop the talk, Jess."

"I know. But seriously, what do you think he's up to?"

"I don't know, but it can't be good."

Chapter 22

Neither said another word until Sean parked his truck in the Free-mans' driveway.

Jessie stared out the windshield while Detective Cramer approached Deputies Lungreen and Anderson, who were now leaning against their patrol car. "I'm scared, Sean."

"Understandable." He reached across and gave her hand a gentle squeeze. "I'm here for you."

For now. She stopped that train of thought before it ran her off the tracks. No sense in going there. It was what it was. "I know."

When they climbed from the truck, Cramer was already shouting orders to the six additional deputies who had arrived from the other sites. In pairs, they scattered to different parts of the property: the barn, the outbuilding, and the house.

"Let's do this," Sean murmured, coming around the front of the truck to take her hand. "We'll wait inside."

Uncle Chad's truck pulled up beside them. Buster bolted out the driver's door before he could close it. "Come back here, you mangy mutt," he hollered, and then laughed. "Hell, let him bother them. I don't care."

Sean gave Chad a meaningful look. "Wait for Nate. You guys stay out here. I'm taking Jess inside."

He escorted Jessie through the back door and into a chair at the kitchen table. She was glad she could only hear, not see, the two deputies searching the house. The sense of violation was already strong.

Sean handed her a bottle of water from the fridge and sat down next to her. He ran his fingers up through the hair at her nape and massaged her neck muscles.

"You've got knots the size of golf balls."

She shrugged. "They feel like baseballs."

His strong fingers tunneled through her hair, sending tingles through her body. Memories of tingles he'd produced in other parts filled her mind. She surrendered to the sensations, wanting, needing to escape for just a few minutes. Sean would be gone soon, and who knew when she'd feel tingles again.

He was still massaging her scalp when Detective Cramer entered the kitchen. The man took one look at the intimate activity and grunted.

Sean's eyes narrowed, his fingers stilled for only a second before he turned her face toward him and claimed her lips in a passionate kiss. She clung to his shoulders, irrationally grateful that he cared more for her than he cared about Cramer's belief in his objectivity.

"Detective Cramer, I found something...odd," a deputy said, walking into the kitchen with a large shoebox in his hands.

"Odd?" Cramer gave him an exasperated look. "What is it?"

"Found this in Hal Freeman's part of the closet." He flipped the lid open. With his gloved hands, he moved the shoes aside and lifted out a wad of twenty-dollar bills. "I counted two hundred dollars."

Jessie gasped.

Cramer shrugged. "Could be his gambling money. Or rainy day stash."

"But I also found these." The deputy reached into one of the shoes and then turned his hand over. A pair of gold earrings rested in his palm.

"Damn him," Jessie muttered.

Cramer scowled at her. "Care to share, Ms. Hargrove?"

She huffed. "The day after Mom went missing, Hal told me those earrings had disappeared off her dresser. And the money is probably my parents' 'quick cash' fund. It's normally kept in Mom's underwear drawer, but it wasn't there when I…I looked for it last Saturday night."

"Why would your father hide this stuff?"

"I think he was planning to accuse Nate of stealing it. We all knew my brother needed money. I'm ashamed to admit that the thought had crossed my mind," she said.

"Jess is right. Hal wanted to point suspicion at Nate for Molly's disappearance by making theft the motive. They'd argued about money Friday morning."

Cramer's gaze shifted between them. "Money's a damn good motive."

She tensed. From his tone, Jessie knew he wasn't referring to the two hundred dollars but to the inheritance, regardless of how meager.

"It stinks in here," Sean growled. "Even the smell of manure would be better." He wrapped his arm around her shoulders and led her out the back door.

The garage door was up, and she spotted two deputies diligently searching through the stacks of cardboard boxes and plastic bins. Her breath caught.

Sean nudged her to a patio chair. "Sit," he ordered, and gently pushed her down. After pulling another chair alongside, he dropped into it.

Spotting them from where they'd been leaning against the shady side of the barn, Nate and Chad started toward the patio. The double doors stood open, noise coming from within proof that deputies were busy inside.

"For the last time, Buster, get out of that goddamn bullshit," Chad yelled at his bloodhound, who was digging furiously at the base of the mountain of manure. Buster raised his head and howled. "Come, boy. Or you're gonna need a bath." As if understanding the threat, the dog bounded after his master, although he took one last, longing look at the pile.

"How ya doing, sis?" Nate asked, sitting down on the patio at her feet. With drawn cheeks and dark circles under his eyes, he looked like death warmed over, but she appreciated him trying to act calm.

"I've had better days. Have they, uh, searched the…rest of the outbuilding?" Her eyes flicked to the darkroom end of the structure.

"Nope. Started with the garage."

Chad swung a chair up next to Sean. "What do ya think?"

"I think we hope and pray."

"Yup, me too."

Two deputies emerged from the garage and headed for the workshop door. A fist closed around Jessie's throat.

One of them jerked the handle a few times before calling to their audience. "Door's locked. We need to borrow your key again."

Nate stood up and fished his keys out of his pocket. He separated the proper key and held it out to the deputy. The guy jogged over.

"Sorry about this, folks." He shook his head. "Real sad about your mom, Jessica. She was a nice lady."

Jessie nodded but couldn't speak. Wasn't it bad enough to lose your mother to an evil killer? To be suspected of the murder was just too much.

The deputy accepted the keys and returned to his partner. After unlocking the door, they disappeared inside.

Jessie counted each passing second with the hammering of her heart. Breathing became almost impossible. She blinked away the black spots dotting her vision. She would not faint.

The thirty-minute search of the workshop felt like an eternity. But when the deputies exited and closed the door, she wished it had lasted longer.

As they turned toward the darkroom door, she whimpered. Her whole body trembled.

Sean scooted his chair closer and rubbed her back. "Breathe, Jess. Slow, deep breaths."

"C'mere, dog. What've you got? Grab him," a deputy shouted.

"You go that way. I'll take the backside," answered another.

The yelling redirected everyone's attention to the two deputies at the barn entrance. One circled behind the manure, and the other darted toward the front. Buster raced into sight from around the manure mountain with something white hanging from his mouth. The dog's long ears swung wildly as he ran toward the side of the house.

Everyone scrambled to their feet.

"Damn, how'd he sneak back over there?" Chad snorted. "Hell, I didn't think he could move that fast anymore."

They watched as the deputies darted after him, separating in opposite directions when they reached the house. More shouting and swearing reached the patio before Buster reappeared in the driveway still carrying his prize. He dropped it to bark loudly for several moments.

"Stop the damn dog," one deputy hollered before coming into view.

"Name's Buster, and he doesn't like bein' called 'damn,'" Uncle Chad said, bristling.

As Buster disappeared behind the manure again with the item, the deputies lumbered to the patio. Bracing their hands on their knees, they panted for air.

"I don't care what you call him, just get what's in his mouth," the older one said.

"He take somethin' of yours?" Chad asked indignantly.

"No. He dug a big hole under the manure. I think he found it there."

Jessie grasped Sean's arm. "What would be under there that's…white?"

He shrugged. "Dead rabbit. Bird. Light gray squirrel. I don't know."

"Aw, hell," Uncle Chad grumbled. "He's gonna need a bath for sure."

Scowling at the old man's lack of cooperation, the deputies took off after Buster again. More barking came from behind the manure. More yelling came from the deputies.

Jessie chanced a glance toward the darkroom. The deputies, who'd been about to enter, were now at the corner of the open garage, laughing at Buster's escapades. They showed no signs of joining the fray.

Sean angled his head toward Uncle Chad. "Call the dog before you piss those guys off."

"Yeah, okay," he muttered. Cupping his hands around his mouth, he shouted, "Buster, c'mere, boy. Come to Daddy."

The dog appeared beside the manure, dropped the object, and barked.

Chad motioned with his hand. "Bring…bring it to me."

Buster snatched the item as the two deputies raced up behind him. After a quick look over his shoulder, he bounded across the yard to the patio. His ears flapped like he was about to take flight.

Jessie's gaze zeroed in, as if through the tunnel vision of binoculars, on the white object in his mouth. Recognition hit like a freight train.

She let out an anguished cry and buried her face in Sean's chest. Her hands clutched fistfuls of his T-shirt as her mind clutched at the fraying thread of reality.

* * *

The back door slammed, and three sets of heavy footsteps stomped across the patio.

"What the hell is all the commotion?" Detective Cramer demanded.

No one answered.

Sean tightened his arms around Jess as he watched Buster stop in front of Chad and drop the dirty white object on the ground.

"What the...?" Chad muttered, and frowned.

Nate stepped around his sister so he could see better and then stared at the object.

"Well?" Cramer snapped.

Sean stabbed him with a surly scowl. It didn't feel as good as calling the detective an insensitive fucking asshole, but it'd have to do. He struggled to rein in his anger. "It's Molly's shoe. One she was wearing Friday."

Jess sobbed against his chest.

"Shit," Chad and Nate said together.

The detective moved closer. Buster growled, and his hackles rose. Cramer stopped and backed up a step. The two winded deputies trudged to where they could see, and the deputies from the outbuilding trotted over. Everyone except Jess stared at the solitary shoe.

"How do you know?" Cramer pressed.

Sean counted to ten. The jerk really needed to work on his bedside manner. Of course, working in LA had a way of making a cop less than compassionate. And confronting Cramer wouldn't help anything. "Read the goddamn file. Molly had a pair like the ones Jess is wearing. The tread will match the pictures of the shoeprints I found that night."

A minute of heavy silence passed.

Detective Cramer cleared his throat. "Bag the shoe. Then secure this whole place. I'll get a team of CSI techs and the medical examiner out here ASAP," he said to the deputies, and then turned. "You folks should go inside."

"C'mon, babe. There's nothing you can do out here," Sean said soothingly.

She nodded and let him lead her across the patio and into the kitchen. Nate and Chad followed silently. Inside, he settled her in a chair at the table. She laid her head on her arms.

He found a bottle of chardonnay in the fridge, poured her a large glass, and set it in front of her. She raised her head and slowly pushed herself upright.

"You okay, baby girl?" Chad asked, his face a picture of sadness and concern.

After sipping the wine, she said, "Okay? I don't even know what the word means anymore."

Sean handed beers to the men who'd claimed two other chairs and then sat down next to Jess with his own. "We're all here for you, Jess. We'll do whatever you need us to."

"I want Hal...*dead*...for everything the bastard's done. I won't be able to live with myself if he gets away with all this." Her determined expression matched the intensity of her words.

"He'll pay," Sean stated firmly.

She turned disbelieving eyes on him. "You can't promise that. They may never even find him. And even if they do, I've read that it's really hard to extradite people from Mexico."

"We...we'll...deal with him," Nate growled.

She shook her head. "We don't have the resources."

"But my friend Jake Stone does," Sean interjected. "We'll find him." God, he hoped he was telling her the truth.

As he took a long drag of beer, he glanced around the table. Everyone looked beaten, emotionally exhausted. Understandably so. He wasn't related to Molly Freeman, hadn't seen her in eight years, but he felt the loss. Even though he'd seen a lot of death since joining the LAPD, the significance of a life ended too soon still affected him. In this case, not only because of his past connection with the victim but also because of his rekindling relationship with Jess.

He studied her. Oddly, she wasn't crying. Maybe she'd used up all her tears in the past few days. Instead of hysterical, she seemed crushed, pulverized by the disastrous events battering her family. Remarkable that she was even hanging on and continuing to function at all.

Sean sighed. Silence cloaked the people at the table like one of those lead-lined covers used in X-ray departments. The weight pressed on everyone's shoulders, but especially Jess's.

Time ticked by. Two additional vehicles arrived, but no one got up to confirm who it was. Drinks were forgotten. Everyone seemed dazed and lost in thought. Over an hour passed unnoticed.

Eventually, the back door opened, startling all of them. Four pairs of eyes stared at the deputy.

He cleared his throat. "Detective Burke, would you come with me, please?"

"I…I want to s-see—" Jess said, leveraging herself up.

Sean gently pushed her back onto the chair. He leaned over and cupped her cheek. "No, you don't. Believe me. Let me do this for you…for all of you."

Her dark chocolate eyes searched his. She released a long, weary sigh. "Okay."

Nate stood. "I should go."

Without looking up from the table, Chad shook his head. "Nah, son. She wouldn't want you to see her like this."

For a moment, Nate appeared ready to argue, but then his male protectiveness deflated, and he sat down leadenly. Sean gave them a brief nod before following the deputy outside.

A stench worse than manure now hung in the air. Not a breeze stirred, letting the late September heat radiate off the concrete patio. Buster lay in the shade next to the house, his head resting on his paws, his eyes soulful. Even the dog seemed to sense the gravity of the situation.

The walk to the manure pile felt like a funeral march. And in a way, it was.

When he reached the far side, everyone stood at a respectful distance from the large hole. He refrained from looking down, praying he wouldn't see what he knew he would.

Detective Cramer stepped forward and motioned toward the spot. "Is this Molly Freeman?"

Chapter 23

Sean closed his eyes for a moment before he turned and lowered his gaze. His stomach clenched because her nasty grave had done ugly things to what had been a pretty woman. But despite her unprotected burial, he could still recognize the face of Molly Freeman. Thank God Jess and her uncle and brother weren't seeing this.

He drew a shallow breath through his mouth. "Yeah, it's her." He gulped. "Cause of death?"

"We think blunt force trauma to the head. There's blood matted in her hair, but we won't know for sure until the medical examiner is done with her," Cramer said.

Sean squatted beside the hole and angled his head. "What's that? It's not the same color as her clothes." Leaning forward, he pointed. "See that speck of blue in the dirt beneath her?"

"Huh?" Cramer crouched next to him and peered closer. "Hard to see. Let's take a look."

The two men moved out of the way before a CSI tech stepped in and carefully rolled the body to the side so another could dig out what was underneath. He scooped the item onto the shovel and swiveled around so Sean and Cramer could inspect it.

Neither touched it, but both nodded.

It was a torn and bloodstained man's shirt.

Sean smiled grimly. *We gotcha, asshole.*

* * *

When Sean walked back into the kitchen, Jessie knew. He didn't have to say a word. The awful news was etched on his face.

"I'm so sorry," he said, kneeling beside her, taking her hands in his.

A sob escaped while curses spilled from her brother and uncle. How could she have expected a different outcome? For God's sake, Hal had confessed. And the shoe alone had confirmed her worst fears, but somehow her heart had clung to a thread of hope. Now even the thread had unraveled.

Her mother was dead. And her stepfather had killed her.

Letting tears run down her cheeks because stopping them was impossible, she managed to ask, "Can they tell…?"

"Yeah, did the asshole leave any evidence?" Uncle Chad finished her question.

"A bloody shirt. I'm sure they'll be able to forensically identify it as Hal's."

The tears came faster.

"How?" Nate asked.

"Head injury."

"D-did she suffer?" Jessie whispered.

Sean pressed his lips together and shook his head. "Probably not."

Whether it was the truth or he was simply sparing her the gory details, she latched on to the reassurance.

"Does this mean they won't search the darkroom?" Nate posed the question she couldn't articulate.

"They didn't show me a murder weapon, so they probably haven't found it. If it's not in there with…her, they'll keep searching."

"Shit," Uncle Chad muttered.

The finality of the gruesome discovery seemed to suck the life from the group. No more questions were asked. Jessie sniffled and sobbed softly, breaking the men's stoic silence. Grief surrounded her, almost suffocating her. She'd lost her mother forever. How was she going to tell Callie that her grandma was never coming back?

Twenty minutes later, the back door swung open, and a grim-faced Detective Cramer entered. No one greeted him.

"First, let me say I'm sorry for your loss. We appreciate your co-operation, but I still have some loose ends," he said.

No one invited him to sit down.

He cleared his throat. "I've upgraded Hal Freeman from person of interest to suspect. Our search, in coordination with other law en-forcement agencies, will intensify. That said, there are missing pieces to the puzzle."

Jessie struggled to keep breathing. Sean squeezed her hands gen-tly.

"It appears Mrs. Freeman walked home after her car died. As I un-derstand from Ms. Hargrove's statement, she believes Mr. Freeman was home, babysitting her daughter, who normally takes an after-noon nap." The detective paused, probably for effect. "Opportunity. Further excavation has just uncovered a large metal floor lamp, most likely a photographer's light. There appears to be blood and hair on the heavy base." Another dramatic pause. "Means. What's missing is motive. Why would Mr. Freeman kill his wife?" Cramer scanned each face deliberately. "Any ideas?"

The kitchen clock ticked off the seconds loudly.

After a full minute of strained silence, Uncle Chad said, "I think the fucker got caught..." He let the unfinished idea hang.

"Caught doing what?" Cramer studied him. "Having an affair?"

Uncle Chad raised his eyebrows and shrugged. "It wouldn't have been the first time he'd got himself in a pickle."

"And Mrs. Freeman caught him in the act by coming home unexpectedly," the detective said.

"I can see that happening," Nate agreed.

Cramer narrowed his eyes at Chad and Nate and then Jessie and Sean. "So why isn't there blood in any of the bedrooms?"

* * *

"C'mon, Detective," Sean said, barely keeping his tone civil. Jess's trembling worried him that she was on the verge of losing it. "Obviously, Hal didn't kill her in the bedroom."

Jess went as stiff as a board next to him.

"If you have a theory, Detective Burke, I'd love to hear it," Cramer said.

Damn, he had to be careful. Lying to a cop in an investigation could get him fired or arrested, to say nothing of the ethical problem. Chad and Nate had just done a surprisingly good job of staying vague. But did it really matter what immoral activity Molly had interrupted? Hal had killed her because he'd been discovered. Being caught had been Hal's motivation.

Jess had made it perfectly clear that she didn't want the child pornography revealed. Justice would be served by having Hal punished for Molly's murder. That's what he would be on trial for, not for what he got caught doing. Did it really matter which path Cramer took to reach the correct conclusion? Did it hurt to encourage the theory he created?

"Okay, let's build on *your* theory, Detective Cramer. Assume Hal was in bed with another woman, and Molly walked in on them. Would he kill her in front of a witness? Don't think so. Maybe he talked his shocked wife into going outside, away from the house, near the barn or the garage. Maybe that's where he stored his photography lamp. No one could see him kill her there. Then he went back inside, told the woman to leave while she could, and shooed her out the front door, claiming his irate wife was waiting in the kitchen. After she was gone, he buried Molly."

Cramer stroked his chin. "The woman would've seen Mrs. Freeman's abandoned car."

"So what? She was in a panic because they got caught. If she even recognized the Buick, all she'd think was that's why she and Hal hadn't heard Molly come home."

"Why hasn't this mystery woman come forward? It's been all over the media that we're looking for Molly Freeman."

"Get real. She's scared," Sean said, warming to the theory.

"Of him?"

"Maybe. Or of being accused as an accomplice. Or he could've contacted her after he split, and they've joined up."

Cramer nodded slowly. "Makes some sense."

Sean shrugged. "It's *your* theory. Arrange it any way you like."

The detective straightened. "Ms. Hargrove, we're going to take the linens from all three beds to analyze for bodily fluids."

She didn't answer.

"Jess?"

She shook her head as if to clear it. "Take whatever you need."

"We also found blood on the tractor, but I don't think we'll have to impound it. The CSI techs—"

The door opened behind him.

"Detective," a deputy said. He glanced at the people around the kitchen table and then back at his boss. He lowered his voice. "They're ready to take…her away. You want to speak to them first?"

"Yeah. Be right there."

"Yes, sir." The deputy held out a set of keys. "We're done with these. Thanks."

Nate raised his hand, and the man tossed them to him. Jess's brother blew out a sigh of relief, which Sean figured reflected what everyone at the table felt.

"Mr. Freeman, Mr. Brown, we're going to be here a while longer, but you're free to go."

The detective and the deputy turned to leave.

"Any sign of Hal's truck?" Chad asked.

Cramer glanced over his shoulder. "Not yet. But we'll find it. And we'll find him."

* * *

"I should pick up Callie," Jessie said once they'd left. "Karla's had her for most of the day." Besides, having her daughter with her would ground her, give her a reason to keep going.

"Are you up to answering Callie's questions about what's going on outside?" Sean asked.

She swiveled her head slowly as she surveyed the kitchen. "I'm not bringing her back here. I'm not sure I can *ever* stay here again."

"You do what you have to, baby girl," Uncle Chad said, patting her shoulder. "Nate and I will hang around here to lock up after all of them guys leave."

"Thanks."

"You're too upset to drive," Sean said. "We'll take your car, and I'll get my truck later."

"Okay. I'll call Karla to let her know we're coming." She rummaged through her purse for her keys as they walked out the back door. Standing together in the shade by the house, she dialed her BFF's cell phone and listened to it ring until voice mail picked up. When Karla was working, she often couldn't take calls immediately. After leaving a brief message, Jessie scrolled down until she found the salon's phone number. "Hi. This is Jessie Hargrove. Would you please tell Karla that I'm coming to get Callie?"

"Hey, Jessie. Sorry, but Karla's not here. She took Callie out for lunch…uh…a few hours ago," the receptionist said.

"How long ago?"

"Almost three hours, I think. One of her customers waited and left. Her next appointment has already been waiting thirty-five minutes. I've tried Karla's cell but just get her voice mail."

"Me too." A prickle of unease raced down Jessie's spine. "Well, thanks. I'll call her apartment and give her a little nudge for her customer."

When she disconnected and started scrolling again, Sean leaned over. "Something wrong?"

"I don't think so. Callie probably just got Karla distracted over lunch, and she lost track of time." God, she hoped that was true.

Sean stilled and frowned. "Where'd they go to eat?"

"I don't know. Karla's apartment, maybe."

"Damn. She was supposed to stay in public places." His frown deepened. "C'mon. You can call on the way."

As they headed for the Camry, he made a quick detour to his truck, popping in the passenger side for just a moment and taking something from the glovebox. Seconds later, he jumped into her car, and they took off, the tires spraying gravel behind them.

"I have a bad feeling about this," he said, stomping harder on the gas. "Where does Karla live these days?"

After giving him directions, she dialed Karla's landline with trembling fingers. With each ring, the vise around her heart tightened. She disconnected and redialed.

When she started to call a third time, Sean reached over and clasped her hand. "Stop, Jess. We're almost there. Get Luke on the phone."

Her hands shook so badly she could barely punch the right buttons. "Luke, we—"

"Put him on speaker."

She did.

"Where are you, man?" Sean asked.

"At the station."

"You're on duty already?"

"No. After I got back from wasting my time searching for the dickhead in San Ysidro, I figured this was the best place to monitor things," Luke said.

"So you've heard?"

"Yeah. Sucks. So sorry, Jessie."

"Yeah, sucks big-time. But that's not why we're calling," Sean said. "What's up?"

"You know Karla was watching Callie today, but we can't find them. Meet us at her apartment ASAP."

"Shit. Drake?" Luke asked.

"Could be." Two minutes later, Sean spun the Camry into a parking space at Karla's apartment complex. "Where's her place?"

"Over there. It's 11B," Jessie said, pointing with one hand and unbuckling with the other. "Thank God she's here. That's her blue Honda Civic in the next row."

"Stay in the car. If you don't hear from me in ten minutes, call 911."

She shot out of the car. "No way. I'm coming with you."

His hands grasped her shoulders before she could close the car door. "I don't know what we're going to find. If Drake's in there, seeing you could make it worse."

"And if Callie's in there and doesn't see her mom, she's going to be even more scared. Callie's fear trumps Drake's reaction. We're wasting precious time arguing. I'm coming."

She wrenched out of his grasp and marched toward Building B. The primal protectiveness of a mother swelled inside. She didn't care how Drake reacted. She was getting her daughter back.

* * *

"Stay out of sight," Sean whispered when they reached the apartment.

Slinking below the two windows in the façade, he inspected them but couldn't see inside because the blinds were tightly closed. A silent turn of the doorknob yielded no results. While yanking his wallet from his back pocket, he inspected the lock and doorjamb for signs of tampering. "Pray the dead bolt isn't locked," he muttered as he slid a credit card between the door and frame. He turned the knob again, and the door opened. Glancing over his shoulder, he gave her an exasperated scowl. "Will you at least stay here?"

She shook her head. "My baby needs me."

"Stay back until I give the all clear, then," he hissed.

She huffed but took a step back.

Sean eased the door open a crack. Paused. Peered inside. Listened. Nothing.

Lifting the back of his shirt, he pulled his gun from the waistband of his jeans. He heard Jess gasp behind him. *Too bad. Better to have it and not need it than need it and not have it.*

Leading with his weapon, he pushed the door slightly to get his arms and head through. No sounds. No movement. No evidence of occupants.

Using his hip, he nudged the door so he could slip inside. He scanned the space twice before advancing into the room. Cocking his head, he listened. Nothing. Maybe he was overreacting. Maybe Karla and Callie had just fallen asleep after lunch. But would they both have slept through the ringing of the cell and landline? No. Besides, his gut told him something definitely wasn't right.

A hand touched his back. Damn, would the woman not listen? He sure as hell hadn't given the all clear.

Turning his head to the side, he placed his index finger to his lips. Jess nodded.

Soundlessly, he glided across the carpeted living room, through the dining area, to the kitchen doorway. Peeking around the corner, he scrutinized the empty room.

He placed each step carefully on the tile as he cut through the kitchen to the hallway. Jess's steps were as quiet as his. *Good girl.*

The two doors on the left side of the hallway stood ajar. He poked his head into the first and found the small bathroom vacant. As he stepped toward the second door, a barely audible scraping sound came from behind the closed door on the opposite side of the hall.

He tensed. His instincts ratcheted up to red alert. Without turning to look at her, he motioned Jess to go back to the living room. When he heard no movement, he glanced over his shoulder. She stood straight as a board, shaking her head. *Stubborn woman.*

He didn't have time to deal with her obstinacy now. The noise in what was probably the master bedroom had paused for a second and then restarted. Someone was in there.

He crossed the hallway in one silent stride. Back braced against the wall, gun in front of him, he inched along the wall to the door. Pausing a moment, he glanced into a small, unoccupied bedroom opposite him.

Whoever was here, however many there were, they were all in one place. Was one of them Drake? Was he armed? Best to plan for the worst-case scenario.

Sean held up his hand, palm out. "Stay," he mouthed emphatically.

After a moment, her shoulders slumped, and she nodded.

Thank God. Now to get in that room without anyone getting shot.

Holding the gun in his right hand, he slowly turned the knob with his left and let the door swing inward. No shots rang out.

But muffled groaning and grunting emanated from inside.

Gun raised, he swung away from the wall to stand squarely in the doorway.

Chapter 24

Jessie's heart almost stopped when Sean froze in the doorway. Her mind could only imagine the worst. *Callie, oh Callie.* Although it seemed he stood motionless for eons, only seconds actually passed before he surged into the room. Not waiting for his all-clear signal, she darted in behind him.

Her eyes widened, and her mouth gaped.

Sean was already helping Karla, but all Jessie could do was stare.

Duct tape bound her best friend as if she were a mummy. A cloth was threaded between her open lips and tied behind her head. Dried blood was caked below her nose, and the side of her face was swollen and bruised. Blood had matted in her hair from a cut near her temple. Tears spilled from her wild eyes.

Unable to move, unable to believe what she was seeing, all Jessie could do was ask in a strangled voice, "Where's Callie? Where's my baby?"

As soon as Sean removed the gag, Karla coughed and then

croaked, "D-Drake's g-got her. I…I f-fought—" She started choking as she gasped for air and tried to talk at the same time.

With his hands, Sean framed her face, held it steady, and placed his a few inches in front of hers. "Easy now, Karla, easy. Breathe. With me. In. Out. In. Out." He nodded encouragement. Still staring directly into her eyes, he pulled a Swiss Army knife from his pocket.

Overcoming her paralysis, Jessie dropped to her knees beside Karla and yanked at the tape securing her to the legs of the chair. Her mind spun out of control. *Callie. Oh, Callie. Is she okay? What's Drake doing?*

"Better to cut it," Sean said, squatting beside her. He sliced through the tape with the pocketknife. "Massage her legs."

Karla's entire body trembled as they worked to remove the tape. She yelped when they had to strip it from her skin. But finally she was free.

Sean lifted her from the chair and laid her on the bed. Jessie ran into the bathroom and returned with a cool, wet washcloth. Sitting next to her traumatized friend, she gently washed the blood from her face. Her heart hammered with the need to ask about Callie again, but Karla was in no condition to be questioned.

"I have t-to t-tell you," Karla stuttered after several minutes, but she was almost incoherent with her teeth chattering so violently.

"Okay, but keep breathing, Slow and easy," Sean said, standing beside the bed.

"D-Drake t-took C-Callie."

"Where?"

"I d-don't know. H-he said…" She tried to swallow.

"Get her some water," Jessie ordered.

Sean dashed into the bathroom and came back with a paper cup.

He handed it to Jessie. "I'll lift her. You help her drink." Together they managed to pour water into her parched mouth.

After a second cupful, she tried to talk again. "D-Drake said…Callie was his…and h-he was taking her…for good."

"To Chicago?" Jessie asked.

"I guess s-so."

"Karla! Karla!" Luke's voice rang through the apartment.

"In here," Sean called.

Karla's brother barged through the doorway and skidded to a halt. Shock and then rage swept across his face.

Her heart clenching at the anguish in his expression, Jessie moved out of the way so he could sit on the bed. Luke took Karla's hand in his and held it to his chest. His gaze roamed over her battered face, and he swallowed hard several times.

"Jesus, sis. I…I'm…" He gulped again. "Drake?"

"Yeah," she whispered. "And he's g-got C-Callie."

"Son of a bitch."

Guilt gripped Jessie by the throat. Her friend had been hurt because of her. The thought revved her heart into overdrive. Sean must've sensed her igniting panic and pulled her into his arms.

"We need to get an Amber Alert out," he said to Luke.

The deputy shook his head sharply as though clearing the shock from seeing his injured sister. "I need info first." He pulled a notepad and pencil from his pocket. "I remember Drake's not that tall."

"Five nine," Jessie supplied. "About a hundred ninety pounds. Blue eyes, darkish blond hair." *Hurry,* her brain screamed. *My baby's out there somewhere with that monster.*

Luke laid his hand on Karla's arm and softened his tone. "Can you tell me what he's wearing?"

She drew a shaky breath. "Jeans. B-black T-shirt. Blue baseball hat."

"Hat insignia?"

She hesitated and then shrugged.

He gave her a loving pat. Checked his notes. "Damn. I need a vehicle description, but he's driving a rental."

"White Nissan Altima. California license 7SAN671," Sean recited.

Three heads turned to look at him.

"What? It's a habit."

"Great." Luke switched back to Karla. "How long ago did he leave?"

She blinked. "Wh-what time is it?"

"A little after three."

Her eyebrows drew together. "We left the salon about noon to go eat at McDonald's. Then we swung by here just to grab the crayons and coloring books I keep for her. Callie and I were inside less than five minutes, but when I opened the door to leave, Drake pushed his way in—with a gun."

Jessie cringed at the fear Callie must've felt. How could her father do such a thing?

Luke massaged his sister's shoulder. "We'll get all the details later. Right now, I just need to know how much of a head start he has."

"I was trying to be back at the shop by one, so probably…two hours."

"Shit," Sean muttered.

"Oh God," Jessie gasped. "They could be on a plane to Chicago by now." Panic gripped her as reality took hold. "B-but he knows that's where we'll look for him. He's got lots of money, so he could take her someplace to hide. Anywhere."

"We'll find him." Sean and Luke exchanged a somber glance. "It just may take a while."

"I know what Callie looks like, but what's she wearing?" Luke asked.

"Oh God, I can't remember." Jessie pressed her fingers against her eyelids, trying to picture what clothes she'd put on her daughter that morning. "I was so upset about the searches…"

"Callie has on jeans and a p-pink shirt with a Minnie Mouse face," Karla said. "I highlighted her hair with temporary pink coloring and curled it."

"Great. She'll stand out." Luke turned to Jessie. "Get me a picture of both of them ASAP."

She nodded, still feeling shell-shocked.

He studied his notes for a moment. "I have all I need. I'll call this in and then take Karla to the doctor."

"You and Jess go to the station. I'll take care of your sister," Sean offered.

Jessie gulped. As much as she wanted to be in the midst of the search for Callie, she really couldn't do much to help at this point. Sean and Luke, as law enforcement officers, would be much more effective. She drew a fortifying breath. "You guys go to the station. I'll take care of Karla."

"No, Jessie. I know where you want to be," her friend said.

"I might want to be there, but I can't really do anything to help. I can help you."

"You sure, Jess?" Sean studied her with concern.

"Yes. She got hurt taking care of my daughter. It's the least I can do."

* * *

The two grim-faced men raced toward the Freeman property to pick up Sean's truck.

"How'd Drake find her?" Luke asked after calling in the Amber Alert info.

"Doesn't matter. I don't blame Karla," Sean said.

"The guy's smart. Gonna make it harder to catch him."

"Yeah. And two hours is a big head start. As Jess said, he could be on a plane already."

"All the airports and airlines in the area will be contacted. We'll get passenger manifests, if necessary. Do you think he's been planning this long enough to have fake IDs?"

Sean stared out the windshield, his detective brain already in high gear. "No. Drake thought he could intimidate Jess into giving him Callie. Kidnapping her is an act of desperation."

"Agreed."

"And I don't think he'd fly out of here or LA, but he could be halfway to Vegas to catch a flight by now."

"Yeah. I don't know if the Amber Alert will reach the Vegas airport."

Sean frowned in concentration. "I'm not sure he'd fly at all. Too many eyes. Too much security."

"So what, then? Drive?"

"Maybe. When we track down the rental car company, find out if they have a GPS locator on the car."

"Right." Luke paused. "Isn't Chicago a big railroad hub? We should alert Amtrak."

"Agreed. And it would be even easier to disappear in a maze of bus routes."

"I can't see rich-boy Drake Hargrove doing the Greyhound bus thing."

Sean tunneled his fingers through his hair. "He won't be thinking like a rich boy. He's a fugitive trying to lose himself among the masses. I also don't think bus depots have nearly as much security screening."

"Might be worth looking at after we eliminate the other modes of transportation. Do you think he's going to Chicago?" Luke asked.

"Not directly, but eventually. Jess told me that his family is politically influential there. He might stand a better chance against extradition or avoiding charges altogether. And of getting a change in the child custody terms on his home turf."

"Wonder if his parents know what he's doing."

"Good question. Of course, you told us his parents didn't even know he was in California. We should contact them again, though, in case they've been in touch with Drake since then," Sean suggested.

"This just sucks. Poor Jessie."

Luke pulled into the Freeman driveway, and Sean jumped out. Several vehicles from the sheriff's department were still parked on the property. Luke's black Ram truck sped away while Sean headed for his F-150. Before he could climb inside, Nate and Chad hurried out the back door.

"Did you drop Jessie and Callie at your place?" Nate called.

Sean resisted the urge to ignore him and get on the road. There was so much to do, and it needed to be done fast. But he drew a deep breath and faced the approaching men. They had a right to know what had happened. "Drake snatched Callie from Karla. We don't know where she is."

"Fuck," Nate spat. "Where's Jessie? Is she okay?"

"What do you think? Look, I've got to get to the station. Call Jess for the details. If you think of anything that might help, tell her."

Without answering any more of their rapid-fire questions, he sped off. His mind raced faster than his wheels.

He didn't know Drake Hargrove, but he knew people. As an LAPD detective, he had learned to read them pretty damn well, too. And he didn't like what he'd read in Hargrove's eyes and body language during their two encounters.

The man was a spoiled rich boy who expected to get his way. When thwarted, he fought mean and dirty. Otherwise, why bring a gun to have a conversation with your ex about child custody?

Jess hadn't explained why he agreed to her having full custody in the first place. Maybe he didn't really want his kid, but in hindsight, the jerk may have thought the concession made him look weak. Sean didn't know, nor care. Drake had signed the legal documents, and Jess was under no obligation to renegotiate the terms. But that wouldn't sit well with a man like Drake. He wouldn't take the time to show how much he missed Callie or to make a reasonable case to change Jess's mind. No, this kind of asshole just took what he wanted. People, rules, laws be damned.

And that's what worried Sean the most. Men like Drake Hargrove didn't compromise or negotiate. They sure as hell didn't surrender.

They went down in a blaze of imaginary glory.

Chapter 25

Jessie sat in a chair beside Karla's bed in an exam room of the Ramona urgent care clinic. Earlier she'd described the latest unbelievable events to Nate and Uncle Chad on the phone. Sadly, it seemed her life had been filled with such events for the past five days. At the moment, mercifully, she felt numb, as if she'd been drained of all feelings. Maybe numbness was a self-preservation tactic that her body had employed instinctively. She didn't know, but she was grateful for the reprieve from the soul-crushing, heartbreaking emotions racking her.

Numbness didn't mean she wasn't worried about Callie, though. She was. Desperately so. But there wasn't anything she could do right now to find her daughter. Sean had already checked in with an update on everything being done by law enforcement. The news had been welcome, although the reason for the high level of activity and urgency wasn't reassuring at all. Drake bringing a gun to her parents' house—not once, but twice—had raised the stakes in the mind of the law. They recognized the extraordinary risk Jessie's ex-husband posed.

When Detective Harlan, the man leading the child abduction investigation, had questioned her on the phone, he'd emphasized that this was a child custody battle gone terribly wrong. This wasn't some random kidnapping by a pedophile or psychopath. It wasn't random at all. Drake Hargrove had a specific, vested interest in the abductee.

In addition, they knew a lot about Drake: exactly where he and his parents lived, what company he worked for, what bank accounts he had, and what credit cards he used. He didn't fit the profile of a disgruntled parent who would simply disappear with the child. Most likely, Drake was racing toward the safety of home base. Once there, he would put up a helluva custody fight. Was he currently so irrational that he didn't even realize that he'd significantly hurt his own cause by forcibly kidnapping his daughter? Such irrationality was dangerous.

In their conversation, the detective had kept coming back to the issues of Drake carrying a gun and assaulting Karla. Both represented a violence factor uncommon in parental abductions, which usually involved stealth and lying more than anything else.

But the detective had tried to reassure Jessie that the worst-case scenario meant her flying to Chicago to retrieve her daughter and him preparing a mountain of paperwork to get Drake extradited to San Diego to face kidnapping and assault charges. Jessie's numb state made accepting that scenario easier.

"You look like I feel or vice versa," Karla's quiet voice broke into Jessie's thoughts. "I don't know how you're surviving all this."

"I have to. For Callie."

"Still, I admire your strength, Jessie."

"You know the saying: What doesn't kill you makes you stronger. Well, by the end of all this, I should be as strong as a bull."

"I think you already are."

Jessie shrugged. "Thanks. Are you sure you don't want any pain meds? The local anesthetic for those stitches is going to wear off soon."

"I better not. When Luke called, he said a deputy would be coming over shortly to take my statement. I want to be clearheaded for that. If I can give them any info to help nail Drake's ass, I don't want to screw up because my brain's foggy."

"Makes sense." She paused. "What doesn't make sense is how Drake found you. I can't figure it out. Yeah, he could remember your name from back in the day, but you have an unlisted landline. How did he find your apartment?"

Karla huffed. "Oh, he was so proud of himself for his little bit of detective work that he had to brag. Get this: He found me through Facebook."

"What? He's a friend?"

"God no. We weren't friends even while you were married. But he has a Facebook account, and he searched for my name."

"Surely you don't have your address open to public view."

Karla rolled her eyes. "I may be blond, but not *that* blond. He saw my cover photo and profile picture."

"So he recognized you in your profile picture. But your cover photo is what?"

"The front of the salon."

"Oh crap." Jessie blew out an exasperated breath.

"With the name of the salon and knowing it had to be in or near Ramona, he easily found the address and phone number on our website. He said he called to confirm I was working but then hung up."

"Why would he be looking for you in the first place? He couldn't have known you were watching Callie."

"After seeing the sheriff's deputies at your place, he went to the coffee shop."

"Of course. News travels fast in a small town. And everyone's been so involved and helpful."

"Yup. Heard all the talk about your mom, Hal, and especially the searches. He knew you wouldn't want Callie around. He remembered my name, decided I'd be the most likely babysitter, and figured out where I worked."

"Let me guess. He followed you to McDonald's and then home."

"Bingo. Give the lady a prize."

They lapsed into silence. Jessie wished they could talk about something else to keep the pain, the fear for Callie from returning.

Karla must've been thinking the same thing, for she asked abruptly, "What's happening with you and Sean now that you know he didn't break up with you?"

Jessie sighed. This topic might make her feel worse instead of better. "What do you mean?"

"C'mon, girlfriend. You admitted you've been spending nights with him at his brother's apartment. Something's gotta be cooking. You two always had explosive chemistry."

Heat rose in Jessie's cheeks. Yeah, the sex was still really hot, but orgasms were fleeting. Just like Sean's time in Ramona.

"I'm glad we learned what really happened back then. Apparently, it's bothered Sean as much as me."

"What about the future?"

She cringed inwardly. This was the part that would make her feel worse. "We don't have one. Not together, at least."

"What the hell? I don't think you ever got over him. Why not give it another try?"

"Because…" Oh God, there were a million reasons why not to get involved again. Having sex with Sean was stupid enough but getting emotionally entangled would just be inviting trouble and heartache. And she had more than enough of both right now. "Because…too much has changed in eight years. I have a daughter, and he doesn't have a clue about kids."

"He could learn."

"How many single guys want to take on the responsibility of some other guy's kid? Dealing with their own is traumatic enough."

"I bet Sean would."

She sighed again. "Besides, his life is in LA. Unlike me and Chicago, it seems to be a good fit."

"Luke says Sean doesn't like LA all that much," Karla said.

"Well, even if he doesn't like the city, that's where the LAPD is, and that's his dream job."

"Dreams change. Haven't yours?"

Jessie rested her head back against the cushion and closed her eyes. Yes, hers had changed drastically over time. Gone were her dreams of growing old with Sean, of a happy family living in a small town, and of running her own child care facility. "I've given up on my dreams, Karla."

"Why?"

Her eyes popped open, and she glared at her friend. "Have you looked at my life lately? Forget about dreams. I'd be happy just to have normal back."

"Have you and Sean talked about the future?"

"No," she said emphatically. "There's no point in getting my hopes up."

Karla cocked her head. "So you have hopes, just not dreams?"

Tears stung her eyes, but it seemed silly to cry over something as insignificant as lost love when her mom was dead and her daughter kidnapped. She raised her chin. "Look, Karla, there's no going home again, ya know. We can't turn back time. Sean and I are two totally different people than when we were in love. There's no second chance. Not for us."

"Jessie—"

"Stop. Please."

When the doctor stepped into the exam room, Jessie silently thanked him for rescuing her. She really didn't want to continue this conversation with Karla. Sean was her past, not her future.

"How's my patient feeling?"

"Sore, but okay," Karla said.

The doctor glanced at the two pain pills in the tiny paper cup. "Don't need these?"

"What I need is a clear head to give the deputy my statement about the assault."

He picked up the cup and folded it around the pills. "Put these in your pocket for later. Those stitches are going to hurt like hell when the local wears off. If you need more, just call, and we'll send a prescription to the pharmacy."

"Thanks. Can I leave now?" Karla asked.

"Sure. Just take it easy for a couple days. And call if you have any problems. The nurse will give you the post-treatment instructions on your way out."

As the doctor shook her hand, a voice called from the other side of the door, "Ms. Johnson, it's Deputy Anderson. May I come in?"

When he left, the doctor held the curtain aside so the deputy could enter. Anderson shook hands with both women and then pulled out his notebook and pencil.

"Uh, Deputy Anderson, Karla was just cleared to leave. She's been here almost three hours already. Would you be able to take her statement at her apartment?" Jessie asked.

Karla gave her a huge smile of gratitude.

"No problem," he said, looking from one to the other. "I'm sure you'd like to get over to the station, Ms. Hargrove. Why don't I drive Ms. Johnson home?"

"What a great idea," Karla said. "I know you've been dying to see if they've made any progress, Jessie. You get going. I'll be fine."

* * *

Sean glared at the map on the computer screen as if his intensity could make the image reveal the desired information. *Where is the son of a bitch?* He glanced at his watch. *Jesus.* Time was flying, and neither the Amber Alert nor their efforts had produced a single solid lead.

No sign of Drake and Callie anywhere.

They'd sent law enforcement officers to all the airports from the Mexican border to LA. Same with the train stations. The airlines and Amtrak had no passengers listed as Drake and Callie Hargrove. Even the bus depots were on the lookout. And with the feds' cooperation, deputies were monitoring the border crossings.

Their only brief lead had been through Drake's rental car, which they'd tracked to an agency at the San Diego airport. But the car had been turned in hours earlier. The man and little girl had ridden the shuttle to the airport terminal but then disappeared. All the terminals had been thoroughly searched, and the airport personnel put on alert. Drake and Callie didn't show up on any of the video footage, suggesting they'd left the premises immediately without ever entering the buildings.

Had they taken a cab? A bus? A hotel shuttle? To where and why? All options were being investigated, but still no sign of the pair. However Drake planned to get to Chicago, he was doing a damn fine job of staying under the radar.

After getting Karla to urgent care, Jess had popped home just long enough to find pictures of her ex and daughter. Copies of those photos had now been shown to hundreds of people with no results.

Sean shoved his fingers through his hair. He was beyond frustrated.

A couple hours ago, he'd called Jake Stone and described the situation. His friend had immediately offered to help. But even his unconventional resources hadn't uncovered their location.

Luke set a fresh cup of black coffee in front of him. "You're going to bore holes in my monitor staring at it like that."

"I don't give a fuck," he growled. Then he shook his head. "Sorry, man."

"I'm right there with you on the frustration scale, buddy."

"Sean. Luke."

They both turned. Jess stood in the doorway, her shoulders slumped, her face drawn, her eyes sunken and ringed with dark shadows. Sean bolted out of the chair, reached her in three long strides, and pulled her into his arms.

"Christ, Jess. You look…" He bit off the rest of his comment. How she looked wasn't really the issue. What it indicated about her mental and physical state was the real point. And her appearance said—loud and clear—that she was teetering on the edge. Beaten beyond belief. Devastated beyond despair.

He tightened his embrace. "Let me take you…wherever you want. Nate and Chad can stay with you."

"No," she mumbled into his chest. "I need to be here. Have you found anything?"

"Just the rental car, like I told you earlier." He ushered her across the office and gently pushed her down into a chair next to the desk.

"Coffee, Jessie?" Luke asked.

"Please."

Sean dropped into the desk chair and scooted in front of her. "Babe, you really should go home or someplace and rest. How about Chad's house?"

"I can't. My baby's out there, somewhere, with…with…" She covered her face with a trembling hand. "Drake wouldn't hurt Callie, would he? No matter how mad he is at me for divorcing him, he wouldn't hurt his own daughter, right?"

Sean didn't want to lie to her, but the truth would definitely freak her out. Since becoming a cop, he'd seen people do plenty of unbelievable things. His faith in mankind had declined precipitously as case after case presented new ways for inhumanity to rear its ugly head. "He's just trying to get Callie to Chicago."

At least that part was probably true. What Drake was capable of doing to achieve that goal, only time would tell.

"If you insist on staying, I'm gonna put you to work. You know Drake better than any of us. How would he get to Chicago?"

"Fly. He's too impatient for any other way."

"Unless he's sprouted wings, we've nailed down all the flying possibilities in Southern California. And all the train possibilities. And the buses."

She snorted. "Buses. No way. The only time I ever knew of Drake lowering himself to ride a bus was when we went to Las Vegas on one of those What Happens in Vegas tour buses with some San Diego State friends before we were married. He swore he'd never do it again."

Chapter 26

Sean watched four additional unmarked vehicles park along the street near the What Happens in Vegas bus station. Eight more deputies spilled from the cars, bringing the total to twelve. Guns drawn and hunched over, they ran toward the outdoor courtyard where Drake Hargrove sat on a concrete bench, talking to his daughter. Sean fought the natural instinct to draw the Glock from his waistband. He wasn't an official participant in this operation, so he'd been relegated to shadowing the group approaching from behind the perp. He exchanged a nod with Luke, who was heading in with the other deputies from the left.

Luckily, most of the customers taking the late bus to Las Vegas had chosen to wait inside. Only three smokers lingered next to one of the trees scattered throughout the large patio. The deputies surrounded the area, taking cover behind benches, trash cans, newspaper dispensers, trees, or anything else offering a hiding place.

Drake remained focused on showing Callie something on his phone. The little girl stood rigidly between his spread legs, barely moving and not talking. Not a peep. Knowing she was a chatterbox, Sean's heart squeezed with the understanding that the poor kid was too scared to speak. And rightfully so.

When all the players were in place, a deputy wearing a bullet-proof vest stepped into the open, several yards in front of the suspect.

"Drake Hargrove! Sheriff's department!"

Drake's head snapped up. Callie jumped and spun around.

"Hands out where we can see them! Face down on the ground!"

The three bystanders were quickly shooed away by other deputies.

Drake yanked Callie closer to him and pulled his gun from under his shirt. He shoved the muzzle against her temple. "Stay back or I'll shoot."

"Daddy, that hurts," Callie whined.

"Shut up, kid."

The deputy held out his hands, palms forward. "Relax, Mr. Hargrove. No one needs to get hurt. I'm Detective Harlan. Let's talk this through…together."

Not saying a word, Drake glared back.

"Let Callie go. You're her daddy. I'm sure you don't want her to get hurt. Just send her over to me."

"Are you fucking kidding me? She's my ticket out of here," Drake said.

Jess's ex surveyed the area. Everywhere, guns were pointed at him. Hopefully, an unnerving sight.

Sean held his breath. The guy had to realize there was no way out. Alive, at least. But Sean didn't give a damn what happened to Drake. Saving Callie was the only thing that mattered. Overwhelming protectiveness swelled inside him.

Hostage situations sucked. Law enforcement faced a high probability of the vic being injured…or killed. Sometimes it depended on logistics, sometimes on the perp's state of mind. Drake didn't seem crazy, but he was sure eaten up by something. Hate? Revenge? Would the asshole really shoot his own daughter rather than surrender?

Sean had an opinion, but he didn't *know* the answer. He doubted anyone did. Even Jess.

"What can we do for you to fix this situation?" Detective Harlan asked.

"Tell my bitch of an ex to let me have my daughter."

"Well, from where I stand, I think it would be hard to convince Ms. Hargrove to allow that. Put the gun down, and let's see if we can come up with some ideas."

"Do you think I'm stupid? My only leverage is this gun and this kid."

A few deputies on the left shifted position. Drake jumped up and whipped around. He pointed the gun in their direction. Everyone froze.

Sean took advantage of all attention being focused on the opposite side of the area and circled out from behind to a position more even with Drake and Callie on the right.

"Stay back. I'm warning you," he yelled at the deputies who had moved.

"Mr. Hargrove, calm down. We don't want anyone to get hurt. Put the gun down so nothing happens…accidentally."

Drake swung back around toward the detective. His gaze darted from person to person, gun to gun. Sean could see his eyes taking on a wild look like a cornered animal. *Not good.*

Gripping her shoulder, he pulled Callie against him, her face pushed directly into his thigh. He put the gun to her temple again. She flinched and turned her head to the side. Sean leaned forward. The movement caught her attention. She stared at him with deer-in-the-headlights eyes, face ashen, body trembling.

Sean nodded, smiled reassuringly. But she didn't react. A wink also failed to get a response. Poor kid was probably going into shock.

A female deputy on the opposite side called, "Ready, Detective."

"What's ready?" Drake shouted.

Callie jerked around to face forward instead of toward Sean.

"We have someone who wants to talk to you," Harlan said. "Step forward, Deputy Klein. She's unarmed, Mr. Hargrove."

A very nervous deputy held up an iPhone facing Drake while she inched several feet closer. Sean couldn't clearly see the face on the screen, but he knew it wasn't Jess.

"What in heaven's name are you doing, son?" a woman's voice called from the phone.

Drake jerked back. "Mother?"

So they'd managed to get his parents in Chicago on a video call. *Good idea.*

"Drake, oh my God, put that gun down before someone gets hurt."

Deputy Klein moved forward. Sean hoped Harlan had lied about her being unarmed.

He reined in the urge to leap or shoot or take some action. Maybe the mom/son strategy would work. He wasn't very hopeful, but he had to at least give it a chance to play out.

"I can't, Mother."

A man's face joined the woman's on the screen. "Listen to me,

Drake. I've got a call in to the best criminal defense lawyer in Chicago. Give yourself up, and we'll fix this. Together."

"No way, Father," he sneered. "If I do, that bitch will get Callie. One hundred percent. I can't let that happen."

Sean's muscles tensed like guitar strings. This tactic wasn't going to work. Drake was too far down Revenge Road.

Somewhere nearby, a car door slammed. Drake whipped his head around. Callie squealed. The entire scene seemed to freeze. Sean's gaze was riveted on the gun pressed against the little girl's head. As her father turned back, he adjusted his grip on the weapon. His finger slipped around the trigger.

Fuck. Time's up. Mommy and Daddy aren't going to solve this. Sean's eyes shifted to Luke. Their gazes locked. Sean gave a slight nod. Luke responded in kind.

"Drake! Drake! What's happening?" his mother yelled from the phone.

"Turn that damn thing off," Drake hollered. He shifted to block his parents' view of Callie and glared at the cordon of law enforcement surrounding him.

"Goddamn it, son, listen to me," his father said. "I—"

Drake spun around. "Shut the fuck up. This isn't about you. I…" He pulled the pistol away from Callie's head and aimed it toward the deputy with the iPhone.

In that split second, Sean took off. With long, running strides, he launched himself across the concrete. As he flew in front of Drake, one arm wrapped around Callie and pulled her beneath him. He broke their fall with his other arm and his knees. Even so, he heard her breath rush out of her lungs when they landed hard a couple feet away.

"Fuck," Drake shouted.

A shot rang out. White-hot pain engulfed Sean's left arm, yet he managed to wrap himself in a ball around Callie.

Time blurred.

Gunshots exploded from multiple directions. A woman's scream came from the phone. Something clattered on the concrete. Drake gave a garbled cry and landed with a loud thud.

Then silence.

Sean gasped for air and waited for the next phase. Seconds later, the singed air filled with shouted orders and running footsteps.

The tiny body beneath him shook violently.

"I've got you, Callie. You're safe now."

Sobs racked her small frame even harder. He hugged her tighter and kissed the back of her head.

"M-M-Mommy," she whispered.

"Hang on, munchkin. You'll be able to see her in a minute."

"Callie?" Dropping to the ground beside him, Luke choked out the name in a panicky voice.

"She's okay," Sean said.

Luke's gaze flicked heavenward for a second. "You're hit, buddy. EMT's coming."

"Just a scratch." But thank God the bullet had struck him and not Callie. Sean jerked his head back toward where he knew Drake's body lay. "Be sure *it's* covered. I don't want her to see."

"On it." Luke scurried away to take care of the request.

A paramedic appeared in his place. "Detective Burke, I'm Scott Talley. Is...?" His gaze dropped to Callie and bounced back up.

"She's good...uh...not good, but uninjured," Sean answered the unspoken question in the man's eyes. "Just waiting for them to cover…it."

The EMT checked out the scene behind them and nodded. "Done."

Sean turned his head to confirm it. A tarp now covered the bullet-riddled body of Callie's father. He released a long sigh of relief and leveraged himself off the little girl.

"Hey, munchkin, we can get up now."

Even though he righted himself to sit beside her, she remained in a tight ball with her eyes scrunched shut. Gently, he grasped her trembling body and lifted her onto his lap. Eyes still closed, she burrowed in as close as possible to his chest.

The paramedic's eyes examined the little girl for any sign of injury. "You're right. She looks fine. Physically, at least. But I better take a look at your 'scratch.' It's bleeding pretty bad."

"Callie, Callie!"

Sean recognized Jess's voice screaming above the din. He scanned the crowd until he spotted her on the perimeter of the crime scene being restrained by a uniformed deputy.

"Ms. Hargrove, you can't go over there," the man yelled.

"The hell I can't. That's my baby." Jess shoved the man in the chest. "Get your fucking hands off me or I swear my knee will guarantee you never father children."

The shock on the deputy's face was comical even from a distance.

"Jesus Christ. Let the woman go to her kid," called another deputy.

The guy jerked his hands off Jess instantly. He looked relieved to still have his manhood intact.

After giving him a ball-shriveling glare, Jess flew across the distance and landed on her knees beside Sean. "Callie, baby, Mommy's here."

"M-Mommy?" the little girl breathed against Sean's chest as if disbelieving of everyone and everything around her.

Jess rubbed her back. "Come to Mommy, baby. You're safe. Everything's…okay." Her eyes lifted to Sean's, telling him everything was far from okay. She desperately needed to hold her daughter to convince herself that she was safe.

"Callie, your mommy needs a hug," Sean coaxed.

She raised her head and looked up at him, fear and shock and confusion mirrored in her huge brown eyes. Then she turned and saw Jess. "Mommy!"

Sobs burst from mother and daughter. Callie sprang off Sean's lap and into Jess's. The jolt was like shards of glass impaling his injured arm, but watching Jess smother the little girl with kisses and encircle her with a cocooning embrace eased the pain.

A second EMT hurried up to the huddled group. "Ms. Hargrove, I need to do a quick exam and then get Callie to the hospital."

"Right. Of course," Jess mumbled.

The EMT wrapped his arm around her shoulders to steady her as she stood up with the crying four-year-old. Jess leaned into the paramedic for support as they walked away.

"Mommy, stop. Stop!"

Callie pushed and squirmed until she forced Jess to let her slip to the ground. The moment her feet landed, she raced back to where Sean still sat on the concrete. She threw her arms around his neck and gave him a loud smooch on the lips.

"Thank you, Mr. Sean. You's my hero." Then she whipped around and ran back to her mother.

Jess lifted the little one into her arms again. She angled her face past the flurry of pink-highlighted blond curls to meet Sean's gaze. A poignant moment froze time and blocked out the horrible scene around them. But then Jess blinked. Once. Twice. Her chest rose with a deep, shuddering breath. Offering a faint smile, she called, "Thank you."

Sean watched Jess walk away. Although he was sure he'd *heard* what she said, it *felt* an awful lot like good-bye.

* * *

After a few hours in the ER getting patched up, Sean made his way to the front desk. He wasn't yet sure how he was getting back to Ramona since his truck was probably still parked at the crime scene. But a ride wasn't his main focus.

"Hi, I'm Sean Burke. I came in by ambulance about the same time Callie Hargrove was brought in. Can you tell me her status?" he said to the lady behind the desk.

"Are you a relative?"

"Uh, no, but I'm a very close friend."

She shook her head. "Sorry, privacy laws strictly prohibit the hospital from releasing patient information to the public without permission."

Sean knew that, but he didn't give up. "The little girl and I were involved in the same...shooting incident. I just want to be sure she's all right."

The woman stiffened, not appreciating his persistence. "Very noble, but still not okay."

"Can you at least tell me if Callie was admitted or if Jessica Hargrove is still here?"

A head shake was her only answer.

Anger flared. It'd been a really shitty day. And damn, even though he'd probably saved Callie's life, this gatekeeper wouldn't tell him anything. How fucked up was that? He considered flashing his LAPD identification and claiming to be a detective investigating the shooting, but he was already in enough trouble with his department, so he dropped the idea. "Look, lady, I just—"

"Sean, over here."

He turned to find Chad Brown sitting in one of the uncomfortable plastic chairs in the ER waiting area. Jess's uncle motioned him over. As he approached, the older man's distraught appearance raised a red flag. Had Callie been injured without his knowing? That overwhelming protectiveness surfaced again. Concern escalating, he grasped Chad's arm. "Is Callie okay? Where are they?"

Chad stood and placed his hand on Sean's uninjured shoulder. "Relax, son. They're fine. Well, maybe not fine, but they're not physically hurt. The ER doctor admitted Callie, and Jessie is stayin' in the room with her. Tomorrow she'll be transferred to Children's Hospital in San Diego. This doctor recommended a kid's shrink do an observation and evaluation. Jessie agreed to it. I just hope she'll get help for herself, too. If not tomorrow, then soon."

"I want to see them," Sean said, his heart in his throat.

Chad nodded. "I understand, but they were fallin' asleep when I left their room about thirty minutes ago. The doc gave them both a sedative."

"Are you waiting here until they wake up?"

"Nope. I'm waitin' for you."

"Me? Why?"

"You need a ride, and we need to talk."

Chapter 27

Jessie lay on the separate pullout bed the nurses had made up for her. Because her eyes refused to close, her worried gaze roamed the dark hospital room as if on guard for dangers hiding in the shadows. The hospital was filled with muted noises, and she jumped at every sound. Shuddering frequently, she fought off the trauma of the day's events.

When Callie moaned in her sleep again, Jessie knew what she needed to do. She slid out of the guest bed and climbed into the hospital bed with her daughter. Since Callie didn't have an IV or any other medical apparatus attached, Jessie didn't think she could do any harm.

Pulling the warm little body into her arms, she realized that holding Callie was the only way for her to believe she was safe. She snuggled closer and kissed her child's forehead several times. Still asleep, Callie gripped her mother's shirt, evidence that nearness was important to her also.

Jessie shut her eyes and tried to shut down her mind. *Not hap-*

pening. Mental videos insisted on playing in her brain. There were several, beginning with finding her mother's abandoned Buick and ending with watching Drake collapse onto the concrete. She sorted through the images until she found one that didn't make her want to scream or cry: Sean making love to her.

The memory flooded over her. Heat spread through her body, burning in strategic spots. Contentment covered her like a chenille blanket fresh from the dryer.

Their mutual desire and need had been explosive, but instead of rushing to reach orgasm, Sean had given as much pleasure as possible. His tenderness and thoroughness touched her to the core. He made her feel special; she felt...loved. No other man had ever made her feel that way.

She sighed heavily. *Damn, I can't let it happen again. It will only make it harder when I have to let him go.* Sean would be returning to LA soon. He would go back to his normal life, and she would try to build a new one. Without him. Again. But this time, she wouldn't make stupid choices like marrying Drake Hargrove. No, she'd focus on giving Callie the best life possible. *How* was still a big question mark. But she'd figure it out.

Already she knew there wouldn't be time for men, for dating, for love. She didn't need the complications when her life was a million-piece puzzle needing to be put back together. Relationships would have to wait. And she was okay with that.

"Mommy?" Callie mumbled.

"Yes, munchkin."

"Is Mr. Sean okay?"

She blinked. Of all the questions her daughter could've asked, why this one? She gulped. "Sure, sweetie."

Lifting her head, Callie glanced around the dark room. "Where is he?"

"Uh, I don't know. Why?"

The little girl shrugged. "I thought he'd be here."

"Well, he might still be in the hospital."

"No, I means *here*. With us."

"Well...uh...why?"

Callie pondered a moment. "'Cause he...likes us."

Jessie blinked again. "You think so?"

"Yeah."

"How do you know?"

"Easy-peasy, Mommy. He treats us nice. Not...not like Daddy." She shuddered in Jessie's arms.

"It's okay, baby. Daddy's not going to hurt us anymore."

"'Cause Mr. Sean's gonna 'tect us?"

"No. Because...Daddy's gone. And Mr. Sean has to go back to LA where he lives."

Callie sniffed. "But I likes Mr. Sean now. I don't wants him to leave."

Fighting tears, Jessie hugged her daughter tighter. "I understand, munchkin. Believe me, I do."

As Callie drifted off to sleep again, she pondered the child's comment *"he...likes us."* Specifically, the word *us* gave her pause. Of course, Jessie knew how Sean felt about her; he'd admitted his love the other night when she'd pretended to be asleep. But she'd never given much thought to how he felt about Callie. Instead, she lumped him in with most single guys, who didn't give a damn about kids, simply because of his awkwardness and uncertainty in dealing with the munchkin.

But Sean had saved Callie's life. Jessie had watched him from inside the patrol car where the deputies had forced her to stay during the operation. He'd thrown himself over Callie and used his body as a shield. His actions were *not* part of the plan. Detective Harlan had wanted him to stay in the car with her, but Sean had told him where he could shove that idea. As a compromise, he was instructed to observe only, not to get involved. Thank God he'd disobeyed.

Tears stung Jessie's eyes. Sean had risked his own life to protect Callie. Exactly what a good parent would've done.

* * *

"Where are we going?" Sean asked when Chad pulled into a dark, littered alley instead of heading to the What Happens in Vegas bus station where Sean's truck had been parked since the shooting. He frowned as the older man drove to the dead end and killed the engine. *What the hell is going on?*

Tensing at the odd situation, he wished Luke hadn't offered to take his gun before the ambulance hauled him off to the hospital. He felt naked without it, and now he didn't have a weapon. But he figured Chad had a gun stashed somewhere in his truck, especially since his rifle was missing from the rack behind the seats. With his left arm bandaged and in a sling, Sean was definitely at a disadvantage, but he could still take the old man—if it came to that, which he hoped it didn't. It would just hurt like hell. And be such a shitty way to end a super shitty day.

"What the fuck are we doing here?" he asked.

Chad sighed before he turned to Sean. "Like I said, we need to talk."

"About what?" Sean gave him a steely glare.

Jess's uncle chuckled. "Damn, you haven't changed a bit. Don't get your hackles up, son."

"Then explain why we're here. This alley wasn't a scheduled stop on the way to get my truck."

"I figure the crime scene might still have cops crawlin' all over, so it's better we talk here, where it's... private."

His eyes narrowed. *Private, secret, or hidden?* "Why's that?"

"So no one can hear, and we won't be interrupted."

"And that would be a problem because...?" He let the words dangle.

Chad pushed a hand through his mop of graying hair. "'Cause I'm gonna tell you what *really* happened to Hal."

Sean eyed him warily. "What the hell are you talking about?"

"Damn, I wish I had a stiff drink right about now. This ain't gonna be easy."

Whatever Chad Brown had to say was weighing heavy. Even in the dark, Sean could see his defeated expression, his slumped shoulders, his exhausted demeanor. Sean's anxiety eased; curiosity and concern replaced it.

"Hey, man, just spit it out. Did you see where Hal went in San Ysidro? Did some drug goons grab him? I know it's a dangerous part of town, so anything's possible."

Chad shook his head. "It's not that simple. I wish I didn't have to tell you, but I do because you got a choice to make. So listen up good."

Sean waited while the guy scrubbed a calloused hand across his face and released another long sigh.

Sounding like each word was painful, Chad began. "Jessie already told ya the part about us findin' the asshole takin' dirty pictures of Callie in the bomb shelter."

"I can't even imagine what that did to Jess."

"It was horrible. I'll never get it out of my head. She won't either."

"I'd string him up by his balls for that even if he hadn't killed Molly."

"Just listen, would ya?" Chad huffed. "After fightin' us, Hal confessed to killin' Molly. Jessie was so upset, she just grabbed Callie, who was asleep, and left. We told her not to call the cops until we got Hal into the house. I know it sounds stupid, but lookin' back, I think Nate and me wanted more time to inflict our own punishment." He paused, stared straight ahead, and seemed to go back in time. "The metal stairs in the shelter are really steep and only wide enough for one person. Nate went up first, Hal right behind him. I stayed down below so I could keep my gun trained on the bastard. Almost to the top, Hal grabbed the back of Nate's shirt and tried to throw him down the stairs. He probably planned to scramble out and get away while I helped my nephew. But as Nate fell, he took Hal's legs out from under him. The asshole practically dove headfirst to the concrete floor with Nate landin' on top of him."

Silence filled the truck.

Sean's chest tightened with dread. "Hal broke his neck?"

"Don't rightly know. It was twisted funny, but his head also had a big dent like his skull was smashed in. There wasn't a whole lot of blood, so I reckon that means he died real fast."

"Shit." A lead weight settled in his stomach. All sorts of potential criminal charges crossed his mind. "Then what?"

"Nate freaked out. He said we'd be charged with murder. Especially him, since you and Luke were already suspicious of him in connection with Molly. And only the three of us had heard Hal's confession. We had no proof." He slammed his hand against the steering wheel. "Me? I wasn't so much afraid of a murder rap as I was Jessie and Callie havin' to face the public learnin' about the nasty picture stuff. Anyway, we decided to pretend Hal escaped."

"So Jess knows?"

Chad's head jerked around. "Hell no. She thinks the bastard got away. That's part of the problem."

A ripple of relief rolled over him. At least Jess hadn't been involved in Hal's death or the cover-up. "Where's…the body?"

Chad exhaled frustration. "Still in the bomb shelter. I 'bout shit my pants when they were searchin' the property."

"Why are you telling me this?"

"We gotta decide what to do with him…permanently."

"You do remember I'm a cop, right?"

"Yeah, but everyone knows you're also still in love with Jessie. And I don't think you want to see her or Callie get hurt—more than they already are."

Great, just fucking great.

"This is how I see it," Chad continued. "Dead is dead. Hal could've got the death penalty if he'd been tried for Molly's murder. You told us he was a convicted felon who escaped, so for sure he woulda been goin' back to jail for a long, long time. Maybe for the rest of his worthless life. I'm afraid the feds are gonna keep snoopin' around and eventually find somethin' that convinces them Hal Freeman was their Ronald Usborne."

"He *was* Ronald Usborne."

"Yeah, I know. But at this point, does it make any difference? They can't put him back in jail. Isn't it more important to protect

Jessie and Callie from the humiliation of people learnin' what that bastard did? Jessie's already teeterin' on the edge of a breakdown. I don't want her to be unable to care for Callie. I mean, Hal killed Molly. Do you really want him to destroy the lives of all three generations of the family?"

Sean bristled. "Of course not."

"And who knows? Nate might be right. They could stick him with murder or manslaughter and put him away. Imagine what that would do to Jessie. Besides, Nate's battlin' his own demons already."

"Agreed." Sean studied the older man. Did he know the source of those demons?

"And then we gotta consider Jessie's concerns. I understand why she doesn't want the pornography shit to hit the fan. But on the other hand, she can't accept the idea that Hal would have a chance to hurt other kids as he did her and Callie. She also needs Hal to pay for killin' her mama. Tellin' her the asshole's dead would solve all that, but it'd also make her part of…uh…you know."

"The cover-up?"

"Yeah. See how complicated it is? What should we do?"

"*We?* Holy shit, don't even go there." Sean shook his head in disbelief. Damn, he had to agree with Chad's points, but that didn't mean he could just ignore his badge. He was a cop who'd taken an oath. He believed in…justice.

Justice. The word rolled around in the maze of his mind. Was there only one way or were there multiple paths to reach that goal? Did justice require all the *i*'s to be dotted and *t*'s crossed? Obviously he didn't condone vigilantism. But if he believed Chad, Hal's death had been an accident, not an execution.

What would be gained by telling the feds or the local cops what had really happened? Would justice be better served or would the truth just ruin more lives? Nothing could erase the past. Nothing would bring Molly back. Was the best result they could hope for be protecting her family's future?

His thoughts flashed back to Jake's girlfriend's case. The legal system, of which Sean was a part, hadn't protected Angela Reardon. Only when Sean and Jake joined forces, broke a few rules and bent a few laws, was true justice served and Angela saved. But it hadn't been a case of the end-justifies-the-means or vigilante action. Working with the PI had simply avoided the constraints and complications of operating within the law enforcement bureaucracy. Something Sean had found extremely effective and refreshing.

Was this another case where justice was best achieved by following a different path?

"What do you want from me?" Sean asked.

Chad looked him right in the eye. "I want you to decide which is more important: your badge...or Jessie."

Chapter 28

Wednesday morning, Jessie and Callie were transferred to Children's Hospital in San Diego. Now it was late afternoon, and Jessie sat in a cheerily decorated waiting room. She'd hardly slept in the bed with Callie, so her batteries were drained. She felt like the walking dead and probably looked like it, too. When a man's shoes stopped a few feet in front of hers, she looked up from the magazine page she'd been staring at in her lap for the past thirty minutes.

"What're you doing here?" she said, and cringed. Maybe her greeting came out barbed because she didn't want to feel the warm comfort created by his unexpected appearance.

Sean pulled back. "Good to see you, too."

"Sorry. My nerves are…still raw." She glanced at the other adults in the room. From their expressions, the child-friendly décor wasn't doing much to raise their spirits either. If your child was seeing a pediatric psychiatrist, a parent suffered.

"Understandable. How's Callie?" he asked, taking the chair next to her.

"Doing amazingly well, considering her father held a gun to her head and threatened to kill her. The doctor said he wasn't going to admit her, but he wants to schedule more visits until he's sure she's not suppressing a ton of emotions. I'm just thankful I get to take her home when she's done with this session."

"Need a ride?"

"I guess I do. A hospital van brought us here." She frowned. "I'm not sure where my car is."

"It was at the Ramona station, but Nate and I got it back to…your place."

She caught his hesitation. Was it her place? Her mother was dead, and her stepfather was on the run, so who was going to live there and take care of it? Would any of them want to? If they sold the property, someone would have to remove all Hal's stuff from the bomb shelter. She shuddered. That someone would definitely not be her. Could she even stand to live in the house, knowing what her stepdad had done while he lived there? She swallowed hard. Had he tainted her childhood home so badly that she and Callie would never be comfortable again?

"Jess?"

She started. "Sorry. I keep doing that—drifting off in my thoughts. It's a good thing Chad and Nate offered to plan Mom's funeral because I couldn't handle it."

"When will it be?"

"Saturday. At our church in Ramona. Luke said the medical examiner would release the body tomorrow." Her voice cracked on the word *body*, and tears burned her eyes. "Sean, I still can't believe she's gone. I need to talk to her about so much, but she's not here. And never will be."

He wrapped his arm around her shoulders and pulled her close so she could lay her head against him. "You can talk to me."

No, I can't. You're part of what I need to talk about. She gave him a smile and a noncommittal response. "Thanks. You were always a good listener."

"I still am. Let it out, Jess. Better to me than a shrink."

She raised her gaze to the ceiling. "There's just so much. I don't know where to start."

"Start anywhere."

She sighed and brought her gaze back to him. "How many scars will all this leave? Where are Callie and I going to live? How am I going to support her?"

Sean's mouth opened, but then he popped it shut without a word.

"What if they never catch Hal? He could be out there right now taking more of those damn pictures. I'll always feel like I'm to blame simply because I wanted to protect my daughter from the shame. Is that fair of me, to protect my own child and leave him to hurt others?"

"You have nothing to be ashamed of. It's not your fault."

"It is if I'm withholding information that would help catch him."

"That particular information might not be significant in the search for a murderer anyway."

"But it might be. How can I ignore the possibility?"

"He's not going to hurt other kids, Jess."

"You don't know that." Why was he discouraging her from coming forward with the truth?

He turned away and pressed his lips together for several seconds. "He'd be an idiot to do it while hiding from the cops."

"I don't have much hope the cops will find him. I think he's already in Mexico. He'll be able to do whatever he wants."

Sean shook his head. "Mexicans don't like those perverts either. Our guys will do the best they can to coordinate a cross-border search."

"But I feel so guilty. I should do something." Jessie narrowed her eyes. Sean had that odd look again—as though he was dying to say something. It wasn't like him to hold back. *What's going on?*

"Give yourself a few days for things to settle down. Maybe after the funeral. If…if they haven't caught Hal by then, we'll discuss it again."

"I guess you're right. They always say don't make big decisions when you're emotionally stressed out." She paused, thoughtful. "And that probably includes looking for a new job."

"Did your boss fire you?" Sean asked incredulously. "You can fight it."

"He didn't fire me. The job just doesn't pay enough to support Callie and me, especially now that I'll have to pay for child care."

"Nate's not working. Could he watch her?"

"For a few days, maybe a week, but not permanently." She sighed. "Life would be so much easier if my dream job ever came true."

"What's your dream job?"

She shrugged. "Doesn't matter. I've given up on dreams. Period."

"Ah, c'mon, share. You always knew mine was the LAPD."

"Okay, fine. My major at San Diego State was child and family development, remember? After I graduated, I knew I wanted to run my own child care or preschool business. When we lived in Chicago, Drake offered to build a small facility in a corner of our property." She closed her eyes. "He had me meet with an architecture firm. I really hit it off with the creative woman who drew up the blueprints. She understood exactly what I envisioned."

"How'd it go?"

Jessie opened her eyes and glared at the floor. "It went nowhere. When it came time to actually put it out for bid, Drake pulled the plug."

"Too expensive?"

She snorted. "We never got an actual bid, but he could've afforded whatever it cost. Reality was that he never intended to let my dream actually come true. From the beginning, it was all just a way to keep me occupied and away from the society events where I was failing miserably."

"Asshole."

"More than you'll ever know." She managed a faint smile. "I keep the blueprints in my nightstand drawer to remind me what an asshole he was."

"Mommy, Mommy," Callie called, skipping into the waiting room with the psychiatrist, Dr. Nelson, close behind. Her face lit up when she noticed who was with Jessie. "Mr. Sean. Mr. Sean."

She ran into his arms instead of her mother's. Jessie laughed at his wide-eyed surprise.

"Hey, munchkin," he said, swinging Callie into his lap.

Jessie introduced him to the doctor.

"Ah, yes, the famous Mr. Sean. Callie's told me all about you. If Mr. Sean doesn't mind watching her for a minute, I'd like to speak with you a moment, Ms. Hargrove."

Before she even asked, Sean motioned for her to go. Once they were out of earshot, the doctor sighed heavily.

"Callie is doing incredibly well, considering…the trauma she's been through."

His hesitant tone raised her concern. "Do I hear a 'but' coming?"

Dr. Nelson grimaced. "Yes." He stroked his chin. "First, I'd like to know…the status of your relationship with Mr. Sean." He looked away as if embarrassed.

She frowned. "What do you mean?"

The doctor cleared his throat. "Are you friends, casually dating, significant others, or…uh…engaged?"

Jessie's mouth dropped open. She glanced at her daughter chattering happily in Sean's lap and then back at Dr. Nelson. "Sean and I dated seriously several years ago, before my marriage. He just came back into my life"—she paused to count—"six days ago." *Oh God, has it really been only six days?* She drew a deep breath to continue. "Unfortunately, it was on the same day my mother disappeared, so things have been too crazy to even think about any kind of relationship. And Sean lives and works in LA. I believe he's going home this coming Sunday."

"I was afraid of that since the personal information you provided about Callie made no mention of him as an adult regularly present in her life."

"That's right. He isn't. And he won't be in the future." She shook her head. "I'm confused, Dr. Nelson. What's the problem?"

"Callie told me that she didn't want to talk about her old daddy."

"Is that unusual considering what Drake did to her?"

"Not at all. But yesterday's events weren't the reason."

"Oh."

Arching his eyebrows, he laid a comforting hand on her shoulder. "Callie only wanted to talk about Mr. Sean. Her new daddy."

* * *

"She said what?" Sean choked on a french fry when Jess informed him of Callie's conversation with Dr. Nelson. They sat at a table in a fast-food restaurant where they'd stopped for dinner on the way back to Ramona. The little girl had eaten like a bird and then run off to play in the enclosed playground.

"I know. I know. Kids, right? They say the craziest things." Jess laughed, but it sounded forced.

After washing down the wayward fry with a long swig of Coke, he leaned back in the booth across from her. God, she looked exhausted. On top of everything that had happened, now she had to deal with the fantasy her daughter had created to escape reality. He couldn't blame the little girl—he doubted anyone would—for finding a "happy place" to help her cope with her real father's heinous behavior. His heart squeezed for mother and daughter.

"How are we going to handle it?" he asked.

Her dark chocolate eyes searched his. For what, he didn't know.

Then she looked away. "*We* aren't. She's my daughter. I'll deal with it."

He rubbed the back of his neck. "I'm not trying to interfere, Jess. Maybe I can help."

She picked up a napkin and started ripping off tiny pieces. When she answered, her gaze remained on the growing pile of paper scraps. "Actually, you can help. But I'm not sure you'll want to do this."

"Anything. Just name it."

"I want you to…stay away from us."

Somehow, she sucker punched him in the gut from across the

table. And yet, her fingers still played with the napkin. All he could do was stare for several painful seconds. Finally, he forced out one syllable, "What?"

"Her fantasy about you being her daddy will fade if you're not around."

"You're serious?"

She finally met his gaze. "Yes."

He wouldn't—couldn't—give up that easy. "But what about us?"

"Sean, there is no us."

"Why not? Now you know I never broke up with you."

She rolled her eyes. "That was eight years ago. You have a different life now. In LA. I...I'll be making a whole new life here in Ramona. With my daughter."

"You do know LA isn't on the moon, right? We can visit each other on weekends."

"Yes. But I have no desire to visit either place."

He shrugged. "I'll drive to Ramona. No big deal."

"You're missing the point."

"Okay. Hit me with it again."

"Callie needs stability to recover from all this. She was still learning to understand the consequences of the divorce, and that was more of a relief than a trauma."

"I think she has it more together than you realize."

"You're an expert in less than a week?"

He shook his head. "Sorry, you're right. That's just my impression. She's a great kid. Can I say that?"

Her eyes glistened. "Of course, and thank you."

He reached across the table and laid his hand on top of hers. "Jess, I don't want to lose you again."

"I wish things were different—I really do—but they're not. My life is in shambles. I don't want any more complications."

"All I am is a complication?"

"Well, a friend, too, I hope."

"A friend who isn't allowed to see you. Can I call?"

She swallowed hard. "It would probably be…easier if you didn't. I'm so sorry, Sean. I feel awful. I mean, you just saved Callie's life—for which I'm forever grateful—and then I do this."

"Yeah, *this* sucks. I don't understand why we can't just date. You know, start over, take it slow. It's not like I'm asking you to move in with me in LA."

"That would be a deal breaker for sure. If it was just me, I could handle the dating relationship, the separation, and the weekend visits. But right now, Callie wouldn't be able to handle temporary or infrequent. She needs permanence, stability, someone she can count on always being here for her. And that's me. Me, by myself. So I have to say no. I imagine I'll be saying no to dating for quite a while. Not just with you, Sean. Oh God, please don't think that I don't…Because…" She glanced down at his hand resting on hers. "Because I—"

"Mommy! Mr. Sean! Did you sees me? I'll do it again." Callie ran up to the table, grabbed both their hands, and pulled them to the playground, ending the conversation.

When they left the restaurant a short while later, Sean automatically drove toward his brother's apartment.

"I'll just need a few minutes to gather our stuff," Jess said.

"What?"

"Callie needs to sleep in her own bed. I'm sure Nate won't mind coming over to stay with us," she added before Sean could object.

Damn, she didn't even want to spend the night together. She was pushing him away right now, this minute, not waiting until he went back to LA. His jaw clenched. He wouldn't go down without a fight. But in front of Callie was not the right time or place.

Chapter 29

Wednesday night, Jessie and Nate sat in the living room of the home where they'd grown up. Both held a tumbler of whiskey on the rocks, although she wasn't sure either was enjoying it. Her brother was grim and brooding, moodier than usual. She wasn't judging, just observing. Nate had to deal with what had happened in the past six days in his own way.

At the moment, she wasn't coping so well herself. She was second-guessing her decision to push Sean away now instead of waiting until he went back to LA. Granted, Dr. Nelson had advised that Callie needed stability and permanence to help her recover. He'd implied politely that a long line of men passing casually through her life could create problems. Well, there had been *no* long line of men since the divorce, and there would be no long line now. But the nice doctor had not said there couldn't be one special man. Yet Jessie had used his warning as the excuse to get rid of Sean. *Why?*

She took a sip of whiskey, closed her eyes, and leaned her head back against the couch cushion. *Is it really just Callie I'm protecting or myself, too?* Her heart ached because she knew the answer.

If she and Sean dated, eventually they would want to live closer together. His dream job was in LA, and she would never, ever ask him to give it up. Which meant one day she'd be faced with moving to LA. She just couldn't do it. Moving to Chicago with Drake had been a disaster. Of course, his wealthy, high-society family hadn't helped matters, but basically, big-city living didn't agree with Jessie. She hated the noise, the congestion, the crime—the list was long.

And because she'd been so unhappy, her marriage had suffered. Would things with Drake have turned out differently if they'd lived in a suburban or rural area? Probably not, since he would still have been a verbally abusive, ill-tempered bully. She sighed. Her marriage hadn't been a casualty of the big city; it had been doomed since she and Drake said "I do."

Sean was a totally different person: respectful, caring, and loving. When they'd dated years ago, she had believed he was her soul mate. *Do I still believe that?* Of course not. Back in the day, she'd been starry-eyed and naïve but not now. He was still a really great guy, but why set herself up for another heartbreak?

Eventually, LA and his job would come between them, and she'd have to recover from another failed relationship. No way did she need that looming on the horizon.

For a while, it would be wonderful to have his strong arms around her, his inner strength supporting her, but in the end, she'd be left with nothing. Better to nip it in the bud now. As she'd told Sean earlier, she didn't need the complication.

"Hey, sis," Nate said softly. "You asleep?"

She started, almost spilling her drink. She'd been so deep in thought that she had forgotten he was in the room. She blinked her eyes open and yawned. "Nope. Awake, but not for long." She massaged her tired eyes with her fingertips.

"I need to tell you something."

"If it's about the funeral arrangements, can it wait—"

"It's not."

His unsteady tone prompted her to lower her hands and stare at him. He looked as bad as she felt. His glistening, red-rimmed eyes held her gaze and wouldn't let go. "You okay, big brother?"

He gulped and shook his head.

"What is it?"

He inhaled a long, tremulous breath. "I…knew."

She drew a blank. "You knew…what?"

He gulped again. "About Hal."

Suddenly Jessie remembered Nate admitting to being at the house that awful Friday afternoon. Alarm sirens went off in her head, but she turned down the volume. "How did you know he killed Mom?"

He blinked for a moment. "Not the murder." He hesitated. "The…the pictures."

Her throat tightened with horror and disbelief. "You knew the bastard was taking pictures of Callie, and you didn't tell me?"

A hate-filled scowl creased Nate's face. "If I'd known that, I would've killed the asshole." He hung his head. "I knew…about you, Jessie. All those years ago."

A shiver skittered over her skin. Humming filled her ears. For a minute, she could only stare at him. Then her brain regained function and filled with questions. "You never told Mom?"

His lower lip trembled while he shook his head.

"You never told anyone?"

Another shake.

Jessie strained to breathe. "How…how did you know?"

He met her gaze. A tear rolled down his cheek. They stared into each other's eyes until the answer came to her.

"You too," she whispered. "Hal took pictures of you, too."

He gave one sharp nod.

"Jesus Christ. It just tears me apart that this happened right under Mom's nose. But Hal was a master of deception. Deep inside, I know I'll always harbor some anger toward her, but I keep reminding myself that Hal is the evil one and Mom was another of his victims. And I have to forgive her for the bad decision she made not to divorce or report Hal, which as a result allowed him to hurt Callie and other children."

Memories of the years of Nate's psychological problems played through her mind. Not only had he been victimized long ago, but he'd also known all this time. And was forced to live with it while she'd been blessedly oblivious. He'd suffered more than she had.

She scooted across the couch to sit next to him. Gently, she cupped his cheek, wiping away another tear with her thumb. "It's okay, Nate. Do you want to tell me about it?"

He blinked, more tears escaped, and he cleared his throat. "Remember, I was only six. You and I still ran through the sprinklers naked in the summer and took baths together. Nudity was…normal. It was fun. We were too young to know something evil could be made of it." His voice broke, so he stopped.

Jessie patted his thigh. "Take your time."

"First, I gotta tell you that he never touched us. You know, in a sexual way. I don't know if he even got off on it or if it was only about making a buck. I can't remember him getting a hard-on or anything, but then, I didn't know to look either. He definitely never got naked with us. I'm not making excuses for him; he was a sick motherfucker for sure. But he didn't sexually abuse us, which I guess would've been even worse."

She swallowed hard. The horrible question that had been lurking in the shadows of her mind faded away. "I agree."

"When Hal took me into the bomb shelter, he said we were playing a special game. He just let me romp around naked while he snapped pictures. He started bringing you down with us, but you were always asleep. Of course, Mom was gone whenever this happened. He kept me from talking about our special game by threatening that Mom would be so angry about not getting to play that she would leave us. He threatened me with that...every...damn...time. Of course, I was just having fun. I didn't realize we were doing anything wrong."

"*You* weren't doing anything wrong. He was."

"Thanks." Nate sighed. "I don't know how long it went on, but then it stopped suddenly. Hal said Mom had found out, and that part fits with what she said in her letter about finding him taking pictures of you."

"Wait a minute." She frowned. "Hal wasn't taking pictures of you, too, when she discovered him?"

"No. I was probably at school."

Her eyes widened. "Did Mom know he'd done the same to you?"

He looked away. His jaw tensed. "Now I don't believe she knew. Her letter to me didn't mention it. But back then, he scared the shit out of me by saying she was so mad that she was planning to put me up for adoption. If I ever said one word *to her or anyone*, I was gone. For years, I thought my own mother hated me."

"Something happened when you were older. I recall your relationship with Hal turning totally negative."

"Yeah. I was nine or ten, something like that. There was a presentation at school to teach kids about inappropriate touching and stuff. Even though Hal hadn't touched us, I suddenly realized him taking pictures of us was wrong, too."

"You still didn't tell Mom?"

He shook his head. "I freaked out. I was so embarrassed. But I did confront Hal. He convinced me that the police would put us in foster care and Mom in jail for not taking better care of us." He pinched the bridge of his nose. "God, I was so stupid."

"You were just a kid. Hal knew how to scare you."

"Yeah, he did a damn good job of it. But I hated him from then on. And I still believed Mom hated me."

They sat in silence for several minutes.

"I'm so sorry, Nate. No wonder you had such problems with depression and stuff," Jessie finally said. "Hopefully things will be better for you now."

He managed a small smile. "I admit I'm happy as hell Hal is…uh…gone. But now I'll never get to tell Mom the truth."

Jessie raised her eyes heavenward for a moment before reconnecting with his. "She knows, Nate. She knows. And she always loved you."

* * *

Around 10:00 Wednesday night, Sean sat on the couch in Glenn's living room, nursing a beer. His second, actually. And there might be another in his near future.

He pulled out his cell phone and called Jake Stone. His friend had already learned from the local news of the discovery of Molly Freeman's body and the rescue of little Callie Hargrove, but Sean filled him in on the behind-the-scene details.

"They need to catch that bastard who killed her," Jake concluded.

Sean's jaw clenched. "It's not that simple."

"You want my help to find Hal?"

"I need your help but not with that."

"Woman troubles, huh, Burke? Let me guess: Jessie."

"In a way." He braced himself. "Look, Stone, I know you have experience in this. What would you need to…fake a suicide?"

A long, strained silence answered the question.

"Stone?"

"Whose?" Jake asked.

"Hal Freeman's."

"Why? You going rogue, Burke? You want the cops to think he's dead so you can go after the SOB personally?"

Now it was Sean's turn to remain silent.

"I don't…do that kind of shit unless I believe in it," Jake said. "Explain why you want to pretend he's dead."

Sean frowned. Why was he hesitant to tell his friend the whole truth? He might not have known Jake Stone very long, but they'd worked well together to accomplish some important stuff. In solving Jake's girlfriend's case. In uncovering Hal's true identity. In discovering the child pornography.

Granted, Stone operated on the fringes of legality, disregarded rules, and ignored bureaucracy, but he got shit done. Good shit. Justice. In some ways, he was envious of the man's operational freedom, and he sure as hell would trust the former CIA spook with his life. Jake Stone wouldn't let him down. Time to go all in.

"That part's not pretend," Sean finally said.

"Huh? What pa—" Jake grunted when the truth hit. "Just the how."

"Yeah."

"You do it?"

"Nope. An accident."

Sean could tell the man was running through the possible scenarios of how Hal had died and probably figuring out why it needed to be kept secret. Stone was nothing if not smart and dangerous.

"The fake suicide doesn't have to completely fool the cops, but it'd be great if they stopped looking for him. Mostly it needs to convince Jess he's dead."

"And clean enough I don't get nabbed for staging it. Don't forget that detail." Jake cursed under his breath. "Do you care where?"

"Not particularly. Away from Ramona would be good."

"What about the body?"

"There won't be one," Sean answered grimly.

"Hmmm." Jake paused for several seconds.

Sean hoped it meant he was planning the fake suicide, not deciding how to tell him to go to hell.

"Get me an appropriate pair of his shoes," Jake finally said.

"Appropriate?"

"Ones he could've been wearing Monday when he…disappeared."

"You mean not dress shoes if he would've been wearing Nikes, right?"

"Yeah. And a pair the cops won't notice missing from his closet, which I'm sure they've already searched."

Sean made a mental note not to take the pair where Hal had hidden the cash and earrings because he wasn't sure if they'd been bagged as evidence. "Okay. Anything else?"

"A comprehensive handwriting sample. Every letter, if possible. And definitely his signature."

"That could be tough."

"You want a credible suicide note or not?"

"I'll get it all," Sean said, but didn't have a clue how since Jess had just banished him. He cleared his throat. "One more favor, Stone."

"What now?"

"I have an external hard drive that needs to disappear. Permanently."

"Not a problem. That just happened to a flash drive of mine."

Chapter 30

Thursday passed in a fog. Jessie focused all her attention on Callie and let her brother and uncle finish the funeral arrangements, field condolences and questions from friends, and run off the annoying media.

Uncle Chad even took the time to go through the master bedroom to box up Hal's clothing and personal belongings as well as his business paperwork. She didn't know where her uncle planned to store it and, frankly, didn't care. After hearing Nate's story last night, she hated her stepdad more than ever. She never wanted to see him inside the house again. The courtroom was the only place she would willingly set eyes on him.

Nate's confession had torn her apart. She'd been protected by ignorance, but he'd suffered for years from Hal's cruelty, physically and mentally. Would it help him recover now that he'd shared his awful secret with her? God, she hoped so. And if Hal was caught, convicted, and imprisoned, Nate might even have a better chance.

Those thoughts drove her back to the guilty burden of not disclosing the pornography if it could aid in her stepdad's capture. She remembered Sean's suggestion to put off her decision until after the funeral. Since she seemed incapable of doing anything but doting on Callie at the moment, that was probably sound advice.

Her heart ached from her decision to push Sean out of her life. Already she felt the void. How could he have taken a place in her heart again in such a short time? Unfortunately, she knew the answer, although she could barely admit it to herself.

She loved Sean Burke. She'd never stopped loving him even when he'd broken her heart. She'd been angry, damn angry, and she had used that emotion to bury the love. But now the revelation of Hal's deception had destroyed the anger, leaving the love to surface again.

How she wished she could tell Sean that she loved him. How wonderful it would be if the circumstances were different and they could have a real second chance. But too many things stood in the way: his LAPD job, her shattered life, her traumatized daughter. If ever there was a bad time, it was now. Hanging on to another chance in the future just seemed like an invitation for more heartache.

On Friday came the news that Hal's truck—at least what was left of it—had been located in a chop shop in Imperial Beach, which wasn't far from San Ysidro and the Mexican border. The discovery four days after his disappearance solidified Jessie's belief that he had escaped into Mexico to live out his days safe from U.S. extradition and punishment. Shortly after the phone call from a sheriff's deputy, she made the gut-wrenching decision to disclose the pornography in hopes it would motivate the Mexican authorities to find Hal Freeman. As painful as the nasty publicity would be, she just wouldn't be able to live with herself if she didn't do everything in her power to put the monster behind bars. On Monday, she would tell Detective Cramer the horrible Freeman family secret.

Friday afternoon, she tackled the heartbreaking job of telling Callie that her beloved grandma was never coming back. The little girl cried a long time before asking about her missing grandfather. Jessie wasn't sure how to answer that question. She ended up ducking the issue by saying lots of people were looking for him. Thank goodness Callie didn't want to know why he'd gone missing.

Then her daughter asked about Mr. Sean, of course. Jessie had foolishly hoped the subject wouldn't come up, but since Callie had asked about Sean several times since Wednesday evening, it shouldn't have been a big surprise. Jessie reassured her that he wasn't dead or missing, just busy getting ready to go back to his real home in LA. Obviously, Callie had thought Glenn's apartment was Sean's home, so the news came as a shock. She crumpled into a sobbing heap in her mother's lap, making Jessie feel like a monster.

Friday night, exhausted and lonely, Jessie cried herself to sleep. There were so many reasons: the death of her mother, the crimes of her stepfather, Callie's exposure to violence and loss, and the failure of her second chance with Sean. She wished with all her heart that he, instead of Callie, was in bed with her. At least they had shared a few special nights in the past week. She would cling to those memories to get through the dark, difficult days ahead.

Saturday morning dawned clear and warm. Moving as if in a trance, she got herself and Callie ready for the funeral. Nate had gone home to get ready but returned half an hour before the limo was to pick them up. Uncle Chad arrived a few minutes later.

Callie was watching a movie in the living room and the adults were sitting at the kitchen table when Jessie's cell rang. She considered not answering but dug it out of her purse after the fourth ring.

"Ms. Hargrove, I have some news," Detective Cramer greeted her.

"I'm leaving for my mother's funeral in a few minutes."

"I'm sorry to interrupt." He hesitated. "But it's about your step-dad. It might…ease your mind a little today."

She stiffened. Had they found the bastard?

"What is it?" Nate asked, placing his hand reassuringly on her shoulder.

She put her finger over the mic. "It's Detective Cramer. Something about Hal."

"You want me to talk to him?"

She shook her head. "Will it take long, Detective?"

"Just a minute or two, unless you have questions."

"All right. Nate and Uncle Chad are here, so I'm going to put you on speaker." She pressed the button and laid the phone on the table. "Go ahead."

"A pair of shoes with a handwritten note stuck inside were found this morning on the Imperial Beach pier. The note's addressed to Jessie, Nate, and Chad."

Her heart thumped unevenly, and she felt the blood drain from her face.

"It's signed 'Hal.' It appears to be…a suicide note."

Her lips began to tremble. "Is it t-true or a r-ruse?"

"We'll have to confirm the handwriting and shoes are his. Maybe we can get a fingerprint match. He probably heard on the news that we found Molly's body, so he knew we had him dead to rights for the murder. Frankly, I'm not completely surprised he took this way out."

Nate cleared his throat and glanced at Chad. "Have you found the body?"

"Not yet. We're going to send down some divers, but they aren't optimistic about finding the body."

"Why not?" Chad asked.

"The shoes were kind of hidden, so they might've been there awhile. And the ink on the note is smeared, probably from the fog. Since the body hasn't washed up on the beach, the tide has most likely already carried him out to sea."

"Good riddance," Nate muttered.

"I don't want to keep you any longer, Ms. Hargrove. I'll have a deputy drop a copy of the note by your house later today. I need the original until we close the case."

"Thank you, Detective." Jessie disconnected.

They sat in silence for several minutes.

Jessie stared at her clasped hands resting on the table. She couldn't quite believe the news. *Is it over? Truly and completely over?* This unexpected phone call had saved her from making the difficult one she'd planned for Monday.

The heinous family secret was safe. No one would ever need to know.

* * *

Sean kept his distance from Jess at the funeral, honoring her wishes by sitting at the back of the packed church. Apparently, most of Ramona wanted to say good-bye to Molly Freeman. Luke and Karla, who was still bruised and battered, sat next to him. She mentioned plans to take Callie and Jess to a friend's cabin at Big Bear Lake for a week. He agreed that getting them out of town was an excellent idea.

Luke gave him the news about the discovery on the Imperial Beach pier. The deputy sounded slightly suspicious that Hal had gone down with a whimper instead of a bang, but he didn't dwell on it. It seemed Detective Cramer and the other authorities were satisfied with the suicide evidence. *Thank you, Stone.*

His heart squeezed as he watched Jess and Callie at the graveside service. When Callie kissed her grandma's coffin and whispered she loved her, there wasn't a dry eye in attendance.

After leaving the cemetery, the mourners congregated at the church's social hall for light refreshments and supportive grieving. News of Hal's suicide was a major topic of conversation. No one appeared to grieve for that asshole. Sean was glad Hallelujah Ima Freeman, aka Ronald Arthur Usborne, was already rotting in hell.

When the crowd started to thin and Karla had taken Callie outside, Sean noticed Jess standing alone for the first time. She looked devastated but strong. Her resilience amazed him. Slowly, he made his way over to her.

"How ya doing?" he asked.

She gazed up at him with glistening eyes. "I'll survive."

"You'll do better than that."

"I hope so." She blinked and turned away.

He drew a fortifying breath. "Look, I know what you said, but"—his fingers gently guided her face back toward him—"I want to spend the night with you."

She covered her eyes with a trembling hand. "Don't, Sean, please." Shaking her head, she continued. "I can't. We can't. Anyway,

Callie and I are spending the night at Karla's apartment, so we can get an early start to the cabin tomorrow."

"Tomorrow? So this is good-bye?"

She lowered her hand and looked him in the eye. "Yes, it is. I'm sure you plan to head off to LA early, too, since you've been gone so long. There's always so much to do after a long absence. Buy groceries. Do laundry. Sort the mail."

Even as she babbled, a tear ran down her cheek. He wiped it away with his thumb.

"Jess…" Emotions strangled the words he wanted to say.

"I'm sorry, Sean. Fate just seems determined to keep us apart. First Hal, and now all of this. You need to…move on with your life, and I need to create a new one for Callie and me."

He swallowed hard. "But…I love you, Jess."

She stepped up to him, put her arms around his neck, and placed her lips over his. Confused but encouraged, he wrapped her in his arms. Closing his eyes, he drank in the taste of her, breathed in her scent, and melded their bodies together. He never wanted to let go. But when she broke the kiss and stepped back a moment later, he released her.

Tears streamed down her cheeks as she met his gaze. "I love you, too, Sean. That's why I could never ask you to give up your dream. Take care of yourself."

She turned and walked out of his life.

* * *

A week later, Jessie gaped when Karla turned into the Freeman driveway. Her eyes widened as she stared at the bustling scene.

At least three dozen pickup trucks were parked along the road, and half the population of Ramona crawled over the property. The air rang with hammering and buzzed with sawing. People with brushes and rollers, some on ladders, were painting the house's white trim. Others were busy planting flowers in the neglected beds in the front yard and weeding the garden in back. In shock, she surveyed the property, her gaze flicking toward the outbuilding. She gasped.

The structure was gone. New wooden framing stuck out of a huge concrete foundation. It appeared much larger than the previous one, but that might've been an illusion caused by the absence of walls. Men with big tool belts and bigger tools covered the area. She spotted Nate and Uncle Chad among the workers.

"What happened?" she cried in disbelief. "Was there a fire?" Her stomach clenched when she thought of the bomb shelter hidden beneath the darkroom. Had it been uncovered by whatever disaster had destroyed the building?

Karla shrugged. "You'll have to ask him," she said, nodding at the man walking toward the car.

"Oh no. What's he doing here?" Jessie murmured.

Sean strolled to the passenger side and opened the door. "Welcome home, Jess." He leaned down to peer inside. "Hey, Karla. Hi, munchkin."

"Who are these peoples?" Callie asked warily.

Jessie turned. Her daughter's concerned expression tugged at her heart. During the past week, Callie had begun to exhibit a general distrust of people. One of the many emotional scars she feared they would have to deal with over time.

"They're friends," Sean supplied in answer when Jessie didn't. "We're making something for you and your mommy."

"Likes a…a present?"

"Right." After opening the back door, he freed Callie from the car seat and plopped her on his hip. "Wanna see?"

Callie nodded enthusiastically.

"Can your mommy come, too?" he asked in a serious tone.

"Sure. C'mon, Mommy." She reached out her little hand, and her eyes showed the first signs of a sparkle since the funeral. "Mr. Sean gots a present for us."

Her eyes burning with unshed tears, Jessie clasped the delicate fingers and climbed out of the car. Her gaze connected with Sean's. She swallowed hard. She should be angry, but she felt something entirely different. "What're you doing here? You're supposed to be in LA."

He wrapped his free arm around her shoulders and planted a chaste kiss on her cheek. "We'll talk later. I want to show you and Munchkin the surprise."

They walked up the driveway together. The crowd dropped what they were doing and gathered along the sides, smiling, calling greetings, clapping.

Jessie blinked in bewilderment. *What in the world?*

When they reached the construction area, Sean stopped. "Do you know what this is?" he asked Callie.

Her lips pursed as she concentrated. "A mess."

Sean snorted. "True that. What do you think it'll be when we finish building it?"

Jessie's chest ached at his sweet, caring manner with her daughter. If only…

Callie frowned. "Is it a house?"

"Close. It's a child care…house. Now your mommy can work here and be with you all day."

Jessie gasped. "What?" She pulled away from Sean's arm and stepped haltingly toward the new construction. "No way. Is…is it?"

Joining her, he rested a hand on her shoulder. "Yeah, it's the plans you had drawn up in Chicago. Revised for California building codes, of course."

She splayed her hand on the side of her face. "I…I can't believe it." Then a nasty reality yanked her down. She leaned her head toward him and whispered, "I can't afford this. How am I going to pay everyone?"

He grinned. "Don't have to. Labor and materials are all donated by the good citizens of Ramona. They even fast-tracked the permits."

"Oh my God." She stood on her tiptoes to whisper in his ear. "What…what about the…you know? Did anyone see it?"

"Nope. Chad, Nate, and I filled it up completely with concrete last Sunday before any of this started."

"Thank God." She drew a trembling breath and turned around. Everyone lining the driveway began to clap. Tears filled her eyes and overflowed while her chest tightened with a sweet ache. Maybe she and Callie would stay here. Maybe they could make a new life where she'd grown up. Maybe the good memories would outweigh the bad. And maybe, someday, she'd find a man who'd want to live with them in this wonderful, caring little town. *Someday…*

She heard movement behind her, and Callie appeared by her side, latching one arm around her mother's leg.

"Why you crying, Mommy? Aren't you happy with Mr. Sean's present?"

"Oh, baby, I am. It's just…just…"

"Jess, I have one more surprise."

She looked over her shoulder to find Sean down on one knee behind her. Her heart did a stutter step. Slowly, she pivoted with Callie still attached to her leg and faced him. "Sean?"

He took her hand in his right and Callie's in his left. "I love you, Jess and Callie. I want to spend the rest of my life with you. Will you let me be your husband and father?"

Callie let go of her mother and stepped closer to Sean. Even though he was kneeling, she still had to look up into his face. "You really wants to be my daddy, Mr. Sean?"

"Yes, munchkin, I sure do."

With a serious frown, she considered his proposal. "You gots to 'mise never to be mean or leave."

He smiled. "I promise."

"Okay, you're my new daddy." She scooted her little bottom onto his raised knee and wrapped her arms around his neck. He hugged her against him.

Sean raised his eyes, filled with love and promises, to Jessie. "One down, one to go. It'd be best to make it a package deal, Jess. Will you marry me?"

She gulped.

"C'mon, Mommy. I loves Mr. Sean."

Jessie dropped to her knees, and he folded her into the embrace with Callie. "I loves Mr. Sean, too. Yes, oh yes, I'll marry you." Her voice cracked with the sweet joy of it. But then she glanced back at the construction, and disappointment struck. "We'll be here, and you'll live in LA?"

"Nope. I quit the LAPD."

"You…you…what? But it was your dream."

"No, Jess. My dream was to marry you. LAPD was my career. But I've decided it wasn't such a good fit after all."

"What're you going to do?"

"Well, Luke offered to put in a good word for me at the sheriff's department, but I told him to hold off."

She gave him an impish smile. "Are you gonna help me with the child care business?"

"Sh—" He swallowed the bad word. "Uh, that would be a no. I'll be too busy learning to be a daddy."

"It's okay with me if you take your time deciding what you want to do."

"Actually, I'm real interested in Jake Stone's offer to join his Rogue Security Agency, but that can wait. We've lost a lot of time, Jess, so we have a lot of catching up to do. And right now, all I want to do is enjoy my dream with you."

ACKNOWLEDGMENTS

My research into the heartbreaking subject of child pornography taught me that the abused child is not the only victim. The consequences can affect an entire family and even multiple generations. By sharing this information through my characters, I hope you will gain, as I have, a greater appreciation for the true magnitude of this heinous crime. All of us must be vigilant as even the darkest evil can be hidden by deception.

I'm sincerely grateful to the dedicated men and women of the San Diego County Sheriff's Department for answering my many questions. Any errors are mine alone.

Thanks also to my talented editor, Alex Logan, and the Forever Romance team for their hard work in bringing my story to you.

Investigative reporter Elle Bradley has been missing for over a month. Until tonight, when she's found by Sheriff's Deputy Luke Johnson as the headlights of his patrol car reveal a naked woman alone on a rural road. Who kidnapped her and why?

Please see the next page for an exciting preview of *Only Obsession*.

Chapter 1

A naked woman dashed onto the rural road barely fifty feet in front of the patrol car. Sheriff's deputy Luke Johnson jerked the steering wheel to the right and slammed on the brakes. *What the hell?* As he stared in disbelief at the person frozen like a deer in his headlights, the crack of gunfire shattered the peace and quiet of the San Diego County countryside.

The woman screamed and dropped to the ground.

"Shit!" Luke stomped on the gas, and his vehicle lurched forward onto the gravel shoulder, spraying rocks from beneath its tires. The shots had likely come from the eucalyptus forest to his right, so he angled the patrol car to position it as a protective barrier between the woman and the trees. A quick check out the window revealed no obvious signs of blood on or around her. Thank God, maybe she hadn't been hit.

Automatically, Luke threw the gearshift into park and set the brake before grabbing his gun and leaning down to scrutinize the wooded area through the passenger-side window. Since the headlights and the moon were the only illumination, finding the shooter in the dense foliage would be nearly impossible, but movement in the heavy brush caught his eye. Zeroing in on the spot, he aimed but didn't fire. Unfortunately, he just couldn't see what was there. Firing blind was not an option.

He continued to scan the trees while sliding back to the driver's side and pushing the door open. Glancing at the woman again, he lowered himself to the ground. "You hurt?" he called to confirm her condition.

Lying flat on her stomach, she trembled convulsively as she raised her head. Her wild eyes blinked rapidly as if she was trying to determine whether Luke was real or a hallucination. Her lips moved but no words came out. Closing her eyes, she shook her head no.

"Stay down. I'm coming to get you," he said.

But she didn't wait for him. She struggled to her hands and knees and crawled toward the car.

Bending low, he scrambled to her side and hovered over her with his gun raised and ready. "How many are there?"

"One." Her answer came out as a whispered croak.

"Who?" he asked, his eyes constantly moving, searching for signs of the shooter.

"A man."

"Name?"

"Don't know."

As they reached the side of the patrol car, the roar of a powerful engine and the crunch of brush came from beyond the trees. Straightening, Luke aimed his gun across the roof of the car, but the noise moved away in the opposite direction. He remained on guard until the last sounds from the other vehicle faded and quiet returned.

"Help me, please help me," the woman pleaded, clutching his pants leg. "Don't let him take me again."

Luke squatted in front of her. "You're safe now. You're gonna be okay."

For the first time, her appearance—besides being naked—registered. She was wet, her smooth skin slick and shiny, her brown hair hanging in dripping strands across her breasts. Her wrists and ankles were covered with red friction burns and purple bruises. Dark circles and long lashes ringed her large hazel eyes. She shivered uncontrollably.

"You must be freezing. Let's get you in the car," he said. "I'll grab the blanket from the trunk and crank up the heat."

Wrapping one arm around her shoulders, he helped her stand and then lowered her gently onto the backseat. But when he opened the trunk, the emergency blanket was missing. *Damn, last shift must've used it, and it hasn't been replaced.* After closing the trunk, he stepped back around to the side of the vehicle.

"Sorry, no blanket, but you can use this," he said, pulling off his jacket and handing it to her.

Since her hands shook so badly that she couldn't put it on, he guided her arms into the sleeves and fastened the front, being careful not to touch her bare breasts. With a sharp exhale, he dropped into the driver's seat, switched the heat to full blast, and got on the radio.

"Shots fired on Old Shelby Road near the abandoned trailer park. The intended victim—white female, late twenties—is safe. I believe the shooter—male, no further description—has left the scene. Send backup and an ambulance."

"No. No ambulance," the woman said. "He...he'll get me."

He twisted in the driver's seat to look at her. "I...we need to get you to a hospital to be examined, miss."

With her eyes still wild and her face drained of color, she peered fearfully at the trees and then back at him. "Can...can you take me?"

He hesitated, but the terror in her eyes persuaded him. "Okay." He shifted to the front again and lowered his voice. "Cancel the ambulance. I'll transport the vic to North County Hospital myself. Notify them that I'll be bringing her in. Then I'll interview her there."

While he reported the minimal information he had about the brief, but serious, incident, he studied the woman in the rearview mirror. She had shut her eyes and rested her head against the cushion. She'd felt so fragile when he had helped her into the car, and now she looked exhausted. And abused. Even wearing his jacket and hugging herself, she continued to shake violently. Probably in shock. Anger at her attacker simmered in his gut.

"Hang on a minute," he said to the dispatcher.

When he swung open the car door, the woman jumped and gasped.

"Just me," he reassured her before stripping off his uniform shirt.

She gaped at him until he draped the shirt across her lap and tucked it in around her legs. When he finished, she managed a faint smile and a soft, "Thank you."

He nodded. "What's your name?"

"Elle." She paused several seconds before continuing. "Elle...Bradley."

He frowned at her hesitation and at the vague familiarity of her name. Why didn't she want to tell him? And why did her name ring a bell? Before he could puzzle it out or question her further, sirens blared in the distance.

"Cavalry's almost here. I should brief them before we head to the hospital. Can you wait a little longer?"

"Yes," she said, and closed her eyes again.

Luke motioned for the two arriving patrol cars to park several yards back from where his sat idling. He brushed off the good-natured ribbing from his colleagues about his lack of a shirt, but he resented their curious glances at the woman in the backseat. He needed to get her to the hospital ASAP, so he explained what had happened as quickly as possible.

"Miss Bradley ran out of the woods and stopped there when I was about fifty feet in that direction. That's also where she was standing when the bastard took a couple shots at her but missed. Not much chance of finding the damn bullets in the dark. We'll have to come back tomorrow. I heard the perp's vehicle—sounded like a large truck—leave from behind those trees. Might've left some tracks or debris. I saw movement in the brush about twenty yards north, but it could've been a deer or coyote." In less than five minutes, he'd finished his succinct briefing. "Shit, I wish I had more for you guys to go on. I'll try to get some useful info from the vic later."

"Where's the ambulance?" asked one of the deputies.

"She didn't want one."

"Why not? You said she had injuries."

"I'm transporting her to the hospital because she's afraid the jerk might get to her in the ambulance."

The other deputy frowned. "Not SOP."

Luke shrugged. "I think she's been through a lot." He didn't want to answer more questions about her, so he abruptly ended the conversation. "Good luck finding any evidence tonight. Call me if you have questions."

A few minutes later, he drove away from the crime scene. The cruiser felt like an oven, making him glad to be shirtless.

"I don't know if you're from around here, but Ramona is a small town. We don't have a hospital. It'll take about fifteen minutes with lights and siren to get to the nearest one," he explained. "You okay until then?"

"Yes…thanks."

As he drove, he stole several glimpses of his passenger in the mirror. Her eyes were closed once again, and her head rested against the seat back. His cop instincts were screaming that he'd seen her before. Or at least seen a picture of her. But where? When?

Elle Bradley. Elle Bradley. Her name played over and over in his mind. Why was it familiar? When had he heard or read it?

Five minutes later, it hit him. He glanced over his shoulder at the battered woman and realized why he hadn't recognized her. She'd looked very different in the photograph. But why hadn't she immediately explained who she was and what had happened? Her behavior made no sense, and even her injuries could be nothing more than window dressing. Suspicion tightened his jaw. Suddenly, he questioned the entire incident. Was it real or staged?

* * *

"I know who you are," the deputy announced loud enough to rouse her.

His words ripped away her cloak of anonymity. She tensed and slowly opened her eyes. "Of course you do. I told you that I'm Elle Bradley."

"But you didn't say you're *the* Elle Bradley, the woman who was kidnapped in Washington about a month ago, the rising-star socialite in DC's inner circles, the fiancée of the son of a high-ranking federal bureaucrat, and the award-winning investigative reporter for a nationwide newspaper."

She sighed with resignation and met his gaze in the mirror. "I plead guilty to the first and last charges only."

"The FBI has been searching for you. Hell, law enforcement all over the country has been on the lookout for you. Your parents and fiancé were on TV several times begging the kidnapper not to hurt you and to let you go. Don't you think you should call *someone* immediately and tell them you're all right?"

His impatient, lecturing tone annoyed her. He wasn't the one who'd just survived a horrible ordeal. This deputy didn't know anything about what she'd endured. In fact, he couldn't know anything meaningful about her at all. Few people did, and she liked it that way. *How dare he judge me?* Resentment bubbled up. "You mean I should tell *someone* that you rescued me so you can get your fifteen minutes of fame."

He switched off the cruiser's siren and swerved onto the shoulder. Then he whipped around in his seat to stare at her hard. "Hell no. I just think there are a damn lot of people out there who are worried sick about you, many who've spent countless hours trying to find and save you. They *deserve* to know you're safe."

Pressing her fingertips against her temples, she shook her head. "I'm sorry. You're right. I just don't know if I'm ready to deal with…with everything. The questions. The spotlight. All of it. None of it."

His expression softened. "The sheriff could call the FBI, and they can contact your family. But don't you think they'd rather hear directly from you?"

The deputy really didn't understand. How could he? It was her family—especially her mother—that she was most *not* ready to deal with. The past month of torturous captivity had injured her spirit as well as her body. She needed time to heal, starting with some anonymous decompression time.

Most daughters would get complete, compassionate support from their mothers but not Elle. Allison Bradley would be more interested in the limelight, the notoriety, the fame of being the mother of a kidnap victim than she would be in helping her daughter recover. And right now, just the thought of coping with her mother on top of everything else was too overwhelming.

Pulling in a deep, fortifying breath, she tunneled her fingers through her wet hair and cringed at the decision she had to make. If her parents learned of her escape from anyone else, there'd be hell to pay. She'd never hear the end of it. They would make it a bigger issue than catching her abductor.

So be it. For years she'd dealt with them, and she'd do it now by calling like an obedient daughter but also by controlling the extent of the conversation. *Calling?* Her mood brightened. "I don't have a phone."

"Use mine."

She huffed. "Do you have to be so helpful?"

"You didn't complain when I loaned you my shirt and jacket."

He had a point. The poor man was half naked while on duty, something she'd overheard his colleagues teasing him about.

"Okay, fine. Give me your phone."

"You're sure?" he asked, pulling it from his pants pocket.

"I guess. You don't happen to also have a flask of whiskey with you, Deputy...Helpful."

"No, ma'am. Just my phone." Grinning, he got out of the car to hand it to her since there was no way to pass it through the protective partition between the seats.

She accepted it tentatively, dreading what she had to do. She noticed the local time on the cell, which meant it was the wee hours of the morning in Washington. But the time really didn't matter. After a few moments, she poked the numbers that would connect her to the center of her family maelstrom.

The phone at the other end rang ten times before a sleepy male voice answered. "The Bradley residence."

"Hello, George. Sorry to wake you. I need to talk to...Father."

"Miss Elle? Is that you? My Lord, are you all right?" the Bradleys' longtime butler asked.

"I...I'm safe." She smiled at Deputy Helpful, who had them on the road again but without the earsplitting siren. "I was just rescued by a very nice deputy."

"Thank heavens. I'll get your father for you. Please hold, Miss Elle."

Had George sensed she wanted to hang up? She almost chuckled at how normal that seemed.

Only a few minutes passed before her mother's voice screeched in her ear. "Sweetie, sweetie, we've been so worried. The stress has been just terrible on your father and me. I was so worried about his heart, you know. And of course, Richard has been miserable. Poor man. First the silly breakup and then your disappearance. You have called him, haven't you?"

Again, normal. "I'm okay, Mother. Thanks for asking."

Strained silence followed.

A click signaled her dad was on the phone now, too. "Elle, are you all right, honey? Do you need anything? What can we do?"

"I'm...okay, considering. I'm on my way to the hospital, but none of my injuries are serious."

"Injuries?" Allison screeched again. "He didn't hurt you, did he?"

Elle drew a deep breath. "Not much. Mostly minor stuff from struggling against the restraints."

"Be sure they get pictures of everything. It'll be good—"

"Publicity. I know, Mother. There's no such thing as bad publicity."

"Where are you, honey?" her dad asked.

"Uh...San Diego County. At least that's what it says on the side of the patrol car."

"We'll be on a plane first thing in the morning. Can we reach you at this number?"

"No, Dad, this is a borrowed cell." She gulped. "Look, I need...some time to recover. Some time...alone and quiet."

"Don't worry, sweetie, we'll reserve the best hotel suite in San Diego," her mother said.

Elle clenched her jaw. "I don't want you two to come. Do you understand? Do not come. I have to go now. We're at the hospital," she lied. She looked up to find Deputy Helpful's puzzled gaze in the mirror. "I'll call when I can."

"Sure, sweetie. We'll contact the FBI, Richard, and the news—"

She disconnected before saying something truly awful to her mother. She kept her gaze downcast so she wouldn't see the disapproval in the deputy's eyes.

They rode the remaining distance in silence. Thankfully, the shakes had stopped, and she finally felt warm. The poor man had probably been baking the whole trip but never complained once. She pushed aside her regret for his discomfort at her expense because she needed to focus on more important things.

Like who the hell had kidnapped her and why?

ABOUT THE AUTHOR

I'm a wife, writer, chocoholic, and animal lover, not necessarily in that order. As a little girl, I cut pictures of people out of my mother's magazines and turned them into characters in my simple stories. Now I write edgy romantic thrillers, steamy contemporary romance, and sexy paranormal romantic suspense. I live in sunny Southern California with my husband, but enjoy traveling from Athens to Anchorage to Acapulco and many locations in between.

You can learn more at:

http://marissagarner.com

Facebook.com/MarissaGarnerAuthor

DON'T MISS MARISSA GARNER'S FBI HEAT SERIES

For San Diego's elite FBI agents, risking their lives is standard procedure when it comes to capturing the city's most dangerous criminals—but falling in love is the greatest risk of all.

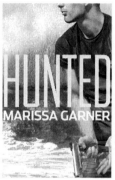 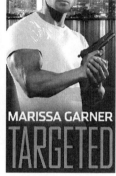 

Available Now

31901062414653

CPSIA information can be obtained
at www.ICGtesting.com
Printed in the USA
FFOW03n0211060118
44368645-44075FF